Arthur Fraser Sim

The Life and Letters of Arthur Fraser Sim

Priest in the Universities' Mission to Central Africa

Arthur Fraser Sim

The Life and Letters of Arthur Fraser Sim
Priest in the Universities' Mission to Central Africa

ISBN/EAN: 9783744752190

Printed in Europe, USA, Canada, Australia, Japan

Cover: Foto ©Raphael Reischuk / pixelio.de

More available books at **www.hansebooks.com**

THE
LIFE AND LETTERS

OF

ARTHUR FRASER SIM

Priest in the Universities' Mission to Central Africa

WITH A PREFACE

BY THE

REV. CANON BODY, D.D.

Canon Missioner in the Diocese of Durham

SECOND THOUSAND

PUBLISHED BY THE

UNIVERSITIES' MISSION TO CENTRAL AFRICA

9 DARTMOUTH STREET, WESTMINSTER, S.W

1897

PREFACE

I HAVE been asked to preface this book, and most readily do so. The request comes to me as a command, made imperative by my love for Sim ; and I obey it in the hope of being allowed to make his influence still more widely felt, especially among the younger clergy of the Church of England.

My first real knowledge of him was gained at the time of his Ordination to the Priesthood. For many years it has been my privilege to minister to such of the ordinands in this diocese to the Priesthood as desire such aid as a retreat can give. Some of the dearest friendships of my life have been made in these retreats, and links have been formed knitting my heart to many which I believe will be eternal. Happy, blessed days—how precious their memories are ! It was in one of these retreats, in 1887, that I first came into close contact with Sim, in the confidence of such a time. The connection then formed between us continued to the close of his life on earth, and, as I believe, lives on within the veil. Dear Sim ! he is to me no memory, but a felt presence still. And as of one living I would write now ; not with the purpose of drawing out admiration for him would I write. I dare not do so in my knowledge that he would forbid this, but for the honour of Him "who is to be glorified in His saints and admired in all them that believe." Sim's beauty of character as a Christian man and as a Priest was not of himself—it was the creation of the grace of God.

In him God gave us a revelation of the true ideal of a Priest's life and character   I do not say that Sim fully expressed that ideal ; but I do say that he did so in such a measure as to reveal it in an arresting degree.

The real purpose of a Priest's mission as towards men is to exercise spiritual influence. Sim certainly had that power of influence. To influence those he was brought in contact with for God and His Church was consciously the deliberate and sustained purpose of his ministry. This record of his life will show how he succeeded in using widely and deeply this conscious influence. But I believe the unconscious influence he exercised was far more extensive and powerful than the influence he consciously sought to bring into play. It was his life and character that was the secret of his power. In the times of his greatest abandonment he had the recollection of a true Priest. He was real and genuine ; he was strong ; he was a man of spiritual power because he embodied his creed in his life—"a living epistle, known and read of all," an epistle " written by the Spirit of God."

He exercised this influence in his ministry because it was begun, continued, and ended in God.

He went into the Priesthood, to my knowledge, quite clear as to his vocation of God ; and in the strength of that vocation and the mission given him of God in his Ordination he lived and ministered. " I am not come of myself : He sent me "— and with this came a definite belief in the grace of Holy Orders. He knew that his Priesthood was to be the minister of the Priesthood of Jesus Christ, and that He who had sent him to his ministry had not sent him forth undowered for it. " The Spirit of the Lord is upon me : He has anointed me." Three characteristics of that ministry were strength, love, and disciplined sobriety. To say this is to say that he lived in the power of the three pastoral virtues, the creation in the spirit of the Priest of the grace of Holy Orders, " power, love, and sober-mindedness." In his work and life, in a very real sense, he walked with God in the sphere and work of the ministry.

This ministerial walking with God rested on an abiding in

the peace of God. This was the secret of that brightness which fascinated all who really knew him. It was more than a natural brightness of disposition : it was that brightness taken up into God and transfigured by His grace. How dear is the memory of that sunlit countenance ! To my mind this face was like that of Stephen—"like the face of an angel." The angels' faces shine because they see God's face. The face of Moses shone—though he wist not that it shone—because he saw God's face. The face of Stephen shone because he saw Jesus at the right hand of God. And Sim's face shone in its brightness because, living in God's peace, he saw God's glory in the face of Jesus Christ. He lived in such a simple, childlike belief in the love of God, he was at home in it, he walked joyfully in the light of God's countenance. His own personal union with God, through the inner witness of the Holy Ghost, was just a simple fact to him. His own continued forgiveness of God was to him abidingly clear. I say this again of personal knowledge. So his life was lived in gratitude to God for His love. He loved Him with a responsive love. He yielded his heart to God, who took possession of it by His Spirit, and shed abroad in it the love of Himself. Sim knew that this responsive love itself was God's gift, and so without pride, but in true gratitude he could and did say, " Thou knowest that I love Thee."

This love expressed itself in entire consecration, at least in will and purpose, to God in the Priesthood. The model of the Priest is Jesus, who, " being come a High Priest, offered Himself." So Sim, by God's grace, in His light, and of His love, laid himself, at his Ordination, wholly and unreservedly as a living sacrifice on God's altar. How touching is his own record of how that offering was made ! At his Ordination he had heard a voice, as distinct as any human voice, say, " Go and suffer for Me." Our familiar name for him was Peter. Ah ! did he not, then, hear the call of Christ to Simon Peter handed on to him : " When thou wast young, thou girdedst thyself and walkedst whither thou wouldest : but when thou shalt be old another shall gird thee, and carry thee whither thou wouldest not. This spake He, signifying by what death he should glorify God. *And when He had spoken this, He saith unto him, Follow Me."* The nature of his call was thus clear to him when, in response to it, he gave himself to God in the sacrificial self-oblation of Ordination. And from that day until his death he consecrated himself to the Lord without reservation. His life was one long act of self-oblation. He was zealous for the Lord.

Underlying this peace and zeal was a deep humility. His low estimate of himself and his powers finds frequent expression in this work. The expression is true to his character. He did not talk about it conventionally: he was lowly in his own eyes. Not only had he a lowly opinion of his power but he had also the humility of a true penitent. All the years I knew him his life was one of abiding and deepening contrition, and by the guidance of this virtue he entered more and more into the penitential life of the Church. The prayers of humble access in our Communion Office express with truth the spirit in which he lived. Like a true Priest, he ministered before God, clothed with the vesture of humility.

And from this humility came an evident purity of intention. He had no selfish ends in life, neither personal nor ecclesiastical. No one could say of him he was playing off his own bat. Those among whom he worked knew that he sought not theirs, but them. Their good was his longing, and that not only for their sakes but for God's. By seeking His people's welfare and happiness as God's Priest, he was promoting God's glory, and to do all to the glory of God was the principle of his life. Beneath that outer life, with its varied interests and employments, this was present. For this he trained the boats' crews, amused children, took interest in recreative and social movements, as well as did his work as a Priest in the sanctuary and in the parish. The sustained beauty of a life which purity of intention gives were seen in him so clearly. Wherever you met him he was one and the same with a beautiful simplicity.

And underlying all was a life of communion with God. He was very regular in his life of private devotion. The three acts of devotion, the practice of which he enjoined on the congregation of St. Aidan's in his last sermon to them, viz., prayer, Holy Communion, and meditation, were helps of which he well knew the power by the regular using of them.

And crowning all there was in him the great priestly virtue of obedience. His obedience to the Will of God revealed to him immediately by His Spirit is seen by his response to His call; conspicuously in his Ordination, and in his going to Africa. His mediate obedience to God, as shown in submission to those set over him with God's authority was sustained from his Ordination to the end of his ministry. What golden words are those of his, " We must be ready to sacrifice a good deal of personal convictions,—at least we do not sacrifice them because we are not responsible,—and then I feel sure our sacrifice of personal feelings will bear fruit in the long run, and we shall be rewarded for giving up these by a very real return of active, real work and energy, and much fruit which we have no right to expect." He gave himself to serve God in obedience, and did so unto death. Zeal he had up to the measure of not counting his life dear unto himself; but it was a zeal purified from self-will, kept in discipline by obedience grounded in humility. He was never a law unto himself. He was a true Catholic. Obedience is an arresting feature in the Catholic character, and this of necessity ; without it the ideal of Catholicism cannot find expression. Its ideal of Christian life is that of a life lived in the associated unity of the Church ; but this can only be when life is ruled by common laws in obedience to constituted authorities by whom those laws are interpreted and made effective; and if this is true of all states of life in the Church, it is specially so of the Priesthood. Sim saw this clearly, and so his life was one of zeal, disciplined by obedience, and loyalty to the virtue of obedience led him along a path of self-sacrifice crowned by the glory of its end.

I have sketched a beautiful character in which self-oblation, love, humility, purity of intention, devotion and obedience, blend harmoniously. But I have sketched Sim as I knew him, and as he lives in my memory, for he *was* a thing of beauty. I have never known a young man more beautiful than he, and in him beauty of character found its true setting in the beauty of his priestly life. Like an " apple of gold in a casket of silver " was he in it, and that not of himself, but by the grace of God.

In this work "he being dead, yet speaketh," as to all who shall read it, so specially to our younger clergy. May the word of his life and letters be blessed of God to raise up a fruitful offspring in whom his character may be reproduced and his work at home and abroad perpetuated. This is the memorial I pray may be reared in this church of Durham to the memory of Arthur Fraser Sim.

GEORGE BODY,
Canon Missioner of Durham.

THE COLLEGE, DURHAM, *July* 28, 1896.

CONTENTS

LIST OF ILLUSTRATIONS

A SKETCH OF THE LIFE

OF

ARTHUR FRASER SIM

MISSION PRIEST

AT KOTA KOTA, CENTRAL AFRICA

Obiit Oct. 29th, 1895

AV

A SKETCH OF THE LIFE OF
ARTHUR FRASER SIM

A RTHUR FRASER SIM was
born on the 2nd November,
1861, at Madras, where his
father was Senior Member of
the Madras Council, and one
of the most eminent men in
that Presidency.

The first seven years of
his life were spent in India,
with the exception of a visit
home for six months in 1865,
and during these early years
it seemed as if he were destined to inherit that constitutional delicacy which is prevalent
among Anglo-Indian children. At
a very early age he suffered a good
deal from asthma, and his parents regarded him as a delicate
child who would require more than an ordinary amount of care
if he were to grow up a robust and healthy man. In disposition he was quiet, but very determined. When very young he
evinced that pluck which in later years formed a marked trait
in his character. An instance is related how that when he
was five years of age, as he and his sisters were one evening
about to be driven to the beach at Madras in a little pony

B

dogcart, and before they had all been lifted into the trap, the pony made off. Arthur, who was sitting behind, clambered over the rail to the front, seized the reins, and managed to stop the pony till the servants appeared on the scene.

In March, 1869, the family came to England, and settled for a year at East Sheen. Then, in the following year, when their parents returned to India, the younger children were left at home, and Arthur began his school life at the Rev. R. H. Cooke's Private School in Cheltenham. Several of his elder

CHELTENHAM COLLEGE.
From Bath Road.

brothers were at the same School, and were, like him, lovable and good fellows, very affectionate as brothers, and great favourites with all. At Cheltenham all signs of asthma or delicacy happily disappeared; so that when Arthur went to Cheltenham College after the midsummer holidays in 1875, he was as strong and healthy as most boys.

He soon found himself coming to the front both in his House and in the College, though he was still a small boy and not yet fourteen. This was due to the fact that his elder brothers, who had preceded him at Christowe,[1] had earned a great reputation for the name of Sim, to his own singular charm of person and manner, and to his keenness and skill at most games and athletic exercises.

In spite of his having no exceptional intellectual gifts, he was diligent in his studies, and progressed steadily in the six years that he was at the College from the eighth class to the second division of the first class. He had a natural taste

THE " BIG CLASSICAL," CHELTENHAM COLLEGE.

and aptitude for botany and drawing, and in later years he rejoiced that he had had the opportunity of cultivating these.

There does not seem to have been any particular period in his school life which can be regarded as a crisis in his faith ; he did not neglect the training received from his mother, and his spiritual life was one of steady growth, which was unaffected by his increasing popularity, deepened by his Confirmation,

[1] Christowe Boarding House.

sustained by his regular Communions, and strengthened by Miss Drummond's [1] influence, and by his close intimacy with one whom henceforward he regarded as an elder brother.

Humanly speaking it was mainly due to his intercourse with this School friend that his wish to devote his life to God's service in the Priesthood grew till it became a fixed determination. Even in those days they used to discuss with deep interest what their work should be in Christ's Church, first at home and afterwards in the mission field. They hoped that this friendship begun at School would be still more closely cemented by at least a year together at Cambridge, whither his friend had gone in 1878. Consequently it was a great disappointment to both when, in the midsummer holidays of 1880, it was decided that Arthur Sim should remain a year longer at Cheltenham. Of this decision he himself wrote at the time :—" I do not doubt that I should learn more in a year at Cambridge than I should at School, nor that it would be a more useful knowledge ; but I am sure that another year at School would make me much more fit to begin such an education. My great failing now is *groundwork*, and a year under —— is, I am sure, the best way of remedying this. . . . But, putting aside all question of work—for I should not go back for that *only*—I cannot help feeling sure that a *similar* opportunity of doing good will never occur to me again. Next term I should be Senior Prefect. . . . Do you

[1] Miss Ella Drummond was an invalid lady of saintly character, who suffered continuously for the last twenty years of her life. Her room overlooked the College playground, and in it she received and welcomed a number of boys on Sunday evenings, or, as she was able, during the week. Her character and influence were such that no boy left her presence without a blessing, and to her Arthur Sim felt that he owed more than he could say.

> " I think of her, whose gentle tongue
> All plaint in her own cause controll'd ;
> Of thee I think, my brother ! young
> In heart, high-soul'd.
>
> That comely face, that cluster'd brow,
> That cordial hand, that bearing free,
> I see them still, I see them now,
> Shall always see ! "

think that a year spent in trying to do good among so many young and forming characters will be a year lost from all those that, please God, we shall spend together in His work after leaving Cambridge? This is not all. Hitherto I have never held anything but a secondary position in the School, and I cannot help feeling that my character, which, God knows, is now weakness itself, would be formed in a mould which, from all the influences that would then surround me, could not but be a mould of strength. You say that School is only a means to an end. This is, of course, true; but I feel sure that the opportunity of using this means to the full should be seized. It is not one, you know, that is offered to every Schoolboy, especially under such circumstances as it is offered to me. I do not yet seem to have said half enough about this point— with me it is, of course, the chief—but I think I have said enough to make you understand clearly what I feel."

In his earlier years at Christowe there were special difficulties, both in the House and in the College, which had to be faced and overcome; and without putting himself forward in any way he was invariably on the side of right principle, and his example was a strength to boys of weaker character, even though in some cases they were his seniors. Later, when he became a leader in the College athletic world, this unseen but strongly felt influence became more marked and widespread. As may be gathered from the letter quoted above, he was keenly alive to responsibility, both as a Prefect and as an ordinary Schoolboy, and yet he never went out of his way to report things he could himself correct or amend. A very interesting feature in his School life was the affectionate and unselfish way in which he treated his younger brother, who was several years his junior, going even so far as to act as his banker—and a very liberal one he proved, too. Yet his brotherly affection was never allowed to interfere with his duties as a Prefect. On one occasion, finding his young brother had been out of bounds, he gave him the usual imposition, and insisted upon its being done.

He took the very keenest interest in all kinds of games and sports, in most of which he himself excelled, for what he lacked in bodily weight he made up by sheer pluck and honest hard work. As an oar he probably established a record as the stroke of his School-boat for four years in succession. As a forward in the College Fifteen he could always be relied on for hard work in the scrimmage, and for making the most of his opportunities in running or dribbling. In athletics he was a good long-distance runner, and carried off several

ARTHUR F. SIM.
Cheltenham, 1879.

prizes for distances varying from half a mile to two miles. He was a strong swimmer, and fair gymnast. As a sportsman, in shooting he could more than hold his own, while he was no mean fisherman.

Only in such games as cricket, racquets, and fives, where quickness of vision was essential, he did not excel. This was due to the fact of his being long-sighted, so that he could not follow the flight of a quickly-approaching object. Yet even of these games he probably knew more than the average boy, and his opinions and criticisms were always those of a close and sagacious observer. Ere he left the School at midsummer, 1881, he occupied the unique position of Senior Prefect, Captain of the College Boat Club, and Captain of the College Football Fifteen; and by masters and boys alike he was universally esteemed as almost an ideal type of what a Schoolboy should be.

CHELTENHAM COLLEGE BOAT.
Winner of Public Schools Challenge Cup at Henley, 1879.
Stroke, A. F. SIM.

In October, 1881, he entered Pembroke College, Cambridge, where several of his greatest friends had already preceded him, and where others were to follow. He was not destined to take honours, not having attained special distinction in any branch of study at School ; but he came up with a definite aim, namely, to seek Holy Orders, and in his social life and in his reading he kept this high aim constantly in view. Rowing, which he took up keenly from the first, was to him more than a pastime, more than healthful bodily exercise—it was a moral discipline. In the regular and hard exertion he found a valuable safeguard for his purity; in training he learnt lessons of self-control; in the multitudinous corrections of "coaching" he developed patience, and as first-boat Captain he realized his responsibility to others, and most faithfully and diligently served the interests of his Club and College.

He did not take a prominent part in any of the religious meetings got up by undergraduates, but he was regular in his attendance at the College Chapel, especially at the early Celebration on Sundays. Though always reserved in speaking about religion, he warmly welcomed an earnest talk with a friend in private, and on such occasions always spoke about himself depreciatingly and of others charitably. Clinging to the great facts of the Christian Faith, he never seemed to be troubled with intellectual doubt or speculation. He "trusted in God and made no haste."

His principal friends were those with whom he was daily associated in the rowing, and he seemed to make no enemies. He stroked the College first boat for four years—1882 to 1885 inclusive—the boat being ninth upon the river when he came up, and fourth when he went down.

In the autumn of 1883 he was selected to stroke one of the University trial eights, and rowed pluckily and well, but was not considered heavy enough for the Putney course. The "*Cambridge Review*," in describing the Bumping Races, June, 1884, says: "Pembroke, though weak in the bows, showed themselves a good crew, and being admirably stroked by Sim, caused First Trinity trouble after entering Long Reach. Here Pembroke drew up, and before long were overlapping a trifle. First Trinity had an excellent coxswain, who staved off more than one shot by good steering. Sim, however, was not to be denied, and his men, rowing pluckily, lowered the colours of First Trinity near the Railway Bridge amid much excitement."

This was Sim's crowning achievement, perhaps, on the river.

9

The College Boat Club showed their appreciation of his services by presenting him with an oar specially painted, and publicly thanked him for the careful and painstaking manner in which he had discharged his duties as first-boat Captain.

Of all kinds of rowing he most enjoyed that in a coxswainless light pair. With one friend in particular, a Fellow of the College, did he delight to row, and, when some six years after they had left Cambridge they unexpectedly met there in the May week, it was not long before they were out on the river together. Sim afterwards, when recounting his various doings in that week, spoke of his surprise and joy at the way that boat travelled on a perfectly even keel, as one of his pleasantest reminiscences of a very enjoyable holiday.

His might seem an uneventful College career; but the powerful influence of his gentle spirit is still felt by many, and his subsequent career showed that Cambridge had been to him a training ground for bearing greater responsibilities and doing nobler deeds.

On his taking his B.A. degree (Third Class, Special Examination in Theology) at Midsummer, 1884, the Master of Pembroke College gladly and affectionately commended him in high terms to Bishop Lightfoot, and he became one of the students at Auckland Castle. Among his contemporaries at Bishop Auckland were two old Schoolfellows, who rejoiced at the prospect of the renewal of their former friendship with him. In one of his letters he gives a brief sketch of his life there : —

"One has an indefinite amount of work to do, so I will give you a sample of the way we spend the day. Breakfast at 7.45 ; chapel, 8.15 ; lectures, 9 till 11 ; reading, 11 till 1 ; lunch at 1.15 ; then in the afternoon we visit three times a week and read the other three days. I generally get a game, and sometimes two, of football in the week by way of exercise. My district is a sort of cosmopolitan one. I visit the parents of the Institute lads. The Institute was built by the Bishop, and it is a sort of club for young men and lads from fifteen years upwards. There are about two hundred in it, so there is lots to do. I generally go there in the evenings and sit and talk with the lads, and I am teaching one of them to read—a slow process! I have a Bible Class on Sunday, and I read the lessons at the Parish Church.

Occasionally I have to preach in a Schoolroom some three miles out in the country, but more often in a tiny little room in the town, where my congregation consists of about four to twelve old women and a lot of children. The latter are never quiet, and to have one of them squalling in one's ear is rather disconcerting, though not to the mothers who are accustomed to it. . . . I have a dear old invalid woman here who reminds me very much of Miss Drummond, and I consequently go in to see her pretty often. She is not such an invalid as Miss D——, as she can get about her room with a little help ; but she has something of the same patience, and is so obviously glad to see one."

Perhaps it was only to be expected that under the influences which surrounded him at Bishop Auckland, and especially that of Bishop Lightfoot, his character would develop more rapidly than hitherto. Such was the case, and he himself, nine years later, recalls the fact :—"How happy," he writes, " those old Auckland days were ! If I have any steadiness or staunchness of purpose, God gave it to me there."

For the month immediately preceding his examination for Deacon's Orders he and three fellow-students formed a reading party at Lake Windermere ; and the others felt that it was due to his example and companionship that the visit proved so profitable and enjoyable. While on this reading party at the Lakes he invited an old College friend, whom he knew to be passing through a time of spiritual difficulty, to come and see him. So great was the trouble, that his friend had all but decided to relinquish the thought of taking Holy Orders, upon which he had previously set his heart. But in the course of conversation Arthur Sim was enabled to clear away the doubts and

PEMBROKE COLLEGE, CAMBRIDGE.
From Trumpington Street.

13

difficulties, and so inspired his friend with his own simple, strong faith that in the end he was ordained, and has always been remarkable for his earnestness and zeal in Christ's service.

On September 20th, 1885, he and four fellow-students were ordained Deacons in the Parish Church at Barnard Castle by Bishop Lightfoot. He had already accepted a title to St. John's Parish, Sunderland, a parish of which it has been said that, as regards squalor and poverty, it has not its equal in the Diocese of Durham. But the hardship and distastefulness of such surroundings, which would have proved a burden to other men, were to him only a greater opportunity for the exercise of his love and self-denial. He rejoiced, too, in the prospect of being once more united in the closest companionship with his old School friend, and it was arranged that as their spheres of work were in a sense contiguous, they should live in the same house.

At Trinity, 1887, he was ordained Priest by Bishop Lightfoot in St. Andrew's Church, Bishop Auckland, the Church in which he had acted as reader while a student at Auckland Castle.

Of his work in Sunderland, his Vicar, the Rev. J. W. Willink, writes :—

" To speak of Arthur Sim's work at St. John's is no easy task ; it was many-sided and very varied in its nature, and every part of it was full of life and energy and love to a most unusual degree. We commenced our work together early in October, 1885, I on my Institution as Vicar, on October 4th, and he as a young Deacon ordained to the curacy at the preceding September Ordination. From the very first he threw himself with boundless energy into the work, and won all hearts by his bright smile and winning ways. Nothing could exceed the attraction of his personal character or the charm of his manner. I remember hearing again and again the same expression used of him by those whose lives he brightened by his visits when weighed down by chronic suffering or by the feebleness that old age brings—' He's like a beam of sunshine wherever he goes.' His first address in the Parish was a delightful one—a carefully prepared speech in answer to an address by one of the wardens at our Welcome Tea. It began well and happily; but shortly hesitation came, then confusion, and then complete and utter breakdown. But with it came a confession of his failure, so delightfully ' taking ' and so entirely natural, and following after came so simple and unaffected a speech, that nothing could exceed the impression produced or the warmth of the delighted applause that greeted him when he sat down. The hold he won that night, though to him the address was an apparent failure which much mortified him, he never lost ; and in the homes of the people, by the bedside of the sick and suffering, in the Schools, and, above all, in the Young Men's Club, he established an influence as deep as it has proved lasting, and as real in the days that followed his departure as it was enthusiastic while he was present in the Parish.

His influence over the very rough class of young men and lads that abound in the East end of Sunderland was extraordinary, and his powers of organization and continued maintenance of night school classes and of periodical concerts and gatherings for the lads were very great indeed—only equalled by their answering love and reverence. One great element that contributed largely to his unbounded influence was his splendid health and great physical strength and skill in many branches of outside activity. His powers as a swimmer in the open sea were the theme of wondering admiration, while a very plucky dive into the River Wear from the Quayside to save a drowning child, which he achieved most gallantly in the face of great difficulty, was rewarded not alone by the Bronze Medal of the Royal Humane Society (and oh ! how distasteful the public presentation of that medal was to him !), but by the respect and deep admiration of the whole of the riverside population.

One great hobby of his was the Lantern as a means of

devotion and instruction, and the use he made of it was very great. The experiments he carried out, and the improvements he was continually adopting, showed how highly he regarded it as an instrument for work among the very poor; and certainly in St. John's his enthusiasm for its use was fully justified by results.

Of what he was to me personally it would be impossible to

AUCKLAND CASTLE CHAPEL.

speak. The unfailing brightness of his sunny nature, the unaffected manliness of his piety, the quiet, deep, true work he was ever doing, his comradeship and brotherly sympathy, and above all, the lofty spirituality of his life, can never be effaced from my recollection. I shall always have cause to thank God, and for more reasons than I can ever tell, that He permitted me to know the joy and blessedness of work for Him with a comrade so true and so helpful, with a brother so loving and

so loved as he ever was from the first day to the last of our
most happy and unclouded association together in the work of
St. John's, Sunderland. He is one of those of whom it may
be said, 'He, being made perfect in a short time, fulfilled a
long time'!"[1]

His Vicar has alluded to his great dislike of the "fuss" that
was made of him after he rescued the boy from drowning in
the Wear. A striking incident in connection with this showed
the true character of the man. At that time he was living
with his fellow-Curate, and they were on terms of very close
intimacy. On the morning after the boy had been rescued,
some man accosted this Curate, and asked him if he had
jumped into the river and pulled a boy out. He replied that
he knew nothing about it. Soon after, meeting Arthur Sim,
the Curate told him of the man's question, but he passed the
matter off in some way, and it was only on the following day
(*two days after the incident*) that he found out that it was Sim
who had jumped in, and had gone home followed by a crowd
of small boys. And later it was with the greatest reluctance
that he accepted the Royal Humane Society's Medal.

Another illustration of the way in which he kept in the
background anything that referred to himself was alluded to in
the sermon at the memorial Service in St. John's Church. On
his leaving School a number of his friends, wishing to give
him some tangible token of their high regard, presented him
with a silver watch, suitably inscribed on the inside case with
the circumstances under which the gift was made. During
the ten years that he lived in the North, not more than two
or three persons had any idea that this watch had anything
of special interest attached to it.

The same reserve was still further illustrated by the fact that
neither at Sunderland nor at West Hartlepool were any of his
cups or prizes for rowing or athletics to be seen about his
rooms. As a matter of fact, he gave them all away before his
Ordination. The only thing of the kind that he retained was

---

[1] *Wisdom of Solomon*, iv. 13.

his Pembroke College oar, which he regarded as testifying to
the prowess of his College boat rather than to any skill or
merit of his own.

ALLEY AND GROUP IN ST. JOHN'S PARISH, SUNDERLAND.

In spite of the press of work in his Parish, he managed to
find time when at Sunderland, and even after he left, to coach
the crew of the Amateur Rowing Club to victory, and no other

Clergyman in the place had such an influence on the young men who rowed there. His efforts on their behalf were recognised and marked by the members of the club electing him a life member, making a presentation to him on his leaving the town, and naming one of their boats the "A. F. Sim." So, too, the St. John's Institute lads named their boat the "A. F. Sim,"' concerning which the remarkable coincidence is related that on October 29th, 1895, the day of Arthur Sim's death, this boat went down and was lost.[1]

Perhaps one of the most characteristic features of his work at St. John's was the round of Christmas festivities for the lads which he organized year by year. For a fortnight—from before Christmas Day until after the New Year—he had some entertainment and either tea or supper for the boys every night, and kept them with him till after eleven when the public-houses closed. Most of them signed and kept the pledge for that fortnight. For some time before they had been learning carols, and on Christmas Eve he was out with them all night, singing at the houses of the different helpers. On one such occasion, a gentleman who knew him intimately went down about 3 a.m. to give the boys some apples and money, and until Arthur Sim spoke, he thought he was one of the lads, with his cap tied down over his ears like the rest; and a happy group they looked in the clear night air with their lanterns. Another work which he arranged among the boys was a Sunday evening instruction class—five minutes' instruction and then a hymn, and so on. This was for those who never went to Church. Often, too, when the classes were over, late at night he would find somebody very ill, and would come back to the Institute, and ask the caretaker to give him some supper as he found he must sit up. On one occasion, when the seamen's Chaplain was sitting up all night with a Naval Reserve man who was dying, Sim got up and came to

---

[1] This coincidence was not generally known till nearly three months after the actual event.

them at 5 a.m. to cheer them, and remained to join with them in the Holy Communion.

It was generally thought, by those who knew him best, that the ties with St. John's Parish were so intimate that he could not be induced to change his sphere of work; but, in the autumn of 1889, when he was invited by an old Schoolfellow, whose life had been closely linked with his, to help him in working up a new Parish and Church in West Hartlepool, he left the decision in Bishop Lightfoot's hands, stating that he would work where he was most needed. The Bishop, in no way undervaluing the needs of St. John's, but recognising that it had had a long period of more or less settled Church life, whereas the district which was to form the new Parish of St. Aidan had been greatly neglected, represented to him that the change would have his approval; and so after much prayer and many heartburnings he decided to help his friend in West Hartlepool. When as yet the matter was *sub judice*, he wrote: —" I don't know how I shall face the awful rupture of leaving St. John's. I trust that if it is right I shall be given courage to do so. . . . May God guide us in this, and make His Will all in all to us ! "

Hence it could not fail but that the renewed consecration of his life should bring him corresponding spiritual power and energy for the wide field of work that lay before him.

Previous to his coming to St. Aidan's in January, 1890, the work of the district had been carried on in a Mission Room; but the Church was approaching completion, and consequently all the machinery and organization for the new Parish had to be thought of and arranged for. In addition to this there were sad arrears, caused by long years of neglect, to be made up. The difficulties to be faced and the responsibility thrown upon his shoulders were considerably increased by the long illness and enforced absence of his Vicar; so that, had it not been for his wonderful power of organization, his ripe judgment and unremitting devotion, this period would have proved very critical in the life of the new Parish. As it was, he showed

himself equal to the demands made upon him, and, in spite of
his having to preach more in those first six months at St.
Aidan's than during the whole period of his ministry at St.
John's, the work grew under his watchful guidance and care ;
consequently, when the Church was consecrated in the following autumn, it fell little short of the high ideal which he had
set before him. At the time of the consecration and afterwards many kindly expressions were volunteered as to the
orderly and reverent manner in which the Services were conducted—a result mainly due to the indefatigable way in which
he had arranged and rehearsed everything beforehand. It was
a source of much satisfaction and joy both to him and his
Vicar that their old School and College friend was able to be
with them, and to preach the sermons during the octave of
consecration. On the opening of the new Church old ties had
to be cemented and further developments conceived and
carried out ; and into both these spheres of work he threw
himself heart and soul, so that the prejudices of the older
worshippers, who had grown accustomed to the simple Services
of the Mission Room, were soon laid aside when they found
the more beautiful Service of the Church conducted with the
same earnestness and spirituality as hitherto.

    In his district he had the visitation of some 3,000 souls—a
work which he carried on with the greatest regularity, diligence,
and perseverance, and wherever he went his attractive manner
and cheerful presence ensured him a hearty welcome. Having
one Sunday School and the Band of Hope under his immediate
control, he did his utmost to make them as perfect as possible.
The choice of suitable lessons was always a subject of deep
thought to him, and every help was given to his teachers in
order that their work might be effective. His devotion to the
scholars was very real, and was reciprocated by a very warm
affection on their part. A touching illustration of this was
furnished in the case of a little fellow of five, who, having heard
that Mr. Sim in his new home in Africa had no sugar, was discovered the following day filling his missionary box with sugar

ST. AIDAN'S CHURCH, WEST HARTLEPOOL.

(From a photograph by A. E. Sim.)

to send to him. In another way, scholars of all ages evinced their regard for him by the numerous letters which they wrote to him in Nyasaland. Of the children he himself wrote :— " They are continuous sunshine in the streets."

As at St. John's, so at St. Aidan's, the lads seemed to occupy the warmest place in his heart, and he was continually devising some new attraction for them. At first he began with a Saturday night "At Home" at the Clergy House, where he would keep them week by week thoroughly amused and interested with books and parlour games for some two hours. Later, when the new Parish Hall was built, he helped to organize a company of the Boys' Brigade with which a gymnasium was connected. Afterwards he learnt book-binding and wood-carving, in order that he might teach and interest the lads ; and even if he were busy with some other duty he would invariably look in before going home to see how they were getting on. For the lads in his own class in Sunday-school his care was unremitting. Rough and undisciplined they were in many cases, but he loved them, and they knew it. One of them had been for some time an inmate of Durham gaol. When it was proposed that the summer treat should be there and the lad remarked that he had seen Durham too often, he felt keenly for him. Another, whose fiery temper had brought him into trouble, and on whom he knew prison discipline was likely to produce a hardening effect, was saved by his care from imprisonment ; and ever afterwards the lad's welfare was a subject of the deepest interest to him.

For the men in his district, which was some distance from the Parish Hall, he took a house, fitted it up, and organized a Working-men's Club, which had a very successful, though unhappily too short a life. In connection with this he arranged a number of delightful and instructive lectures on popular subjects, with limelight illustrations, and several Social Evenings such as had not been known in that part of the town within the memory of man. A summer trip also in connection with this Club, organized by him, and for which he

curtailed a short holiday in the South of England, is remembered still as a red-letter day by the men and their
wives.

But these more secular organizations were only steps to win
those who participated in them to higher and better things,
and he proved their usefulness by the hold he had upon the
lads who came to his Bible Class, and by the way in which
he was able to gather them round him for preparation for
Holy Communion on the great festivals. Into his dealings
with men and lads when preparing them for Confirmation he
threw such an amount of earnestness, affection, and direct-
ness, that he won their entire confidence, and was enabled to
give them such a grasp of Divine truth as to make their Confirmation very real. This work was a great joy to him, and he
was deeply grateful for the opportunities it afforded him. Of
the Confirmation of 1891 he wrote :—" We have so many
adults ; it is such a privilege helping them, and they are so
earnest." That of the previous year was held on a Saturday
afternoon, and he realized the great danger there was of some
of the candidates, especially the lads whom he had prepared
and who were very dear to him, being tempted to visit places
of amusement of a more than questionable character. As a
counter attraction he arranged a Lantern Service for them in
the Parish Hall. The subjects were sacred ones, most of
them being scenes in our Lord's life. One of exceptional
beauty formed the text for a short address. It represented
" The Good Shepherd who giveth His life for the sheep."
The lion, which would have attacked the flock now feeding in
safety, was slain, but at the cost of the Shepherd's life. The
love of Him " Who loved them and gave Himself for them "
was spoken of with an earnestness which could not fail to take
effect.

Allusion has already been made to his use of the Lantern
at St. John's, and his experience and skill in this direction
were highly valued, not only parochially but by his brother
Clergy in West Hartlepool, so that he was in constant request

to illustrate addresses and lectures. His knowledge of every detail connected with lantern work was complete, and his skill and taste as a photographer enabled him to make a large collection of valuable slides. He mastered the intricacies of modern cameras and lanterns. Before he left for Africa he had devised and constructed an oil lantern without any fixings

ARTHUR F. SIM.
West Hartlepool, 1892.
(*From a photograph by T. Braybrook.*)

of leather or wood, so as to defy the ravages of the white ants. The subsequent success of this lantern was a source of great satisfaction and delight to him, and he looked forward to its proving a useful adjunct to his work among the natives. His method of conducting these Services was always reverent and impressive. He refrained as far as possible from using words of his own, and adhered closely to the inspired word of Scripture, supplemented with suitable collects and hymns.

The taste and skill which he exhibited in work of this description found further expression in the decoration of the Church for the great Festivals; and it was in a large measure due to his direction that the result invariably proved so pleasing. Although he himself would never admit that he possessed any decorative ability, or that he was an authority upon such matters, yet those who worked with him were always glad to defer to his opinion; and the harmonious colouring and simple dignity of St. Aidan's Church are a lasting witness to the correctness of his judgment. Whatever decorations were in hand—whether for some Festival in Church, or for some tea or entertainment in the Parish Hall, he was always at the beck and call of those engaged, and so busily would he be kept occupied that sometimes he would go without his evening meal.

He was himself of such an essentially buoyant and cheerful disposition that he seemed always to be intent upon making others happy. When, through illness or some other cause, his Vicar was what he would call "dowley," he would lay himself out to cheer him up. And with what energy and zest he would strive to make the treats and trips of the children and lads as bright and as happy as possible! Yet no one enjoyed those occasions more than himself,—till the next day, when he was often sore and stiff with the exertions he had made.

His large fund of general information, his knowledge of natural history and of architecture, his cheerfulness, equable temperament, and unselfish interest in everybody and everything around him, made him at all times a most delightful companion, but especially so on any holiday trip; as, for instance, when Bishop Lightfoot took him and his two oldest friends to Norway in the summer of 1887.

For him certainly,—

> " All things were fair, if we had eyes to see
>   How first God made them goodly everywhere."

He had a large fund of quiet humour which generally found its expression in harmless chaff, and he enjoyed the fun as much as others if the laugh was against himself. Occasionally, however, it would take a more practical shape, as for instance, when he would snapshoot with his camera some friend in a ridiculous position, or when, as once happened, he materially increased his Vicar's score by making his little terrier run off with the cricket ball from the fielder.

A failing of his—not a very serious one—absent minded-ness, used often to afford him and others considerable amusement. If he went out with a walking-stick and called at any house, he invariably came home without it. An umbrella he never used—it would have been too expensive. On one occasion he found himself in Church without his sermon ; and on another he put on two surplices, one over the other, thinking that the topmost one was his hood.

Though knowing little himself of bodily suffering, he was always deeply touched by any sign of it in others, and it quickly called forth his earnest sympathy.

> " The quiet happy face that lighted up
>   As from a sunshine in the heart within,
>   Rejoicing whomsoever looked on it,
>   But far more whomsoever it looked on."

These words might well be applied to him in the homes of the sick and the sorrowing. This sympathy of his encouraged his people to tell their troubles to him, and many a careworn heart found relief in doing this. His care for their bodily needs was no less real than for their spiritual good. None that were really in need of help ever applied to him in vain ; even those whose distress was the result of their own wrong-doing were relieved in sickness, and so tender-hearted was he that not infrequently he was imposed upon. To this day tramps call

at St. Aidan's Clergy House and ask for Mr. Sim, with the tale
that they "knew him at St. John's, Sunderland."

His watchful care for those who were tempted was that of
one who felt the awful responsibility of his priestly office.
When he knew of young girls in danger of being led astray,
who in their own homes were unlikely to learn anything of
what was pure, and over whom he imagined a woman's influence would be most powerful, he would ask those whom he
trusted to look after them.

In the autumn of 1891, a Sunday scholar, who had always
been delicate, became seriously ill. She was prepared for
Confirmation, and the rite was privately administered by the
Bishop. His care for her bodily and spiritual needs was
unremitting — books, pictures, and delicacies to tempt the
capricious appetite were taken or sent, and very few days
passed without a visit from him. On the last night of her
life he stayed beside her for hours, soothing and cheering her,
for she was very restless, until the end came about midnight.
A dreary walk homeward through drifting snows brought on
a severe attack of influenza ; but his kindness made a deep impression on the heart of the mother, hardened though it was
by poverty and the cruelty of her husband, and she presented
herself as a candidate for the next Confirmation.

Early in 1892 he was asked to visit a young girl in the
Parish who was dying of consumption. She was very beautiful,
and seemed the embodiment of Ruskin's ideal of English
maidenhood—the loving helper at home, and the kind friend
of those in distress. For three months he ministered to her
constantly, teaching her until death was looked upon as the
"Gate of Life Immortal." In Easter week the end came,
and for the last time he visited her. The distressing cough
had ceased, and all noisy grief on the part of those to whom
she had said good-bye was checked by her calm, peaceful face.
Then in the quietness his voice rang out :—" I am the resurrection and the life," " I am the Good Shepherd," " Yea
though I walk through the valley of the shadow of death, I

will fear no evil, for Thou art with me." Then followed the Commendatory Prayer, and in a few minutes all that belonged to this mortal life was over, and he went back to a meeting of young happy girls without any sense of incongruity, only realizing more intensely the closeness of the unseen world.

Very different from this was the scene in another house where he ministered. A man, who went to his work in a state of intoxication and who was warned of the danger he incurred, was killed. The son had that morning been sentenced to a month's imprisonment for theft, and when the father's remains were carried home the wretched wife had gone to the theatre. Yet even in such an atmosphere his presence was welcomed, for words of loving sympathy for the bereaved were spoken. And now the widow, dying herself, speaks of him with the deepest gratitude.

Nothing could exceed his care for the poor and aged members of the congregation. Everything that could brighten their lives was done at any cost to himself, and after he left the Parish very few mails arrived without some kind remembrance being sent to them.

Two old women, both earnest Christians though not members of the Church, were for two or three years the objects of his care, and his visits were looked upon as the bright spots in their lives. Another old woman, a cripple, hardened by cruel usage from a brutal husband, and who for nearly forty years had never entered a Church, declared that she would do so in order that she might hear his last sermon. A wonderful tribute surely, for she was wretchedly poor, and could only walk by the aid of two crutches.

So deep was his joy in ministering to the suffering and sorrowful, a joy which he first felt in the quiet of Miss Drummond's sick room at Cheltenham, that he regarded the blessedness of helping others as one of the sources of truest comfort in time of sorrow. This he used to teach, and one of his workers, who in a time of bereavement was urged by him to visit and help a poor fever-stricken woman, tells how she proved then, and in times of deeper sorrow, the efficacy of his teaching and the truth of the words,—

" A child's kiss set on thy sighing lips shall make thee glad ;
An old man helped by thee shall make thee strong ;
A poor man served by thee shall make thee rich ;
Thou shalt be served thyself by every sense of service which thou renderest."

As a preacher, there were some who were inclined to criticise him adversely because occasionally he lacked fluency, but he always possessed that first essential of a good preacher, namely, earnestness. His sermons were carefully, thoughtfully, and prayerfully prepared, and as a rule written out in full, after which he would make an outline and preach from that. But whether the subject matter were good or indifferent —it was never bad—one invariably felt the truth of what Bishop Lightfoot once remarked : " Let Sim go where he will, his face will be a sermon in itself."

On the last Easter Day in the old Mission Church, when the room had been tastefully decorated in a way that satisfied even his artistic ideas, and the Services beautified so as to welcome the Day of Resurrection, there was a large crowd of earnest worshippers, for during the preceding week the love of Him, " Who liveth and was dead," had been set forth in earnest words, and it was a glad thanksgiving. The sermon, preached from the text "That I may know Him and the power of His resurrection," was an inspiration. No one who heard it and knew his life could doubt that the words were those of one who had that knowledge and power.

During Lent, 1893, the life of the prophet Elijah was taken as the subject of his addresses. The grandeur and faithfulness of the strange mysterious life were beautifully shown ; nor was the human weakness lost sight of, and God's call " What doest thou here, Elijah ? " was both an incentive and a warning.

In the autumn of the same year he gave a course of addresses to the Girls' Guild on the Holy Communion. This he looked upon as the mainspring of its work. The last of these addresses was given on the evening of his return from a Retreat, and was unequalled in its deep spirituality.

Unless away from home he always took the children's addresses at the monthly Services in Church. His last one was on April 22nd, 1894, when they were urged to make " Jesus only " the aim of life.

On March 18th he preached the last of his course of Lenten addresses. The subject was " Perseverance." To attain this grace the means recommended were : Looking to Calvary for courage, to heaven for confidence, within for humility, to God for sanctity.

On April 15th he preached his last sermon in St. Aidan's. His text, " Christ is all," was surely the key to his own life. He spoke, to use his own words, "as one who in all probability would never stand there again," of his own sorrows, the deepest being the fewness of the regular communicants ; and of what to him had been the greatest helps—Prayer, Holy Communion, and Meditation.[1]

Referring to the Farewell Service on April 26th, when the intensity of his feeling was such that he could barely finish reading the first lesson (Isa. lxi.), a working-man afterwards remarked " That was the best sermon Mr. Sim ever preached in St. Aidan's Church." The reply was " No ; the best sermon he ever preached was his life here during the last four years."

The great aim of his life seemed to be that God in all things should be glorified, and that those under his care should be helped. To do this no trouble on his part was spared ; his time was cheerfully given, and those who worked under him were encouraged and helped. Every effort was made to bring the Services to the highest state of perfection. It was his desire that the one great Service, the Holy Communion should be magnificent, and he believed that it would be best

[1] See Appendix.

to set it before the congregation in all its glory rather than
wait until they were ready for it.

In a way it was a great trouble to him that he could not
devote his whole time to parochial work, but when he felt it
to be his duty to be otherwise occupied, he ungrudgingly gave
the time. Thus it was due to his devotion and unceasing
labours as Honorary Secretary that the local branch of the
Missions to Seamen Society was pulled through a very critical
period.

In a similar way, as local Honorary Secretary for two years
of the Universities' Mission to Central Africa, he gave a tremendous impetus to the interest in, and work for, that Society
throughout the town.

As Chaplain to the Stranton Lodge of Freemasons and
Grand Provincial Mark Chaplain he exercised a wide and
healthy influence over those with whom he would not otherwise have been brought in contact.

Upon two occasions he took part in special Missions. The
first was in November, 1889, at St. John's, Weymouth. His
share of the work there was the Meditation at the Daily
Celebration and all the Children's Services. These latter he
managed admirably, and they were a great feature of the whole
Mission. He also took a certain number of dinner-hour
addresses, and visited many sick parishioners. In this Mission
he assisted his Vicar most readily and willingly, in the absence
through illness of another, on the shortest notice and almost
without any time for preparation. Those associated with him
remember it as a very happy time in every way.

The second occasion was in January and February, 1894,
shortly before he started for Africa, when, among the Seamen in
the Liverpool Mission, he assisted his oldest friend. He was
appointed to undertake the work at Garston, one of the out-
lying Seamen's Mission-rooms on the Mersey. In reply to a
letter of welcome sent before his arrival, he wrote: " I am a
poor, weak man. I have no gift of speech. I am not eloquent,
and feel very unable in myself to undertake so great a work.

But having been selected by others, I feel that it is a call from God, and that therefore I shall have all my wants supplied by Him who calls me to this great work." During the Mission he and the Lay Missionary at Garston were closely associated in the work, and became staunch friends. Of Arthur Sim the latter writes: "The moment I saw Mr. Sim I felt sure I was in the presence of a man who lived much upon his knees ; and the longer I knew him the more I loved him, for of him I could say ' He is a man after God's own heart.' When having tea at my house I asked ' When do you intend returning from Africa ?' He looked at me over the table and said with a smile ' Never ! I have been called by God to go out to Africa, and there I intend to remain until I am called hence.' I was much struck with his patience while listening to the story of sorrow and sin which some of the seamen had to tell him, and his cheerfulness under difficulties. On one occasion our oil lantern would not burn, and do what we could the pictures would not come out. I was very much put out about it, but he only said ' Do not be concerned ; we can talk about Jesus in the dark without the picture '; and he did so. When the congregation had dispersed and the gas was turned up, we saw ourselves as black as sweeps, for our faces were covered with soot from the lantern. On seeing this Mr. Sim laughed until he could scarcely move, and as there was no time to wash, he went to Liverpool by train as he was. His first sermon at Garston was very simple, but it won the hearts of his hearers. He said ' I have nothing new to tell you. I have come to you in the name of the Lord, and of Him only do I wish to speak.' Mr. Sim said of the Garston congregation that they were the most attentive people he had ever seen, and that he felt sure God was blessing the work there."

The Rev. Edgar Lambert, who worked with him in this Mission, writing of his great helpfulness to him personally, adds : " His instructions and conduct of the Intercession Service and Sunday Bible Classes at Hanover Street Seamen's

Church were all done with a power which struck me as being greater than he had been able to exercise in Sunderland days, and his whole tone was one of deep spirituality."

He himself regarded these two Missions as two of the happiest and most spiritually helpful experiences in his life.

But so great was his devotion to the work of St. Aidan's that he wrote during his last holiday : " I am enjoying myself immensely here, but am longing to be back with you all." And shortly before his departure, when he had been obliged to go away unexpectedly for a few days, he wrote expressing the deepest regret that he was unable to be present at the Band of Hope Meeting. This devotion on his part made the indifference of others a source of deep regret, and he felt profound pity for those who, merely for the sake of some worldly advantage, would give up work to which they were called.

If there was one thing that disturbed his equanimity during the time he was at West Hartlepool, it was the number of tempting invitations to important spheres of work elsewhere that fell to his lot. As he himself repeatedly said, he had no ambitions in that direction, and he was so contented and happy in his work at St. Aidan's that he would not contemplate the thought of leaving till he was sure of God's call. In the end that call came to him with no uncertain voice to devote his life to God's service among the heathen in Central Africa. He had been greatly impressed and influenced by the words of the late Bishop Smythies when he gave an address, in 1890, in West Hartlepool, on the work of the Universities' Mission. From that time forward he studied the history, methods and principles of the Society with ever-increasing interest and enthusiasm. Another thing that helped him to realize the call was that at his ordination he had heard a voice, as distinct as any human voice, say " Go and suffer for Me "; and he felt that so far his ministry had been singularly devoid of hardship and suffering. Referring to his decision to offer himself to the Universities' Mission, he wrote : " I only feel that I am doing here " (at St. Aidan's) "what many other men could do who could not go out to the Mission Field. I do not for one moment feel a bit worthy of being a missionary—rather, I feel exceedingly presumptuous in making the offer ; but I believe I have a good constitution, and I think I shall be ready to fill any menial position. . . . I have no ambition to have a living of my own, and no desire to settle down ; and in the meantime one's youth is slipping by, and I should like to make the most of it that one can in God's service. Thus it was that the strong drawing I have long felt towards the Universities' Mission took a definite shape ; not that I don't feel that such work as I have at St. Aidan's is just as grand as any other; yet, if God has marked out another sphere for me, it is not the grandest for me. One is always preaching about self-sacrifice, and this seems a call to put one's theories into practice."

As the time drew near for his departure, it was characteristic of the man that his one desire was "to slip away without fuss of any kind "; and when it came to his knowledge that the congregation were getting up a presentation to him he persistently refused to receive it. Consequently for a time there was a deadlock, till at last he yielded so far as to accept silver Communion vessels for his future Church, and a cheque to be devoted towards forwarding his work in Nyasaland.

Then as for the actual departure—what, in a sense, could be more thrilling than the Parish Hall packed with those whom he knew and loved best, assembled to hear his last words ? What could be more touching than those few workers assembled in the railway station in the early morning to give him one last grip of the hand, and to wish him farewell in silence ? What could hearten him better than the sight of those men and lads among whom he had worked, lining the railway wall at the ironworks and blast-furnaces as the train passed ? Yet the feeling stirred by these incidents was in a degree superficial compared with the deep solemnity and impressiveness of the Farewell Services in St. Aidan's Church. Certain it is that no more soul-inspiring Services have ever been held in that Church. From the oldest to the youngest all were deeply moved at the spectacle of that true Priest of God offering to

ARTHUR F. SIM.
Kota Kota, 1895.

his Master at His altar, in a more literal sense than he had ever done before, "himself, his soul and body, to be a reasonable, holy, and lively sacrifice unto Him."

Of his wearisome journey and his life and work in Africa

extending over a period of eighteen months, a record is furnished in the most interesting and graphic letters which follow this brief sketch. Perhaps it goes without saying that those who read them will do so with mixed feelings—on the one hand of intense admiration for his marvellous devotion, his simple reliance upon the Will of God, his realization of the Divine Presence, his deep humility, his righteous wrath at the hypocrisy and injustice around him, his wondrous sympathy with the downtrodden native, his large-minded grasp of important administrative questions, his cheerfulness, and his varied ingenuity and skill ; and on the other hand of pity for that lonely life cut off almost completely from those of his own colour and blood and from all sources of direct personal sympathy, stricken again and again with sickness, and finally yielded up to his Maker when his hopes seemed brightest. Of a truth, it was for him throughout a very real taking up of the Cross, and nothing but the belief that it was the call of God to him would have induced him to undertake it.

Of all his letters perhaps none contains more cheerful allusions to himself than his last, in which he speaks of his " cast-iron " constitution, and the prospect of a temporary alteration in his plans owing to the illness of some of the staff, and the deaths of Bishop Maples, George Atlay, and Joseph Williams. He had already passed, as he thought, fairly well through the worst months of the year, and was beginning to consider himself more or less acclimatized. After this letter a few weeks intervened. Then, on Jan. 15th of the present year, came a rumour of his dangerous and hopeless illness nearly three months before. It was indeed hard at first to believe (for he himself had been so explicit and careful in arranging for any such news to be cabled home), even when the authorities at Zanzibar telegraphed asking if the report of his death had been confirmed. But two days later no room was left for hope or even doubt, and every one who had known Arthur Fraser Sim " sorrowed for the word that they should see his face no more."

> " Death takes us by surprise,
>   And stays our hurrying feet ;
> The great design unfinished lies,
>   Our lives are incomplete.
>
> But in the dark unknown
>   Perfect their circles seem,
> Even as a bridge's arch of stone
>   Is rounded in the stream.
>
> Alike are life and death
>   When life in death survives,
> And the uninterrupted breath
>   Inspires a thousand lives.
>
> Were a star quenched on high,
>   For ages would its light,
> Still travelling downward from the sky,
>   Shine on our mortal sight.
>
> So when a great man dies,
>   For years beyond our ken,
> The light he leaves behind him lies
>   Upon the paths of men." [1]

The following week particulars of his last illness were received from his fellow-worker, Mr. J. G. Philipps. On October 18th he had an attack of jaundice ; later, an attack of fever supervening, his condition became hopeless, and he passed away in the very early morning of Oct. 29th, 1895, within four days of completing his thirty-fourth year.

> " To me the thought of death is terrible,
> Having such hold on life. To thee it is not
> So much even as the lifting of a latch ;
> Only a step into the open air
> Out of a tent already luminous
> With light that shines through its transparent walls.
> O pure in heart ! " [2]

Throughout his illness he was nursed with the most solicitous care by Messrs. Swann and Philipps, and his native teacher, William Kanyopolea : and every effort was made to secure the services of a doctor, but without success.

[1] Longfellow.   [2] Longfellow's *Golden Legend*.

He is said to have spoken but little during those last sad days of suffering, but his last words were "Wash my feet," which he repeated several times. Doubtless his mind was dwelling upon that scene in the upper chamber in Jerusalem, where our Lord washed His disciples' feet on the night before His crucifixion. Reading these words however in the light of a sermon he had preached in St. Aidan's, they were the oft-repeated prayer of a true penitent for a cleansing from whatever sin might shut out the clear vision of God. The following verses, referring to these words, were very familiar to him :—

> " Many waters go softly dreaming
>   On to the sea ;
> But the River of Death floweth softest
>   To thee and me.
>
> We have trod the sands of the desert
>   Under a burning sun ;
> Oh ! sweet will the touch of the waters be
>   To feet whose journey is done !
>
> Unto Him Whose love has washed us
>   Whiter than snow,
> We shall pass through the shallow River
>   With hearts aglow.
>
> For the Lord's voice on the waters
>   Lingereth sweet :—
> ' He that *is* washed needeth only
>   To wash his feet.' " [1]

So closed the earthly life of this true saint of God—a life so natural and simple, and yet so full of a deep reserve that Bishop Lightfoot's words at his Ordination were amply verified. "There are depths in Sim," remarked the Bishop, "that I cannot fathom." He was a Christian so loving that his heart went out instinctively to all men, with the result that he was loved by all. Clergyman and layman, rough seaman and well-bred gentleman, trader and commissioner, found him to be just what his best friends knew him.

[1] *Ezekiel* and other Poems.

He had such steadfast faithfulness, and so strong a sense
of responsibility, that one always felt that these characteristics
would have carried him through actual martyrdom without a
flinch.   He seemed the embodiment of the text : " In quietness and confidence shall be your strength."   No talk, no
show, just quiet strength all through.   He was never given to
bemoaning the wickedness and weariness of this world, but
rather he was wont to dwell on its beauties and goodness, and
to enjoy both : —

> " He loved each simple joy the country yields,
> He loved his mates "—

He had an implicit belief in the existence of good in all,
dormant though it might be, alike in professed atheist and
degraded savage ; and if it was impossible to say a good
word for a fellow-creature, then he remained silent.

Words written of St. Aidan in a short sketch of his life, prepared at the time of the consecration of St. Aidan's Church,
might be written with equal truth of Arthur Fraser Sim : " He
was a man of the utmost gentleness, piety, and reasonableness,
and full of zeal towards God.   ' He left a splendid example to
the clergy of temperance and purity.   His life was absolutely
consistent with what he taught ; and this commended his
teaching to all men.' [1]   He did not seek or love this world's
wealth.   .   .   .   The saint, whose memory those who worship in this Church will ever hold in reverence, will be best
honoured by the determination to imitate the example he set
of a simple, devoted Christian life, full of zeal for the Lord,
and full of love to the brethren."

To few men is it given to have such an abiding realization
of the Divine Presence - the natural result of his habitual
purity of heart and mind.   Of this purity his life-long friend
has written: "I cannot remember one single occasion on
which any unclean or profane utterance fell from his lips.   I
shall always think of him as one of the purest souls possible."

The presence of God was in him a living power, sanctifying

[1] *Bede* III. 5.

him and making him patient and strong for labour, sorrow and suffering. It was the source of his constant cheerfulness and contentment in varying circumstances; and it preserved him from all fretful anxiety about the future. Hence death was to him a thing in no sense to be dreaded; it was the drawing aside of the veil which hid the sinless beauties and glories of the unseen world; it was the opening of the gate to a life of greater joy and fuller activity where the Priesthood begun on earth would be continued through eternity.

> " 'He is not dead,' but only lieth sleeping
> In the sweet refuge of his Master's breast,
> And far away from sorrow, toil, and weeping.
> 'He is not dead,' but only taking rest.
>
> What though the highest hopes he dearly cherished,
> All faded gently as the setting sun;
> What though our own fond expectations perished,
> Ere yet life's noblest labour seemed begun;
>
> What though he standeth at no earthly altar,
> Yet in white raiment, on the golden floor
> Where love is perfect, and no step can falter,
> He serveth as a Priest for evermore.
>
> O glorious end of life's short day of sadness!
> O blessed course so well and nobly run!
> O home of true and everlasting gladness!
> O crown unfading, and so early won!
>
> Though tears will fall, we bless Thee, O our Father,
> For the dear one for ever with the blest,
> And wait the Easter dawn when Thou shalt gather
> Thine own, long parted, to their endless rest."

"He asked life of Thee, and Thou gavest him a long life even for ever and ever." Ps xxi 4

LETTERS OF
ARTHUR FRASER SIM

" Letters are the best materials for history, and to a diligent reader the best histories in themselves."

BACON.

" I saw a Saint.—How canst thou tell that he
    Thou sawest was a Saint?—
I saw one like to Christ so luminously
    By patient deeds of love, his mortal taint
Seemed made his groundwork for humility.

And when he marked me downcast utterly
    Where foul I sat and faint,
Then more than ever Christ-like kindled he;
    And welcomed me as I had been a saint,
Tenderly stooping low to comfort me.

Christ bade him, 'Do thou likewise.' Wherefore he
    Waxed zealous to acquaint
His soul with sin and sorrow, if so be
    He might retrieve some latent saint :—
' Lo, I, with the child God hath given to me !' "

C. G. ROSETTI.

(Printed by kind permission of the S.P.C.K.)

LETTERS

THIS and the following letter give A. F. Sim's views re-
garding the work of the two Parishes in each of which
he ministered for over four years.

Letter to T. C. G——, dated,—

Sunderland, August 11th, 1888.

MY DEAR——,

I must just write a line to you to say how glad I am that all
is settled, and that you are coming to us in October. When you
come we must have many consultations as to the division of labour.
Last winter almost the whole of every evening was taken up by
my lads in a Night School. I got part of Monday for a Band of
Hope, and Thursday for Service and Choir practice. Yet both on
Monday and Thursday I had to get away from these before nine
to be in time for prayers at the Gymnasium. Now I consider that
the lads are the pleasantest feature of our work, and I feel I should
be selfish to keep it all to myself! I think we might go partners
in it. I need not give you a long account of it. Next winter we
are going to amalgamate the work among the lads, at what went
by the name of the "British Workman." Last year we had two
places going, with the result that one was neglected. Alterations
are going to be made, to make the "Workman" (or "Church
Institute," as we shall call it) suitable for its new requirements.
Subscriptions to the amount of £60 have been collected for this
purpose. We purpose having a Night School there, a weekly
Concert, and a Bible Class (rather a lot to fit in). It means some
one there every night. There is another little organization (growing, I trust) among the lads, viz., a Communicants' Guild, once a
month.

Among the children of course we have Sunday Schools and a
Band of Hope. These want careful supervision. The Sunday

Schools are not at all satisfactory. In short they want looking after thoroughly. This one of us must do. Hitherto I have had a Bible Class on Sunday afternoon, which prevented my taking any part in Sunday School work ; but I have left that off now, and intend when the winter comes to start one on a week-night. The Band of Hope I think might be made a useful organization. You see all we do among the children is done in Day School (mighty little), and on Sunday afternoon. Well, I think the Band of Hope might be an extension of Sunday School work on two week-nights for an hour on each.

Then there is the Temperance work. I agree with what I imagine your sentiments to be in regard to Temperance, from something the Vicar let drop. I am not bigoted ; I am an abstainer, but have taken no part hitherto in Temperance work. That has been B——'s line. I could not do it because of want of time. I am positive you won't be many weeks here without realizing the need of special means to meet a special disease and sin. Drink is the curse of almost every house. Last winter our Temperance work was poor—meetings small, pledges few, corporate union unrealized. Something must be done, and you and I must do it ! Perhaps we can invent some new method—something after the manner of a " Fathers' Meeting," social intercourse—a sort of conversazione every Saturday night. Tea and coffee ! All the better if we can. I don't think much of the old sort of Temperance meetings. They are very slow, to my mind, and not adapted to the needs. Now Band of Hope work and Temperance work ought to be done by laymen ; but they are so hard to get. Then there is a heap of work to be done among the soldiers. That was B——'s department, and I know nothing about it ; but there it is, and there is enough for one man to do in barracks alone. We have an excellent Scripture reader there, who is half butler to the Vicar— an old soldier's servant.

Then there is work among the girls corresponding to work among the lads. We have a lot of splendid ladies who help us in this. I think however more might be done. There ought to be an institute for them, which they might use every night. They are very rough—worse than the boys, far ! I think it is mostly on the surface, and that they have an innate sense of modesty which forbids them proceeding beyond certain limits ! Now we cannot expect the Vicar to undertake any work that needs his continuous superintendence and presence. His hands must be free ; he is the general.

And now about the Church Services. First of all, you know how unfortunately our Church is seated. It would cost £1,000 to reseat facing East, because any such scheme would be incomplete unless it included considerable alterations in the Chancel and the removing of the organ. I myself would rather see this done than anything else. However, there it is, and we must make the best of it. Of course, as long as the choir is in the gallery, we cannot have any (or, at all events, much) dignity of worship. The Services are hearty, at least. I myself should like a daily Service, and so would the Vicar ; but I don't think many would come to it, and hitherto it has not seemed possible. I think it is his ambition to have it—yet doubtless where the arrears are so great we must be patient and content to move slowly. As to the evening Communion, I don't like it, as I told you. I consider that as a memorial feast it may be celebrated in the evening ; but we hold it to be more than that, do we not ? However, I know W—— is aware of my views, and I do not hold myself responsible. I am afraid we must not expect this to be changed, at all events in the immediate future. We must be patient. I think we must be ready to sacrifice a good deal of personal convictions. At least we do not sacrifice them, because we are not responsible, and we have made known our mind on the subject. And then I feel sure our sacrifice of personal feelings will bear fruit in the long run, and we shall be rewarded for giving up these by a very real return of active, real work and energy, and much fruit which we have no right to expect.

Then there is the Church Army. I will not say anything about it, except that to be really efficient it needs close clerical superintendence.

There, now I have done something to unburden my mind ! I did not intend to write so long a letter. But having begun I had to go on.

I am sure I have not frightened you by the list of what lies before us : but rather my purpose has been to show you that I am determined to work shoulder to shoulder with you ; indeed, if we do otherwise, we shall fail altogether. I look forward very much to having you as a fellow-worker. How much better a "fifteen" plays when the men are well together ; and a boat's crew well together is a different thing from a scratch crew, is it not? And so I look forward to next year's work, because I am confident that we shall be able to work together. Knowing this, "Courage rises with danger," and I begin to feel eager for the fray !

Ever yours sincerely,

A. F. SIM.

Letter to R. H. M. C. about coming to St. Aidan's as the new Curate, dated,—

West Hartlepool, *Feb.* 23*rd*, 1894.

MY DEAR,——

I must write and tell you from my point of view what I think about this Parish and the work here.

(1) My Vicar is an old Cheltenham friend of mine, and we live together on the most intimate terms. . . . Bishop Lightfoot sent him here nine years ago to make a new Parish ; and with great difficulties to face he has succeeded, and the new Church is three and a half years old.

(2) About the work. The population is almost entirely artisan, most intelligent men—the pick of the artisan class. They are awfully kind and warm-hearted people, and I think very receptive.

The children are my delight—very quick and intelligent—and I think we have them well organized, and under fairly good discipline.

What I think is the charm of it all, is the fact that the work is *developing*. No old-fashioned prejudices hamper you. The people have not been overdone, not "Gospel-hardened," ready and glad to receive you, and grateful for help and sympathy. It is not quite impossible to learn to know them all. I have got round two or three times to nearly all the houses in my district since I have been here, besides other visitation. This gets harder every year, it is true.

There is ample scope for fresh work, and fresh development of old work, but you will be quite free to work on your own lines— a Mission Room, a working-men's Club in a district with a bad name, but full of good and nice people, about a mile from the Church, where we have a Day School, which, in spite of the class of people, has got the " Excellent Merit Grant " for ten years.

Development in the way of Communicants' Guilds for men `we have a strong one for young women`, and one for married women

—improvements in the Sunday School, and in the catechising of the children—all these want attention in the future. There is plenty of material to go upon, but you must remember that we are young, and that the Church has fearful arrears to make up in this town, and especially in this Parish.

A *beautiful* (though plain) brick Church with much stone facing, a very satisfactory choir—very sweet in tone—a hardworking choirmaster who is a great treasure to us—these make Sunday a perpetual delight, and to be away a sorrow ! With charming and easily pleased people to work among during the week, and children who are a continuous sunshine in the streets, you will wonder how I can leave such a paradise, and I often wonder myself. I have been *very* happy here, and know that it will be a tearing of the heart strings when I go. You know I have offered for the Universities' Mission to Central Africa. I have done so under the conviction that it is God's call, and so I must bear the parting among other tokens of the Cross. . . .

However do come and stay for two or three days.

Yours, etc.,

A. F. SIM.

Letter to E. L., dated June 19th, 1893, announcing his intention of going to Central Africa.

MY DEAR——,

It has long been on my mind to offer for Foreign Mission work. This has been more and more with me of late until I feel it to be a call from God, and I should be doing wrong to put it away from me. I have been now two years Secretary here for the U.M.C.A., and I have a great admiration for that Mission. My place here, with plenty of notice, could be filled, as far as the work goes, pretty easily. Of course it might be more difficult for M—— to get a personal friend. There is nothing on my sisters' account that need keep me at home. I am painfully aware of how little I have to offer in so grand a cause—the best is an iron constitution for that trying climate. Acquaintance with their work leads me to imagine that it is eminently pastoral work, looking after children in the Schools, and extending the work by persuasion and personal influence into the neighbouring country. It is work of the first importance, and there are few so little hampered by home ties as I am—there are comparatively few who can go out—and therefore to those who can, it is an imperative duty. I am filling no post another could not fill in England. I know it is a grand ambition to have a Parish of one's own to live for, and, if necessary, die for ; but there are plenty to do this, and there seem to be few enough to go abroad. One is not a grander or nobler work than the other—both are in God's service, and that makes both grand. For myself, I have no ambition to settle down to a " living," and I could work on here contentedly to the end of my days. But others, who cannot go out, can do all that needs doing here—could take up the work where I leave it, develop it, start afresh, and do more than I can. I should hate the parting with all here, and even more the fuss that it seems to make when a man goes out, but that would not last long. I have tried to count the cost, but it seems impossible to do so. I know that at least it means personal devotion. The heat, the climate, the fever, all must mean doing work under difficulties. The language is said to be a very easy one—men have learnt it to preach in it in six months.

I am very grateful for the time I have spent here, and I feel that the experience gained in these last three years will make a great difference in my character. . . . You see the thought has been with me for a long time now, and latterly is seldom from my mind. Will you write me all that strikes you about the matter, and will you pray over it ? Farewell, dear old boy,

Yours, etc.,

A. F. SIM.

Letter to Bishop Hornby, dated November 9th, 1893, offering himself for work in Nyasaland.

MY DEAR BISHOP——,

Two, getting on for three years ago, I made up my mind eventually to offer my services to the U.M.C.A. About four months ago I mentioned the subject to P. M. Wathen, when he was here speaking ; and then when I was in London this summer I saw Travers and the Doctor. Of course Wathen and Travers don't know much about me ; they said that my services would be acceptable. The Doctor said the Mission ought to be glad to have so strong a man. You knew me a little in Sunderland. Since those days of many mistakes, I feel I have made, by God's grace, some progress, and now it is my sincere wish to devote myself to Him and His Church more whole-heartedly. I know that there is more than I

can do to be done here, but not more than others can do who
would fill my place, while so many others have home ties which I
have not, which make it hard or impossible for them to go out.
So it comes to this—I have offered my services to the Mission. I
have told my people at home, and now the Parish knows all about
it. For a long time I was quite unsettled as to my destination,
not knowing that it was necessary for me to make the choice. I
am willing to go where I am most needed, and thought I should
be sent to Bishop Smythies to be sent where he thought fit. But
Wathen and Travers say that if I want to go to Nyasa I must offer
myself to you—this is why I am writing. These men both say
Nyasa is more in need of men ; so I write to ask you will you
have me? You know me a little, and I know myself a little, and
that little is quite enough to convince me of my utter unworthi-
ness of so great a task. And this feeling long held uppermost
place in my mind and prevented me offering myself before now.
I have no gifts—devotional or mental—to bring, but I have a strong
carcase, and a placid, easy-going temperament, which I imagine to
be of some value in the tropics.

Now you will legitimately want to know my convictions on
matters of Churchmanship. Here our teaching goes further than
our ritual. I would not die for a point of ritual—I regard it as
the greatest of external helps. First comes the Truth as to the
Presence of the Divine Head of the Church and the Power of His
Holy Spirit, and ritual is an essential to us for the clothing of
these deep truths. In itself it must be dignified and understanded
of the people. I enter into this in order to assure you that . . .
Church was never in my rawest days the ideal of worship, and also
because I know how essential a mutual understanding is, where
men have to work together. I feel that I could render you complete
and implicit obedience—as I feel in turn that you would be a help
and a guide and a true Bishop to me. For myself I have long felt
the paramount importance of the Lord's command, " Go ye and
teach all nations "—it can be fulfilled by those who must stay at
home—but I should not have a quiet conscience if I did not at
least offer myself to Him for its literal obedience. The U.M.C.A.,
its principles and its sphere — and I may add, its men, for I know
several —has long been a great attraction to me, and for two years
I have acted as correspondent for this Deanery. I don't pretend
to realize at all what the work is like, or what the difficulties are.

I suppose much isolation and much fever are the sacrifice one has to make ; but it seems useless anticipating them. I have prayed for the spirit of obedience. I anticipate also much counter-balancing happiness and joy in the progress of truth and light, and in the visible fruit of work.

Will you write to me, and (if you can) say you accept my ser-vices, for I long to be settled as to my future ? And, if you can do this, will you say something about outfit ? How many books to take is my chief difficulty. Of course all my books are at your service, and perhaps I had better make a list of them and let you scratch off what are useless. Will you say also something about the route I should take (of course I should like to see Zanzibar on my way and all the well-known work there). As to date—next summer is the earliest date M—— expects me to be off. I want to associate this Parish as much as I can in my movements ; I must not therefore leave in bad odour, by leaving my place un-filled and a double share of work behind me. This is to be my English home—all that I leave behind, I shall leave here—and if ever I return, I shall come here first. I can't say how deeply at-tached I am to these people ; and, from the way many of them cried when they heard of my intention, I believe they are attached to me. I could willingly and gladly stay here all my life ; but I don't think I should be obedient if I did so. I am busy with Swahili, which I presume is essential wherever one goes.

Tell me if there is anything I can do for you, or (if I come) any-thing I can bring with me for you. Pardon the unlimited use of the first person singular—it is almost necessary in a letter of this kind.

If you see cause to refuse my offer, you must consider the letters that follow as if they had not been written.

Ever yours in our Lord,
A. F. SIM.

Letter from London, dated,—

April 28th, 1894.

MY DEAR TEACHERS,—

I cannot refrain from writing you a line, which I hope will reach you to-morrow, Sunday. You will not miss me half so much as I shall miss you. I am very homesick, and my constant thought is of the dear friends I have left. I had to speak for the Mission at a meeting in Cambridge on Friday night. But how could I speak of what lies before me, with a heart so full of what I have left behind? I think my words had for their text—" Go and work in the North if you want to know what happiness is !" A poor advocate I made for the Mission ! The good Bishop Selwyn, late of Melanesia, was there, and gave me his blessing and much kind encouragement and advice.

Cambridge was looking its best—every tree out in its freshest, greenest, spring clothing, the lilac in blossom, and *nightingales* singing at mid-day ! But it only made me sadder. I yearned for the black trees and black roads and warm hearts of my home. And yet, ought I not to thank God that there is so much to give up ? Far better this, than having neglected God's bidding, to spend a longer time with you and forfeit His blessing. I know I shall be repaid a thousand-fold by increased faith in Him, and dependence upon Him, and I trust deeper knowledge of Him. Of course I saw Mr. K—— in Cambridge. He was very full of his time at St. Aidan's, and it was a comfort to pour out one's woes into a sympathising North Country ear !

And so I have filled almost my whole letter with myself. I don't think I need ask you to give Mr. C—— a hearty welcome. After all it is not the man who sits in the big desk for whom you work. It is One higher than he who commits His little ones to you for teaching which they would never get at home.

And the Vicar—you will rally round him, and support him in every way, and make the work easy for him—I know you will do this. If God has taken me away from you, I know He will not let the work go back or suffer in any way. I should so much like you to feel that you are sharing in my work. I know your kind hearts feel my going, and so we have a common ground to start from. We each take a share in a sacrifice—and to me that is the real, the only sacrifice—the leaving the Parish. I shall meet with nothing compared with it in the future, I am quite sure.

And now give my love to those dear children. How much I shall think of them and miss them.

Ever your affectionate friend,

Arthur F. Sim.

Worthing, *April* 30*th*, 1894.

My Dear——,

You must let me write you a line, as it is a great comfort to me to do so. I am feeling the parting more than I can tell.

Perhaps I did not sufficiently count it in the cost. I do not expect
to get over the pain till I have settled down to work again among
my new people. I celebrated at eight yesterday, and was with
you all in heart, as I believe you were with me, and all through
the day my heart was full of you. I do feel God's goodness in
this especially, that He has given me so much to give up again to
Him, and I believe I am not presumptuous in thinking that some
of you feel my going, and, if so, can share in the "sacrifice." I do
not feel that I have *left* St. Aidan's, and I should like to feel that
you have permitted me to go, and have given me to God for this
work. I go out from a very dear *home*.

Yes, I am confident that God will repay me by added faith and
dependence upon Him, and in many other ways—no one can help
being the gainer by doing His will. To neglect His bidding can
only mean in the long run to forfeit His blessing, and that would
be misery indeed. Among His blessings to me, I count most
precious the friendships He has given me all through life ; and I
count your friendship, and may I say it perfectly honestly, your
example, as among His greatest gifts and privileges. I feel it
would be ungrateful not to acknowledge this to you. And now
I know I need not remind you that I depend upon your prayers
to help me to meet and fight the temptations of a tropical climate
and the consequent lassitude. With very kind remembrances,

Yours, etc.,
A. F. SIM.

May 2nd, 1894.

MY DEAR——,

I return to town at 4.30 this afternoon, and spend most of
Ascension Day with Mrs. R——. I shall try and see P—— to-
morrow. This is the inscription I have had put on the Communion
vessels : " To the Glory of God, The Gift of St. Aidan's, West
Hartlepool, in memory of February, 1890, to April, 1894."

A. F. S.

I found a perfect bundle of letters awaiting me here from those
dear people. I could never have believed how home-sick I should
feel. I doubt if I shall get rid of the feeling till I get to definite
work again. I am rather unsettled as to my departure now, owing
to a hint of the C——'s coming home on the 8th, in which case
I shall not start till the 10th, and see them in town.

To-day C—— is making his way North. I do trust the people won't sicken him by quoting me. Tell him to have patience. I will write to him. I am sure he will make his way in time, and his work will be thorough, and—if only in the Schools—much more valuable than mine has been. I ought to write a line to the Day School teachers, for I never got a chance of thanking them, though, of course, I am not supposed to know that they took any part in the " Present."

I wonder if you have stored away my books yet. I shall regret the George Eliots, and when you have time I should like you to get them out, and such devotional books as Body's " *Life of Temptation and Justification*," and " *School of Calvary*," and send them.

My brother, a practical man, is now employed in showing me how to make bread in a saucepan ! He has made me a present of a lot of tabloids, also dentists' forceps and books relating to life and expedients in camp.

Yours, etc.,

A. F. SIM.

London, *Ascension Day*, 1894.

MY DEAR——,

I leave London, *via* Folkestone, for Paris, on May 8th. Life seems changed for me now. It is hard amid the bustle and leave-taking to realize the missionary aim and spirit. I trust to find time on board ship for quiet contemplation. This part of the going forth is very unpleasant and horrid. I have just received yours written yesterday. Do not let what I said about " your example" pain you. It is not what one is, but what one is trying to be, which is the inspiration of life, and the influence in example. How far short we come ! And yet it is easy to see the far-off look in the eye of one whose aim is where Christ sitteth at the right hand of God. Browning is often very fine. He says :—

" What I aspired to be, and was not, comforts me :
A brute I might have been, but would not sink the scale."

If I may venture to advise you, let me pray you not to dwell too much on the failure to attain the great ideal. Look onwards and upwards, and not at your feet. If one could do this more, no doubt our pathway to the goal would be more direct, and our footsteps less faltering. We ought to regard as nothing what others

see in us and say of us. If the aim is true, the inspiration of our
lives will be strong and pure ; and if the aim is Christ, our humility
will be real and true, and contrition abiding. But melancholy and
despair and lack of glorious hope are wrong and out of place in
the Christian's life.

I am just off to St. Peter's, Eaton Square, for High Celebration
—I was with you this morning at eight.

Yours, etc.,

A. F. SIM.

Paris, *May 9th*, 1894.

MY DEAR——,

You see I am on my way now. I can't realize what it
means at all, and it is no good trying. I am in God's hands, and
I must leave the future to Him. I saw Bishop Hornby in London.
He wishes me to go to Unangu—the new station—fifty miles from
the Lake. There I shall have my wish for complete pioneer work.
But of course this may be changed when I get there. There is
some fear of the Mission being turned out " neck and crop,"
because the slave dhows of the chiefs on the Lake are being interfered with by the gunboats.

I left London at 11 a.m. yesterday. Most of my relations were
down to see me off. Here I am with friends, and we are " doing "
the place ; but when I have time to think I have to confess to
a homesick feeling. I doubt if this will wear off till I get settled
down to work.

We saw Notre Dame this morning and the Sainte Chapelle. In
neither was I much impressed, but that is the way with such
prejudiced Britishers as I am ! What is meant for the gorgeous
is tawdry to my eye ! This afternoon we went for a drive in the
Bois de Boulogne, which I enjoyed very much. It seemed like
miles of Surrey woods, and it was so warm and bright.

To an outsider and a complete stranger it seems as if religion
were at a very low ebb here ; but it is impossible to judge. I
believe that the long and the short of it is that the Priests are
uneducated and rather despised. I imagine things are different
in country parts, such as Normandy and Brittany. A man told
me to-day that the best Priests are the Jesuits- they are more
educated. An Englishman naturally despises a foreigner ; but I
must confess that the young men seem somewhat despicable—very
fat and lazy-looking ! The best-looking are the artisans. The

women are painted and powdered! This as a matter of course; but my taste is very insular. Give me the dear old North Country for freshness and energy and life and enthusiasm.

On Tuesday morning I went down to St. Matthew's, Westminster, for my last Communion in England. The Bishop of Nyasaland celebrated, and gave me his blessing. The Bishop of Lincoln communicated, and I knelt next to him, but I did not recognise him till I was coming away. Mr. L—— also spent the previous night in town, and communicated on Tuesday morning. How good God is to me! There are such good men who have not this privilege. The truth is, that work is work wherever our lots are cast, and some are called to one sphere and some to another; but it is all work for God, and may not be compared one sphere with another.

If ever your lot brings you to London, let me commend St. Matthew's to your notice. It is an ideal Church—two daily Celebrations (7 and 8)—a large staff of Clergy, who live in the adjoining Clergy-house, and some slum work. It is in Great Peter Street behind the Army and Navy Stores. What charmed me was that they bind "*Central Africa*" with their Parish Magazine. It is the London home of the Mission. I hope you will get a Report; it is very interesting.

Remember me most kindly to the teachers and every one, and give my love to the children.

Yours, etc.,

A. F. SIM.

Letter dated,—

Marseilles, *May 12th*, 1894.

MY DEAR——,

Just a line of adieu to Europe! I shall be with you to-morrow—hoping to have a Celebration on board. The news of Bishop Smythies' death is a terrible blow to us all. God knows best. It is doubtful if the doctor will permit Bishop Hornby to return. Remember us; it is a heavy cloud under which we start. I am very well, as are all our party, five in number. I am very happy, considering; but I feel lonely and strange sometimes. Time goes very quickly with Swahili, and letters and thoughts. I don't try to realize what it all means—time enough for that later on. One has to leap in the dark when He bids us, and I know He is here and there as well as with you.

Yours, etc.,

A. F. SIM.

Marseilles, *May 12th*, 1894.

MY DEAR——,

Here I am—all safe—after a night's sleeplessness in the train from Paris. I don't want to analyse my feelings. I look forward to having plenty to do on board. I know nothing of the passengers, as none have turned up yet. Our party is as " *Central Africa* " described it—very nice. Others are coming belonging to the Consulate at Zanzibar.

It is a terrible blow to Miss Mills to hear of Bishop Smythies' death. We are awaiting a telegram confirming the news in answer to one from me at eleven o'clock this morning.

Give my love to all my friends.

Yours, etc.,

A. F. SIM.

Whit Monday, 1894.

MY DEAR——,

I had better begin a letter to you, and then I shall have something ready at Port Said to send off. We are very comfortable on the whole, and not at all crowded. I have only a boy in my cabin, which gives us two empty berths, consequently I have unpacked almost all I have with me. Yesterday did not seem like Sunday—still less like Whit Sunday. It was too rough for Service, and we had no Celebration. They won't allow Service on board. There are four French Fathers, and even they are not allowed. So we are dependent upon one of the ladies' cabins—a pretty big one—and that means their clearing out in good time ; hence, if they are ill we are " up a tree." And they were all ill on Sunday except Miss Mills who is an exceedingly good sailor—as good as I am.

This morning, however, we managed a Celebration, and though it was rolling a little, all turned up, and all happened without accident. Mr. C——, S.P.G. missionary at Madagascar, celebrated, and we used my big Vessels. Our time was 8.30, which would be about 7.30 with you. The clock is puzzling just now. Our party, as you know, consists of Miss M——, Miss C——, Miss F——, Sister D——, and myself. Mr. C——'s party consists of a Miss K—— and a Miss N——, both going to Zanzibar to be married. There is another English girl bound for Kurrachi, and one or two other Englishmen. I don't think there are more than six or eight first-class passengers, and of them only one couple and two men are English. My French is wonderful. Three of our party can speak French, and as they have all been mostly *hors de combat*, I have been interpreter in general! And now I am going on deck for a breath of fresh air. As you know, the French meals are at extraordinary times : 6.30 a.m., *café complet* ; 10 a.m., *déjeuner* ; and 6 p.m., *diner.* They rather suit this lazy board-ship life. We have had such a struggle for our cabin boxes. They were all shoved as they came into the luggage hold, and my boxes were at the very bottom, so I spent most of Sunday morning "down-pit," hot and dirty. I spoiled one of my only pair of European trousers !

These good ladies keep me on the move fagging for them ! But I have silently struck, as I intend, if possible, not to let this time pass in utter laziness.

We passed the Lipari Islands this morning, and saw Stromboli to the North of us. We get through the Straits of Messina about 5 o'clock this afternoon.

I can't help thinking about you all, and what you are doing at different times of the day. Tell A. D—— how useful I find her little pen. I had a patent ink-pot given me in London, and with that and A——'s pen I am quite furnished. So with E. A——'s card-case. I have carried my tickets in it all the way from London, or I should certainly have lost them. I am very comfortable, and should be very happy, but that I feel rather like a stranger among strangers. This is, I am sure, very good for me. Those people would have spoiled me very quickly. I think some of even the best men are a little in danger of this, and you can see it in their constantly talking of themselves. And this I am doing I find. I fear I have always been given that way.

Will you give my sisters my news ? I have told them to write to you and let you know where they are. If they are moving about very much I can't write to them, so I should like you, if not too much trouble, to send my letters on to them. "Skipper" might like to see them. If I can cut down the number of letters I write I shall probably be able to write better ones. I suppose Mr. J—— has left you now. I should like to hear that Mr. D—— was settled. I think he had better come out to me. He would enjoy this part of the business, the bright sun and the deep blue sea. Sitting on deck is a perfect delight, but it is rather a snare. I can't work there, or even read. I shall take this up again to-morrow. This

time last year (Whit Monday evening) we had just returned from
Mr. L——'s field with the Band of Hope children. I wonder if
you have any such fun going on to-day. I have an impression you
have a cricket match on. Now I am just going to say my Office
on deck, and then off to bed.

Whitsun Tuesday.—Absolutely nothing to say—out of sight of
land—300 miles yesterday, and 304 to-day. We saw the coast of
Italy yesterday, and very pretty it was. The atmosphere here is so
clear, and the sea so blue ! I have plenty to do, writing letters
and learning Swahili and eating ! I don't think I shall do much
novel-reading.

Thursday.—We are due at Port Said this evening, and letters
have to be posted this afternoon, so I will sit "tight" and finish
this and a few others I am writing. We had hoped to meet Mr.
Travers at Port Said. He was with the Bishop when he died; but
I hear that we passed the "*Peiho*" last night, and so our hopes are
vain. I am longing already for letters from the Parish. If you
write, as you must, don't consider any detail too trifling to tell me.
And now remember me to all those dear people—the children, the
teachers, the choir, the lads. I am so glad to hear of the success
of the Rummage Sale, and I am glad that my old things came in
useful. I wonder how the Library is getting on. I hope it will be
a success. Tell me whether you are using two bookcases or only
the one. How does the Londoner settle among the Northeners ?
I hope to see him looking quite young again when I come home.
Give him my love. One of the ladies, Miss F——, knows his
people, and has an uncle at, or near, Tadcaster.

Yours, etc ,
A. F. SIM.

Letter to E. L——, dated, —

s.s. "*Amazone,*" *May* 15*th*, 1894.

MY DEAR,——

Time goes very quickly, and I have plenty to do between
writing and doing Swahili and thinking of you all. I should be
very happy, and I am. I feel rather a stranger among strangers,
but I am old enough not to mind that very much. We are a good
number of English, and all are nice. . . . We have the run of
the deck, and are well treated. *Déjeuner* at 10 and *diner* at 6
is rather a long interval, and I wish I had a private store of biscuits. I can't describe what we have seen—the country about

Marseilles was very pretty, and the sea is so blue, and now it is smooth. The peep at Corsica was very fine, and Italy at the Straits of Messina very pretty. The brilliant colouring was quite a revelation to me, and it interprets a good many pictures one sees in galleries, *e.g.*, Moore's sea pieces, and those vivid landscapes, green and blue and white and red. . . . Bishop Smythies' death is a sad blow. Who will be found ready to occupy what seems to be so dangerous a post? A young man, and yet wise and very strong. . . .

Yours, etc.,

A. F. SIM.

S.S. "*Amazone*," *May* 21*st*, 1894.

MY DEAR——,

It is awfully hot—94° under double awnings, and not a breath of wind. It is behind us (the wind), and consequently we are breathless. I have on cricket flannels, my thinnest shirt, and your silk jacket. Still I don't mind it very much, and don't feel very stupid and lazy; but it is stifling downstairs, and I am writing on deck with a pair of blue spectacles on which Mr. C—— gave me, and A. D——'s pencil. We had great fun at Port Said. It was dark when we arrived. We had a few things to buy, such as biscuits, to keep the life in us between 10 and 6, and some cigarettes. The bargaining, at which C—— is an adept, was great fun, but I fear I shall make a bad hand at it. It seems that you have to pretend you don't want the thing at all, and go out of the shop, and then after an interval the seller follows you to another shop where you may be, and offers you your thing at a lower price. We got some excellent cigarettes at 3 fr. per hundred. The coaling was done with wonderfully little dirt or inconvenience of any kind. Suez we did not reach till the evening of the next day, having many delays in the Canal. There we did not go ashore, nor were the merchants allowed on board. The new Consul-General of Zanzibar came on board at Suez. He is a very nice fellow, very young looking, speaks most languages under the sun, including Russian and Arabic. He has brought a horse and two men on board. He is an Eton man, and so we know a good many men in common, including H——, P——, D——, etc.

Yesterday we got leave to have Service. We had two Celebrations in the ladies' cabin, at 8 and 8.45, and at 11.30 we had

Matins, three hymns, a sermon out of Aubrey Moore's book, and a collection for the Sailors' Widows' and Orphans' Society. So it was more like Sunday. The Romans had their Service in the same place early, and the Captain said if the Mahommedans asked him he would let them also have the same place. In the evening (Sunday) the Frenchmen got up a sort of concert, which however they conducted on the third-class deck. One of the *garçons* remarked that we each amused ourselves in our own way. I perspire sitting still! We are all grinding at Swahili, and it is a grind. We saw plenty of flying-fish yesterday. We are due at Aden on Wednesday about 3 a.m., but we stop at Obok on the way. I wonder if I shall see E. B——.

May 22nd.—We had the most awful swelter last night. A strong wind sprang up, and they closed the ports—some of the men slept on deck. They begin swabbing the decks at 3.30, and they won't allow you to bring your mattress up. So I concluded that I would try the cabin, and the result was that I was in a bath of perspiration all night, but I slept like a top. This morning the hot, strong wind has gone down, and we have just a breath, which is much better. I think to-night if it is so hot again I shall try the deck. Everybody says we are very lucky not to have it much hotter here. I don't feel the heat very much, but the question of dress is occupying my mind rather now. I was very much taken with the Arab garment at Port Said—a long sort of gown from the neck to the heels, like a cassock. Like a duffer I have not kept out any white "ducks," except one of your pairs, and they are so big for me that I can't wear them. However for the present I am luxuriating in your tussa silk jacket and a pair of cricket flannels—an awful spectacle, but every one else is the same! I shall post this at Obok. I wonder when you will get it. I doubt if there is any good trying to find my sisters; they will be off by the time this reaches England. Please remember me to all my old friends. There is absolutely no news, but you will see from this that I am still alive and kicking. Have I told you that my boat leaves Zanzibar on June 2nd? So if we are up to time I shall only have three days in Zanzibar, as I think I ought to push on. Any delay would mean a month at least, and I suppose they will be short-handed at Nyasa, so I had better get on as quickly as I can. I shall feel rather an incubus at first I fear, not being able to talk the language. I was told that Swahili is no use at Nyasa, but I

have no other books to learn anything else, and at Unangu, where
Bishop Hornby thought I ought to go, they speak Yao. However
I think I can't do wrong in learning Swahili. I often look at my
choir photo and think of you. At about 9 p.m. with us on Sunday
you were just going to Church, gathering up in the choir vestry.
Tell me when you write all about the cricket, and what you and
the others are doing. Don't forget that I am anxious to know
who is E——'s successor and T——'s, and who is to take B——'s
place, and what B—— is going to do, and any other changes that
may be in contemplation. Remember me to old C——, and
E—— too if he is not gone. I will try and write my impressions
of Zanzibar, when I am there, for the Missionary Association. I
shall leave a little money (for I have very little) with Miss Mills
or one of the others for African curiosities. I wonder what the
carriage will come to. I had best direct them to you. With all
best wishes,

Yours, etc.,

A. F. SIM.

S.S. "*Amazone*," *May* 24*th*, 1894.

MY DEAR——,

We got to Aden at six yesterday night. It was rather an
eventful time. First we had to attend a wedding ! The lady was
to have been married at Zanzibar, but her impatient *fiancé* met
her at Aden, and having arranged matters before our arrival he
wired to her at Obok, and on our arrival we had to go off straight
to the Church, which we reached about 6.20. The bride meanwhile changed her dress at the hotel. We had a long, long wait ;
finally, at a little after eight, when all interested had read through
every possible law relating to such marriages in British Colonies,
the happy event took place, and the girl we knew when we started
as Miss K—— is now Mrs. C——. The elder C——'s brother is
the bridegroom ; he is a Vice-Consul in Zanzibar.

Well, after the wedding I went up to the R.A. Mess and sent a
message in to E. B——, Esq. They were at Mess, and I am afraid
I robbed the poor chap of half his dinner. I was quite too disrepu-
table to make my appearance at the table, so we sat in the ante-
room and talked. What an awfully slow place ! He keeps life
going by dreaming of a shooting expedition to Somaliland, whither
he intends to make his way about July if he can get leave for two

months. His ambition has been fired by the success of a brother
officer there, who slew two lions and an elephant, besides countless other game. So I trust you won't be minus a nephew before
the end of the year. The rest of the party meanwhile had gone
back to the hotel to drink the bride's health. B—— saw me back
to the steam-launch at 10.30. Aden is relieved from utter destitu-
tion and absolute misery by being very beautiful. You have seen
it. We saw it in sunset colours, and it was very lovely. I have
unpacked my cabin-boxes entirely, and, as you can imagine, my
bunk is a litter. I always was tidy, wasn't I ? So I am going to
begin packing. I shall commence by sewing up my dirty clothes
in the old canvas which covered one of my boxes. We hope to
reach Zanzibar on Tuesday the 29th, a day before our time. My
party and Mr. C——'s party are the only English in the 2nd class
saloon, and the Consul-General the only Englishman in the 1st ;
all the rest have left us for Bombay, etc. You can see from my
writing the state of collapse I am in ! It is hotter than ever I
think, though we are promised a cool night.

May 25th.—We have just got round Cape Guardafui (look it out
on your map), and are heading a little West of South. It is much
cooler, and we are enjoying the beginning of the monsoon, which
means that the boat is pitching a little. It will probably increase,
and very likely our ladies will have to seek the seclusion that a
cabin grants. But it is such a mercy it is cool. I think no one is
overcome yet, though two or three have retired from active life.
We are off the Somali coast. I believe there is a good future for
Somaliland, but now the people are very jealous of strangers.

May 26th.—We are having some rather dirty weather. It is the
monsoon. It is such a pity, for all the ladies are ill, and it means
no Celebration or Service to-morrow : it also means that the ports
are closed, and the cabins are awfully stuffy. I'm afraid we shall
not get into Zanzibar till Wednesday or Thursday. I hear there
is a " Union " boat going to the Cape ten days after we are due,
perhaps I shall go on in that. It will give me more time in Zanzibar.

May 28th.—Yesterday was very rough and only the best sailors
survived, which, for my reputation's sake, I am glad to say included myself. We had no Services. To-day it is better. On
Saturday we only did 225 miles, yesterday 240, and to-day 247.
We are nearing the line, expecting to cross it about 6 o'clock to-

night. The evening begins at 6 prompt. I miss the jolly English twilight which you are enjoying. I often sit and think what you are doing. I shall be thankful when this time of inactivity is over. The hours on board this ship are very funny. We have what amounts to two enormous dinners each day, at 10 and 6. I am quite accustomed now to go starving between the two—very bad for one I think. I sometimes long for a decent cup of tea and a hunch of cake ; I haven't tasted any since I left England. The tea is horrid on board, and the milk is condensed and therefore sweet. The women-folk fare worse than I do.

May 30*th.*—We are off Pemba now, and hope to land at Zanzibar to-night. The old ship had to stop for an hour early this morning, something got heated. We have been putting on the speed in order to land to-day. It is absolutely calm and we have varied the entertainment with tropical rains. It did come down. I sat in my mackintosh, as we all did, under a double awning ! I wish I had Mr. F—— here to pack for me ! You will imagine I am awfully gloomy from the tone of this letter ; it has been rather hard to be cheery. Snap-shots are out of the question under the awning. I shall post this on board and write again in Zanzibar. We have seen the usual flying-fish, a whale and a grampus, a sun-fish, etc., etc. Will you make any use of this you like ? Give my love to all at St. Aidan's. I do so long for letters ; I wonder if I shall get any !

Yours, etc.,

A. F. SIM.

Letter to St. Aidan's Parishioners, dated—

Mbweni, *June* 1*st*, 1894.

MY DEAR PEOPLE,—

I hasten to write to you before all the novelty has worn off. We arrived at Zanzibar on the 30th. It was quite dark, except for some lights on shore and on other ships, and the Sultan's electric light predominating all, so that I have no impressions as to what the harbour is like. I was heartily thankful to leave shipboard life. It is enough almost to damp all one's zeal to have three weeks of that sort of inactivity. I read nothing but my Swahili books ; but it was always difficult to concentrate one's attention to work. Five or six of the missionaries and the ladies came on board. We sent them all ashore, and I waited with Mr. Faulkner (the General Manager of such things) to get out the luggage and take it ashore. This took us nearly two hours. When we got ashore the luggage was all piled up on the sandy beach, and porters carried it up to Mkunazini, about ten minutes' walk. In the meantime we sat on the boxes until the first party of carriers had gone and returned. When I got up to the Clergy House the ladies had gone to their separate abodes. Mr. Brough came in from Mbweni (4 miles) on his bicycle, and he took charge of me. I was told off to stay at Mbweni (where I am at this moment). I got something to eat at Mkunazini, and then rode out here on Mr. Brough's bicycle, while he borrowed another (Mr. Faulkner's), and we rode together. It was pitch-dark, and except that the road is perfectly pure white I should not have known which was road and which not. It was the strangest ride I have ever ridden. The streets (!) in Zanzibar are about six feet wide. They wind about at their own sweet will, and are not lighted except by the shop lamps. Everybody seems to live in public; every house is wide open to the street with no glass. Of course we led our iron horses through these streets. Eventually we mounted. Mr. Brough's bicycle has not been oiled since it came out! So off we went. How am I to describe the strange sounds? The road and the neighbouring scrub were alive with fireflies, and the air full of sound—frogs croaking, crickets, etc., chirrupping, an occasional owl hooting : one, a cricket, makes a sound like a phantom bicycle bell (old-fashioned sort !). Well we reached our destination safely, calling at Kiungani on the way to leave letters which had come by our ship. The rains have begun, and the road was a quagmire in places ; but we had no light and could not pick and choose, so we rode through everything. Immediately we got in a perfect deluge came down. We came straight to the Clergy House here, fifty yards from the Girls' School and Home. Mr. Key is in charge. He is the only married Priest in the Mission. Mrs. Key gave us (J. Brough and me) cocoa, and we went to bed. It is the cool season and is really very pleasant. Of course I am wearing my white " ducks," and when I want to look decent, I put on a white cassock ; it covers all blemishes in my attire ! The least exertion makes me perspire as I never have done before. The ride simply bathed me ! I know now something of what the puddlers feel, but I never suffer from thirst. There are always oranges and bananas and lime-juice (very different from that bottled stuff you buy in England) to be had. I have not had a headache since I left home, and don't intend to ! How am I to describe this lovely place ? Oh, how I wish I could transplant you here ! What a place for a Sunday School Trip ! What flowers (and it is not the flower season) and what butterflies and trees ! You can't see forty yards for trees—cocoa-nut mango, cassarina, acacia, oleander, and countless others that I don't know the names of. If Mr. L—— wants to keep the boys out of his fields, let him plant a cactus hedge—six feet high and spikes from the very ground ! A boy who has just left Eton, and is going for two years into the Chartered Company's Police in Mashonaland, joined our ship at Aden, and he is waiting for the same ship as I am. I am going to get him here next week. I shall make a butterfly net, and we will make a collection to send you. And now I must tell you about the Mission here ; and first you must understand that the photos you have seen give you no idea of the place. That of the Church is good. The prevailing colour in-side is a yellowish white. The present Church was only meant to be the chancel of the future Cathedral. It is smaller than it looks in the photo ; I should not think it held more than 400. The choir wear red cassocks, which set off their black faces and bare feet—altogether very nice. The singing—well, it is hearty ! I don't know what Mr. D—— would say to it ! They shout, and don't know much what a "head-note" means, and yet it is tune-ful. Of course they sing in Swahili. The English Services are led by an English choir of the residents here. It is all very wonder-ful to think that twenty years ago thirty thousand slaves were sold annually on that very spot ! Such merry children they are, always laughing, not a bit " hadden doon," so reverent in Church, and yet when they grow up sometimes so disappointing. Their idea of the marriage tie is so slack. It is the one problem. In Zanzibar, round the Church is the Clergy House, with Miss Mills' boys (about forty), and next door the Industrial Boys (thirty-eight), under Mr. Lister, and then the Hospital—a beautiful little place. In a few days Miss Mills' boys are going to be moved. Mr. Brough has built her a lovely house at Mbweni. Then the Clergy House, which has been threatening to tumble down for the last twenty years, is going to be pulled down and rebuilt. They are building another house and Chapel in the native quarter to be worked by two men : they will meet Mahommedanism mostly, as well as

much heathenism. This won't be ready for some time yet. Then
there is Kiungani, a mile and a half out of Zanzibar on the coast,
where, you know, all the boys are, and where Samwil Mhesa [1] was.
(By the bye, I am going to send him a present, a lamp I think,
and a knife, and one for his future wife !) A party is going up to
Magila next week.

Archdeacon Jones-Bateman is at Kiungani, and until a new
Bishop is appointed he is the head of the Mission. I hope to stay
over Sunday at Kiungani. And then there is Mbweni (which
means "The Girls' Home")—remember it is an estate (*Shamba*),
I was going to say of hundreds of acres. There is a village of
natives—about three hundred freed slaves, who work for wages
for the Mission. Building is the principal work, which means
also lime-burning, carrying sand and stone, quarrying, etc. There
are carpenters' shops, such as a contractor in England like Mr.
H—— requires. The villagers also till the ground for themselves, and grow rice, maize, mahogo (like tapioca), sweet potatoes,
and such like. They live in native houses—one or two rooms
thatched from roof to floor. They have their own Church and Parish
School for boys ; the girls go to the big School. Then there is
the Girls' School—a boarding School of course. I think most of
the girls are freed slaves. Some are Shamba (village) children. I
haven't been over the School yet, though I hope to go this afternoon. They have a Chapel attached to the School where they have
a daily Celebration—English and Swahili on alternate days. This
is at 6.45. Mr. Brough built the Chapel.

I am staying at the Clergy House, about fifty yards from the
School. Mr. and Mrs. Key live here and Mr. Brough. Then the
Clergy and others in the town use it very much as a place of rest,
if they feel fever at all or are done up. One of them, Mr. Fir-
minger, walked out with me last night and intends to stay till
Saturday evening.

We have just had lunch (11.30), and I am sitting in the baraza,
or open-air sitting-room, over the porch. It has a roof of corru-
gated iron and then thatch on the top of that and is of course
delightfully cool. About twenty yards from me is a bush eighteen
feet high—a mass of magenta flowers—bougainvillea ; another to

---

[1] A native boy, whose maintenance is undertaken by the scholars of St.
Aidan's Church, West Hartlepool.

the left of mauve; right opposite, an oleander, and on all sides crotons of a thousand variegated leaves. Flying all about are Java sparrows, much more cheeky than English sparrows ; and now and then one gets a glimpse of a brilliant little bird—one a coppery black, with a brilliant scarlet shirt front, cut in fashionable proportions ; another with a yellow breast and shiny green back. The flowering bushes are thronged with butterflies of every hue.

The Shamba is extended by Miss Thackeray's purchase of Sir John Kirk's estate. It is of course her own property,.but every one regards it as Mission property. She has a good many freed slaves living on her Shamba. The sea is immediately below us. I could flip a pebble into it from where I am sitting, about forty or sixty feet down--a steep slope covered with greenery. The children were bathing a few minutes ago. Their ordinary garment is a sort of bathing-gown, so they just walk in, and such a row they make ! How their dress dries I don't know ! Perhaps it just dries on them.

The road out to Mbweni goes a little further to one of the Sultan's palaces. The present Sultan has only one wife, but all previously had many, and these palaces were then useful. The road is the only one out of Zanzibar, and was made by the Mission in Bishop Steere's time. The Mission keeps it in repair and the Sultan pays for it. It is a very good road—fourteen feet wide, very smooth and white.

I went into town yesterday to unpack my things, with a view to re-arranging them. The Miss Nicoll, who came out in our ship, was married at three in the afternoon. Then in my efforts to find young Mr. S—— (of whom I have spoken before as coming out here next week for a few days), I came across a sailor who hailed from West Hartlepool—a Greek married to a Seaham Harbour woman, and living in Christopher Street. It was just a little breath of home. He was as much pleased as I was, and expressed a wish that he was walking down to the Park instead of in the streets of Zanzibar ; in which I agreed, though I should prefer Stockton Road on my way to Longhill ! My ship leaves on the 9th. There may be an invalid with me until I get out at Chinde ; then I shall be alone. I am going on by the Union line. I have had no letters yet from home since I left Marseilles, and I don't know when I shall get any. I need not say how much I long for them. The French mail South), is expected in to-day : letters of course will not come by it, but they are expected by the British India boat.

June 2nd.—I went in again to town yesterday to do some shopping, and then in the evening I tried another mode of progression to bring me home, viz., a donkey! Mr. Brough and I rode out together. It was great fun as the donkeys were quite willing to go. It is not so warming as the bicycle. I confess I would rather ride a horse ; I was in mortal dread of landing over the donkey's head ; however the stirrups were a great help.

Now I have told you nothing of my impressions of the actual missionary work here. How can I pretend to judge of it in these few days? All a stranger can see is the School work and the rows of happy boys' and girls' faces. The Industrial Boys' School is in splendid hands under Mr. Lister, and it has I should think a great future before it. The work on the Island is mainly educational—preparing teachers, etc., for the Mission stations on the mainland. There is preaching in the streets, and there is this new work in the native quarter about to be set on foot. The Services are really beautifully rendered in the Cathedral ; the attendance is of course chiefly that of the staff and Schools. There are English Services on Sunday and sermons in English ; of them I shall be able to judge to-morrow. I think the work suffers from the constant and unavoidable changes in the staff, through fever. Men are always wanted and taken from their proper work to undertake that of some sick man who has had to go into the hospital. For myself I would rather go to Nyasa than stay here. What I long for is real mission work. The Priest-in-charge at Mbweni has something more like Parish work at home, only his parishioners are black.

I have no doubt a missionary's life is full of endless little duties : almost everything he does he must do himself, or at least superintend. I intend spending some time over my boots with a rag and some grease this morning ! When I am about to leave the haunts of civilization (not before) I shall get the Treasurer (Mr. Davenport) to cut my hair. There is a good deal of "cut" about his work, but there is little hair left to tell the style ! It has the advantage of being cool !

The French mail is in, and so this letter must go almost at once. You will see from what I have written that I am very happy. I shall be much more content when I am at work. I am afraid I shall be very useless for some time, because even the little Swahili I have learned will be almost useless at Nyasa, where they speak Chinyanja or Yao.

When shall I write again I wonder. I will try and send a line to tell you whether I reach Chinde in safety. In the meantime I know you remember me in prayer, as I do you every day.

Ever your affectionate Friend,

ARTHUR F. SIM.

Letter to E. L. ——, dated—

Mbweni, *June 4th*, 1894.

MY DEAR——

I spent Sunday at Kiungani, but saw only a little of the Archdeacon. I communicated at the Swahili Celebration, and then went into Zanzibar for the English Service. There are very few English residents ; most of them seemed to be there. It is rather awful the way everybody gets fever. You can make no certain arrangements, for you can never count on any one being well two days together. Dr. Palmer is Priest-in-charge at Mkuna-zini (in the town) ; he had fever on Sunday, but had to take work with his temperature at 102°. One of the ladies from Mbweni has been taken into the hospital to-day, and half a dozen others are on the verge of, or just out of fever. In Zanzibar there are three places : 1. The hospital (new) for natives and the staff—no room and no time for any others. There is another good hospital in the town. 2. Then there is the Clergy House, and forty little boys under Miss Mills. 3. The Home for Industrial Boys (thirty-eight) under Mr. Lister, a layman. These are apprenticed to tradesmen in the town, and so they have trades—a few to use in the service of the Mission, others to get their own living afterwards. Then of course there is the Church. At Kiungani there is the Boys' School (a mile and a half South of Zanzibar), one hundred and thirty boys ; four miles South of Zanzibar is Mbweni, the Girls' School ; and fifty yards from it the Clergy House, where I am staying. To-morrow there are four weddings coming off, between three boys of Kiungani and one of the Industrial boys and girls at Mbweni. On the mainland there is a settlement at Dar es Salaam (eight hours by steamer) of the people from the Mbweni freed slave village. Mbweni is three-quarters by half a mile, but it is too small to support all the people. They are employed in building,

etc., by the Mission ; but for the most part they ought to be able
to grow enough food to feed themselves and their families. It is
hoped that ground may be got in English territory on the mainland where superfluous families may be transplanted. We have a
native Deacon working at Dar es Salaam, who is doing very well.

June 6th.—The weddings came off in great style yesterday ; all
was very nice. The newly-married and a few friends communicated. I have never seen an English wedding so reverent and
orderly. The Church was packed. One can't speak too highly of
the work that is going on here. Much has to be left undone for
want of funds, and much is half done by reason of the constant
sickness of the men. The poor fellow who preached on Sunday is
in hospital now, dangerously ill. I hear that Wimbush has been
sent home very ill ; this is the last of the Sunderland lot (seven
men). I offered to wait here for a month to take Dr. Palmer's
work ; he had proposed a holiday journey to Magila, but Tyr-
whitt's illness prevents it. However they think I ought to go on to
Nyasa. I am quite fit and in no way disappointed with the work—
on the contrary. But it will require a wise man to be Bishop ; the
problems of heathenism are so fearful, and the question as to the
development of the work requires the greatest wisdom and fore-
sight. . . . Pray for us. I can imagine it is hard to say one's
prayers properly here sometimes, owing to lassitude. Farewell.
Give my love to M—— and the bairns.

Yours, etc.,
A. F. SIM.

Union s.s. "*Pretoria,*" *June 9th,* 1894.

MY DEAR——

I am now on my way to Chinde from Zanzibar. I left on
June 9th, and expect to reach Chinde on June 14th ; then I put
myself into the hands of the Lakes' Co., and trust eventually to
reach Nyasa in a month's time.

I was glad to see the life in Zanzibar, though it was rather
horrid being so idle while men and women were being knocked up
all round one with over-work. While I was there Miss Willion, a
nurse in the hospital, died after three days of great anxiety. She
died at 6.30 p.m., and was buried at 9 a.m. the next morning. It
was a very solemn thing. I was present at the early Celebration.
One felt rather the risk to life ; so many were either on the verge

of fever, or in the hospital, or just out. Miss Willion had been out only a year. The Clergy and nurses suffer most : perhaps both are over-worked. The laymen are perhaps more sensible ; and yet they all, even the healthiest of them, bear their scars. Two of them have had a temperature of 107°, and one of 108°, and live to tell the tale !

Before leaving I heard that Wimbush was on his way home, so perhaps I shall never get to Unangu, but have to stay in Likoma. At any rate either will be better than Zanzibar—I mean more of the real thing. The only post I covet in Zanzibar is Priest-in-charge at Mkunazini (town). I would make the men take more care of themselves, and the nurses too. I think it is such a pity they should be teetotalers there. I would make them drink a light wine. At present they only drink under doctor's orders. I feel sure that high living is the secret of long living there.

June 14th.—At Quilimane. We stopped at Mozambique at twelve on Monday, the 11th. After tea I went ashore with the two first-class passengers, Mr. H—— and Mr. S——, who joined the "*Amazone*" at Aden, and have come on in this boat. The latter is going to Mashonaland and the former to England. We walked round the island, and came to the cemetery at the far end where Ellis Viner and Pollard are buried. Such a barren, bleak place— about one and a half miles by half a mile—all sand, and an old fort at one end. We took the Portuguese Bishop and a Priest on board there : they gave him a salute of fifteen guns ! Here we are anchored twenty miles from Quilimane. A tender takes passengers and cargo ashore, and then takes the Chinde passengers and cargo, and we (two passengers) spend a night on board the tug. Chinde, forty miles from Quilimane, at the southern mouth of the Zambesi, is the head-quarters of the Lakes' Co. I believe they take charge of me, and in time hand me over to the Zambesi mosquito and the hippopotamus fly ; the latter has patent pinchers warranted to go through any clothes !

And now farewell again. It is more than a month since I have heard from any one, except old K——. I got a letter from him, dated May 11th, at Zanzibar. I long for news. How is all going ? Remember me affectionately to all old friends.

Dominus Vobiscum.

Yours, etc.,

A. F. SIM.

African Lakes' Co., Chinde, *June 21st*, 1894.

MY DEAR——

Here I am waiting again. I suppose on the whole I ought to consider myself lucky—eight days in Zanzibar, five days in Quilimane, seven or eight here, and who knows how many at Blantyre or elsewhere on the way. It is horrid waiting. Even at Zanzibar, where one was among one's own people, I felt useless and out of place ; and here they are all Presbyterians, but they are very kind. From Zanzibar I have had a companion. He is the most insufferable bore I have ever met, and I consider my life a burden until I shall have seen the last of him at Mandala. He is the worst of all bores, a religious one, and starts the most solemn and-sacred questions in the presence of those who take no interest in religious matters ! It is at least a capital lesson in patience. At Quilimane, forty miles from here, we were handed over to a small tug-boat. This was on Thursday last, June 14th. And from the "*Pretoria*," which anchored outside the bar, we were taken into Quilimane (twenty miles), and there we remained till the following Monday. Imagine my sentiments on being transferred to this little dirty tug-boat—passengers and crew living and sleeping in a cabin aft not quite as big as my study ! Ten of us in all ; the table and floor were called into requisition ! The captain was a dear old man. The chief engineer delighted my ears the first night with a choice selection of " Billingsgate " and worse, and the crew giggled at his coarse jokes. But he never uttered another coarse word after the first night and we lived on the best of terms and played a rubber or two of whist and now he has the loan of some of my books. He is a type of the man who comes out here. What good word can you expect for Missions from such men ? And they tar them all with the same brush, dealing out accusations of all kinds with a lavish hand. The pity of it is they get such ready credence at home. One of the passengers, who lives at Chiromo (in the Zambesi Flotilla Co.), accused the Blantyre Mission of all kinds of villainies. I do not believe one word of it.

Saturday, June 23rd.— I expect to get off on Monday. Once I reach Likoma, I feel it will take horses to get me away with this tedious journey before me. I haven't told you how we came here. Last Monday, the 18th, we left Quilimane in the tug-boat " *Union*." Oh, that Quilimane bar ! We left at 7 a.m., and reached here at

5 p.m. (forty miles). I did not think I should ever know what sea-sickness was. I was not sick, but was not far off it. Three of the crew were worse than I was ! The whole time we had water swilling round on the decks, and constantly one or other gunwale was under water. I have never experienced such a queer business, and could not have believed a boat could live through it ! Well, we got here all right, and the skipper comforted us by saying it was nothing to what it is sometimes ! Here we are lodged in a grand house specially built for passengers by the African Lakes' Co., but there are no appliances. So I have been very busy, with another man, doctoring, building, digging, carpentering, etc., etc., and just now cooking.

Really there is no time to do all there is to be done ! Doctoring ! Both the African Lakes' Co.'s men living in this house have been ill with fever—no doctor ; the temperature of one was 106°, of the other 105°, and we can't get it down at all. He is so sick. Three men in the tug " *Union* " I had to doctor ! I haven't had a pain in even my toe yet, but I fancy the journey up will try me—it does most people. Chinde is an awful place. The British have a concession of a square mile from the Portuguese. The Portuguese are very much in the background, but all goods are taxed. It would be a good thing if they could be bought out. Chinde is all sand—loose, fine sand—such a labour to walk in ! Nothing will grow except in the marsh. There are perhaps fifty white men and a growing village of blacks. The Lakes' Co. is the biggest, but there are two or three other trading Companies. Everything is fearfully dear here owing to Portuguese taxation. Last night I dined with the Consul, and met the captain of the " *Blonde* " cruiser and the naval lieutenant, who came on a visit to Chinde and nearly got drowned crossing the bar in their pinnace. Capt. F—— was captain of the " *Ariel,*" and lunched once at 31, Norfolk Street in 1886 ; he remembered F——, W——, L——, etc. He talked twenty to the dozen, and I enjoyed the evening not the less for a rubber of whist. To-morrow I am to take Service on the " *Mosquito* " gunboat, at 9.30 a.m. I am glad of the chance of meeting a few " shell-backs." I don't brood much, but when I begin thinking of home there is a sort of longing for the old familiar faces. It is a capital discipline this. One is nobody here—as one ought to be—only those dear old people in a big town somewhere in the North tried to make one think differently. While I am writ-

ing you are just drawing stumps ; it is striking six.   I am writing
in my bedroom by the help of a flickering candle.   It is quite dark
at 6 p.m.

The sermon I preach to-morrow will be my first since leaving
home !   I am yearning for news from you.   The last news I have
heard was the Derby winner and Mr. Mundella's retirement !   Is
the Church disestablished in Wales ?   Is the Government still un-
changed ?   What has happened in West Hartlepool ?   What is
happening at St. Aidan's ?   Have you forgotten my existence ?
Next week you will all be at Auckland.   I left a telegram to be
sent in time.   I hope Mr. Davenport won't forget it.   I also wrote
to the Bishop, but he won't get it till too late, I fear.   And now,
good-bye again.   God bless you a hundred times.

Yours, etc.,
A. F. SIM.

Letter to E. L——, dated—

Chinde. *June 24th,* 1894.

MY DEAR——,

This morning I took Service on one of the gunboats ; the
Consul and a few other English came on board, and I am to
take Service here (at the African Lakes Passenger House) this
evening at 7.30.   I enjoyed meeting the "shell-backs" very
much.   .   .   .   On Friday coming over the Chinde bar the steam
launch of the "*Blonde*" was pooped and her fires put out ; she
had to anchor for two hours and relight them.

It is shocking the way Europeans treat natives, and worse the
way they speak of any good work among them.   I am afraid it
must be confessed that the native is lazy and stupid ; but he has
not been accustomed to work, and I think half his stupidity is
due to his not understanding the orders given to him, and he is
flurried and bothered by the Englishman's hasty temper.   I hope
Bishop Hornby will be able to get a man for the river to work
among the English.   It was not what I came out for ; but the
Bishop was just sounding me I think, and yet it is important
work.   .   .   .

June 25th.   I went to breakfast with Capt. Carr, of the "*Mosquito*," this morning.   It was a comfort to hear him speak well
of the two boys he has had for a year from the Mission in Zanzibar.   .   .   .   I still maintain rude health, and have had no reason

to complain of the African climate yet. I am comforted by the
anticipation of a bad bout when I do get the fever! I hope I
shall get some shooting on my way up the river. Buffalo,
lions, and buck abound at Chiromo. One of the officers on the
"*Herald*" gunboat shot five lions the other day.

Yours, etc.,

A. F. SIM.

H.M.S. "*Mosquito*," Chinde, *June 30th*, 1894.

MY DEAR——,

Mail day will always be a mixed pleasure ; it makes me
think of home in rather a depressing way. The officers on board
this gunboat got their letters yesterday (there are only the captain
and the doctor), and both of them were very quiet all the evening,
talked of retiring from the service, and so on. It is not time for
me to begin complaining yet. I expect when my first three years
are up I shall long for home too much to resist the temptation of
a visit to the old folks. Alas ! What changes there will be ! If
only one could find things just as one left them. Well, I can't tell
you anything yet of missionary work. My time seems just to
have been spent in constant delays, of which I am thoroughly sick,
though this little time on the "*Mosquito*" has been very pleasant.
Both doctor and captain are very nice men.

Of all the many missionaries who pass through Chinde the only
ones I have heard a good word for are our people. Of course that
may be in consideration of my presence. However people are not
sparing of condemnation. But if missionaries are doing no good,
the ordinary trader does a great deal of harm. I am not going to
give my "well-considered opinion" of the native till I think I
know something of him. But from the little I have seen of him, I
am afraid he is a low character ; still that is no reason for desert-
ing him. At any rate the children ought to be redeemable. . . .
You will be glad to know, as I daresay you guessed before, that
the Mission is worked on Catholic lines. It is astonishing to find
the ritual so reverently and carefully carried out as it was in
Zanzibar. The language, on the whole, rather lent itself to such
purposes, I thought. No one here speaks Swahili. The little I
know is quite useless : a few words are the same, and the construction is similar, but otherwise I have to set about learning a
new language from the very start. And now I have said enough

about myself. I do miss you all more than I can tell, and sometimes faithless regrets come into my mind. One is so apt to
forget that one works for Eternity. Except for my friends, what
have I given up? In Africa one has to lay hold of every luxury
that comes in one's way. Poor living is specially productive of
sickness, and I believe that even absolute teetotalism is bad for
one. I cannot feel that I have chosen poverty; all my wants are
supplied; I even have a gun and a rifle, and have already shot
at hippopotami—without success! Please tell me all about the
people whenever you write, who is sick, and who is well, and if
any die. And please remember me to all my Longhill friends.
Often I wish I had one of those boys with me, G. T——, for
instance; we could talk about old times, and one would not be
so lonely. There are such a lot of people I ought to have said
good-bye to before I left, but there was no time. If only I could
have had these wasted days there instead of here! I do hope the
Sunday School is keeping up. The Band of Hope is of course
over. Remember me if you will to　.　.　but it would take up
all my paper if I named them all. I never forget them, and often
sit in a "brown study" thinking of the dear old place.

Yours, etc.,

A. F. SIM.

Chinde, B.C.A., *July 2nd*, 1894.

MY DEAR——,

I am to leave Chinde to-day and it may be some time before
you hear from me again. I am still on board the "*Mosquito.*"
Capt. Carr has been awfully kind to me. I have been his guest
since last Wednesday. I have been here nearly three weeks. It
seems an interminable time since I left Zanzibar. I long to reach
the end of my journey. This is an awful hole, though I daresay
that is because I have nothing to do. There is a cement tennis-
court, and a level place in the roughest field imaginable, which in
the wet season is a marsh, where they pitch a wicket and play
cricket. They are ambitious and intend to level the whole field.
I still maintain my resistance to the fever and I hope I shall long
do so. Indeed I never felt better than I do now, but I am living
like a lord here.

I was awfully glad to get some letters here, and your two papers
—the "*Strand*" and the "*Picture Magazine.*"

I expect I shall reach Likoma about the beginning of August ! I have in other letters described the various beauties of this place. I have had a shot at hippo from the boat and seen crocodile ; hippo-shooting when they are in the water is literally snap-shooting with a rifle, and generally at a hundred yards. So it is no wonder that we did not "bag" the wily hippo. The whole ship's company were armed ; it was a perfect fusilade. I have taken some photos, but have no chance of developing or printing them till I get to Likoma.

The doctor reports a case of blackwater fever on board this morning. This seems to be the most deadly form of fever. The skipper at this moment is getting his hair cut by a bluejacket. My hair was scientifically cut by one of the laymen at Zanzibar, and I shall go till I can get a bluejacket on the Upper Shiré to do it for me. It is funny to think of you looking forward to winter ; at least it is past midsummer, and probably it will be August before you get this. When you write please send me plenty of gossip.

Yours, etc.,

A. F. SIM.

On the Zambesi, *July 5th*, 1894.

MY DEAR——,

At last I am on my way from Chinde. We started yesterday at 2.30 p.m., and got as far as where the Chinde river branches from the Zambesi. This morning we have been delayed till 10 o'clock by fog. I am on a stern-wheeler, fairly fast, and would be comfortable if we were not so crowded—three ladies and five men ! The ladies have one cabin to themselves about the size of a pill-box, and we take the saloon, which, with five of us, is pretty thick ; but I have what I consider the best place, across the door in my camp-bed. Indeed it was rather cold this morning. I wished I had another blanket. It is quite a mistake to think Africa is always broiling. I am so thankful for my Norfolk jacket, which you remember I was nearly leaving behind. In fact once I was reduced to wearing my thick great-coat. It is getting hot now (10.30), but the breeze is cool. The presence of the ladies involves manœuvring to get a "tub." I think shaving is a superfluous luxury. Here we are on the Zambesi (about a mile broad) with

two native pilots to pick out the channel, which winds about the
whole breadth of the river. Hippos and crocodiles are on every
sandbank, but they disappear when they see us.

July 7th.—It will take us ten or eleven days from Chinde to
Chiromo, where we tranship into house-boats, and get paddled up
as far as Katunga's ; thence we go by land to Blantyre, and thence
by land again to Matope ; then the lake journey begins. Our
party consists of Dr. and Mrs. L——, Miss S——, for Bandawe,
opposite Likoma, Mr. I—— and Mrs. P——, for Tanganyika
(they are of the London Missionary Society, I think) and a Mr.
C——, a sportsman who distinguished himself last year by shooting two white rhinoceros, which are very rare. There are a lot of
natives on board too. The English crew consists of the captain
and the engineer. We are towing two lighters. Though we are

A BRANCH OF THE ZAMBESI.

all going up under the auspices of the African Lakes' Company,
this boat belongs to the Zambesi Flotilla Company. I think it is
faster than any other boat on the river, except of course the gunboats. Business is not very solid here. Everybody is waiting for
the coffee, of which great things are expected. Sugar too is a
good thing, and there is one very big concern, with electric light
plant and a miniature railway, at Mopea, near Vicenti, which last
we expect to reach to-day, and where we shall lose Mr. C——
who is a very nice fellow. The river here is about a mile or a
mile and a half wide, but sandbanks are very frequent, and our
course is consequently a zig-zag one. On these sandbanks croco-

diles frequently lie. We shoot at them, and they immediately wriggle into the water. I feel sure they are often hit, but they are such a pest that it is almost a duty to try and exterminate them. Hippos too are rather numerous, but they are hard to kill, so we scarcely ever shoot at them. We burn wood in these steamers, and consequently our clothes often get burnt by a falling spark. I have a hole as big as half a crown in one of my karkee coats. Mrs. L——'s umbrella had half of one side burnt and the white cover too. Every morning we have been delayed by mist till about 10.30. This morning the mist cleared about 8 o'clock, and we got away early. We draw into the side every night at sunset, about 5.45. The boys go ashore to sleep, lighting fires and making a lot of noise. You can't imagine how cold and wet the mist is in the morning. The decks are as wet as if it had rained heavily, and it is bitterly cold. I have taken to sleeping in the wheel-house ; the saloon is too crowded for my taste. This is a very badly-fitted boat. All the glass is out of the wheel-house windows, and so I stuff them up with anything I can find handy, generally spare sail-cloth. We have just passed the "*Henry Henderson*," the Blantyre Mission boat. She is engaged in traffic as much as in Mission work, and carries passengers for the Lakes' Company. We are in sight of the Morambala Mountains. They are about 4,000 feet high I believe ; otherwise the horizon is as flat as it can be. All that we see of the banks is a fine sand. I daresay it is mud at the bottom of the river, but even the sand seems most fertile.

Sunday, 7th after Trinity.—Another Sunday on my journey. I spend much of my time on Sundays thinking of you. To-day we put into a wooding station, so after saying Matins to myself I went ashore and executed the enclosed sketch,[1] which you may send to next year's Academy if you like.

The boat, or rather the upper deck of it, is in the foreground. I am sitting on a high bank, and looking down upon it. Mrs. L—— and some others are distinguishable to an artistic eye, and in the distance are the Morambala high lands. That part of the picture I consider good. Now we have put off again, and are just going to have breakfast (11.15 a.m.). We have tea and bread and jam at 7 or 8 a.m., afternoon tea at 3, and dinner at sunset. We haven't stuck on a sandbank yet. There is a monkey and a

[1] See next page.

mongoose on board; they are great fun, but monstrous full of fleas.

Monday, July 9th.—We reached Misongwe (above Vicenti) last night, and slept there, though it was early to anchor; but we had finished all our bread, and so waited to get palm-wine yeast to bake fresh bread with. Mr. C—— left us there. Isn't it funny, when we were talking last night, he said: "Do you know anything of Cheltenham?" and it turned out he was at school there from 1884 to 1887. Then he was in the Bechuanaland Border Police, and through the Matabele Campaign. I believe there are several old Cheltonians out here. So we talked about the old School till late at night. We put a half-caste passenger ashore at Misongwe against his will. He had stolen a bottle of whisky and

(*From a sketch by A. F. Sim.*)

a pair of new boots; so he will have to make the best of it on a desert shore (more or less).

July 15th.—We are nearing Chiromo now, which is the furthest limit which this boat can reach, owing to the lowness of the water. We have been aground a dozen times to-day, perhaps more. Once all the black boys were sent into the water to find where the channel was. The country is hilly here; nothing very high, but reminding one of the Perthshire hills. All seem to be clothed with trees to the top. To-day I have my first experience of fever.

Three of us arc seedy ; mine is very slight, a bad headache and aches in the bones, very like the " Flu." I am not surprised at having it, the broiling day and the bitterly cold mist at night drenching everything, clearing up between 8 and 10 each morning.

I post this at Chiromo, which is a British station. There is a lot of life in this river—hippos, crocodile, ibis, crane, kingfisher, fish-eagle, etc., etc.

I think of you people many a time, and wonder what you are doing. I shall be at Likoma I daresay at the beginning of August.

July 15th. 8th Sunday after Trinity.—Another Sunday on my journey ! This makes five since I left Zanzibar, and only Communion once. I feel a heathen. Ever since landing at Chinde I have been among Presbyterians. My touch of fever is still on me, chiefly in the head ; temperature 102°. I shall take fifteen grains of antipyrine to-night and sweat it out of me. We are off the boat now. It is a comfort not sleeping on the floor with sore bones ! Tell me all the news. Love to all of you.

Yours, etc.,
A. F. SIM.

Letter to Miss H. A. S——, dated—

Mandala, Blantyre, *July* 23*rd*, 1894.

MY DEAR——,

The river journey is a roughish business, and one only has the barest necessities in the way of clothing, etc. Everything else is stowed away in lighters towed alongside. I may well say that I am more than half way now. I expect to leave this very soon, and then the last stage of my journey will have begun.

Zanzibar	arrived May 31st,	left June 9th.
Quilimane	„ June 14th,	„ „ 18th.
Chinde	„ „ 18th,	„ July 4th.
Chiromo	„ July 14th,	„ „ 16th.
Katunga's	„ „ 19th,	„ „ 21st.
Mandala	„ „ 21st.	

Now my next stage is thirty-five miles by *machila* in one day ; then up the river in a house-boat to Fort Johnston, six or seven days from here, and there our own steamer meets me. Quilimane was a roughish experience—eight of us in a little cabin in a tug-

boat for four nights doing nothing ; and that delay wasted a fortnight for me, for I just missed a steamer coming up. . . . We
came to Chiromo in ten days—nine passengers, and two Englishmen to work the boat. It was too crowded ; three ladies made a
great difference in such cramped conditions. The cabin was so
full that after the first night I slept in the wheel-house, which was
exactly my length, on the floor ; the cork mattress came in most
handy. It was awfully cold and unwholesome, so that when we
reached Chiromo four of us had a touch of fever. . . . We
slept a couple of nights at Katunga's, delayed by the rain. How-

TRAVELLING IN A MACHILA.

ever we started on Saturday at 11.30 and reached here at 8. The
machila is a hammock slung on a bamboo—a not very comfortable
mode of travelling, especially if the boys let you down a few times.
You lie flat and two men carry you : eight men go to one *machila*.
They do the twenty-eight miles between Katunga's and Mandala
in about eight hours. However I did not like being carried,
so I got out and walked most of the way, and felt thoroughly
tired out when I got in here in pitch darkness at 8 p.m., but
very much better for my walk, for I had a headache all the way
from Chiromo, solely from want of exercise. You can't imagine

what a civilized place this is, and it is quite cold. It is funny that
no one ever told me to provide warm clothing. It was very cold
on the river in the early morning, and it is always cold here—as
cold as English spring weather about April. There are fir trees
growing, wide roads, some brick houses, and wood fires all day
long ; pine apples (not ripe yet), papai, coffee, guavas, oranges,
lemons, limes, mangoes (not ripe), cabbages, etc. I believe anything would grow. Everybody is mad on coffee—it is the coming
thing. . . . Everybody is Scotch here. This is the centre of
the Scotch Established Church Mission, and very civilized. It is
also the head station of the African Lakes' Company. They are
the principal, in fact *here*, the only trading Company. Of course
English things are very dear ; labour is cheap, and that is all.
The best food, besides fruit, is tinned ; it is really very good. The
African fowl is the staple food ; what a beast it is, tasteless and
tough ! All African meat is the same ; it is only eatable in rissoles
and done up. The native eats no meat, but only rice and maize.

July 24*th.*—There are sixty or seventy Europeans here. I
dined at the Manse last night—quite an English home, charming
people. Fancy a sale of work here on Wednesday taking £140,
and a concert in the evening. I dine with the Administration
Agent to-night, by name McMaster ; he says he is remotely connected with the Vicar. . . .

The road to Matope, *i.e.*, the thirty-five miles ahead from here,
is rather disturbed. It often happens that men with loads are
fired at, and yesterday a man was seized by a lion. . . .

Yours, etc.,
A. F. SIM.

On the Mission boat "*Sherriff*" on the Upper Shiré,
July 30*th,* 1894.

MY DEAR——,

It is 7.30 ; we stopped at 6, put into the bank, lit a fire,
boiled soup and water, and now I have finished dinner at the
fashionable hour of 7.30. No one ever felt so like Robinson
Crusoe as I at this moment. I am monarch of all I survey, having
parted from the rest of my fellow-travellers at Blantyre. They
went on ahead of me while I waited for the Mission boat. I
have a crew of ten boys ; all but two are Christians, and they are
catechumens. I have a teacup and pot (Mr. F——'s gift), a

saucepan, and a slop-bowl. In the latter each course is served. I have also a knife, fork, and spoon all in one. My provisions for a week consist of four tins of soup, two tins of corned beef, two of condensed milk, tea, butter (in a tin), cocoa, sardines, sugar, and salt. I bought eight eggs this morning for two boxes of matches, and at the British Central African Administration Station exchanged a box of sweet biscuits for half a tin of water ditto, half a loaf of sodden bread, and a piece of cake. So I am now luxuriating in fresh bread ! I am sitting in my shirt. It is chilly early in the morning, but very hot here in the daytime—a change from Mandala, which was never oppressively hot. The boat is about eighteen or twenty feet long. My house in the stern is thatched with reeds and grass. I can sit on my chair in it, but cannot stand upright. I spread my bed on the bottom boards, and have my bath and all my meals in it—of course each in its turn. I don't know what I should do without Mr. S——'s filter. Oh, the mosquitoes ! ! ! Each day I boil water, and have tea and biscuits about 6, then prayers, and off about 7 (prayer in Chinyanja with the boys). They know morning and evening prayer by heart. My part is that of a worshipper in a foreign language. I could take prayers, but the only Prayer-book has most of the leaves torn out ! What remain I take. The Scripture consists of the first nineteen chapters of the Acts. None of the boys speak English, so I make them talk slowly while I look out each word in a dictionary ! I want to reach Fort Johnston on Thursday. There I expect to meet Madan on his return from a visit of inspection, and Matthews, skipper of the "*Charles Janson*," who is ill, suffering as Wimbush was in the legs ; he is almost paralysed. Seeing therefore that there was a sick man in the case, I felt justified in starting from Matope on Sunday afternoon. I left Mandala on Saturday at 7.30, and reached Matope in a *machila* at 4.20, thirty-six miles (good travelling I think).

July 31st.—I have just finished an aldermanic dinner—gravy-soup, fowl, tomatoes, and bread the same old bread, it won't float in soup, but perhaps that is the soup's fault, and jam. We called at a village to-day where there were two or three catechumens, and one old man caught a fowl and presented it to me—alive of course. In return I gave him a handful of "'bacey." The fowl remained alive till half an hour or less before I ate part of him ; the boys got the rest. I ate him off the top of a biscuit tin to the tune of a hippo grunting like a gigantic pig a little distance off.

About ten this morning we passed Madan and Matthews, who were in one of the African Lakes' Company barges, which was towed by the gunboat "*Dove.*" I am sorry not to have had a talk with Madan ; we could only shout at each other for a moment in passing ; but it is much better as it is, for they have plenty of room, which is indispensable for a sick man. I don't know how they would have done in this little boat.

Now we have had food and prayers, and are putting out again in the dark to reach another village a little further on to sleep at. The boys probably know where they can get a good reception and an empty house to sleep in. Last night the house was small, and four of them had to sleep on the boat—rather a hard bed on the top of iron-bound boxes. It is too dangerous here to sleep ashore ; many man-eating lions are about. The only game I have seen are crocodiles, at which I have fired with varying success, and rats, which for cheek beat English rats and mice hollow. They spend sleepless nights within a few inches of my head, and no doubt would examine me if it were not for my mosquito net. The mention of the net makes me think of Mrs. C—— and all her kindness to me. I am reserving myself for a letter to her when I reach Likoma. I hope many letters are on their way to me. I have not had a chance of getting any yet except those few at Chinde, but I expect them. The boys are singing such a funny chorus. They always sing these catches, or chants, whenever they are on a journey. No doubt it is to while away the time and keep their "hearts up," but also no doubt to frighten away beasts. I seem to be sitting in a cloud of gnats and other insects, not to speak of mosquitoes ; no doubt my candle attracts them. I wonder what some timid people I know would say of the beasts of the night here—spiders seven inches long (and they sting) hornets of various kinds, jiggers which bury themselves in your feet and legs. I have escaped the worst of these charms so far.

August 1st.—The boys went on so late last night that I spread out my bed and went to sleep. They were making such a row, singing and talking at the top of their voices, that I had to tell them to stop, and then the next thing I remember is 6 a.m. this morning, when we were moored along the shore, but all the boys were sleeping on board. I don't know how they can manage to

sleep in such hard beds ! We went on immediately, and did not
stop till 9 a.m. In the meantime I shot an enormous bird, standing four or five feet high on stilts, with a huge beak, red and
black and yellow. I have preserved the beak, and the boys have
eaten the bird. I can't use my shot-gun, as I have no cartridges
loaded : otherwise there are plenty of birds to shoot—duck, geese,
waders and divers of every kind, pigeons, enormous fish-eagles,
hawks, vultures, and kingfishers. The game is extraordinary, but
you have to go for it, and that I have no chance of doing. We
are now in a very wide part of the river called " Pamalombe
Lake." The hills on either side are lovely : one might be on a
Scotch loch, only it is more magnificent. The black boys and the
hippos and ibis, etc., make it different.

August 2nd.—We reached Fort Johnston last night. The boat
is still my home.

Sunday, August 5th.—I am still at Fort Johnston waiting for
the "*Charles Janson.*" With affectionate remembrances to all,

Yours, etc.,

A. F. SIM.

Fort Johnston, *August 7th,* 1894.

MY DEAR——,

I am yearning for letters from the Parish. Yours dated
May 23rd I have just received. How I long every Sunday just
to be in my old place for a few minutes. In my letters I have
mentioned very few by name, because they are so many, and I
could easily occupy the whole letter with messages ; but I presume
you want to know what I am doing. I have purposely been most
egotistic, but I know you will understand. I should like you to
keep my letters after they have gone the round. But never mind
about it. I should rather like to read them when I get back, if
ever ! Tell my old pals to write to me, C—— about the Parish ;
E——, if you see him, about his new work ; C——, but I fear that
is too much : T- —, G——, C —, and C——, if he would. Let
them ventilate Missionary ideas. Also make my old friends in
the Parish write. Remember however that what costs you 2½d.
costs us 6d. postage. But I will try and answer all letters I get.
And now farewell.

Yours, etc., ·

A. F. SIM.

On board the Mission boat "*Sherriff*,"
Fort Johnston, *August 7th*, 1894.

MY DEAR——,

I posted my last letter to the Vicar on Sunday, August 5th, from here, so I must tell you about my stay in this place. I might have gone on by the s.s. "*Domira*" to Likoma last Saturday, but I asked the price of the passage. £15, if you please. The African Lakes' Corporation has a monopoly, so I determined to remain here until the "*Charles Janson*" turns up. She has been undergoing repairs, hence the delay ; but I hear that she is ready for sea now, and I am expecting her any day. There are three general boats on the Lake besides the two gunboats and the "*Charles Janson*," two belonging to the African Lakes' Company, and one to the Germans, half gunboat and half trader. The German boat is in now, and sails again on the 12th. I think if the "*Charles Janson*" does not turn up by then I shall take passage in the "*Wissmann*." In the meantime here I am. My house is a reed and grass roof over the stern sheets of this twenty feet boat—at least four feet high in the highest part, and six broad at the broadest. However I can get my chair in and my bed. I lie along the bottom boards at night. I am quite a Robinson Crusoe, and my meals are rather scratch. I am moored at the Mission Station at Mponda's opposite the Fort. The two officers at the fort or Boma, Captain Robertson and Dr. Harper, are awfully kind and give me the run of their house ; and I have had a good many meals with them on the strength of their hospitable treatment at Likoma. I have had boiled fowl twice, eggs, and bread. Such bread ! I have no oven, and native pot gives the bread a wonderfully unbreadlike taste. I have tinned things as well. To-day I went out shooting with Dr. Harper. We got one difficult shot each, and came home with nothing. Such walking—grass eight and ten feet high, scattered trees, stalking on hands and knees. There is evidently plenty of game if it were only visible. The heat was very great. This evening I tried to get some duck, but saw none. I shall try again. I go down or rather up to the Lake about two miles, and trust to getting overhead shots. Alas ! I have lost a precious box. Mr. H—— made it to hold my despatch box. It has all my little treasures in it, and among others, my caps. So at present my shot-gun is useless, though the doctor is going to give me two hundred caps. I am in wonderfully good health. Except for that little touch of fever at Chiromo, I have scarcely had a headache. Mponda's is a big village or town, with perhaps 5,000 inhabitants. The Mission keeps two teachers (native) here, but the people at present have just got in their grain crops, and are employed in drinking pombé and dancing! So the teachers have no scholars. The buildings consist of a School and two teachers' houses. The crew of the boat, eleven boys, sleep in the School. One of these boys is my cook, but his ideas of cooking are very hazy. I think he has been appointed cook because he understands most English! Oh, his bread! He blossomed out in what he called scones to-night. He was going to make them of flour and water in a frying-pan which I have borrowed. I persuaded him to add a couple of eggs and some baking-powder. It turned out a sort of pancake half an inch thick. If I haven't indigestion soon it is good testimony to my digestive organs! The fowl is invariably killed just before he is cooked, consequently he is very solid eating! I have never managed more than the wing as yet. To-day one of the teachers got me a few bananas. Alas! that "scone"--it taxes even my internal arrangements. We have had School for a few boys while I have been here. I can't say they are clever. It is just an infants' class for married men! Alphabet and words of one and two syllables! On Sunday we had Service. Of course I was no use. A few heathen came when the bell had been sent round the town. I spoke through one of the teachers' interpretation. It was a new experience. I won't express any opinion of the Mission work until I know more of it. My estimable cook at this moment, 10 p.m., is fishing off the boat. I occasionally hear struggles, as of some mighty fish being landed. I hope he won't tumble in. There are many crocodiles here. They keep out of sight in the day, but sneak up to the watering-places at night. Many people have been taken in this way. The "dug-outs" (canoes) are rather cranky vessels ; it reminds one of being in a lightship again. Yesterday, going across the river, an old crocodile was swimming alongside of the canoe about twenty yards aft. I had no gun with me. No doubt it would have been a dangerous experiment to have shot at him ; one flap of his tail would have upset the canoe.

August 9th.--The "*Charles Janson*" came in last night, and all in a hurry I came on board, so I must close this in the same haste, as the letters are going ashore almost immediately, and we are off. From what Mr. Johnson says I am bound for Unangu, remaining a few days at Likoma, and then the Archdeacon goes with me to Unangu. I am glad of this. It will be real Missionary work, and not all school work. It is rather a squeeze for three passengers on board, but I am heartily glad to be practically at the end of my journey. However I feel that my holiday is over. I am glad of it. This sort of do-nothing life is most demoralising. And now "farewell" till I get to Likoma.

Yours, etc.,
A. F. SIM.

THE PREACHING TREE AT LIKOMA.
People waiting to sell food and firewood.

Letter to Mrs. G ——, dated —

Likoma, *August*, 1894.

MY DEAR——,

Here I am, very happy in the prospect of plenty of work, and very well. Fever of course comes, but unless it is serious no one takes any notice of it. . . . This station is a bright, happy place. The Archdeacon is very nice, full of fun and kindly chaff, wholly given up to his work, and we all get on very well together. . . .

Most of our work is in German or Portuguese territory. Indeed the Germans offered Bishop Smythies a price to clear out; but he realized his indebtedness to this people, and of course such a thing could not be dreamt of. The Church here is temporary, with stone walls and mud for mortar; but it is seemly and reverent; no seats in the nave, two or three forms in the choir and a harmonium. There is a picture of it in the May "*Central Africa.*" . . . You don't know what a languid, careless sort of person an Oriental is—no energy, so leisurely. I suppose one must go slowly. I am learning Arabic characters. What Swahili writing is done is written by an Arab clerk in Arabic characters. I suppose I must expect and rejoice if I get opposition from the Mahommedans. It will I think be better than the listless callousness of the pure heathen. . . . I have three little chaps sitting on the floor by me here looking at the pictures in the "*Century.*" I think a few picture-books would be useful for these youngsters. A picture of a big town calls forth the exclamation, "*Steamer!*" the steamer being their idea of wonderful things. . . . Remember me most kindly to all my friends. Tell the ladies that if only they could see these poor people I think they would work hard for them. Perhaps it is our prayers they need more than anything else. Ignorance and superstition—not more than two or three years ago they burnt four women alive for witchcraft not a mile from here. The Archdeacon only knew of it after it was done. Yesterday a great palaver was held about witchcraft, some men demanding payment for an alleged case of witchcraft. The Archdeacon dismissed them summarily. Now, please remember us in your prayers.

Yours, etc.,

A. F. SIM.

Letter to Mrs. C——, dated—

Likoma, *August* 15*th*, 1894.

MY DEAR——,

. . . I shall try and gather a few curios here for the Parish Hall, as I think you ought to have a Missionary Museum; but the cost of sending things is very great, and the natives make nothing very original. . . . No one can take an interest in

Missions until they know something about them. I have experienced, even in my short time, what reliance to put in travellers' tales about Missions. Most outsiders know nothing about the work, have no sympathy with it, and often live such lives as will not bear the light which Christian Missions throw upon them. . . . The Makanjira business is rather misrepresented in England. They have certainly been routed, but they have fled to the hills, and are I believe quite capable of giving plenty of trouble still. Of course if the English had been driven off trouble would have resulted, but Jumbe's death is a matter of much greater importance. It was he who supplied Makanjira and Kalanji with slaves. Now the fear is that the Yao chiefs on the East side of the Lake, now that the source of supply is stopped, may take to raiding the lake shore villages where most of our work lies. In fact there have been some cases of seizure and robbery, both of people and of cattle. . . .

Here at Likoma each man has his separate house, but we all have our meals together. Prayers every morning at 6.30. ; Holy Communion every Thursday, and some other mornings, at 6 ; breakfast at 7 ; lunch at 12 (generally rice-pudding) ; tea at 4 ; dinner at 7. So we don't do badly when there are any stores in hand. These sometimes run out, and now we are very short of sugar and salt. It is a pity Europeans can't do with less of these home-made luxuries.

Please remember me most kindly to the ladies at the Sewing Meeting, and remember how much I value letters.

Yours, etc.,

A. F. SIM.

Likoma, *August 15th,* 1894.

MY DEAR——,

. . . I am completely happy at the prospect before me ; whatever it is, it will be somewhere to the "Front." . . . I have opened my letters, and my thoughts are too full of the dear old place and faces to think about anything else. I am full of thankfulness about the parish news. I think I see the Parish going ahead. The Rummage Sale and the Bazaar are good news. Poor Longhill! I do hope Mr. C—— will do better work there than I did. Oh, if only one could look back at one's ministry with satisfaction! What a humiliating retrospect it is! May God give me strength to be braver for Him here ! I rather dread the language difficulty. If I go to Kota Kota I shall have to know three languages, and at Unangu two. Chinyanja is easy, Yao is hard, and Swahili is rather hard ; but the difficulty will be not to confuse them. . . .

What a pleasure it is getting back to settled Church life ! The journey up the river was long and tedious, and very demoralizing ; I feel I have reached a haven of rest. The mail makes me feel a little home-sick again, but I am very happy, and I feel I am wanted here. The work at Likoma is very prosperous on the whole ; the School work is specially bright, and the children are very affectionate ; I think I shall get to like them. . . .

I am sorry to say that the doctor seems to be suffering in the same way in the legs as Mr. Wimbush and Mr. Matthews. The Archdeacon too has numbness in his legs. Is it not a strange form for malarial fever to take ? I find, I confess, everything most comfortable here. Certainly the houses are airy, and it is cold in the mornings and evenings. This is the healthy season it is true, but I feel as well here as I ever did in England. . . .

Remember, me most kindly to all the teachers, and to the children also. New faces will begin to creep in, and soon I shall be a stranger to most of them ; never mind, I shall not be jealous.

Yours, etc.,
A. F. SIM.

Likoma, August 18th, 1894.

MY DEAR——,

. . . Now about Kota Kota. We went over there, the Archdeacon and I, by the "*Charles Janson.*" We started on Thursday, called for a ship-load of wood, picked up Mr. Glossop, dropped Mr. Johnson at Msumba and slept there ; then off at 6 a.m., and reached Kota Kota at 2.30 (we had to anchor nearly a mile from the shore owing to shallows . We made our way up to Mr. Nicholl's house (British Central African Administration Agent), some way from the shore, at Jumbe's old house, and found him with his Sikhs and many old chiefs and head men of the town (Jumbe's brother among them) seated in his baraza. We talked with Mr. Nicholl about our business, and found that the Scotch Mission's plans were rather vague still. So we called the headmen together ; the future chief came too after some delay, as " he was saying his prayers "), a young, rather delicate-looking man, very shy. But Mr. Nicholl said the real man of power was and would be the old chief's brother ; he seemed a kindly, good-natured old fellow. Mr. Nicholl and Mr. Glossop left us to have our talk ; the natives were very nice, except perhaps one man. We did not ask for an answer until the new chief was "enthroned," but they were well inclined—at least so we thought. Jumbe had frequently asked Likoma to send a teacher. He seemed to prefer the "Bishop's people" to any others. And so, after looking at prospective sites, we came away, leaving Mr. Nicholl a bundle of papers, etc. One of Jumbe's youngest sons, a child of four or five, attached himself to my big finger, and when we got to the boat he wanted to step in too, much to the people's amusement. And so it is at present settled that I am to go over when the German steamer returns on September 3rd (or before, if an opportunity occurs). It turns out that Swahili and Chinyanja are the two languages required there. If only this scheme can be carried out, I shall be a remarkably lucky person, and a privileged person too, to get such an interesting and important place to work up. I like the idea of starting from the beginning.

Saturday, August 18*th.*—We returned last night, or rather 3 a.m. this morning, from Kota Kota, travelling through the night. There was a brilliant moon—a lovely scene—so we sat on deck (the Archdeacon and I) till we fell asleep, and about twelve went below, and I did not awake till 5.30 a.m. I spent Saturday preparing a sermon for the English inhabitants of the station, and took a walk with Mr. J. Williams at 4 o'clock. The island is very pretty, the Lake so blue, and the opposite shore four to six miles away and so clear. You can see the hills on the West side, thirty-five miles away, so clearly sometimes that they seem not more than five miles off. I am anxious to develop my photos, but I daren't just now while the moon is so bright ; you can't keep the brightness out you see. Saturday night I had just a slight touch of fever, and on Sunday felt that I was still human !

Sunday, August 19*th.*—The programme for to-day is : Holy Communion, 7 a.m. ; breakfast, classes, heathen preaching. Christian Service (Matins) ; lunch, 12 ; catechising, 2 ; tea, 3 ; English Evensong, 4.30 ; dinner, 6 ; and Chinyanja Evensong. Pretty full day for two Priests.

September 10*th.*—It is nearly a month since last I wrote in this

diary—a month more or less uneventful so far, spent in packing for
Kota Kota (I seem to have done little else than pack and unpack
since I came to Africa), learning Swahili, spending some time in
bed with fever, which last has taught me to be careful. But the
great event of the month to me is my coming here (Kota Kota).
I left in the German steamer on Sunday, September 2nd, after
Communion, with William, a native teacher, and a native cook
and his wife. We arrived before sunset—4.30 p.m.—and here I
have been since, living with Mr. Nicholl, sharing expenses and
sleeping in a native hut, living in the open air under a grass shelter
from the sun. Again I am waiting, learning Swahili, native habits
and patience. Jumbe II. is enthroned, and they are holding a
seven days' pandemonium in the village, half a mile away. When
this is over I shall approach Jumbe with my petition, and I hope
to buy a site and begin building at once. The old men (or elders)
say it will be easy to get a school, but not to " wash with water "
(or baptize). We shall see. No doubt a long, weary waiting lies
before us. This place is much under Arab influence. Old Jumbe
was a half-caste Arab. There is a mosque here and an Arab
School. I purpose beginning the School at once, and as soon as
possible begin itinerating work in the many villages around. This
is a big Parish ; for sixteen miles to the South, with but few
breaks, villages continue, owning Jumbe's chieftainship, and there
are many thousands of people. Last Friday Jumbe, a young man,
was enthroned. Mr. Nicholl and I were present. We went to his
private house and waited till twelve o'clock, Jumbe retiring about
a quarter of an hour before to be robed. Then we proceeded
very informally to an old tomb, the resting-place of one of his
forefathers really an old house, for they bury great men in their
houses here. In the baraza, or verandah, was set the throne, a
saddle-back chair presented by Mr. Nicholl for the occasion. The
new Sultan approached, robed in a long white kanzu. First, the
Arab Sheik, or holy man--an old rascal who will shortly find himself in durance vile—said Mahommedan prayers, to which the
people responded. Then the *Waziri*, or Prime Minister, old
Jumbe's brother, took up the ceremony, first clothing him in a
long black Arab "*joho*," or coat, embroidered with gold : then a
coloured cloth over his left shoulder ; then a fez and turban—each
with some words as a kind of ceremonial. Then followed an un-
merciful pulling of his right ear with words to the effect that he

was to have neither eyes nor ears for any but his head men ; and finally a speech by the " Installing Master," or *Waziri*, in which the new Jumbe was reminded of his predecessor's example—never to turn even a child away from his baraza, never to listen to any one who smoked " *bhang* " or drank " *pombé*," and to remember the honour due to grey hairs. Mr. Nicholl congratulated him on his accession, and shook hands with him in the name of the English people; and after he had given him a present of two trusses of calico (£15 cost price) we departed, but not before I got a photo of them all.

And here I am waiting, and learning Swahili, and enjoying Mr. Nicholl's company. He is one of the oldest and most experienced Africans in British Central Africa—a well-read man and thoroughly conversant with native manners and politics. We see something of the slave trade. A few have taken refuge here. Really the Government is powerless to stop it while the road to the coast lies through Portuguese territory. One, a woman with a baby, clung to my skirts as we were going into the village the other day. Mr. Nicholl sent her up to the Boma, or fort, which is becoming a City of Refuge. Another came in a slave-stick ; five women fled here from a neighbouring chief who was going to put them to death.

Now I have written as much as will go for 6*d*. We expect the "*Domira*" soon. She will take our letters down to Fort Johnston.

Yours, etc.,

A. F. SIM.

Letter to Mrs. F——, dated,—

Likoma, *August* 23*rd*, 1894.

MY DEAR——,

I don't think I can say I enjoyed the voyage. It may serve to make me more contented with my lot now ! Likoma is a desert island as far as vegetation goes, sandy and stony, and yet not so bad as I was led to expect. It is only four miles from the East coast. We have two boats manned by native Christians constantly running to and fro, so our own barrenness is supplemented from the mainland. We can never well starve, since we can get supplies from any part of the Lake by means of our own steamer or the German steamer which calls every month. No account of Nyasa would be complete without mention of the work of the

steamer "*Charles Janson.*" She is simply and solely a missionary;
she only brings up our passengers and loads from Fort Johnston
because she has to call there in any case. And her work is endless and unremitting. Two Priests are on board, Mr. Johnson and
Mr. Glossop. They visit the lake shore stations, sometimes remaining a few days at one or another, preaching, taking classes, and
superintending the school work and the teachers. How thankful
I am that our Mission sets its face against dabbling in native
politics. The only cases we consent to hear are those relating to
Christian discipline. I hate to hear people talk of Missions as
forerunners of English civilization ; they may be this, indeed they
can't help instilling a regard for the English name, but it is very,
very secondary to mission work. Don't you think so ? The
truth is there is no time for the missionary to civilize, except only
as the Message of Peace and Love civilizes. Better preserve
our people as good Africans than make them bad Englishmen.
We have no time for improving the breed of sheep, or intro-
ducing Cochin China fowls, and so on, and we must be content
with the barest necessities to which we have been accustomed in
England. What we have to do, as I conceive it, is to educate a
Christian people and a Christian standard of right and wrong, and
eventually a Christian Native Church, remembering our heritage
as a Catholic Church and handing it on to them. Don't be
frightened, we are not fearful ritualists here !

I hope to get what building there is to be done completed by
Christmas, when the rains will begin. In the meantime I shall
work very hard at Swahili. No doubt I shall be able to begin
preaching through an interpreter at once. I am promised a very
clever boy (or rather man) as teacher ; he speaks English very well,
and Swahili and Chinyanja are his native tongues ; he was in
England for eighteen months, which spoils any but the very best
characters. I won't say anything yet about the Africans as a
whole. I know I shall feel the responsibility of the work tremendously. In England character is formed by the atmosphere one
lives in, and the result is at least not utterly negative or evil.
Here the Christian teacher has to create the atmosphere ; all
outside his gate is heathen, bad, weak, indolent, selfish, irresponsible. No one I am sure can quite count the cost of the life of a
missionary among savages ; so you see how we need your prayers
and sympathy, and in what lines we need them.   .   .

It is too much I fear to ask you to write once a month, isn't it? I should so much like to hear Sunderland news regularly, and your letters are so chatty. Good old Sunderland! I got the account of Durham regatta from Mr. McM——. Please congratulate any you see who belong to the crew or Club.

If you see any St. John's folk remember me to them, and give my heartiest congratulations to Mr. M——. And now farewell.

Yours, etc.,

A. F. SIM.

Likoma, *August* 26*th*, 1894.

MY DEAR——,

. . . Mr. Nicholl is an old African and an interesting man, a bit of a naturalist, fond of growing things for experiment. To be in touch with the only European at Kota Kota will be of importance. He is a Scotchman I believe, and he understands the native. The oldest Anglo-Africans are the most ready to confess how difficult it is to understand Africans. . . .

I am but human I find, and have to be ridiculously careful about chills. I suppose one must go easy at first and be careful. I daresay Kota Kota in the wet season will try me—anyhow I mean to try it! . . .

Jumbe's funeral was not over when we were at Kota Kota. He had been dead two or three months. They bury people in their houses; the women do the mourning, and abstain from washing all the time! The houses are afterwards burnt down.

August 27*th*.—Joseph Williams,[1] a dear old layman and one of the oldest members of the Mission, is going back to Unangu, having been here partly on a holiday, and partly for stores. So the school yard is a scene of bustle. He has about forty loads, goes across in a boat, and starts from immediately opposite this. . . .

I want some saccharine. Sugar[2] is very dear here and we almost do without it. Can you get saccharine in powder? a few ounces will last a long time. . . .

You did not tell me if my wire from Zanzibar arrived at Bishop Auckland on St. Peter's Day. I left it to be sent in time, but of

---

[1] Joseph Williams and Bishop Maples were drowned in Lake Nyasa through the capsizing of the "*Sherriff*," on Sept. 2nd, 1895.

[2] A St. Aidan's scholar, five years of age, having heard that Mr. Sim had no sugar, was found by his mother filling his missionary box with it to send to Kota Kota.

course I was far away at Chinde then.   I wrote at the same time
and the Bishop would get my letter shortly afterwards.

And now farewell.   Remember me to all.

Yours, etc.,
A. F. SIM.

Letter to R. T.——, dated,——

Likoma, *August 27th*, 1894.

MY DEAR——,

We want a bricklayer, builder, and mason very badly here

BISHOP'S PALACE AT LIKOMA,
Where A. F. Sim stayed.

now.   The Archdeacon intends starting soon to build the permanent Church.   Our mortar is made from mud taken from white
ant heaps.   It hardens, but won't stand rain, and so houses have
to have wide eaves.   I don't know if the Church is to be built like
this.   Lime can be got at Unangu, a long way off.   Of course
there is plenty at Zanzibar : there everything is built in Oriental
style.   .   .   Zanzibar is beautiful, but most relaxing and un-

healthy. Mbweni is lovely—such trees and flowers and butterflies and fruit! This is a barren desert in comparison; really
very little will grow here. . . .

I can't tell you how I rejoice at being sent to a new place; it is
just my dream. Kota Kota is a large town, with 2,000 or 3,000
people perhaps, a good deal of Mahommedanism, a mosque I
believe, and an Arab Sheik, or sacred man. . .

One has to be awfully careful, especially about bathing. The

Likoma, looking eastwards towards the mainland with part of the Archdeacon's house,
and boys playing football.
(*From a photograph by A.F.S.*)

houses are open three feet from the eaves, and the walls are only
reeds, so they are little protection against the wind if it blows. I
shall build differently at Kota Kota.

Water I think will be a difficulty there. The only place I
shall be able to live at is a long distance from the Lake, and there
it is very shallow, and I expect, owing to there being a large town,
somewhat unwholesome; but I believe water can be got in wells.

Won't it be interesting starting from nothing, and doing every-thing with one's own hands almost? My place must be out of the town ; I could not live in health in it, but I shall have a preaching shed in the centre of the town. It will be best also for the School to be away from town influences. . . .

Likoma is quite a village with between twenty and thirty houses. Each European has a separate house. The Church, a dining-room, school, dormitory, carpenter's shop, printing office, store, two hospitals (European and native), library, store for combustibles like lamp oil, large new industrial house, and the ladies' part for girls in a walled space adjoining—these make up a large village. . . .

Let me break it to you gently ! You see one must give up some-thing in the Mission field, so with many struggles, and many inward questionings, and many fallings away, I have now definitely and decidedly broken off the habit of shaving ! Yes, it is more than a week old now, thick, brown, stubbly, and promising well —in fact, I can pull it ! . . . Remember me most kindly to all the lads and children. How I wish I could have two or three of you people out here ! I expect great things of Kota Kota ; would that I were more worthy of so great a work ! Give my love to all the teachers, and to all my old friends among the men.

Yours, etc.,
A. F. SIM.

Letter to Mrs. C——, dated,—

Likoma, *August* 30*th*, 1894.

MY DEAR——, . . .

It is no good being too enthusiastic. The people at Kota Kota do not want us. I don't think they would put up with us, if it were not for secondary considerations. In old days, when they were raw heathen, they would welcome the missionary much more readily than they do now. It may be a long weary time before I get any hearing. . . . Swahili is the court language, but I expect the common people, formerly slaves, and still slaves to all intents and purposes, will speak the Lake language, Chinyanja. . . .

September 9*th.*— I am now writing from Kota Kota. I am sleeping in a native hut and living in the open air under a grass thatched shelter from the sun : rain, of course, there is none at this time of year. The native hut shelters myself and teacher, as well as sundry other beings, less human, but who "owe their existence to human negligence!" However I am alive and well. I had a touch of fever at Likoma, which has taught me to be careful. All the ills of Africa are due to chill. I imagine the pores of one's skin must be intensely sensitive here. The sun has a peculiar burning heat, almost smarting. This and the next two months are the hottest in the year. The rains come in December, and April and May are the unhealthy months. . . .

I am staying with Mr. Nicholl, who here now watches the course of political events. . . .

How strange it seemed early this morning, when in my native hut I was celebrating Holy Communion with my three native Christians, to hear shouting, singing (so tuneless), dancing, and firing of guns all the time! Can you picture it? I think not; and yet this drumming is a characteristic of native life. One wants a phonograph more than a camera to reproduce Africa to the English mind.

Sounds are never absent—human beings, insects, birds, and at night beasts join to make a continual buzz. The animal world is only silent when the sun is at its height. This (Kota Kota) is an interesting place—a flat plain with a few hillocks at the back of the village and a range of high mountains two or three days' journey to the West. . . . I am thankful to find that my teacher is a good joiner and has a straight eye—most wonderful in an African. I get up about 6.30, have a cup of tea, dress, have prayers with my three natives, breakfast at 9.0, read, write, do Swahili, or some useful work till lunch at 1.0, go on doing ditto till tea at 4.0, then a walk and dinner at 7.0, a smoke and bed at 10.0 or even 11.0. Among all this comes in every day a baraza, or audience, when most of the headmen come and sit and talk to or stare at us. Sometimes they have things of state importance to discuss. They are very nice old fellows though rather a nuisance, of which I shall not get rid till I build my house. I pick up Swahili sounds, though, by listening, and I can generally follow what is said more or less. I am thankful to be well here; what would it be to be boxed up all day in my hut in a bed! but my native teacher is a brick and ready to do anything for me. We have peace to-day as Mr. Nicholl gave out that Sunday was our sacred day, and this they quite appreciate. To eat we have soup, fowl done with curry powder or native onions roasted, a pudding of rice, cornflour, or ground rice, an occasional cake, pancakes, and bread made with hops (boiled and left to ferment). Biscuits, salt, sugar, tea, fruits (there are very few native fruits here), these are all imported. We have too tinned meats, jams, soups, potted meat, etc., but tinned things we avoid as long as possible. . . .

My hair is cropped like an escaped convict's—no brushes, no razors, no looking-glass !

Yours, etc.,

A. F. SIM.

Letter to E. L., dated,—

Kota Kota, *September 9th*, 1894.

MY DEAR——,

Here I am in a large—perhaps the largest and most important—town in Nyasaland. Jumbe is dead ; long live Jumbe ! The original old Jumbe fifty years ago was a coast Arab, conquering the place and enriching himself with the profits of the slave trade. . . . This is a most interesting place. Jumbe, compared with his purely native neighbours, was an enlightened man. He planted many trees, even cocoanut, thereby breaking down the superstition that cocoanuts will only grow near the sea. A single mango tree of Jumbe's planting exists in the village. . . .

I have seen some tusks of ivory more than six feet high, weighing more than 100 lbs., and measuring round the curve more than seven feet. These are in the possession of an old Arab here, a courteous old rascal, and a thorough-paced slave dealer. There are many such in the town, but as they can't get leave to cross the Lake their stings are drawn. Their slaves are afraid to report themselves. . . . If only the African Lakes' Company would make it worth the Arab's while to take his ivory down to the coast by the Zambesi ! Instead of which this Company has descended to being a kind of big agency for European travellers and missionaries. Their prices are enormous, and everything bought out here is purchased at a premium of seventy-five per cent. The route up the Zambesi and Shiré is practically in their hands, and here too they charge exorbitantly—£35 from Chinde to Likoma for passengers, and I don't know how much per ton. The price from Southampton to Zanzibar by the Cape second class in the Union boats is £35. I should think that the future of these parts is in their hands. . . .

I went down to the "palace" yesterday and had a talk with

Jumbe, and told him the purpose of our coming here. He was very nice about it all, and promised to help me in everything, and to name a price to-day. He is being led by the nose I feel sure by an oily money-grubbing headman, whom we have both had reason to suspect of forcing prices. So this man came up to offer the site for 1,000 rupees—quite an exorbitant price. One could buy quite a large coffee estate for this in the Shiré Highlands. I have told him I can't and won't give more than 300 rupees.

They cannot realize at all one's disinterested motives, and it is no good attempting to make them understand them. We are very fortunate in Central Africa in the administration of the country. Not a drop of liquor is permitted to be introduced, and people will not be spoilt in that way. . . .

Mr. Nicholl and I generally read a bit of the Swahili New Testament at night. He knows the Bible thoroughly, and is by no means sceptical as so many of the laymen out here are, or pretend to be. My general reading is Scott's poems, Tennyson, Shakespeare, and an occasional novel from Likoma. In this picnic state of existence I have not thought it wise to open my book box yet. White ants have already attacked my Gladstone bag and boots, and if I had many things lying about I should certainly lose some of them. . . .

Kota Kota grows a lot of rice, and that is its main source of revenue. The people work in the rice fields for the five months of the wet season, and then they have done work for the year. They never work *hard*, but they do grow their rice. Women hoe, men helping them when it suits their majesties : and when the rice is ripening all the children in the place are occupied in driving away the birds. Will you send me some seeds? I should like to try and grow some English vegetables—vine seeds, tomatoes, wheat. oats, barley, Jaffa orange, turnip, radish, Spanish onion, cabbage, cauliflower, beetroot, and almost any flower seeds to experiment on. They should be well dried, or they will combust on the way. The soil is I suppose sandy. Are there such things as potato seeds? They would certainly grow here I think. . . .

Do not forget to pray for me. I need your prayers I can assure you.

Yours, etc.,

A. F. SIM.

Kota Kota, *September 12th*, 1894.

MY DEAR——

I don't think the day will ever come when I shall be able to wean my thoughts from the old place and old friends. Remember me always most kindly to all the Longhill teachers, and the children and the people at Longhill that ask after me. I am sitting in the open air with an oil lamp wired together where it is broken, and threatening to blow out now and then! Mr. Nicholl and I are living in native huts, out of which he has bought the original inhabitants (human I mean—certain others refuse to budge!). My hut, into which I have almost to crawl, is divided into two—my native teacher sleeps in the outer portion and I in the inner. Can you imagine what a point the life and noises around me gave to my intercessions last Sunday morning, my first here, as I celebrated? But I never forget the *Eucharistia Conjuncti*. It seems more real I think among these surroundings. . . . Mahommedanism holds sway here ; I don't mean that they are good Mahommedans, even from their point of view ; but they think that they are serving God very well as it is, and they are at least permitted to have many wives and a few slaves, if they can keep the latter from the British Agent's eyes. This place is important owing to the fact of its being the natural starting-point of the ferry across the Lake. Here Arabs came with ivory and slaves and went across in dhows ; and, once across, they were safe, being in Portuguese territory. Such a thing as liberty, as we understand it in England, is quite unknown here. Their ideas are altogether Oriental. Liberty of thought, or action, or speech, is an idea that has never entered their heads. A sort of feudal system I should say exists. The serfs, for the most part, are those captured in war. This means a system very different from what we understand by the "slave trade," and, until Christianity introduces the system we are accustomed to, I doubt if a better one than the feudal could exist. It keeps a people, unacquainted with law except in a rudimentary form, under obligations which at least answer to the restraints of law. The heads of the government under the chief are the "*Wazee*," or elders, or headmen, each of whom is responsible for order, etc., in his part of the village, or community. But slaves there are in the bad sense ; some, three women and one man, have taken refuge here. One came in a slave stick ; another hung on to my "skirts" when we were walking down the village last week ;

five women came the other day under fear of death for some crime they were accused of. They were wives of a chief living two or three days' journey from here, and next morning one of them wanted to marry one of Mr. Nicholl's boys, pleading as one desperately in love ; the boy is about sixteen, and she perhaps seventeen. Death, selling into slavery, fines, and sometimes cutting off ears, are the only punishments practised here. Mr. Nicholl is going to build a Boma, or fort, with a ditch and stockade round it on this spot, a little raised above and commanding the town. Here there will be a garrison of forty soldiers, Sikhs and Makuas (natives). To-day the crews of four dhows have come up to be registered. They will in time be given a British flag, and so be liable to search, etc. What seems to me to be the weak point politically here is the fact that for the Arab merchant the only road to the coast lies through Portuguese country, and this with the Zambesi and Shiré offering, one would imagine, every facility for cheap and rapid delivery to the coast. Arabs get ivory away to the west of this, bring it here, cross the Lake, carry their ivory to the coast by means of slaves, and perhaps sell their slaves when they are done with them. Such men are in the town now, but one of them, who has paid £120 customs on his ivory, has three hundred people with him. Are they slaves or not? He calls them his "children," *watoto*. They know they can leave him and take refuge here if they want to. I imagine they are dependents of his, slaves if you like, or serfs. He treats them well, goes slowly, does not overburden them, feeds them, and defends them. They in turn carry his ivory, feel no sense of degradation, and are quite contented and happy. They come from a country two or three months' journey from here, South West, of which this Arab is the chief, and with which the British have some sort of treaty of long standing.
. . .

September 13*th.*—To-day we went down to the village at 7 a.m. to see Jumbe let out of "Coventry." He and his wife sitting on a *kibanda*, or couch—he with a very English and old umbrella over his head, and she fanning him—were carried round the place followed and preceded by a howling mob. I got a few snap-shots. . . . Farewell !

Yours, etc.,

A. F. SIM.

Kota Kota, *September* 14th, 1894.

MY DEAR——

. . . The place is practically Arab, though I don't think many are earnest Arabs. The people are well disposed towards the British Administration, and specially towards Mr. Nicholl, who manages them very well. How strange it seemed when celebrating, in my native hut yesterday (Sunday morning), to hear the sounds of drumming and shouting and firing guns going on all round us. Nor could one help making the future of this place the intention of one's intercession. Do remember how much I long for letters, and do not let a mail go by without writing, or getting some one to write. I do like the newspaper cuttings. If I have money enough in your hands for it I should like an occasional novel—new ones I, mean, which people are talking about. I wrote you a letter with some wants in it last opportunity. I hope you will send saccharine. Is salt concentrated in any way? These things are almost necessities to me, and we are always running short of them.

Sunday, September 16th.—Now I am bargaining with Jumbe for the land. He asks 1,000 rupees. I am not going to give more than 300 rupees, and that is too much I think! Jumbe is nice enough, but he has a "go-between," who is an unmitigated money-grubber. I hope to get it settled early this week, and then I shall begin to build at once. It is very hot—about 90′ now—and it will be hotter. I find that a white cassock is a convenient garment in a hot climate.

Monday, September 17th.—I have concluded my bargain to-day for the land—about what I should consider twenty acres for 300 rupees. It is dear as things go out here. I daresay I might have got it for less if I had bargained; but I want to have the old men on my side; and besides I paid half in calico at a fathom a rupee, which is a gain to us. I have to draw up a written agreement or title-deed in Swahili about it. . . .

I am getting an inconvenient reputation as a doctor. We were told this afternoon that an old fellow was dead, and this evening a man came up to say he wanted medicine! I went down just now, after dinner, with William, and gave him brandy and opium and a blister of oil of peppermint, so I expect that the report will be true to-morrow that he is no more! His house is a round hut about the size of your study, divided into two, and nine people were in it. By-the-bye, I suppose he is our rival. He is the Mahommedan teacher in the place.

They all say that our medicine is better than theirs, and so they attribute the advantages of European civilization to our superior medicine !

September 18*th.*—All the morning has gone, and I have done nothing yet. I daresay a hundred people have been up here this morning, and among them an Arab with a lot of people to be registered as not slaves. They are no doubt domestic slaves, but that is really a different matter. Anyhow they know they can get liberty and protection if they wish.

No ! the old fellow is still alive, and, strange to say, better, and wants more medicine. .   .

Now please give my love to all my old friends.

Yours, etc.,

A. F. SIM.

Letter to S. F. S——, dated,—

Kota Kota, *September* 25*th*, 1894.

MY DEAR——

My memory is playing me tricks ; it is the way of Africa to do so, but I hardly expected it yet, so I cannot remember whether I have written to you recently or not. I attribute it to a slight attack of fever I had at Likoma. One goes to bed and imagines oneself in another world, only to awake and find that some things of the old original have escaped one ! Let me, before I go on to other things, tell you how useful I have found your filter. The other day one of the men found a kind of leech in the drinking water, about six or seven inches long and the thickness of fine wire. We bottled it in " Hennessy Three Star " !   . . .

I am going to try and get volunteers to build my house ; but one of the principal headmen has been allotted to do my work. A sort of contractor he becomes, but he has no idea of time ! I have drawn plans, and that must come to something ! I wish I had you to help me. My house is of course to be built of mud and reeds and trees and *chirodi*, or the midribs of the raphir palm, with grass for roof, and bark rope for nails. Bad weather is experienced from North and South. The West faces a beautiful view of the village and Lake. The baraza will be at first my School. I have a beautiful tree for a preaching tree. The site is at present occupied by a village. I am inclined to keep the village, as it may help to form a nucleus for my work and also for workmen. .   .   .

I

Trees are expensive here, as men have to go a day's journey to
get them ; and for a 12 ft. wall I shall want at least a 16 ft. tree.
The population here is countless, but I am very hopeful of ultimate
success. I am amusing myself just now with a charming little
monkey a few weeks old, but monstrous full of fleas ! I paint him
with paraffin now and then, but they soon come again. William,
the teacher, has an aviary full of young birds. . . .

Tell me about digging wells. I propose beginning with a square
pit, 8 ft. by 8 ft., and as deep as necessary ; if very deep, go down
with a smaller hole. Oh, if I only had you and your men and
machinery ! I don't think the water is very far down, but I
expect no pressure, as there are no springs here. It will be a rope
and bucket business, but it will be cleaner than the public water-
holes. The only water-springs are hot and slightly sulphurous ;
we soft boiled an egg in one in seven minutes. They are about a
mile from here among a beautiful grove of trees, so you may expect to hear of Kota Kota becoming in the distant future the
Harrogate of Africa ! The people bathe and wash clothes in the
water. In one place it springs out from a crack in the solid rock,
and the rock is almost too hot to bear your hand upon it. In all
probability I shall not have time to dig a well until after the wet
season, which will give you time to send me instructions. In
digging I have hopes of coming upon a marble, which might
make good lime. It would be a tremendous boon to the whole
Lake-side if we could get lime to build with. I have seen chips of
a white opaque stone, which looks like marble, but I dare not build
hopes too high upon my scanty knowledge. One never gets such
a thing as a plank here—all solid trees. Imagine the value packing cases have in consequence ; tables, shelves, everything level is
made of them. We have made a draught-board out of a box-lid,
and eventually used ink for the black squares, after trying Condy's
fluid and pencil. Our draughtsmen are rupees and pennies. Mr.
Nicholl is better at the game than I am ; we get intensely absorbed in it. Mr. Nicholl is in much the same predicament as I
am about building, only he has been here three months. I helped
him to make out his Fort to-day, about 100 yards square. One of
his men shot a guinea-fowl to-day, which we hope to have for to-
morrow's dinner. We feed very well on the whole, and our cook
can make really decent bread : it is best toasted however. No
African meat has any fat upon it, so we have to use tinned fat

from England. Flour, sugar, and salt are the luxuries which generally run out. When I arrived at Likoma they had no sugar and salt, and very little flour, so they mixed native meal with what they had. This might be bearable in England, but here it is dangerous to lower one's diet. Perhaps some of the sickness there of late is due to this. My own stores are getting very low, but I expect more by next week or the week after. I should be quite happy if the building were begun. I have a crowd of patients were, but I can do them very little good; yet still they come. One very bad arm I managed to cure with iodoform and carbolic. But more frequently their diseases are incurable. It is rather an inconvenient reputation to have, especially as my store of medicine is rapidly diminishing. This letter has had rather a disturbed progress. We have killed two scorpions, and watched a batch of ten houses on fire. I should say there are at least two fires in the village every week ; this alone makes it impossible to build there. . . . I am rather seedy, in bed, and can't finish.

September 28th.—Temperature 105° and going down.

Yours, etc.,

A. F. SIM.

Kota Kota, *September 26th,* 1894.

MY DEAR M——,

I am still learning patience. I told you I had bought my land ; it is the very best site in the whole place I think, though I fancy 300 rupees was more than I need have given. And now I am waiting for building materials. Things are managed strangely here. A headman is appointed to look after your work, to squeeze what he can out of you I suppose. Mr. Nicholl's man and mine have both left the town, ostensibly to cut trees and *chiwali* ; I believe my old fellow is off on a smuggling expedition. It is curious that he timed his departure at the moment his dhow was blown North to his village, instead of coming in here to discharge. Never mind, I have drawn some beautiful pictures and plans, and of course that is the first step. . . .

Michaelmas Day.—So far I had got when I was seized by the " enemy " and put to bed with a temperature of 105·4° and rising. My fevers don't last long. I feel rather pulled down to-day, but my temperature is very nearly normal. It is very like a sharp attack of influenza, but the effects are not the same.

October 2nd.—I think that last remark was rather previous ! I have been back and forward to bed, and can hardly hold my head up now. I thought I could write a little, but my very arms seem too weak. I suppose it is the first real fever I have had, though I have been to bed with fever twice before. I have eaten nothing for four days, and of course I am weak. There is very little comfort in a native hut under these circumstances ; but William is a capital and most willing attendant, and one doesn't want much except drink—lukewarm water and tea tasting strongly of the very strongly-flavoured milk of these parts. There are cows here, but their milk is very tasty ! My head is still singing with the effects of the quinine, and I can't write straight, so I shall stop for the present.

October 5th.—Pardon the above complaining spirit. I am quite well again to-day. Events move suddenly here. The gunboats captured three dhows from this place, containing 240 slaves and 2,000 lbs. of ivory ; so they have taken away Mr. Nicholl, who ·is a magistrate to try the case, and I am left alone. The officers thought there might be a disturbance here, and advised the Likoma people to send me off ; but I apprehend no danger, and the "*Charles Janson,*" which came in here for me this morning, has gone away again without me. Alas ! they have taken William to interpret in this case for Capt. Robertson. I very unwillingly let him go, but it is in a good cause, and perhaps the delay won't be very great. It is a serious question this slave capture. I don't know who is implicated in it. I hope not Kalanji of Unangu, as it might be the cause of unpleasantness. Dr. Hine is in a difficult place. Unangu seems to be a station on the route to the sea-coast, and no doubt Kalanji levies taxes upon all passers-by. So I am absolutely alone here for a few days ; it is a good thing for my Swahili I have no doubt. Of course I have Mr. Nicholl's servants and the Sikhs, but without William I cannot get on with my building. Mr. Glossop has had a mail more than I have, and gave many hints of interesting news, including the Bishop's resignation. Personally I am very sorry, but it is as we expected. There is good news of Mr. Wimbush: *i.e.*, it is not his spine which is affected, which also reflects credit upon other people's spines whose legs were affected in the same way. By the way, I am in the middle of a long and interesting (! letter to the "*Mail.*" I think I will write a second later on telling about this place. It will interest some of my friends who do not hear my news through you. It is funny to think of your reading now my news from Chinde—how long ago that seems to me now! I hope you have given me a full account of the reunion on St. Peter's Day. I haven't even heard of that yet! The very last news here is the birth of Prince George's baby! And now you will be making ready for the Confirmation. It is to be in St. Aidan's I suppose, and by the Bishop of Durham. We shall some day be able to telegraph to you. A bit of the line is complete; this is Mr. Rhodes' business. It will certainly come here when it does get as far, and then on to Bandawe, Tanganyika, and so on, starting of course from the Cape. One or two of our Likoma boys are already engaged as operators between Blantyre and Chiromo. Then it goes into Portuguese territory; and that is where Lord —— made a blunder in letting the Portuguese fix it up. It may be the cause of disturbances yet. I think I had better send you my effusion to the "*Mail*," and then you can correct my mistakes.

Sunday, October 7th.—How can I thank you sufficiently for your budget, and especially for the scheme of monthly correspondents. It was a coincidence getting the news of the Consecration of St. Aidan's Gateshead on the day it was fixed for. I was enabled to be with them in spirit, and to-day they are holding high festival. Dear M—— too, his waiting is over. I had a grand letter from W——, giving a full account of the choir trip, and a drawing of Middleham Castle and antiquarian researches. Altogether I had nineteen envelopes and crowds of papers. What a lot I have to answer! I hope they will all be patient. The mail somehow has stirred me up; I don't feel so homesick as it generally leaves me. After all those letters one feels as if the eyes of Europe were upon one, and nerved to do desperate things.

You ask for subjects for intercession. After the appointment of the new Bishop (and pray that he may be first and last a saintly man, able to stir us up to a sense of our real privileges), for myself I would have you pray that I may have zeal and grace to love these poor savages. It is a very hard spiritual combat, deprived as one is of all the adventitious aids which have surrounded one so long. Except for a couple of Sundays, or three, at Likoma and two at Zanzibar, how long is it since I have worshipped in a Church, and how long since I have done so in a language I understood! And now I am spelling out the Holy Eucharist in Swahili, and

Matins and Evensong in Chinyanja, in a circular hut divided into two, 12 ft. in diameter, and 9 ft. in the centre, and walls 5 ft. in height. But I do feel the sense of the *Eucharistiâ Conjuncti*, and that little Service every Sunday morning is my greatest joy. (Last Sunday I was too ill to celebrate.) For the work, pray for these semi-Mahommedans ; how hard to reach them, so wrapped up are they in the sense of their own excellence !

Most of the people think I am in the midst of a famine. There is plenty here, and plenty of locusts too, but they are too late to hurt the crops. They haven't been known here in the memory of man.

And now the Bazaar is on the top of you. May it be a great success ! And the Harvest Festival, that may be to-day, the first Sunday in October. Who are your preachers ? I wish I could look in upon you.

Now cricket is over and football beginning, and the sun here is vertical at midday ! All those people are constantly in my mind, tell them ; but it would fill the letter to name them all ! Don't forget Capt. and Mrs. L——, and Mr. and Mrs. B——. I find the former's telescope most useful in spying out which steamer it is coming in. I shall be able to see better still from my new site. Remember me to the choir. What a jolly trip ! What would I give for a dive now ? I daren't here ; it would certainly bring on fever. I have done so though with no ill effects. Henley Regatta must have been grand this year. I have sealed up the children's letter, so I enclose the scorpion, a very small one, in this ; show it to them. My village is cleared of native huts now. I hope to begin building at once. With affectionate remembrances to all.

Yours, etc.,

A. F. SIM.

Letter addressed to one who was working under a sense of spiritual loneliness.

Kota Kota, *September 30th*, 1894.

DEAR——,

. . . Honestly speaking I do think a missionary must at least make up his mind to bear the cross of loneliness. I don't want to be hard on you, but I want to be straight. Do you not think there is a little of the "spoilt child" about your spirit of viewing things? I treat it the more seriously in view of the confession you make to me of spiritual deadness which you feel. I am not afraid of lack of spiritual perception, especially out here, but I am frightened at running loose, lack of self-discipline and self-restraint. The vocation of God should ever be before our hearts to restrain us ; a lack of discipline leads to coldness. Are you getting any moments apart, alone with God? Are you preparing faithfully for your Communions ? Without this no one can be recollected. I would in all humility recommend you to get a quarter of an hour daily about noon before lunch in your own room, or in *Church*, and if you have to make a sacrifice to get it so much the better. I would at least use part of the time for intercession ; take your list with you ; add to it, if necessary ; especially remember those who have gone before. This helps one to realize the Communion of Saints, that infinite spiritual temple of which ours is so small a niche. This is the only antidote I know for loneliness.

Well, now, I don't think you will be angry with me. You have given me your confidence, and I should not be dealing fairly with you if I did not put before you what I feel. I am not scolding, and what I say, I say with all the solemn responsibility of the Priesthood committed to me. I know well, and deeply deplore, the lack of spiritual provision made for white people out here ; but that places a responsibility upon the individual to supply the deficiency. . . .

There now I have said more than you ever bargained for. Remember however that I speak in all kindness. . . .

Yours, etc.,

A. F. SIM.

Letter to F. C. M——, dated,—

Kota Kota, *October 5th*, 1894.

MY DEAR——,

The spirit moves me to write you a line to congratulate you on your accomplished work. I wonder if it is envy I feel, waiting here delayed by a hundred causes, the principal one being the shilly-shallying way of these old ruffians who pull the strings here. I expect I am feeling something like what you felt in the days you had to wait and wait. I am building too, but it is only a mud house. How far off is the day when a Church shall be built here too, and though probably a mud one, yet one from which voices and hearts may join in the hymn of praise which is now going up from St. Hilda's? Do write me a letter and tell me all about it yourself. I celebrate every Sunday for myself and three Christian natives; but it is in a mud house, in which I can just stand upright, with all the village heathen sounds around—drums and shouting and dancing and guns. "*Oceano divisi*" indeed, but "*Eucharistiâ conjuncti.*" . . .

As to the new Bishop—O for a saintly man !—that is what we want. It is the most demoralising place, this Central Africa. Patience, trust, zeal, love for these poor lust-eaten savages—how hard it is ! A man to encourage and raise his Priests in spiritual things would of all others be the man for us. And who for Zanzibar? It is a difficult berth, and wants a firm and sympathetic man with an iron constitution. . . .

The so-called slavery here, at its best, is but the old feudal system, but its worst feature even then is that the slaves, or serfs, are content with their position. In English law here the position of a slave is disregarded, and he obtains the same justice as a freeman. Mahommedanism makes rascals of men who would otherwise be simple savages. Smooth-faced and smooth-tongued, they are untrustworthy to the core. They don't drink, but that is their one virtue. Anyhow there is no *spirit*-drinking in any part of Africa that I have seen. "*Pombé*" is very light muddy beer, rather sweet. It seems to have no ill effects beyond making people silly and sleepy and stupid while under its influence. No, not drink but lust is the African's crime. . . . I am sure you will enter into our difficulties, and pray for us especially in the Eucharist, and ask one or two of your faithful people to do so too. I expected to find the life difficult, and I am not disappointed that it is so ; and yet was it not difficult in England? How much of one's religion is sentiment only after all ? Here it is rugged and bare, stripped of all sentiment. Perhaps one mistakes this for difficulty. The atmosphere too—how much does one unconsciously depend upon atmosphere ? Here what an atmosphere it is ! Heathenism, cruelty, deceit, lust, greed. Atmosphere must be made round about each Christian station—trustfulness, love, chastity, unselfishness—it is a big burden for unworthy, weak shoulders to bear.

What a miserable picture I have been drawing ! I am rather

"dowley" to-day, all by myself, and only just recovering from a rather bad attack of fever, having been ill for a week. I will try and write more cheerfully to-morrow.

October 6th.—The mail has come (such a splendid one, nineteen letters for me !), and consequently I am set up. I have told you how I rejoice at your good news, and though mine is a mud hut, and yours a late Early English Church, God above is the same to both of us.

I have spent this morning entertaining some Arabs, among them Selim bin Nassur, who has come here to cross the Lake with at least £2,000 worth of ivory, and how many slaves ? I know he is a murderer, yet he is so pleasant and so meek and so polite, butter wouldn't melt in his mouth ! And so they all are, these Arabs, the greatest ruffians unhung when they have the power in their hands, but to speak to, the politest of gentlemen ! What material for Christ is this ! What a regeneration is needed here ! Alas ! most of the headmen are the same. Though pure blacks, or half-caste, they are thorough-paced hypocrites and humbugs. "O generation of vipers !" My hope is in the bairns and the raw heathen. . . .

Abdallah Nakaam is waiting to be ordained. His case is an interesting one. He is the son of a Christian chief, Barnaba Nakaam of Chitangali on the Rovuma, a Yao. To Barnaba Kalanji of Unangu has sent a message of peace. Abdallah is of course a free boy, and has volunteered for work at Unangu, knowing what difficult work it is. This is as it should be. A few others are coming on, and these are the hope of the Mission. They are picked men, and are carefully trained and subjected to the hardest tests, under which a man soon shows what he is made of. Fancy, there are two girls at Mbweni who have declared their determination never to marry, but devote themselves to the work of God. To those who know the African, and the African woman especially, it is almost incredible. They are quite women now, not mere girls, and would in the ordinary course of events have married long ago.

. . . Tell me all the Sunderland gossip. Those men must have rowed well to win the "Grand" at Durham. Please give them my respects, and clap them on the back. It did me good to hear of it. No rowing here. The "dug-out" (canoe) is a monstrosity, heavy as lead, and as cranky as a lightship. They mostly

pole them along, like a Thames punt, when the water is shallow
enough. The dhow sails best right before the wind. I have
never been in one, and shall take my smelling salts if ever I do go
aboard !

   . . . *October 12th.*—I have just got over another attack of
fever, not very bad—temperature about 104°. It knocks one's
feeding arrangements astray, and I am getting a most gracefully
slim figure. . . .

I have made a bargain for 300 trees and 100 bundles of bamboos and grass for £7 10*s*. for my house. This is all the building
material I want. I think it is fairly cheap. Labour will come to
a shilling a week, or one fathom of calico. . . . I have seen
some tusks of ivory 150 lbs. weight and 7 ft. long. Fancy carrying a tooth like that in your head, and fancy having toothache in
it ! . . .

I am getting so fussy and anxious to have the building finished.
I spent most of to-day over at the site. How hot it is ! The sun
has not the same effect as it has in England. My hands are red
and blistered with prickly heat. The sun is too hot to brown you ;
it boils you ! Some of the mothers work with their children tied to
their backs. I saw one to-day, fast asleep, a mass of flies. . . .

Good luck to you, and God bless you in your new advance.
Give the boating men my love. I saw a Tyneside man when I
was at Chinde who rowed against our second boat at Durham.
He is the son of the old boy who rushes about the bank at the
Regatta always. I forget his name, but he is, or was, secretary.
He has a sort of working-man's job. . . .

                    Yours, etc.,
                      A. F. SIM.

            Kota Kota, *October 5th*, 1894.
MY DEAR——,

   I don't think I am homesick, though you people are always
in my thoughts, and sometimes when I have fever I think of
what a home-coming would be like. This waiting is such depressing work, so you must put down my grumbling to it. I expected
to find Africa a hard life, and I am not disappointed. It is not
the roughing I mind : I don't know that it is so very rough always,
but it is a life in which much grace is needed. You see one is
deprived of so many supports—sympathy (direct sympathy at

least), atmosphere, surroundings ; but perhaps these formed too
much of one's religion at home. Here it is bared of all adventitious aids. I know it ought to be a grand discipline, and by God's
grace I hope it will ; but how easy to fall short ! St. Paul is a
help. What an example for a missionary ! An example always
to be kept in mind.

And so Bishop Hornby has resigned. I am very sorry, but it is
as we expected. May his successor be a saintly man to stir us
Priests up to a due sense of our privileges ! This is what we
want. No Retreats out here, no spiritual bracing—we are apt to
become self-dependent and self-absorbed. Self is more present
in the desert than among men. Pray that we may have grace to
keep *self* under and turn away to God.

. . . Fancy, you will be getting this at the end of December,
the wet season here. I shall (D.V.) be in my house, with a thriving School, and the beginnings of evangelistic work in hand. Very
hot and wet it will be I am told. Then the trying season follows,
with cold and malaria—March, April, May—the season for blackwater fever and all horrors. . . . We are just as short-handed
as we can manage now. I was in mortal terror that the " *Charles
Janson*" was coming to take me to Likoma to take up the reins
there, but they have left me alone, and I am intensely relieved not
to be away for some one else's work. . . .

You are in Church at this moment. I often think of this, especially on Sundays, and I ask God to hear your prayers for me, which
I know are not infrequent. Perhaps you are decorating these days
for the Harvest Festival. I wish I could hand in some of these
grand palm branches which grow here, and of which we partly
build our houses. How grand they would look about the altar
and font !

Twentieth Sunday after Trinity.—The " *Domira* " came in last
night, and brought me such a budget of letters. How grateful I
am I can't tell you. I am feeling quite stirred up by the sympathy
and kindness of everybody, and not at all homesick now. . . . I
wish I could tell more of actual missionary work. It will be long,
long, weary sowing I am sure. I expect most from the children,
who are especially bright here. The Swahilis are tinged with
Mahommedanism, and will listen and assent, but that is all. The
actual heathen aborigines are better material than they. These
last outnumber the Swahilis, and are the despised among the

Swahili people. St. Paul made most progress among the despised and poor. . . . How am I ever to tackle the girls here? Yet how necessary it is. It is a problem of the future. I shall never try and persuade any one to come out here ; God only can do this. It is too great a responsibility. How trying it is I can't tell you. Perhaps to a young man who has few ties in England it may be different ; but the misery of finding one had made a mistake would be too great to bear. . . . A letter from —— inspirits me ; it always has had that effect. And at this moment you are in Church. Oh, for a glimpse of you all !

October 8th.—Makanjira has not come in. In fact a *Safari* (caravan) of his is at Mwasi's, three days' journey from here, with ivory and gunpowder, the sinews of war, from the Portuguese on the Zambesi. Mr. Nicholl hopes to catch this man at the head of the caravan, as he once tried most treacherously to kill Lieut. Maguire. The latter only escaped miraculously. I expect he will get away unless the gunboats keep a sharp look-out. Mwasi sends assurances that he will keep him, but I expect he is like the rest—an old humbug, getting presents from both sides !

And now farewell. Continue your prayers, especially for grace for me, and for wisdom to do God's will in the Mahommedan problem.

Yours, etc.,
A. F. SIM.

Letter to the Editor, " *The Northern Daily Mail.*"

Kota Kota, *October 7th,* 1894.

DEAR SIR,—

It is not my habit to "rush into print," but, since I have no one to find fault with and only friends to listen to me, I feel it in some measure a duty, but more a pleasure, to write in a few lines, which you may care to insert, the impressions gathered during my short experience of Central Africa. And first let me protect myself by saying that I do not hold myself to any expressions I may use. I shall probably change my mind about many hastily gathered ideas ; in fact the oldest Anglo-Africans confess the most ignorance as to native habits and character.

First, as to my own movements—the journey. It is enough to make one forswear England altogether. The time in my case was three months and five days ; but this is variable. It has been done in two months and a half. Nearly two of my three months were spent from Chinde to the Lake. The Zambesi, like all African rivers, is very shallow and very wide. As it approaches the sea it branches into many mouths, and in course of time these vary, each wet season causing some change in one or other of them. I believe I am right in saying that during the last thirty years the navigable mouth has changed three times. In Dr. Livingstone's time it was to the South of the present one ; a few years ago Quilimane, to the North, was the only port ; and now Chinde, between the two, has replaced Quilimane. I have seen all three mouths, thanks to the kindness of Capt. Carr, of the "*Mosquito*" gunboat. At the first there is but one Portuguese house left, occupied by a half-caste Goanese trader, or he may be a Portuguese Government official. If so, I beg his pardon.

Quilimane is rapidly being deserted by all but its Portuguese inhabitants, and Chinde is growing in importance every day. Of these however Quilimane is still the most pretentious, with its beautiful verdure and its stone or rather concrete houses. Of course all these are in Portuguese territory, and herein lies the weak point of British Central Africa. At Chinde the British have a concession about a square mile in area, part of which is a "transit concession," where goods lie in bond awaiting transit. Chinde I ought to know particularly well, as I was kept waiting there more than a fortnight, until a steamer came in to take me up the river. At least in my own opinion I know more than enough of it. A sand spit (sand silted up by the river, and six inches deep of loose sand) makes the most unpleasant road material I know of. One's progress is almost like that of the boy who had to go to School backwards. But my time at Chinde was made as pleasant as possible by Captain Carr, who made me his guest on board the "*Mosquito*," and took me for a trip, as I have said, to the Kongoni or southernmost navigable mouth of the Zambesi. The gunboats on the Lower River, as we call all that part below the Murchison Rapids on the Shiré, are intended for all emergencies in connection with the presence of the Portuguese, and also such contingencies as may arise with the natives in our own sphere below the Rapids. They are stern wheelers, drawing eighteen inches or two feet— built at Yarrow's on the Thames, as, indeed, all the Portuguese gunboats also were. The latter has seven gunboats on the Zambesi. Besides these there are perhaps seven or eight English trading boats running passengers and cargo up the Shiré as far as the shallows will permit. In my case this was as far as Chiromo, the first British station on the left bank of the Shiré. The journey up the Zambesi, where the banks were far away on either side for the most part, with nothing to be seen except one continuous line of tall grass and reeds hiding a perfectly flat country, was the slowest part of the whole. It seemed that during the days we spent in Portuguese territory we were passing a country deserted by human beings. But this changed when we passed the boundary between Portuguese and British country ; and one evening, when we put into the bank to sleep, two of us strolled up to what looked like a superior native village. It turned out to be the home of a Russian who had been some years at Tete, but according to his story he had been robbed of everything he had, and turned out of the place by the Portuguese. I heard afterwards he had killed one of his men in a fit of temper ; but then he only spoke French, and I may have misunderstood him. He was a hunter, a trader, and a Polish officer. Of course you will agree with me in my conclusion—a banished patriot.

I think one reason for my dislike of the journey up the Lower River, at least, was the way the native was treated and spoken of. He gets credit for no virtue, and generally the *chikoke* (hippo-hide thong) for every vice. Talking of hippos or their hides, we saw many hundreds of the owners of these ; indeed in the Upper River they are a source of danger to traffic when the steamer is exchanged for a small boat, and if interfered with they will follow and attack such a boat. Crocodiles too are countless. We considered it a duty to fire at all within range, and between us accounted for perhaps eight. By the bye, as far as Misongwe, a trading station six or seven days up the Zambesi, we had a hunter with us who, a year or two ago, killed three white rhinoceros, and brought home their skins and skeletons. One is to be seen in the Natural History Museum, South Kensington, and one at least in Mr. Leopold Rothschild's natural history collection. He had been sent out by a syndicate to obtain specimens and make observations. He started from Misongwe to reach Mashonaland and Matabeleland, and so beat round to the North-East. He was the more interesting to me as having been at my old School. We had therefore much in common, and had a long talk the night he left us.

Enterprising young folk who see this will want to know something of the prospects of British Central Africa as a place to emigrate to. And so, with all the presumption of a new comer, I will proceed to give my views. You see I do not consider myself a full-fledged missionary yet, so I am not begging nor recounting my interesting cases! Well, as to "prospects"; even a new comer can see that this is not a place for a poor man yet. The only prospect is coffee, and for that a man must have capital, and he must have patience to wait three or four years for any return. And after all the district in which coffee is successfully grown is limited, and I suppose land will be going up in price. I believe it is true to say that plenty of labour is to be had if properly sought for. All the hopes for the future of British Central Africa, from a trader's point of view, are centred in coffee. A few years now will settle this question. Sugar and tobacco for local consumption are grown by one or two enterprising men, but I don't believe they will repay the cost of transport. Only one man is known to have made money, and he has been nearly twenty years in the country. His land he bought "for a song." The present rates for transport down the river are almost prohibitive.

This alone seems to me to be suicidal in those who are responsible; but here of course I can only speak as an amateur. I know nothing of the other side of the ledger. But apart from the opening up of the country to European trade, the whole question of the slave trade in these parts might almost it seems have been settled long ago, if only the managers of these Companies for transport had seen their way to divert the ivory trade from its present route, and had opened up a cheaper method of transport to the sea down by the Shiré and Zambesi water-way. At present I think I am right in saying that no ivory, save only such as is paid in Customs duty, goes down by this route. I have no doubt I should be doing a great injustice to those responsible for this state of things if I left the matter here. One cannot help thinking that this is a cause worthy of the sympathy and help of our home Government. Freights are exorbitantly high, because the capital laid out on the still meagre plant has been enormous. And the Zambesi is a closed highway; and this water-way, which seems to a novice like myself the very solution of the slave traffic difficulty, in an enormous district whence slaves are annually taken in large numbers, is useless, all for want of timely help from the home Government. Sir, I hope you don't belong to the " Little England Party." If you want to continue a supporter of it, let me advise you never to leave little England. But here you will say I am trenching on politics. If however Commissioner Johnston gets all he wants in England, perhaps it is not too late yet to divert the native trade down the Zambesi, and so put an end to the *raison d'être* of the traffic in slaves.

Well, I have run on in advance of my subject, and I must re-trace my steps to Chiromo, and when I come to tell you about Kota Kota, I will perhaps revert to the slave question, but that will probably be in a subsequent letter. Chiromo is on the North bank of the Ruo at its confluence with the Shiré, with Bishop Mac-kenzie's grave on the South bank, and a post office and by this time I suppose a telegraph office on the North! One could not help contrasting the picture drawn in Bishop Harvey Goodwin's "*Life of Bishop Mackenzie*" of that sad, lonely death scene, and the picture which I saw before me. But thirty years work many changes in new countries, and in thirty years more Cook's agents will perhaps be bringing brain-tired invalids from West Hartle-pool to the hot springs of Kota Kota. I was glad to leave Chi-romo, impatient as I was to reach my destination, and perhaps my first touch of fever there made me the more glad to get away. But what a place it is for game—countless buffalo and all kinds of buck. There the record number of lions shot in a single day was beaten by Lieut. Hunt of the "*Herald*" gunboat—five—all with-out moving from his place. They had scented out a buck which he had shot, and surrounded him while he was resting and waiting for carriers to take his buck home. It was good luck, perhaps, but it was also good shooting and pluck.

From Chiromo we had another four days of discomfort in what was termed (on the *lucus a non lucendo* principle, I suppose) a "house-boat." The "house" (a straw-thatched covering in the stern, in which none of us could sit upright) was supposed to hold three at night, asleep. We were only once under this shelter together, compelled by rain. Fortunately one of the three had a tent, and so we forgot our discomfort, though the poor owner of the tent had high fever all the way. But let us forget the past. Katunga's, the end of the " Lower River " journey, brings back visions of drenching rain and a disconsolate party of travellers making the best of it over a smoky fire, roasting peanuts and reading papers dated 1893. Then we went on to Blantyre, starting too late in the day, owing to the rain, to arrive before sunset— twenty-eight miles up hill, perhaps 2,000 feet. The journey to Blantyre is made in *machilas* (hammocks slung on poles), but I had such a bad "crew" that I preferred shanks' aid to theirs, when once a few humiliating obeisances to mother earth had taught me their worth. But Mandala repaid all the discomfort. I was last I think to arrive. Imagine my feelings when I found a group gathered round a blazing fire in a brick house with a real chimney, the first I had seen in Africa, a long table laid with a clean cloth, and the promise of good things to follow. After falling upon our host's wardrobe, I soon set to work upon his larder.

Blantyre (Mandala is a part of Blantyre) requires description. Blantyre is the name of the Scotch Established Church Mission Station. Mandala is the name given originally to Mr. Moir's house, and now appropriated to that part occupied by the African Lakes' Trading Corporation. Situated in the Shiré Highlands, 2,800 feet above the sea level, you can imagine what a pleasant change it is to a river-wearied traveller. Bracing and cool, it reminded one of the old country, and the unlooked-for rain and wind did not lessen the illusion. It is the oldest English station in British Central Africa, and has had I suppose the best chance. Here are roads and brick houses, and a really ambitious and picturesque brick Church, the work of Mr. Scott, the Scotch Established Church Missionary, himself its architect, builder, contractor, foreman-bricklayer, clerk of the works, and all. Here—will you believe it? I saw with my own eyes a dog-cart and a tandem of handsome Arab ponies, and to prove it I photographed them! Here during my stay the Mission people had a sale of work, and cleared £140 in the afternoon, besides further orders. And in the evening a concert was held at the "Boma," or fort, and the "new song" was "Mrs. 'Enery 'Awkins!" Fancy people in dress clothes, if you please! I went to the magistrate's to dine. He answers to the respected name of McMaster. Both he and his charming wife come from the sister isle.

Blantyre is famous for good fellowship and civilization. It is regarded as the metropolis of Central Africa. But to me its chief charm consisted in its bracing atmosphere, its trees, its gardens,

K

its roses these last blooming all the year round—the loveliest
"gloire de Dijon" I have ever seen. Surrounded by hills clothed
with verdure to their summits, except where here and there rugged
granite rocks peeped out, it reminded me of parts of Scotland, and
the nationality of most of its inhabitants went far to maintain the
resemblance.

Nearly everybody is Scotch out here. Blantyre is the centre
of the coffee plantations. The Shiré Highlands as yet are the
only lands opened up by the planters. A fund of continual interest to me was the experimental garden of the Lakes' Company,
full as it is of all manner of fruits and flowers, many of them
familiar old English friends, as well as many Eastern and tropical
trees and plants. The blue gum grows prolifically there—introduced of course—and many pines and firs and cypresses. Blantyre is a busy place. The hum of work is continuous. "Hum"
is not the word. Such noisy workers as the Atonga and Angoni
make more than a hum. They cannot go a walk without singing.
Their song is after the fashion of a sailor's chanty, and, like him,
the more they sing the better they work. The song, somewhat
tuneless, consists of a refrain or rather a recitative, which is taken
up rhythmically by the rest in a chorus. The sounds of Africa are
as characteristic as the sights. The drum, the dance, the songs
at night are incessant. They must be a merry people if one could
only get at their inner life.

And now my "few lines" have become enough for two insertions
already I fear. I wonder what your readers will gather from these
impressions. Not a very attractive picture I think. Well, I don't
mean it to be. To the missionary this has no great weight. I
would not be responsible for drawing any one out here by glowing
accounts of the country. There are one or two favoured spots, of
which Blantyre is one. And yet what would I not give to have as
companions and helpers here one or two whom I know in West
Hartlepool? Perhaps I am "cutting my own throat" by drawing
a somewhat gloomy picture of this place, but unless he is called to
it by the voice of One greater than man, as I say, I would not
undertake the responsibility of persuading any one to come out
here. May I conclude with the heartiest of good wishes to the
place where I have left a big (the biggest) part of my heart, and
remain   Yours faithfully,

                                        ARTHUR F. SIM.

Kota Kota, *October 7th*, 1894.

MY DEAR BOYS AND GIRLS,—

I don't want to keep you waiting a long time till I can answer all your kind and jolly letters separately, so I shall write immediately to you all, and then perhaps I shall be able to polish you off one by one. How nice it was to hear from you I can't tell you. I read and re-read your letters and try and think I am back again among you all. How jolly to think of those trips ! Edith I see has not lost her love of mischief; fancy hiding behind the bushes and nearly getting lost ! No wonder boys are easier to manage than girls. I see you want me back to keep you in order ! Well, here I am, writing in the open air under a grass thatch ; but it is late, and the sun isn't shining, so I am using a candle ; and the table I made myself--how those joiner boys would laugh at it ! It was straight when I made it, but it has a strong inclination to the East now ! Its legs are young tree stumps, and its top packing cases with the old name still printed on, and the old nail holes in the middle and at the edges. All my tables will have to be like this ; what a good thing I watched joiners at work in England ! I would rather have some of you boys to do my joiner work for me, then you couldn't laugh, and you girls to do my sewing and washing. I haven't an iron, so nothing ever gets ironed ! I marked one of my white cassocks the other day on the outside of the collar, so now any one can see what my name is, but no one can read here ; they most likely think it is an ornament, or a badge of honour at the back of my neck, or a charm against stiff neck !

My house[1] is mud with a straw roof; its door is so low I have almost to crawl in. There is a door-way, but no door. I and my teacher, William, and a small boy live in it. It is our Church too ; we have prayers there morning and evening, and on Sundays I celebrate Holy Communion there ; how different from St. Aidan's ! Yes, but it makes us remember that God is the same. The people here are mostly Mahommedans, and they will be very hard to win for God, so you must pray for them all the more earnestly. I have such a big Parish—sixteen miles South, four days' journey West, and seventy miles if I like North. I daresay I could go more than seventy miles South and not find a white man. You see I have not gone to Unangu, and I am glad. I would rather have

[1] See other side.

all my own work to do, but this place is in frequent communication with Unangu. I sent a letter to Mr. Williams the other
day, and wonder if he will ever get it. The children are very
nice here, and one or two old fellows with sores, which I have
healed with iodoform and carbolic acid, are attached to me. I
think I shall get them to come and live with me when I have
built my house. I shall build a beautiful big house—twenty feet

My hat

This is my house

(From sketches by A. F. Sim.)

high in the middle, forty-five feet long, and sixteen feet wide without the verandah.

The verandah will be the School at first. Inside it will be
divided into three ; one end my bedroom, the middle my sitting-
room, dining-room, etc., and the other end will be the Chapel.
Then I hope I shall have a big school next year, and be able to
build a School separate from the house. I have a lovely playground for the boys, and a splendid "preaching-tree." The
village is just below it, and behind the tree I shall have my garden.

There are thousands of people here. They seem to do nothing; only the women work. And they all sing and dance in the evening, especially moonlight evenings; and they blow off gunpowder —in guns and out of guns. One of the men, who came to me with an awful arm, had it blown up with gunpowder—his gun burst. I thought it would never heal, but it is quite better now in only three weeks. The explosions of gunpowder often wake me up at night; I think the place is being attacked. I wonder where they get it all from. I don't think they drink very much here; but they do a little, I know, and there are two "*pombé*" shops (native beer), like public-houses. The people are not poor, and would buy anything useful if some one would start a shop here. They have bought miles of calico from Mr. Nicholl, the magistrate. He is away now. Of course it is not my business, or I could sell the clothes off my back at a good profit if I liked. They love biscuits and tea and sugar and, strange to say, soap! Even little toddlers will sometimes beg for soap. It is two rupees a box of yellow soap here. I don't know what it is in England. All our sugar and salt and flour come from England, and sometimes—even since I have been here—we have to do without all these. I'm so glad I don't like sugar in my tea, but I think it is an improvement in puddings. Butter is a rare luxury; we get salt butter from England in tins. I used to hate salt butter, but I like it now! Bread is not made with yeast, but with native beer. Flour is mixed with "*pombé*" and water and put out in the hot sun, and it rises as if it were made with yeast, but it has a funny, bitter taste. However we are glad when we can get it at all. We have no oven; the cook makes it in a big cooking-pot like a bread jar!

This place is not like Zanzibar for flowers or trees. I fancy you would think it rather desolate. But there are more trees here than at Likoma. There are some cocoa-nut trees, and one mango tree, and plenty of bananas, but no apples or cherries or plums or strawberries. I intend to grow some pine-apples though. I shall enclose a few photos in this, some by myself, and one or two by Miss Palmer, at Likoma. I have taken a lot, but have no paper to print them on. I will enclose a tiny scorpion. I killed two on the table last night. Full-sized ones are two and a half inches long, and they sting with their tails worse than a hornet. I think they fall down from the roof of this shed where I am writing; I hope one won't fall on my head some day.

Monday, October 8th. I have spent most of the morning getting jiggers out of my toes. They are like tiny little fleas, and lay their eggs in your feet, and it is very hard to get them out ; you must get all the eggs out or they will make such a sore place. They leave a hole behind them as big as a pea. I have wrapped my toes—those where the jiggers were—in carbolic acid, and I hope that will kill them if any are left behind. The natives call them "*Malakenya.*" This morning I had a visit from some Arabs who are staying here. Selim bin Nassur is a great chief in his own country, and has come here with thousands of pounds' worth of ivory. And I suspect most of his people are slaves, but they daren't say so. His visit was a friendly visit, but I expect he came to see what goods the "*Domira*" had brought. The people here are honest I think. I expect a visit to-day from the Sultan and a lot of men from Marambo's country, a month's journey from here. They want to go across the Lake. I wonder how many of them are slaves ! They must wait till Mr. Nicholl comes back. People who travel here are never in a hurry, and don't mind waiting ever so long. Sometimes a runaway slave comes up here, but generally they are afraid to say they are slaves. Their masters might put an end to them. Most of the people are slaves, or rather serfs, here. I asked an old man the other day how many slaves he had, and he answered without the slightest hesitation that he had forty. When the owner of slaves goes about and a slave meets him, the slave kneels down to let his master go past. This will only be put an end to slowly and gradually, and not completely till the people become Christians.

I have also been cutting my hair this morning and my beard with Eva and Ida H——'s scissors.

And now, dear boys and girls, good-bye for the present. I will try and write to you each separately. Do not forget to pray for us out here.

By-the-by, there is no famine here. Plenty of locusts, but they are too late to do much harm.

Ever your affectionate friend,
ARTHUR F. SIM.

Letter to E. L——, dated—

Kota Kota, *October* 9*th*, 1894.

MY DEAR ——,

You ask me to tell you of my spiritual combat rather than the details of my work. Well, it is a difficult life, and needs all the grace prayer can win. Prayer itself is difficult. Perseverance is a strain in this relaxing climate. One never gets the spiritual bracing of a grand Service, or the sympathy of steadfast souls, except when the mail comes, and last mail has braced me wonderfully. But I think God is nearer to me, and somehow I feel nearer to those who have gone before, who have influenced my life and led me indirectly to this step. And now it is slow work learning a barbarous tongue, building houses, and bargaining for materials with people who only want to "squeeze" you. But I am encouraged in my Swahili work. I can carry on the ordinary conversation now almost. I look out a word in the dictionary when I am puzzled. The people are surprised when I do so, and when one word reveals the meaning of a whole sentence, I think they regard it as magic. The other day, when talking with my building "contractor," one of the headmen, I asked if white ants were numerous here, and he said, "Yes, but the white man will overcome them." All the machinery of civilization is *dawa* to them. They have little or no ambition to reproduce it among themselves. The Arab alone has civilized the raw heathen as far as he is raised above his normal animal life, and the Arab's civilization means added lust, and cruelty, and deceit. . . These are the people with whom I have to deal here. "Who is sufficient for these things?" The "lad with five barley loaves and two small fishes" comforts me. . . .

How *can* the missionary take the same care of himself as other Europeans? Granted, if he could rise at nine and breakfast at ten, keep indoors during all the heat of the day, take a stroll in the cool of the evening, and feed on unlimited luxuries from England, then he would not so often have fever. When I have been the guest of such people I too have felt well. But the missionary must be up at daybreak, and work whether he feels well or not, putting off bed till his temperature is 104 sometimes. Don't be afraid for me; I am intent upon living and not dying. My hard time has not come yet, and I am taking life easily, and still I get fever ; but so does everybody. Germs accumulate and break out at intervals. No one escapes it. There is not much at Blantyre because it is so bracing there ; but here there is nothing to brace you.

And now farewell. I need your prayers, and I know you need mine so I don't forget.

Yours, etc.,

A. F. SIM.

Letter to Mrs. C——, dated,—

Kota Kota, *October 11th*, 1894.

MY DEAR ——,

I seldom spend a whole evening without writing at least a line to some one of my many dear friends in the dear old place. The steamer has gone, and I had only time to write a few (nine) letters by this mail. . . .

There is work here for a large staff of mission workers. It is an enormous district, but of course I must cut my coat to my cloth, and begin with a native teacher and myself. I hope to do a great deal to influence people by visiting them in their houses, talking to them of the things of God, gathering families together round me, and so on. . . .

How many changes will there be when I return ? How many old faces gone, and new ones in their place, say, in five years' time, if God spares me ! If I keep my health I do not wish to return before I have really done some work here. Three years (the three first) are not enough to settle people in our holy faith. Nor could I willingly leave unless there were some one to take my place ; but it is premature to talk about returning. . . .

Each slave has to do a certain amount of work for his master, such as hoeing and sowing (perhaps for a month in the year building , or bringing trees or other material for building. In return for this the master provides his slave with a wife and such security of tenure as he has. In the hands of a good master the burden is not great, and the best masters are those who have most slaves, for then the work required is spread over the greater number. But in the hands of a lazy or avaricious man, who has only a few slaves, I can imagine it is very galling. For instance, the other day in Mr. Nicholl's absence I was paying his men for work done, and the master of one man (an utter rascal, who owes a debt of eighty rupees to the Administration for one of his shady transactions), when his slave was paid, seized all the twelve fathoms of calico without a word of remonstrance on the part of the poor man. However I let the big man know my mind, and told him that in England he would be put in prison for such a thing. One cannot, on the other hand, judge of all these cases, as the man may be his debtor, and may have pawned himself to this master until the debt was paid. The poor fellow's abject face was the thing I fear which stirred my indignation.

It is very difficult in this intense heat to settle down to really hard work. I shall so enjoy going round preaching and talking to the people when I am able. It is far better than a sedentary life. I hope I shall be able to stand the sun as time goes on. I had a threatening of fever again, for the third time since I came here, the other day, but I took thirty-five grains of quinine and felt quite well next morning. I wish you could see some of my patients ; they have the most awful sores I can possibly imagine. Poor things, it is little I can do for them except to make them wash them in carbolic acid and water. If ever I return to England I should like, above all things, to go through a medical course. . . . April and May are the unhealthy months ; if I get through them I hope I shall be in a fair way towards acclimatisation. But there are other tortures—prickly heat, that torture of tortures, the jigger, which gave me two festered toes for nearly a month, and flies and mosquitoes. Value a letter, please, according to the cloud of flies which surround one as one writes, and you will treasure it indeed ! I have many visitors, whom I turn to account by reading Swahili to them, and thus practising upon them. The completion of my building is my present horizon. Then all my woes come to an end.

Yours, etc.,

A. F. SIM.

Letter to C. H. B ——, dated,—

Kota Kota, *October* 14*th*, 1894.

My DEAR ——,

How better can I employ an hour on this blessed Sunday morning, devotions being ended, than to sit down and write to and think of you. while you in turn are just preparing for morning Service somewhere? I am sitting under a grass shelter, and over that a vertical sun, for it is midday here. No, I have no fixed roof over my head yet, and if these wretched people delay much longer the rains will find me in a proper fix. . . . A small mite sits at my side on the floor, watching me with wonder, and awfully pleased to run an errand now and then. Yes, I can get fond of them. I can hardly believe how rapidly and how entirely the prejudice against the black skin disappears, and the faces of these people are by no means hideous. Many have the sweetest expressions, and then one cannot help feeling the intensest pity for them. . . . The dear Bishop—how proud I felt (and always feel to belong to the Durham diocese) to see the estimate of his work in the " *Manchester Guardian* " ! . . . No one actually escapes the fever. If you are strong it does not bring other complications with it as a rule. A weak heart or liver or anything wrong with the spleen means death after one of these attacks of fever sooner or later. There was a good deal of fault to be found with the houses at Likoma, but that is being remedied now. . . .

October 18th.—Here is a small crowd of patients, mostly with horrible sores of long standing. One man wants a sheet of paper to make *dawa* (medicine), *i.e.*, to write or get written texts from the Koran, and tie it round his neck ! How long I shall be able to go on I don't know, as my iodoform is rapidly diminishing, and my bandages were finished long ago. . . .

To work this district properly there ought to be two Priests, and some ladies for the girls and women. I believe that would be the Roman Catholic method. I always rather regret that we do not come across any of their Missions out here. A party of eleven— six men (including a Bishop) and five sisters—went up the other day, but I did not see them. Their station is somewhere on the high plateau between Nyasa and Tanganyika. I should like to have a personal acquaintance with their methods. They are generally accused of buying slaves to start work upon. *We* get them for nothing, but our experience has been that freed slaves form the worst material. . . .

I am preparing for hard times in the rainy season, having concluded a bargain to-day for a ton of rice, which I intend to store against these rainy days. Some men brought in a rum beast to-day, after the coon sort, awfully shy and wild. I have kept it knowing Mr. Nicholl's fondness for curiosities of this sort. I hope to effect some mission work by gathering clans together. People are very clannish here, and the town is divided up into clanships with an elder at the head of each. I want to make Jumbe discontented with his indolent, lustful life, and I mean to urge him to build a house out of the slums of the town, and make a garden. His predecessor had three hundred wives. Most of these by right descend to his successor, but for some reason they refused, and I suppose they will be scattered among the villages in time. Doubtless most of them are slaves. My gang of labourers, let me triumphantly remark, are *free*. Witness the amount of work they have done! My attaché (Wadimayu) calls them heathens, he being a self-righteous Moslem. Wadimayu has a good eye for the main chance ; but he has energy—the only man among them who has. I employ him therefore, though I daresay he will "do" me. I simply must hurry on with the work, teacher or no teacher, or the rains will be upon me. Then it is impossible to build, and still more impossible to live without a building. . . . Much of most days is spent in entertaining strangers, *e.g.*, an Arab merchant here ; the headman, Baruku by name, an old rascal, slaver, smuggler, etc. ; Msusa, an honest old ruffian, who does not beg, and is generally somewhat of a North country man ; Mwenge Kombo, a fat old clown, with little or no influence, but a first-class eye to No. 1 (I think he poses as court jester, with any amount of energy, but no brains to direct it properly) ; old Marengo, whose village is further South three miles from here ; then there is dear old Mwenge Waziri, old Jumbe's brother, who used to have great influence in the old man's time, but is quite deposed now. He spent a whole day with me lately, and I gave him lunch. I think the old fellow, for whom I have no little pity, is quite fond of me. Then there are other younger men, and Jumbe himself—the Sultan, as he is styled —not a great person, but rather sharp and clever. Perhaps in time the missionary may be able to help these people to see that life was given them to make use of, and is worthy of nobler uses than they put it to. You see I have the *entré* into "the 'ighest sassiety" when I am ready to make use of it. I could now read to them, but it wants more than that. It wants a firm treatment of sin.

October 24th.—Still alone—the building progressing, rain threatening.

Yours, etc.,

A. F. SIM.

Letter to W. W——, dated,—

Kota Kota, *October 20th*, 1894.

MY DEAR ——,

I enjoyed your description of the choir trip more than I can say. It went far to set me on my feet again when I was very seedy and despondent. I wish I had you here to help me to build. Site lovely ; close enough to the town, yet raised above it 80 or 100 feet ; about twenty acres, with a fine clump of trees on it right in the middle ; bounded North and South by gullies filled with water in the rainy season : East slopes down to the village, North an imaginary line marked out by ant hills. My house and teacher's house I am now starting with. Mine—walls, trees three feet into ground, with fork at top to carry wall-plate, eleven feet high, trees crossed by bamboos tied with bark ; in between filled with mud, and plastered outside and inside, making wall more than a foot thick. The wall-plate will consist of the straightest trees I can find, cutting short lengths, if necessary, and joining them with wooden pegs. This is to carry roof joists. Such wood it is, with grain like a wire rope. And there is no wood big enough to make a plank of. The adze and axe are the only tools to work this iron wood with. Roof beams—I don't want uprights in the middle of the house if I can help it, so will these do ? They are crossed with

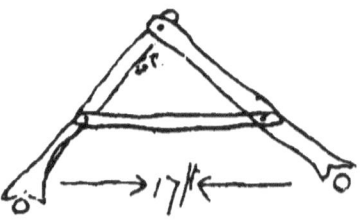

(*From a sketch by* A. F. SIM)

bamboos, and have grass for slates. I have now made the drawings. I know you would demand cloisters and lavabo ; the latter is impossible for want of water, but the former is not impossible as School and place of merchandise, etc. There are no shops here ; people bring things to sell. If ever I do build a Church I shall think seriously of a grass cloister for heathen Services and hearers'

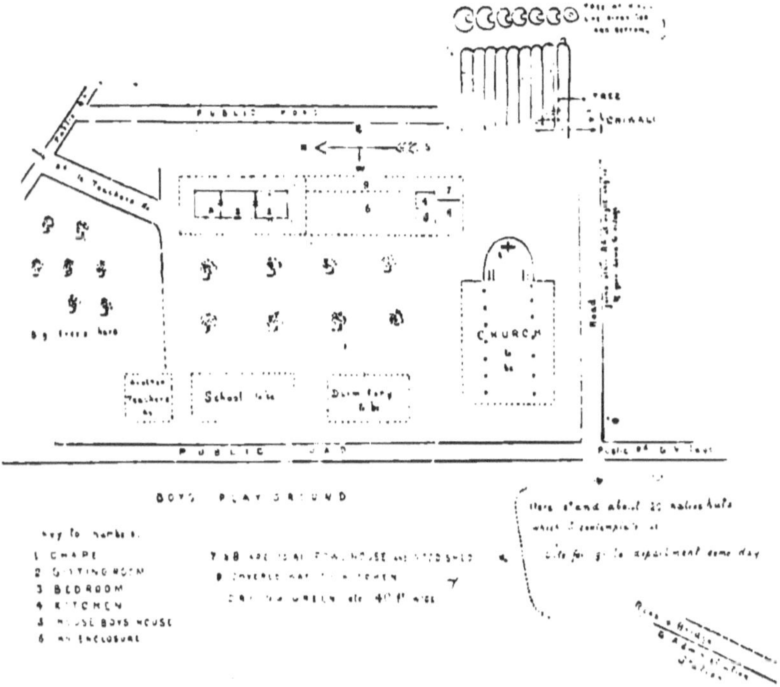

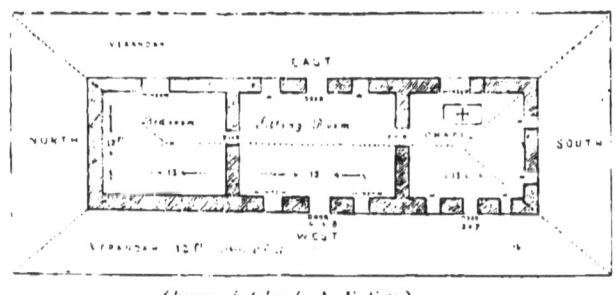

(*From sketches by* A. F. SIM.)

classes. Hearers are those whose earnestness is being tested, while for a year they are being taught the elements of Christianity.

The store-room will come under South end of verandah probably, and I shall change the Chapel to North end. Of course there is no glass for windows, only something to keep the wind out. The

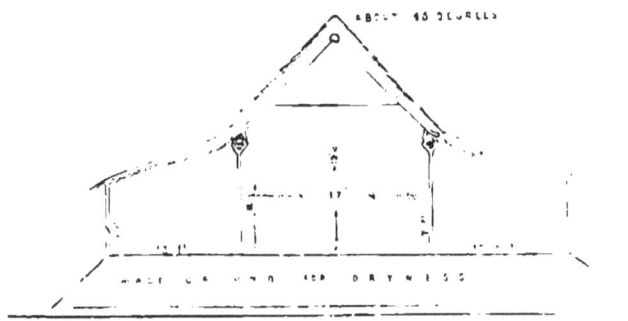

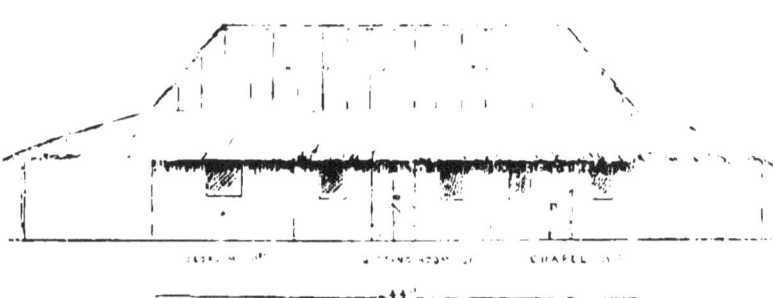

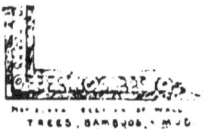

(*From sketches by A. F. Sim.*)

doors will be patent I expect! I hope to get hinges from Likoma. Rain does not and must not touch the walls owing to the verandah.

Well, there is still plenty to say about the building and tools and materials. I have over 100 people working at my site now

11 men, 36 women, 47 boys, and 21 girls—105 all told, ages varying from 5 to 60 ! They do as much as half a dozen English boys would do in the same time. The men have hoes and hoe up the ground, and the women and children carry the soil on their heads in baskets to the site of my house to make a false foundation. This they will eventually trample down and beat with rammers until it is as hard as a brick and smoother. Into that I stick my uprights 3 feet deep. Hoes are the only implements in use yet. I may introduce a pick and a spade next week, and even a crowbar. If I had gunpowder, I think it would expedite matters in the way of blowing up an ant-hill or two, or at least loosening the ground, which is as hard as bricks now. As to my joiner work, I spent £5 on tools before I left London, and thankful I am to have them. I wish I had a grindstone. My square is in a box which has not arrived yet. I should like a blacksmith's rig out. There are blacksmiths here, but they only make knives, and spears, and arrowheads, and native axes. I don't yet know where they get their metal from. I am preparing furniture for my new house—tables, and chairs, and wash-hand-stand. While I write I can hear a hyena howling about a hundred yards off, and sometimes I can hear the hippopotamus in the Lake, nearly a mile away. . . .

October 22nd.—The building operations are going on, and they have nearly finished the ground plan of my house ; then they will begin watering it and beating it down, dig the holes for the trees, and make the walls. I have a bad time with jiggers ; two toes are festered, and I can hardly walk. The site is nearly a mile from here, and the road is rough. I am puzzled how to make a chair. You will say make a Glastonbury one, but how am I to work the wood ? Here's a tip for getting up in the morning :— Get a laying hen to make her nest under your bed, and if she is a robust person with strong maternal instincts and a broken voice, I am sure you won't sleep much after that hen wakes ! I have tried it. At daybreak (6 a.m.) she began, so I heaved a tin match-box and hit her on the head, but she came back ; a slipper almost dislocated her wing, but still she returned ; a boot, which nearly went through the mud wall, everything at hand went, even a tobacco pouch, but she got the best of it, and eventually I got up. Try it ; it is worthy of the Patent Office. Besides she provided me with part of my breakfast two mornings running. The same hen haunts me during the

day, but I keep a collection of clods handy, and when she comes
round she gets one. I know her among a hundred. She filled
me first with pity, then admiration, now I marvel at her !

October 28th —Mr. Nicholl and my teacher came back on Thursday, and very glad I was to see them. The latest news of the
slaving case is that thirteen slaves were released ; no more would
say they were slaves ; no doubt many more were, but that is their
business. All three dhows were confiscated. We expected some
unpleasantness or a row here when the news came, but somehow
these people are peaceful enough. If they had been Yaos I have
no doubt there would have been a row. Fortunately Kalanji's
dhow was not in it. If it had been confiscated, possibly Dr.
Hine and J. Williams in Unangu (of which place Kalanji is chief)
might have had a bad time of it.

By the same token Kalanji's dhow brought over a cargo of gunpowder the other day, all German made. A good deal of this
Mr. Nicholl has taken to keep in bond lest they should sell it in
the interior, contrary to the Brussels Treaty. Staying as I am up
here with the magistrate, I get a good insight into all these affairs,
and a fair idea of the people's character who are concerned in
them—good old rascals most of them, though they don't mean it,
and know no better. . . .

The trees are coming in for the houses. What an awfully
crooked eye these people have ! I make them use a line, and
still they go zigzag to the end. They have dug the holes for the
trees all crooked ! They dig the holes with a bit of stick, watering the mud and soil to soften it, and then with a pointed stick
digging it out, and emptying the hole with their hands. They
get a fathom of calico for a week's work—worth here about a
shilling. I used to think this was "sweating," but working as
they do I am changing my opinion. I scarcely think it is worth
more. For two fathoms we can get forty pounds of rice, so
that it is wealth to them. There is a tremendous demand for
sugar and salt here. They have none, though they can grow
splendid sugar-cane. They use it for their drink, "sherbet"—not
the fizzy stuff you get in England, but a still, syrupy stuff, which
I have seen but not tasted. They also grow tons of ground nuts,
of which beautiful oil can be made, and with which olive oil is
adulterated in Europe. They also grow sesame seed, which
makes splendid oil. Castor oil and cotton grow too, but they

make nothing of the latter. I should like to have the means of developing these industries here. They would pay to export, but there is plenty of ivory in the country, and many of the natives want these things. . . . The sun is scalding here ; it does not brown me, but raises blisters on such parts as are exposed to it. I am a mass of bites too from various insects. . . .

With all best wishes.

Yours, etc.,

A. F. SIM.

Kota Kota, *October 24th*, 1894.

MY DEAR M——,

I have found immense pleasure in re-reading those letters that came by last mail and the papers. I think I know more politics than I ever did in England. . . .

Stick to St. Aidan's, old chap, till I come back, and I will be your Curate if you will give me the price of grub and a new cassock once a year ! Life after all only begins at thirty. Stick on, and perhaps I shall be back again some day, and we'll have good old times again.

I am determined to carry on the school work here in Swahili. Mr. W. P. Johnson for some reason has a great prejudice against Swahili. . . .

It is exceedingly hot here now—about 100 in the shade, with often a hot wind blowing. Our drinking water, which we cool by evaporation, won't go below 71°, and that feels icy to our heated palates. . . .

I am single-handed, and I hope people will remember that. I think I have been an almost exemplary correspondent. What do you think ? . . .

One of my patients died last week. Ulcers and sores are many and dreadful, and my *dawa* is giving out. I asked one old man how he got his finger twisted out of its proper place, so that it sticks out of the back of his hand. He said, "God sent it." Another—a woman—I asked how her sores came, and she said she had been very wicked. On my way to the site from here I have to pass a point where three roads meet. There is always a collection of broken cooking pots there. They are filled with something trifling for somebody who is sick ; it is *dawa*. Many, indeed most of the people wear charms, which generally take

L

the form of some nonsense written on paper, and folded up and
sewn in cloth, and tied round the neck, head, arm, or affected
part. I was surprised at the number of people who came to ask
for writing paper, and only discovered the other day that they
wanted it for *dawa*. One boy writes some bosh in Arabic on bits
of paper like this and sells it for a fowl. That young man will
make his mark some day ! . . .

The Archdeacon is to go home early in December. . . .

Yours, etc.,

A. F. SIM.

Kota Kota, *November 2nd*, 1894.

MY DEAR M——,

This is the first day of the thirty-fourth year of my life.
What an awful thought ! How long to have lived and done so
little ! . . .

Now I am writing placidly surrounded by Jumbe and his
courtiers, with an old coast man ostentatiously telling his beads
on the other side of the table—no doubt wondering what he can
make out of us. Jumbe is sitting on a chair and the rest on the
ground, sixteen all told. It is a breach of etiquette for any to sit
on chairs in Jumbe's presence. This does not apply to Europeans
of course. Those who are accustomed to Arabic writing are
always astonished at the rapidity with which we write. They talk
of the "pen flying" ! These people come up here, Mr. Nicholl's
place, out of courtesy, and sit for hours sometimes. We simply
go on with whatever we are doing. They are terribly patient. I
trust they will not favour me in quite the same way when I am in
my own place. . . .

Well, the walls of my house are up, but not mudded yet, and we
are rather short of trees, which come in slowly. Next week I
hope to have the roof joists on, and some of the mudding done.
If all goes well a fortnight should see it finished. . . .

A sad affair has happened here in the death of Dr. Mackay,
of the gunboat "*Pioneer*." He was killed by a lion—horribly
mangled—and buried at Likoma. No doubt the November
number of the "*Nyasa News*" will give an account of it.

November 11th, 25th Sunday after Trinity.—Mr. Nicholl, magistrate of the South of the Lake, has gone to Likoma to settle some
feuds among the heathen there. I do not expect him back till

about the 20th. William has had a bad attack of fever; so the native is not free from it you see. And at this moment I have a temperature of 102°, but I trust to a strong dose of quinine to ward off anything higher. The framework of both houses is just finished. I hope to begin mudding to-morrow, and to finish it by the end of the week. Mr. Nicholl too is busy with his house, which will, as it should, be grander than mine. Mine would be half the size but for the Chapel. . . .

I cannot write under this restraint. The men from the "*Domira*" are here, and are going to stay to dinner with me, and my head is buzzing with quinine. I feel I shall make a poor host. I hope it does not sound very fearful all that I say about fever. It is the natural order of things, and nobody thinks anything about it out here. Water is very scarce. The lake water is not drinkable here owing to its shallowness and the large town that washes in it. Our drinking-water comes slowly filtering up in deep holes dug by the people. It is the colour of milk, but is said to be very good. . . .

And now the Bazaar is over and the Harvest Festival, and I suppose you are preparing for the Confirmation. I am glad to hear about the schools. Remember me most kindly to Mr. L—— and indeed to all the day school teachers. And now farewell. Remember me to all my old friends. This is only a line to say I am well and flourishing.

Yours, etc.,

A. F. Sim.

Kota Kota, *November 19th*, 1894.

My dear M——,

When this boat comes I expect it to bring a cook, William's wife and two children, and possibly Mr. Corbett as well as Mr. Nicholl on his return. The rains are beginning; for two nights we have had rain, and it threatens again. The first night we were all unprepared, and I got a ducking in my bed, so you can imagine how anxious I am to have a solid roof over my head. We have been much delayed by want of trees, etc. Mr. Nicholl has been very good to us, and given us everything we wanted; but that is unsatisfactory, and I don't like taking from him. It is the way of these people, they know nothing of punctuality, or the sacredness of contracts ! There are some at home something like them, are there not? There are some rather disquieting rumours in this place just now. Jumbe seems to have been seized by a frenzy ; he has already killed five innocent men who had been friends of his predecessor's ; and this morning he tried to take his brother's life with a revolver, which Mr. Nicholl had given him. Mr. Nicholl is away at Likoma still, though I expect him back by this boat, I think to-morrow at the latest. There are many problems and complications to be worked out here, by reason of the change of circumstances through the coming of the English power. Jumbe is a young man, and is surrounded by a lot of young men, like Rehoboam of old. These youngsters ape the Swahili, or Arabised coast-man, in a life of indolence and lust. In old days the slave-trade was their source of wealth, and fighting their only occupation. Now they have neither wealth nor occupation. The present Jumbe is not at all satisfactory to my mind. He has treated the old men of his father's court with scant ceremony. He seems little inclined to follow Mr. Nicholl's advice, though he owes all to him. I hope Mr. Nicholl will try him and depose him, and I think rule in the interregnum himself with a few more soldiers. Baruku is the richest and most powerful chief in this town, more so than the Jumbe I believe. Two or three days ago he went off with all his goods and people to another place belonging to him, Bua, as if in disgust, and in the middle of the night. As he had to pass my site, some of my people saw him, and thought it was war, and made ready for flight. To-day I hear he is back again with a lot of Angoni, his friends. Now the Angoni are the scourge of this part of the country, a warlike tribe of Zulu origin.

November 23rd.—Here is the steamer. Yesterday the Angoni chief came to see me—such a wholesome contrast to the Swahili—a big man, with a head-dress like a top hat, five inches high, all of his own hair. He has promised to come up and give a war-dance outside here. Poor Mr. Nicholl, he will have a bad time of it when he faces Jumbe's sins, as I hope he will do firmly. The future will be beset by difficulties if he doesn't do something to teach Jumbe that he cannot do just as he likes. He has besides seized an Arab here, and refuses to let him go except for a ransom of ten women ! When he treats a powerful man, as this Arab is, like this, he is guilty of a grave error of policy, because these men bring the ivory to the place, and are its principal merchants. . . .

I am very fit indeed just now except for prickly heat. It is very hot : there is a strong wind blowing, though I think it only makes it hotter. . . .

Yours, etc.,

A. F. SIM.

Kota Kota, *November 6th,* 1894.

MY DEAR BOYS AND GIRLS,

I don't know how I am ever to answer your letters one by one ; but because I write to you all in one letter, you must not give up writing to me separately. I can t tell you how much I long

W KPE LE AT KOTA-KOTA.
(*From a photograph by* A. F. SIM.)

for letters out here : and it is so nice to sit night after night with a budget of home letters, to read and re-read them till I almost know them by heart, and think of what you are doing. You know that the sun comes to us here two or two and a half hours before it comes to you, so when you are going to bed I am snoring in my bed, and when you get up I have finished breakfast and am busy with the work of the day. Well, my house is not finished yet : I hope in a fortnight it will be. I am longing for it to be finished, for I can't do any missionary work here, nor much other work, there are so many interruptions. People come every day in great numbers to see the magistrate ; they sit and talk, or do nothing but stare and watch us ; it is not easy to do anything then. I go every day to where I am building and give directions, and sometimes, nay often, I have to lend a hand. I should have to be there all the time if I had not a capital " foreman " in my teacher —William Kanyopolea. He is there all the day. My work-people would do nothing if some one did not watch them, and even then they rest more than they work. But they only get a shilling a week for what they do : I don't think it is worth more ! I had a " strike " the other day for more pay ; but I was glad to get rid of all my women and children, for I had nothing more for them to do. So now I have about twenty men left. The mud floors are finished, and all the trees in the walls are up, and now we are to make the roof. Then comes the putting the mud on the walls, and the grass on the roof, and then my house will be finished. Such a beautiful mud house, with walls 11 feet high—but I have told you all about that, haven't I ? The place I have chosen is such a lovely spot. I like it more and more every day I see it, and Mr. Nicholl is quite envious of it. My poor little monkey has left me. The captain of the German steamer took a fancy to him, and begged for him ; and as he has two others I thought it would be happier with its friends. He was the funniest little mortal. He had no other monkeys to teach him how to do things. I used to feed him with a spoon when he first came. When he got bigger I gave him a cup full of milk ; his only idea of drinking it was to stick his head right down to the bottom of the cup, and then he would come up again half drowned. Mr. Nicholl and I used to laugh at him till we cried ! One day the men brought in such a funny beast. Mr. Nicholl said it was a lemur. It was bigger than a cat, with a long tail and grey woolly fur, large round eyes, and hands shaped like a man's all four. It was so wild and savage. At last he escaped from his cage, and I was rather glad. Are you fond of rats ? Come out here if you are. They are so cheeky they don't mind you a bit, but will come and sit and stare at you. I caught one in my hand last night, or rather it ran into my hand.

This is November 8th, and I am alone once again, only I have William with me this time. He takes all the building work off my hands, so that I haven't to be out in that scalding sun all day long.

Mr. Nicholl has gone to Likoma to try some people who have been shooting at each other, and stealing cattle. They are not Christians, but heathen.

We have to be our own doctors and dentists here. The other day Mr. Nicholl would not let me pull out one of his teeth, but pulled it out himself! If ever I have to do that I shall do it with a piece of string and a red-hot poker. You know how, don't you? All the best dentists do it that way I am told! And now good-bye. Here is the steamer, and I have no time to write any more.

Ever your affectionate Friend,
ARTHUR F. SIM.

Letter to Mrs. P——, dated—

Kota Kota, *November 12th*, 1894.

MY DEAR ——,

. . . Likoma is four miles from the eastern shore, about five miles long by two and a half broad and of irregular shape. Its principal products are mahogo (tapioca), stones, large and small, one palm-tree (borassus), and many baobab trees, which always testify to a poor soil. The population, about one thousand in scattered villages along its shores, live on fish and mahogo. The Mission station is built in proximity to the only harbour, a capital one, and faces the eastern mainland. Two small islands block in the harbour, which is consequently almost land-locked, and the view from the Mission station, which is on high ground, is very pretty. . . .

November 17th.—To-day the boys and William are having their first lesson in football, and by the shouts and excitement I should imagine they appreciate it. I hear them shouting "goal" and "touch," so I fancy they are also making progress. May they make similar progress in other things! . . .

What changes there are in West Hartlepool! It makes me sad to think of them all. . . .

Yours, etc.,
A. F. SIM.

Letter to A. E. M ——,

Kota Kota, *November 12th*, 1894.

MY DEAR DOCTOR,—

It has been long in my mind to write you a line, and now I am more or less settled it is time I did so. You will be interested to know something of my movements, and what I can tell you of the natives and my prospects, their diseases and my diseases, etc., etc. I have been a good correspondent on the whole I think ; but most of my letters have gone to West rather than to Old Hartlepool, and once, not long ago, I made so bold as to write a letter to the "*Mail*," thinking that there might be some who would care to hear about me and this out-of-the-world country. In steering clear of missionary work, of which I don't know enough yet to speak; and in trying not to be too personal, I felt I had made rather a bosh of that same letter. I am very, very fond of West Hartlepool, and I should be exceedingly sorry to be forgotten by my old friends in the town. My feeling has always been that it is my home, and I shall always do what I can to maintain my connection with the old place. I am so thankful always for those nine years of English parochial work, not only for what it has taught me, but for the deep friendships it has made for me. I pity from my heart the Missionary who comes out here immediately on his Ordination. He has none of those ties which only spiritual contact can make in England ; and here, how many years will it be before one can look for such sympathy as one gets from the spiritually-minded at home ? I have heard of men such as these going wrong out here. Detached from what is spiritual, and without roots in hearts elsewhere, without the force of a hundred prayers offered almost daily for him, I cannot be surprised that some men (no, I know of none in our Church, and no ministers in any other Church, only teachers, etc.) should fall away. I can feel a deep pity for and sympathy with the layman — trader, administration agent, or what not — all alone, and surrounded by Heathenism. So many of them find refuge in what they are pleased to call Agnosticism, and that I fear becomes a cloak for evil living. And yet we have much to be thankful for in British Central Africa. No liquor is allowed to be sold to the natives, and on the whole the European example might be worse. There are some exceedingly nice men, and some with the real

interest of the native at heart. Some, it is true, seem quite unable
to see any good point in the native, and curse him and kick him
for what is really their own fault, for the simple reason that they
can't make themselves understood. In his own way a native is
very self-dependent. Every one of them can build a house, saw
very neatly, and so on, and if treated properly, will serve his
master like a dog ; but when he comes into contact with cork-screw,
table knives, forks, table-cloths, and napkins, a dozen different
sauces, tinned meats, and fish, what wonder if he makes some
mistakes? Sugar and salt are temptations to him, but he is
honest on the whole—very. He has no little self-respect, and keeps
himself clean ; he loves soap, and hates a tear in his cloth. But
European civilization is not fitted for the African native, it generally spoils him. The Arab has a far greater affinity for him, and
his Oriental manners suit him far better. The native can never
hope to be a white man, but he can aspire to Arab ways. The
Arab is his ideal of a native gentleman. The European (*Mzungu*)
is a great bully, who bustles him about and introduces all manner
of strange implements and habits. He (the native) hates regular
work. The *Mzungu's* bell goes at seven, and twelve, and two, and
five ; he would prefer to begin at daybreak, and go on leisurely
all day long, bothered by no bells, eating when he felt inclined,
and resting when he wished. There are one or two tribes that
seek work with the European. They are the best workers from
our point of view. They "sign on" for six months with the
Europeans at Blantyre—with coffee planters and trading companies. They get four fathoms of calico a month and their food ;
and for that they work pretty hard I think. A fathom of calico is
supposed to be worth a shilling out here, and of course the native
can buy a great deal more with it than we could in England with
ten times its value ; and after all, native labour is but slow, poor
stuff. An English apprentice-boy could do as much as six of
these fellows in the same time I think. Well, I am like all new
comers, only too ready to form opinions and express them. The
truth is native races differ very much, and what is true of one does
not hold of all. I am here in the midst of an Arabised town,
where the autocracy aspire to Mahommedanism and Swahili, or
coast civilization—a civilization the result of Arab influences.
There is nothing good to be said for it as it exists in its native
perfection—cruelty, guile, indolence, lust. It is no doubt some-

what picturesque. What is to come to these people? The absolute heathen is much better off, because, though despised by the Swahili for it, he has a certain amount of work to do. Indolence is the mark of the Swahili gentleman. He will fight to get possession of slaves and the produce of the field, but work he will not. His slaves do his work, plant his fields, build his houses, etc. If in battle he gets possession of slaves, he sells them ; and this has been the curse of Africa. And now what is to be done? The problem is to be worked out here. Things are changed ; the Mzungu has come with his soldiers, fighting is put an end to ; already three out of four dhows have been confiscated for carrying slaves. The Swahilis' source of wealth is gone; he has not the acumen to find out any other source of wealth, and so the Swahili, conservative slave-trader, the rich, indolent gentleman, hates the Mzungu. The downtrodden, timid, stupid, superstitious aboriginal is benefited. For him there is a hope where a firm government can protect him. Will he ever rise to independence, and shake off his timid cringing to the Swahili (but not exchange it for an European yoke)? These are problems for the future. There are plenty of signs of the Swahili's hatred of us. They quite recognise that our coming is their going. They meet our workmen cutting trees, and chase and threaten to kill them. Irresponsible ones among them taunt our people, and say they will kill the Mzungu and all his people.

I feel I ought to say something about your line of business, though the steamer which will take this has already cast anchor.

The fever—no one is quite free from it. I imagine it is malarial. One's perspiration when in the throes of fever reeks of the same smell which the marshes have ! Temperature rises very rapidly ; in a couple of hours one goes up to 106°. I have had only one attack like that, though I have had several days in bed with it. When I feel it coming on, which is generally at night, I take twenty grains of quinine, and sweat all night, and generally wake up quite free from it, but with a buzzing in my ears, the result of quinine. Sometimes however the fever gets the better of me ; but even after the worst attack I have had, with my temperature 106°, I was perfectly well in a week. It is very like a sudden burst of influenza, which comes and goes and leaves no effects apparently like influenza does.

The people who come to me are those who have ulcers and

wounds of every description. At present I am out of medicine. I am using permanganate of potash and vaseline.

Farewell. I had better send this off when I can. . . .

Yours ever,

A. F. SIM.

Letter to C. H. R——, dated,—

Kota Kota, *November*, 1894.

MY DEAR ——,

I can't tell you how much I appreciate letters ; they give me back-bone. As you can understand, one lives upon them ; they are the only breath of sympathy that reaches one. No, except for the thought of all you people at home, this is not a hard life. Perhaps hardships may be in store for one, but hitherto, except the lack of sugar, salt, and tobacco, it has not been hard living. No milk often enough, and nothing but the tough African fowl for meat, and a mixture of flour and native meal once for bread, are things one forgets as soon as they are over. No, the only hardship I have yet experienced is an occasional "go" of homesickness. Even the frequent fevers have their counterbalancing boon —one feels so jolly thankful when one is free from them. The mosquitoes and flying and creeping things are a little gruesome. . . .

A whole year is generally calculated as time spent in starting upon missionary work, and I daresay I shall be quite that before I can speak at all fluently. It is a horrid language to understand, for these people talk so fast ; and it is monstrous to read, because so many vowels come together and each must be pronounced. . . .

A man whom I have employed, a servile kind of chap, has sold the same woman four times. Each time she has run away from her new master and returned to the original. Eventually she made a complaint to the Mzungu (European). In Mr. Nicholl's absence that was myself, so I let him out on bail till the magistrate's return. To-day I have been receiving customs for imports —calico and gunpowder. . . .

The Swahili, even more than the Arab, is the enemy of all progress, and consequently the enemy of the English in the country. The two cannot exist together, as his whole idea of life is to possess slaves, and slaves are his revenue. . . .

My teacher's house is finished but not dry yet. Twice a part of the wall has fallen because white ants have eaten the bark rope, and the mud, being wet, has fallen out. White ants are everywhere. They have destroyed my Gladstone bag, and they started on my shoes. It is simply impossible to put anything that is not tin upon the ground. But, worse than this, they almost invariably attack seeds and young trees, especially if you water them. Tell S—— I am going to see if wheat will grow here, but I have no seed yet. Nothing grows at Likoma ; they get even their firewood from the mainland. Here the soil is richer, but scarcely rich enough for wheat I fear. . . . The "former" rains have begun, and the whole face of the country is changed as if by magic. I have found some lovely white and scarlet lilies. . . .

I have quite lost the odium for a black skin, and I can fondle a black child as readily as I could a white one. I forget people are black, and the features of those here are seldom after the ordinary negro type. Many boys are nice looking. I have a jolly little fellow for a servant at three fathoms of calico a month and food, and a jolly Christian boy full of fun for a cook. How they go for a football ! . . .

Oh ! How hard to realize Christmas ! It is cool, about 70 to 80° ; this is because of the rain, but there are no Christmas cards or parties. I must begin to think of a Christmas pudding ! How you fellows will fill my mind ! I shall think of the New Year's party at the Vicarage last year. How shockingly rude we (M—— and I) were ! There are times when the thoughts of the old place and the dear old folk and the beautiful Church and Services fill me to overflowing : but I know I shall get interested in this work. If I may be permitted to see some fruit in changed lives, then I know I shall become absorbed in it. . . .

There is no escape from fever—it is like the white ant. About once in three weeks is my average, but it is nothing to be alarmed at. I am sound in vital parts, and it has nothing to attack yet. . . .

In developing native industries the Arab has a great pull over the European. He takes what he finds and improves it : but the Englishman despises what he finds and introduces impossible luxuries, such as glass windows, beds, mattresses, and countless other things, which the native could supply if he only knew how. . .

Tell S—— they do grow wheat on high levels. At Blantyre Buchanan grows a lot. The Archdeacon had a contract with him, but sometimes it fails. . . .

Yours, etc.,

A. F. SIM.

Kota Kota, *November 20th*, 1894.

MY DEAR ——,

. . . Some thirty of the Angoni (who are Zulus) are in the town on a friendly visit to Baruku. They brought a letter from the Scotch missionary of their place—merely a letter of introduction to any European who might be in charge here. It got about that this letter was from the Mzungu, warning us that Jumbe had called these Angoni to help him to fight the Wazungu. So I have had Jumbe up here to-night in a great state of mind to know whether the letter really said so ! Our people are often taunted with being Wazungus, and a party of them was attacked and frightened out in the country, where they were cutting trees. . . .

The Angoni are famous for their dancing, and as they are going to dance this afternoon I think I shall go down and see them. If they are all decked like their chief, it will be a weird sight. . . .

My medicine is finished, and so is my tobacco ; my watch has stopped, and I have lost my calendar ; but I am well, and it is wonderful how easy it is to do without these things when you have to. I shall begin keeping a tally of the days on a stick soon. Farewell.

Yours, etc.,

A. F. Sim.

Kota Kota, *December 1st*, 1894.

MY DEAR ——,

I am conscious of the fact that St. Andrew's Day brings Foreign Missions specially before the minds of Church people at home, and what a power that knowledge is to me it is hard to tell. I have quite a congregation of Christians here, for when the German steamer came she brought two carpenters and their wives, and another cook for myself, and William's wife and two children. That makes nine natives besides the two children. The carpenters' wives are only catechumens as yet. We had Matins at 6.30 a.m., and Evensong at 9 p.m. On Sunday we are to have Service twice in this house with Mr. Nicholl. Of course we shall have the Celebration in the hut as before. Prayers are said in a mixture of Chinyanja and Swahili, as there is a dearth of Prayer-Books. . . .

During all the excitement with Jumbe I had a rather bad turn of fever—temperature 105·4°—and I am only feeling quite fit again now. This is the third high temperature I have had here, and I suppose it is a fair share. . . .

December 12th.—I have written a letter to the Archdeacon, which will reach him in England, beseeching him to go North and visit my dear old Parish. Oh, that in time, as this station develops, I might have two ladies here ! I am sure that there is work for them. Poor girls, how much they need a sister's sympathy and guidance ! They are for the most part mere articles of furniture. The late Jumbe had three hundred so-called wives—most of them taken in war and torn from what they call their homes. Then there are minor difficulties to be faced. Other knowledge than teaching is mostly gained in a short time ; cookery (especially invalid)—and yet how different cooking is here, with no kitchen ranges, no lard, no fat, no yeast ; surgical knowledge—bandaging, treatment of ulcers, use of syringes, poultices, carbolic acid, iodoform, and how to make a very little go a long way ; further—how not to worry or overwork, and how to think nothing of fever ; hardship—there is no great hardship—only when one's heart is at home, that is my only real hardship. Otherwise the journey out has been the only hardship to me ; but mine was exceptionally long and tiresome. . . .

My old friends are too numerous to mention, but I think of them all very much, and often bring them to mind as I in imagination pass my eye down the congregation in Church from the pulpit. I see them all again, and it does me good. . . .

It will be hard to keep Christmas with no Church furniture, but we must do our best ; and, deprived of all associations, perhaps Christmas will not be robbed of its real joy. I wish I could send you some of these lovely lilies for your decorations. I have discovered the loveliest vermilion lily I have ever seen—a large cluster of small flowerets, bigger than a cricket ball. When it seeds I shall transplant it and send some seed home. How lovely it is here sometimes ! And it is always picturesque. To-night I ... outside : the full moon had risen and was hidden behind the clouds, but it was reflected in the water with the deep shadows of the trees below us as a foreground and the silver lake and the mountains on the opposite side as a background. The atmosphere is most wonderfully clear. Those hills must be forty miles away, and yet one can see every crack and fissure, almost every tree. . . .

I have a swarm of bees on my "Estate," and the other day one of them was ungrateful enough to sting me—where do you think? On the very tip of my nose. Well, I rubbed earth on it, and felt little or no inconvenience. . . . I wish you a most happy New Year in the real sense.

Yours, etc.,
A. F. SIM.

Kota Kota, *December* 1*st*, 1894.

MY DEAR ——,

Great things have been happening here since my last letter to you. I think I told you of Jumbe's little jokes, and how he had killed five strangers who came to the town in the late Jumbe's time, and how he also attempted to take his brother's life, missing five shots at him with a revolver. Well, when Mr. Nicholl returned that same evening, yesterday week, he tied up the young man, and sent the German steamer, which had just brought him in, to call the "*Pioneer*," which happened to be at the other side of the Lake. And so on Saturday morning at ten the "*Pioneer*" steamed in, and the villagers in a fright streamed out of the town. On Monday morning the Jumbe and his principal adviser were carried off to Zomba to await his trial, and he will probably find amusement for his lazy hands at Chinde eventually. Now an interregnum has been declared, and Mr. Nicholl is Jumbe for the time being. There was little fuss. Of course everybody seized some weapon; my rifle and gun (loaded with empty cartridges) were both called into requisition, but not a single attempt was made to rescue the prisoner. Mr. Nicholl was quite wise and cool and allowed a certain amount of access to him; but the young Jumbe was too unpopular to excite much sympathy. The old men are glad he is gone. . . .

December 6th.—Since I wrote last Mr. Nicholl has been very ill. It has been a most awfully trying few days. . . . Finally the German steamer came in, and he went off to Bandawe, seventy miles from here, to put himself under the doctor there. Next day I took to my bed for a bit with a little touch of fever. I am all right again to-day (December 7th).

December 8th.—Again a heap has happened in my small world.
First the mail on the 6th.   Such a splendid budget again!
Enough to cheer one on one's way for quite a month.   More of
this hereafter.   Then, as I have said, getting Mr. Nicholl off at 5
a.m. on the 7th.   Then at sundown in comes the "*Charles Janson*"
with Archdeacon Maples on board, not without warning.   I was
on the look-out for them.   Then just at dusk, most unexpectedly,
in comes the "*Domira*" on her way South, and I had not a single
letter ready.   I don't think I shall actually have missed a mail,
because my last letters only left a fortnight ago.   Poor old chap,
I fear all the changes will distress you fearfully, especially C——'s
loss.   They are distressing enough to contemplate from a distance
like this.   Shall I recognise the old place again when I return?
. . .   All the English residents out here are awfully sorry Bishop
Hornby has had to resign.   They liked him immensely. . . .
The Confirmation is over.   What an anxious time it is!   I trust
you are pleased and gratified with at least apparent results. . . .
If I were to get a year at home any time I wonder if I could go
through a course of elementary surgery.   Can you send me a book
on anatomy and physiology?   I might do something in the way
of reading out here.   Remember me to the choir men and lads,
and to Mr. H——.   Oh, for another sing with them, or I would
as soon sit and listen! . . .

Let me retract all the nasty things I have said about Africa.   It
is lovely now.   The waste places are green, and there are a few
such flowers lovely lilies.   When they seed I will send some to
you for hothouses.   I have nine Christians in my lot here.   On
Sunday afternoon (December 9th) we went for a picnic to the
hot-water springs.   I thought we might find some lilies or other
flowers.   And didn't we, with their bulbs two and a half feet below
the surface!   A few ferns too ; lilies with masses of huge white
flowers in bunches ; another with a lovely round head of small
vermilion flowers, bigger than a cricket ball ; another with a single
huge violet flower like an iris, only very short, and a much bigger
flower : some other lovely flowering shrubs too, and many labiates
of all kinds.   And yet I don't suppose this is a very rich country
for flowers.   With the rains I have put in seeds turnip, onion,
potatoes, sunflowers, etc., etc., and melons.   Many are already
showing above ground, but, alas! there are many locusts about,
which may cause us trouble.   This is a great rice-growing centre,

and it would be a terrible calamity if we had the locusts later on. I have taken the precaution to buy a ton of rice ! . . .

Now a word about the Archdeacon's visit. He is on his way to England about the Bishopric. They want him to be Bishop, and so do we, but he himself is very loth. He called here to see me, and for a final talk on his way South. He was pleased with what I had done (more than I am), but the principal thing he said was that I should be undisturbed here, unless the worst came to the worst, and no one was left at Likoma. I am very thankful to find myself more or less secure here. I hope when he returns I shall require more help. My ambition is, when I know both languages, to move about a great deal. I have a very wide district— 2,000 square miles. I have not begun preaching yet, and don't think I shall till I get into my house and begin the school work. Even then it must be by interpretation, for these people are distinctly bi-lingual. I believe it will be intensely interesting work. The Archdeacon and Mr. Corbett came ashore about 8 p.m. They came up here, and we talked till 4 a.m. Mr. Corbett felt the mosquitoes, and he went under my curtain and fell asleep. Then the moon had gone down, and by starlight we tried to find the boat. We naturally lost ourselves, and had to knock up some one, and when we found the boat, the boys had gone ; so we went back to find William, and there were the boys with oars and rowlocks ! They got off after one hour and a half hunting about in the dark. I could not persuade them to remain till daylight. . . .

So a good deal has happened in my little world. Another thing, which I have forgotten to tell you, is that we have moved into a house with a roof on it and walls. It was very roughly built for the Sikhs, who are under a temporary shelter in their tents. Mr. Nicholl's house is only in the rib stage. He is using palm trees (borassus). I could not run to that. Perhaps I shall when I build my Church. This house is about forty feet long. Mr. Nicholl's bed is at one end, and mine at the other ; but big as it is it is lumbered up with Jumbe's treasures, which seem mainly to consist of mattresses. With William almost all the building bother is taken off my shoulders. He is there all day—comes over at 6.30 a.m. and 9 p.m. for prayers, and sleeps there in a house he bought for a fathom of calico ! For one hoe, without handle, we can buy forty loads of grass ! A load at its big end is a good six feet in circumference, and about seven or eight feet long, tapering to nothing.

M

I am sadly in want of Altar ornaments (cross I have), candlesticks and vases. My little Chapel shall have the best I can make out for it. I should like a *Longfellow.* I shall never bring myself to beg in the pages of " *Central Africa.*" . . . I am abashed, and blush at the circulation my letters have ; being at a good distance, and with a flowing beard and moustache (!), perhaps you don't notice my blushes. . . .

I can't say how much good a large packet of home letters does me. It makes me feel as strong as a horse in no time. You ask me what my difficulties are. At present the enervating, zeal-sapping delay is my chief difficulty. And of course the absence of sympathy here I feel very much—more than I can tell. And yet your letters bring warm hearts very near to me. I have been here more than three months now, and am still some distance from a starting-point. I fear I have failed to send you any Christmas cards this year. There is a poor choice of them here ! I wish I could send you a cartload of these lilies for decorations ! Wouldn't they be lovely ! One bunch would fill one of the vases. I shall send you some seed later on when it is ripe. . . .

I wish you could see the lightning here. It is magnificent almost every evening. Sometimes at night a deluge comes down —a good portion through the roof—and then I have to get up and cover everything destructible, and myself too. But I have moved my bed, and trust I may escape a dripping to-night. I cannot wonder at having a cold in my head with this. Here is the rain, a deluge, and it can rain out here. I wish I had a rain-gauge to measure it. It is just coming down in sheets. In a moment I expect it to be dripping in on my head. It is a strange sight to see the clouds of the kungu fly on the lake. They look like dense clouds of black smoke. The natives eat them, baking them in little cakes. They are feasting on locusts here, boiling them and drying them. . . .

Yours, etc.,

A. F. SIM.

Kota Kota, *Christmas Day,* 1894.

My DEAR ——,

I must write you a line, if it is only a line, to wish you a Happy New Year, if I am too late for Christmas wishes. How strange it is here ! Can you imagine Christmas among my sur¹ roundings ? I am trying to picture you getting up with a sore head, having been kept awake half the night by the bands and waits ! Perhaps snow on the ground, probably one of those jolly old slushy, sleety days, which one only knows how to relish when you have little else than sunshine and a dry, baked desert under your feet ! Well, we have done our best. Last night—Christmas Eve—we had carols (fancy carols !), "While shepherds watched,"

END VIEW.

SIDE VIEW.

(*Sketches by A. F. Sim.*)

"Hark, the Herald Angels," and "Once in Royal David's City," in Swahili, to the old tunes. And William, who has had eighteen months in England, turned up with an armful of Christmas presents for Mr. Nicholl and myself. Then this morning at 7 a.m. we had our Celebration, when we had the Christmas hymns to the dear old tunes, still in the old round native hut. The Christmas tunes alone reminded me of Christmas more than anything else. Then I sent William and the carpenter boys with my rifle and Mr.

Nicholl's to shoot in the country ! And now I am expecting them
back every moment. They took some of my workmen with them,
and a lot of biscuits and a tin of jam ! The plum-pudding ! It
wasn't half bad. Only it was served up for breakfast as if it were
a cake ! Poor Mr. Nicholl is much distressed because he cannot
touch it. Indeed he is very seedy, and has spent all the day in
bed. Altogether it is the strangest Christmas I have ever spent.
It has been fine nearly all day with very hot sunshine. . . .
Among other things I sowed some peas and French beans, and
the melons are doing splendidly. Potatoes too are coming up,
and so are the sunflowers ; but we have a terrible lot of locusts.
People are getting very anxious for their rice crop, which of course
is the staple food, and indeed wealth here. I have kept a certain
number of people at work to-day, who, poor things, know nothing
of Christmas Day and what it means yet. I trust in three days'
time my walls will be finished. Then I shall light big fires and
try and dry them, so as to get into my house by January 4th.
Then, please God, my active missionary and school work will
begin. Really my house is a beauty. I am awfully pleased with
it. . . .

The doors and windows will be rather primitive. Doors here
are made of the *chiwali* palm, the section of which is like this :—

These are cut the length of the door and fitted together like
this :—

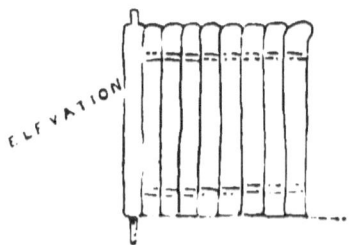

The left-hand end one is a tree stem, and the ends of it are pivots which fit into a socket top and bottom, and so it forms an exceedingly strong and useful hinge. The *chiwalis* are strung on a bamboo, which passes through each (*vide* dotted line) and which is wedged into the wooden upright at the left of picture ; fastenings are primitive. I don't see why I should alter this. They are capital doors, not beautiful, but easily and quickly made, and very fairly light considering their thickness. People here have no windows ; indeed, their houses inside are pitch dark except when the door is open, or they stifle themselves with a fire. So I have no native precedent to go upon. My house will have big windows, and I shall try and make shutters out of old boxes to shut at night. Perhaps if I take to photography very vigorously I shall in time have enough spoiled plates to make a glass window or two ! The nights are cold; and you must keep the night air out or risk fever. I have had a cold in my head almost since the rains began, and can't get rid of it. . . .

January 4th.—We have had a lot of excitement here. Mr. Nicholl has taken over the entire government, and announced that there are to be no more Jumbes, so the excitement has been great. I think the people are pleased. Feudal government continues. Slaving—capturing, buying, selling—will probably end in hanging. *Mwavi*, or poison test, is to be treated as homicide in future if a man dies of it. Messages of peace, ambassadors, etc., etc., are coming in and going out. We might be a great nation ! At the Baraza yesterday ambassadors from Unangu said they wanted a present for their chief. Mr. Nicholl said, " Let him come and take it," only a little more politely. However he satisfied them with friendly messages and promises of help in the matter of the ferry. We hear that many caravans are in Kalanji's country, afraid to cross as they hear we are in an uproar here ! The report is that Mr. Nicholl is a fierce man ! It is the dhow business that has given him that name no doubt, though he did his best to get them restored. However, a little patience will I think show them what is good for them.

Dr. Hine is a very widely read man. He has Abdallah Nakaam, a native Deacon, with him now ; he is a Yao, and an excellent preacher ; I am told he ought to be a great help. The Yaos are a very difficult, insubordinate, cheeky people to get on with. My cook was with Dr. Hine some time ago, and he says

they used to have about ten boys and three or four grown people !
It must be very heartbreaking work. I told you the books had
arrived, but I haven't taken them out yet ; we have no room here.
· · ·

And so farewell, dear old chap. God bless you and your work
and your people this New Year. Keep your heart up. Separations
are only temporary.   Yours, etc.,
                                                            A. F. SIM.

Letter to Miss H. A. S——, dated,—

                                  Kota Kota, *December 25th*, 1894.
MY DEAR ——,

A merry Christmas to you from me and the mosquitoes.
The latter are so keen on their message that they will rapidly
drive me to bed. O for a good shiver in a warn? overcoat ! O
for a good old storm of snow and sleet ! . . .

One hears of strange superstitions here. At every cross-road
you find broken pots, which sick people place there, with flowers
in them, for their betterment. Graves are marked by these broken
cooking-pots. To break one is a great calamity, and to do it purposely means that you wilfully break up your home and all its ties.
I think the cooking-pot has belonged to the dead man or woman.
To-day they sacrificed a bullock to get rid of the locusts. Mahommedanism certainly winks at native superstitions. They are indeed
very deeply rooted, and are entwined with all the details and
relations of life. There are also some curious customs, *e.g.*, the
lip-ring, a bit of brass tube or cartridge, or a solid round thing
half an inch or more stuck into the upper lip ; also the nose-ring,
stuck into the side of one of the nostrils ; ears too are pierced
even in men ; women when very stylish have six or seven studs

NATIVE WOMAN'S EAR
— TO STUDS

in their ears. Then there are the tribal marks. The mark of these people is two long cuts on both sides of the face from the temple to the chin. The birds here are decidedly interesting—more so than the flowers. All the crows have a pure white breast and neck. The moths and butterflies are, many of them, lovely. But oh, what creeping, and crawling, and flying things ! Mosquitoes in the evening are the bane of one's life. . . .

I have told you not to think of my fever ; the attacks take me very gently. I shall quite get over them soon, and I have not had any since the last ! . . .

It is very interesting to watch the oil of English justice mingling with the vinegar of Swahili semi-civilized savagery, or rather not mixing, but trying to make the best of it. Mr. Nicholl goes to Fort Johnston to try Jumbe, and in his absence I shall be a sort of Vice-Sultan. His collecting witnesses has been rather trying, as his principal witness, who escaped when her three companions were killed, has gone off to a place seventy miles away, and all the time she was supposed to be safe. However he has plenty of evidence to convict the young man upon. . . .

No African meat has fat, not even the pigs ; only elephants and hippos have, and as we don't get them every day we have to depend on tinned stuff from England. It is these things that make living expensive here. Fowls are 2*d*. or 3*d*. each, but one eats three or four a day, including soup. . . .

Farewell. A Happy New Year to you all.

Yours, etc.,
A. F. SIM.

(*Sketch of Kota Kota and Lake by* A. F. SIM.)

I have not finished enclosed picture, as I did not put in the opposite mountains. It is rather a fancy picture, as I wanted to get all the eye full upon one sheet of paper, and I could not see the middle distance from where I was sitting. It was raining all the time, as it is most times now. The trees on the left are an " impression " of my site as seen from here. The native huts and a woman pounding corn with a wooden pestle and mortar are seen everywhere, and the man is usually reclining. I have not got any paper to paint on, though I have my paint-box.

Letter to A. D —— and E. C——, dated,—

Kota Kota, *December 31st*, 1894.

MY DEAR ——,

I have so many letters to write, and so little time to write them in, that I must answer both your letters together. I want to wish you both, and all your two families, a Happy New Year. . . . Oh, these mosquitoes ! There are five trying for the same place on my nose, and I am sitting with my legs in a mail bag like a big sack. I am afraid I shall be driven to bed, where I sleep under a muslin curtain, as every white man has to do. . . .

We had a picnic the other day with the eight or nine Christian natives whom we have here from Likoma. It was to a very beautiful place, where there are hot water springs—so hot that once I boiled an egg in them. We took biscuits, coffee, jam, and tinned fruits ; but they liked the sugar best, and did not care for the tinned fruit a bit. After tea we hunted for lilies—such beautiful white lilies, very large, and so sweet to smell. The boys made a fire by rubbing two dry sticks together. We had no matches, and it took them half an hour to get fire.

The people here have such funny superstitions. The other day Mr. Nicholl was very ill, and they said he had been bewitched. He had a big white stone with a lot of Arabic on it, which they insisted was the cause of all the mischief, so they took it away. Some time ago Mr. Nicholl was away, and at that time Jumbe had an evil conscience, and was not at all anxious for his return. So he tried to prevent it by throwing a charm into the Lake to stop the steamer returning ; but unfortunately it came in that very night, and Jumbe found himself in prison, and now he is sent off to be tried for murdering some people. So now Mr. Nicholl is Chief, or rather, as he says, the Queen is Chief, and he is Viceroy. Jumbe meant to have attacked the white men, and had half a ton of gunpowder hidden away, which Mr. Nicholl has seized. The Mahommedans have no conscience, and would kill every white man in the country if they were strong enough. They think us fools for being kind, or honest, or just. These are the people I am going to try and win for Christ, so I do need your prayers. It is only God who can win them. . . .

We have some funny cookery sometimes, though on the whole we do very well. Fowls constitute our principal meat, but they are not English fowls. Thrice my men, who go out to cut trees or bamboos for my houses, have brought in a hartebeest, as big as a calf, not very nice to eat, but a change. Sometimes too we have had a guinea-fowl. It is very difficult to get about now, as all the streams are full of water. I am building a bridge at my place. The rain makes the country look very pretty, and the grass is six, eight, or ten feet high ; but in the dry season the country is like a desert. Thank F—— for his nice letter. I was so glad to hear he was going to be confirmed, and I pray that he may become a constant communicant and a firm and steadfast Christian lad. I know he will have many temptations in the shops, but I hope that he will show a good example.

Please remember me to all in your two families and to all my dear friends. I am not often but always thinking of you all.

I beg leave to introduce you to some of my tormentors. Please look at their noses, long and sharp, made of specially tested steel for sticking into you ! Good-bye again.

Yours, etc.,

A. F. SIM.

Letter to E. L——, dated,—

Kota Kota, *January* 1*st*, 1895.

MY DEAR ——,

The first time I write that date this year let me greet you and wish you all blessing and happiness for the year. . . .

The young Jumbe, who has just been deposed, had an elaborate scheme for restoring the old state of things (*i.e.*, killing and slaving); to do which of course he would have to get rid of the *Wazungu*. However he began a little prematurely by killing four or five men

when Mr. Nicholl was at Likoma. These things are very hard to dis
cover here, and had it not been for my teacher we should not have
known of them ; for however much the people may wish to side
with the whites, they would never tell about anything like this.
So in the case of the gunpowder, it was discovered by a mere
accident by one of Mr. Nicholl's workmen, who belonged to a distant tribe friendly to the white man. Though the whole town
almost surely knows of everything that passes (for they are the
veriest gossips and they talk openly in a crowded baraza of all
that is doing), the white man never gets to know anything. In
the killing case one of my employés told my teacher, who, of
course told me, and I told Mr. Nicholl directly on his return. The
young Jumbe was sent for, and when faced with it drew his dagger
and tried to escape ; but a sentry was posted at the door, and
collared him very cleverly. . . .

The young man's scheme depended upon our ignorance or folly,
or he would never have come up to the Boma when sent for. He
was going to get out of the town and, with this half-ton of gunpowder, attack the station. Some damage no doubt would have
been done, as there are only fourteen soldiers here and no defences.
If he had succeeded in killing us or driving us away, he would have
gained his end. But if he had failed he would have gone up into
the mountains, as Makanjira and two other recalcitrant chiefs have
done, and this would have led to a lot of trouble and fighting. So
you see there was something providential in his capture, as a
number of little "accidents," so called, point out. His capture was
effected quietly and without resistance, partly because the young
fellow was unpopular with the headmen, and partly because Mr.
Nicholl threatened to shoot him if any violence were shown or
offered. I was in a raging fever all this time, with a temperature
of 106°. But there was little or no excitement, though all the soldiers were under arms three days and nights, and all who could
armed themselves with guns. . . .

The Administration, while forbidding buying and selling and
capturing people, recognises a kind of feudal system. Each headman has his people, and he is responsible to the Government for
their good order, etc. They pay him certain dues (a percentage
of their crops) and he can call on them when he wants a certain
piece of work done. This is not liberty as we know it, but without
a large force of soldiers and much expenditure no other way of

governing the people is possible. Peace and security are assured
to the "common people," and that they have never had before.
To do away with this feudal system would be to revolutionise the
country, and might lead to serious outbreaks. Probably the first
case of slaving that occurs after this will end in hanging. So, but
for the friendship of the two principal headmen, we might have been
living here in some danger. The young Jumbe had it in his mind
to kill all the old headmen who had been his predecessor's sup-
porters and councillors. With such peace and security assured,
these people might in time develop some trade in rice. . . .

I tried to vaccinate myself to-day, but the vaccine had coagulated
and would not run, so I made holes in my arm to no purpose.
There is plenty of small-pox at Fort Johnston, Blantyre, and
Bandawe, North and South of us, but only one case so far here
that I know of. The careless way in which these people go in
and out of the house and to other people's houses is enough to
spread the disease through the whole town. We shall have to
take measures for isolating these cases. All my little Christian
flock have been vaccinated recently, and some of Mr. Nicholl's
servants. I think, if the disease spreads, we shall make a fever
hospital, and nurse these poor things the best way we can, using
all those who have been vaccinated as nurses. If it comes, it
may be a God-sent opportunity for making the spirit of Christianity known among these people. At present I think they place
us in the same category with the Arabs, etc., and look upon us as
a grasping lot owing to the imposition of taxes, which, between
ourselves, I think are pretty heavy. . . .

In a week I hope to be in my house ; then, please God, active
work will begin, both school and preaching, and when 1896 comes,
what will be the effect ? I know you will pray for this place this
year—perhaps specially for the Mahommedan element ; for the
British Administration, that it may have wisdom ; for me, that I
may have tact, and zeal, and health ; for my teacher, that he may
have increase of the missionary spirit. Pray too that my coming
here may really draw me closer to God. I often wonder if I have
made a "sacrifice" at all ; certainly it is only in the friendships
and sympathy left behind. And yet the letters, unexpected,
affectionate, thoughtful, and the number of them, fill me with
happiness, and in some measure supply the lack of sympathy here.

I wish the bairns could have seen some of the stolid old fellows this morning dancing and greeting Mr. Nicholl as their new Governor, or Jumbe, with branches of trees in their hands and shouts. They were most grotesque, though solemn all the time. I suppose their actions and postures meant something, though they conveyed nothing but the ridiculous to my mind—old fellows whom one would never suspect of such frolicsomeness. Fancy Mr. Gladstone, Lord Salisbury, and so on, betokening their rejoicings by dancing wildly along Piccadilly ! . . .

I hope you are going to send me some seeds from home ; but I trust I shall never get like some missionaries here who seem to become mere farmers and improvers of the material fields, instead of sowing and watering the true harvest fields. It cannot fail to interest one—the planning and laying out a new station, reclaiming the waste places and making all kinds of shifts without the necessary tools, but I trust that interest may be only very secondary. Dr. Hine has a native deacon, a Yao, to help him at Unangu. The Yaos are the most troublesome and unpleasant people to get on with, but when won they seem to make fine Christians. We have the most to do with them in our Rovuma stations and at Unangu. The lake shore people are Nyasas, different from Yaos, and very much bullied by the latter. The Yaos are the most numerous tribe in Central Africa. The people here are *Wa Nyasas*, and their rulers are coast Swahilis. . . .

Farewell, and a Happy New Year to you and yours !

Yours, etc.,
A. F. SIM.

Letter to Mrs. P——, dated,—

Kota Kota, *January 5th*, 1895.

MY DEAR ——,

. . . I am busy now preparing my first Swahili sermon. I have to write it out in English, translate it into Swahili, get William to correct it, and when I preach it in Swahili he translates into Chinyanja. As you can imagine, I look forward with some degree of trepidation to this first venture. I shall go round to the different barazas and preach that same sermon, gathering as many people about me as possible. I expect February will be here ere I begin my School . . . William has been simply invaluable to me for my building work. Of course I could not have done without him,

or at any rate it would have cost me three times as much. He
and his family—wife and two bairns—are in their house now.
Hitherto we have been content with Daily Prayer and Celebration
on Sunday. . . .

To-day I have made out the papers for a dhow, sailing to-
morrow, with eighty-three souls on board, and I have paid over a
hundred men their wages for nine weeks. It took me all the
afternoon till dark. Poor fellows ! I thought they looked a
downtrodden lot. They are all slaves—few of them but will have
to give all or part of their wages to their owners ; all or most of
them were taken in war long ago. This state of bondage cannot be changed all at once, as these poor fellows are not ready
for freedom yet. They would cease work altogether, and famine
would be the result. . . .

I really think the old open slave trade is dead. There is some
done still, but compared with the old state of things it is nothing.
No doubt a slave would still fetch here thirty or forty rupees, but
there would be immense risk in transporting him owing to the
gunboats. One of the confiscated dhows has been sent to ply as a
ferry-boat between here and the opposite shore with passengers
and ivory. So there are only two dhows sailing from here, both
under pretty strict surveillance. . . .

January 19*th.*—Mr. Nicholl came back on the 15th, and to-day
we have had a trial, a case of attempt to poison some Germans.
One of the Likoma boys was wanted as a witness, so they brought
the case over here to Mr. Nicholl . . .

And now farewell.

Yours, etc.,

A. F. SIM.

Letter to W. W.——, dated,—

Kota Kota, *January* 8*th*, 1895.

MY DEAR ——,

. . . I am not in my house yet. I never expected to be so
long out of it, but I have had endless delays in getting material to
build with. Well, now the door and window frames are going in—
such warped and twisted things made of quite green wood. Still
they are mortised and tennoned. My teacher has taught one or
two handy men how to make them. They first use the adze, then

a jack-plane, and though they may be straight and smooth at first they soon warp out of shape.   I shall begin storing wood for my Church and School so that it may be seasoned some day.   Of course I have no glass in my windows, but I shall have shutters

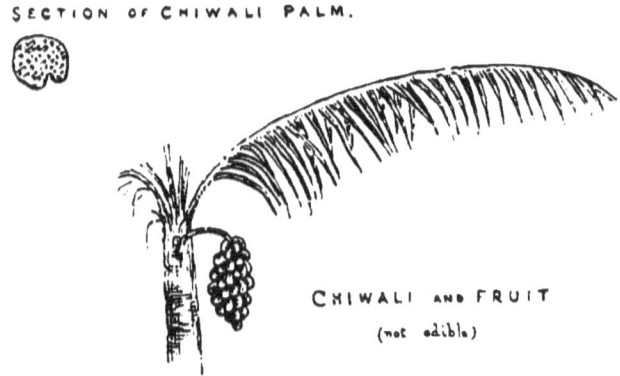

SECTION OF CHIWALI PALM.

CHIWALI AND FRUIT
(not edible)

made of the midrib of a palm tree leaf called *chiwali*.   Some of them are thirty feet long, very strong and light, with wiry fibrous grain.   I have used them entire for my roof.   I have only made use of four of those couples I spoke of in my last, and two uprights

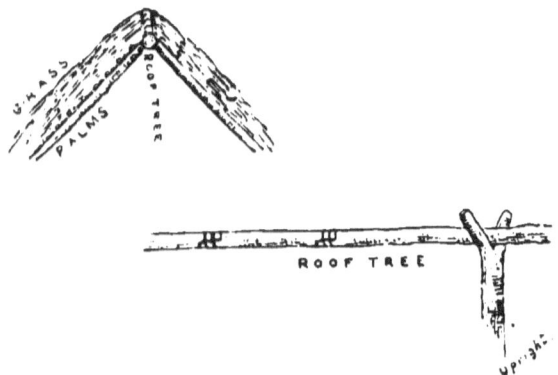

ROOF TREE

springing from the partition walls.   A roof tree runs along and chiwalis are tied with the bark of a tree to this after having been notched. The roof tree is made of three trees joined with nails and iron hoops off the boxes and bales we get our things in. The walls have trees for uprights about two feet apart, then bamboos nailed and tied (I dare not trust the bark tying owing to white ants, so I sent to Likoma for nails) on both sides of the uprights, and between these stones and mud, plastered with mud outside and inside.

Including the baraza, my house is just forty feet wide—eighteen feet inside measurement without baraza. It is thoroughbred pure native, except such improvements as windows, tables, and chairs, and they are native made under my direction. . . .

January 10*th*.—This afternoon I put on my mackintosh and a pair of leggings and went for my usual constitutional. Alas ! my poor mackintosh has all the collar and part of the tail eaten by rats. The women have done a big bit of the verandah with a last coating of mud, and I have great fires lighted in the rooms to dry the mud as soon as possible. I generally find a little crowd round each, doing nothing but keeping each other and the fire warm. They are awfully lazy beggars, although there are excep-tions ; but what more can one expect for six feet of calico a week ?

January 13*th*.—It is rather my style I fancy that the very first new year in these foreign parts I should find myself without a calendar. I have had to make one for myself, with tables of lessons, etc. We do our best to make Sunday as like Sunday as it may be. We have a Celebration at 7 a.m., using half a native hut for the purpose. Then we have Matins and Evensong with plenty of hymns and chants, of which you will be glad to know " Kelway" is generally one. This morning " Hail to the Lord's Anointed" was our hymn. I expect in days to come this hymn will be our favourite processional through this slave town, as the third and fourth lines run :—

"Who comes to set free, to make all free,
To break the fetters of sin, to do justice only."

I was just going to boast that we managed to keep pretty quiet on Sunday, when, behold, here comes a whole ship's crew of one of the dhows to get their *cheti*, or sailing papers. Of course I shall send them away with a "flea in their ear," as it is supposed to be generally known that this is "God's day." A dhow is about the size of a rather small fishing smack. It has one sail, and carries about ten or twelve sailors and a passenger list of about eighty. The last passage one of them made, she sailed about 8 a.m. with such a cargo, met head winds, anchored about eight

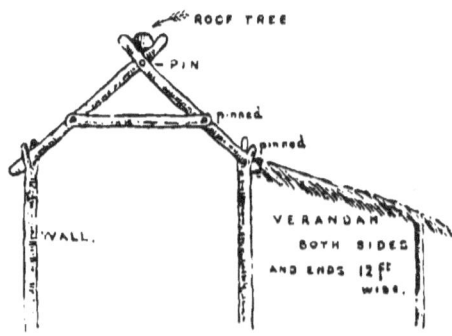

miles off, and the last I saw of her she was being enveloped in a thick, drenching rain, which quickly hid her from our eyes. The rain lasted all night, and they had no awning—what a terrible time they must have had, poor things!

Please set to work at once to draw me plans for our Church, and reckon upon uprights or pillars not more than twenty feet high above ground and no wood you can make a decent joint with.

I should get palm-trees for the pillars a foot in diameter. Then we might square these for the crossbars, and mortise and tennon the second upright which carries the roof-tree. Give me an apse at both ends (for I think that is the simplest form of ground plan), a chancel at East end long enough for a choir, at least four steps higher than the nave and not more than twenty feet wide, and a baptistry at West end. You need not give us a tower or an organ chamber ; and one straight line for roof of nave and chancel will do. I want to build the chancel soon, perhaps next dry season ; but the School will have to come first I think. . . . And so farewell. Write often.

My letters are my friends out here.

Yours, etc.,
A. F. Sim.

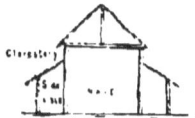 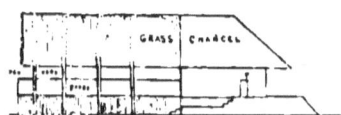

Kota Kota, *January* 11*th*, 1895.

My dear M——,

. . . I daresay I shall make a habit of enclosing other letters in yours, because if, as I have often done, I write eight or ten letters a fortnight, this comes to 5*s*. or 10*s*. a month ! And as the Mission pays for stamps perhaps one ought to have some consideration for their funds. . . .

The town is very quiet. Most people are away at their shambas hoeing. We have not had a great deal of rain yet. I thought it would have poured every day of the rainy season. One great difficulty in sowing here is that when the sun comes out after rain the ground gets baked at the top, and it takes a sturdy plant to push its way through such a hard crust. I planted many seeds which have not shown themselves, and I think they are done for. We are still fearing evil days from the locusts. I hear that at Fort Maguire the Administration are feeding the people ; still there may be other reasons for this. The war frightened all the people away, and as they are returning in considerable numbers now doubtless the food supply is scarce. . . .

For myself I am well, though I don't like to boast, for if I say I have not had any fever lately (which is the case), I am sure

N

to have an attack to-morrow. But I have had to have considerable recourse to chlorodyne of late ! The immortal jigger isn't
dead yet. I had one taken out of my foot yesterday. In the
meantime I am getting on with Swahili and beginning to think
of my course of preaching. My door and window frames are
rapidly approaching completion ; the kitchen, cook's house, etc.,
are in course of building. I might have been feeding on pine-
apples all this time but for the symptoms which I have mentioned
above. Dr. Prentice sent me a basketful, but I have had to give
most of them away.

I am writing to your nephew, E. B——. He seems very keen
to try this part of the country. Expense and time will be against
him. There is plenty of game. I don't hear of many lions,
though there must be plenty not far away. Mr. Nicholl has sent
out four parties of elephant hunters ; besides bringing ivory they
are to get a present for every young live wild animal they bring
in. So in a short time I may be having a lively time of it !
There isn't a chain in the place, let alone a cage ; I sincerely
hope they will not succeed in this latter scheme ! I had a present
sent me the other day of the side of a fine young hippopotamus.
I could not bring myself to eat it, but the natives about the place
disposed of it soon enough. Before I forget, let me say or suggest
a thing which has long been on my mind. I don't like to see the
Magazine cover without my name, as if I had entirely left the
Parish. Would it be ridiculous to put me down under C——'s
name as Missionary in Central Africa ? I daresay it is sentimental
and egotistical. However I throw it out as a suggestion of my
own wishes, for I don't feel at all as if I had cut all connection
with the Parish ; on the contrary, being far away seems to draw
me in spirit much nearer than ever.

January 16th.—The above matter I leave to you. If you think
it is a bit of sentimental nonsense don't say anything about it :
but if you think it will serve any good purpose by helping to
keep up people's interest in Foreign Missions—well and good.

Well, the day before yesterday the "*Domira*" returned, and to
my surprise brought back Mr. Nicholl, whom I didn't expect for
three weeks or more. Whenever he goes he leave matters more or
less in my hands. I have had to administer martial authority—
tying up a Sikh and two Makua soldiers for fighting. I have
passed a dhow through the customs' house and taken about £40 in

customs. I have also had to administer justice in another case. One man stole another man's wife and ten goats and four hoes, and tied him up ; so I got the man and made him restore all and. pay a fine ! I am so thankful Mr. Nicholl returned, for yesterday a Makua soldier was murdered in the town. The murderer has run away, as indeed we hear all the men in that part of the town have, so little do they know of our idea of justice. But the right man, who is well known and has a large following, will certainly be hanged. Well, I should not have liked all this business on my hands.

In the meantime Jumbe has been convicted of misrule and sent as a prisoner to Zanzibar—outlawed in fact. . . .

January 18*th.*—Poor William is suffering from a bad foot, very bad, and so the building suffers a little. I have sent three of my best men with the shooting party. I am expecting some of the blue-jackets up to tea this afternoon, and have had a big cake made specially for them. The murderer hasn't been caught yet. It is a good thing the gun-boats are in on the whole. They serve as a wholesome reminder to the youngsters who are mal-content. People wonder we haven't had our throats cut here ; we have no fort. Mr. Nicholl has just begun it. But it is really quite quiet and safe. Perhaps another man than Mr. Nicholl might have made a row. . . . The gunboat officers have gone off shooting for two or three days. There are only two out of four left. Poor Mackay, as I told you, was killed by a lion, and Captain Lyons died of fever. I do trust no accident will happen to these two. They are such nice fellows. I went on board the gunboats this morning to see the men ; they seem a really nice lot. I hope I shall be able to have Service with them on Sun-day. . . .

Later.—The German steamer brings news from Likoma of poor Butler's death on Tuesday. It is very sad—a few days' illness. But Dr. Robinson had told him he ought to go home, and he refused. He was, in his line, a most able and useful man— the schoolmaster at Likoma. All of them write under the sense of a great shock, poor Miss Palmer especially. Thinking he was much better they all went to bed leaving three native boys to watch him—young men rather than boys—and they came to say he had " finished to breathe." And so he died, as Pearson did, in his sleep. The houses at Likoma cannot altogether be blamed

for his death, as his house was mudded up to the very roof; it is
an unhealthy time of the year.

Well, dear boy, I wish I could tell you more of mission work
done. I can't say how much I long to get to it, and this waiting
time is very trying, not to my health but to myself internally.
I cannot think that I could possibly have begun any sooner. . . .
Of course if I had been at Likoma or even Unangu I should have
had something to do in the missionary line, but here all has had
to begin from the beginning. . . .

And now good-bye, with all affectionate remembrances to old
friends.

Yours, etc.,

A. F. SIM.

Kota Kota, *February 2nd,* 1895.

My DEAR ——,

At last you have got my letters from Likoma. It is a comfort to hear from you in answer to something I have written. I
always unconsciously find myself living in the time your letters are
dated. Thus I often have to remind myself that it is February '95,
and not November '94. . . .

I trust that for certain I shall get into my house next week.
What has delayed me now has been William's illness. I dared
not go in until my windows were in, and these have taken time
to make ; only William or I could make them, being out of the
ordinary native run. So I have been making window-frames,
mortising, and tennon-cutting. The shutters are made of those
chizuli palms I told you of split : they look like Venetian blinds !
Working with my sleeves turned up under the verandah (never in
the sun my arms where they were bare are quite red, as if sun-
burnt. The sun itself would have blistered them as it does my
hands. Sitting as I am now in the cool of the evening writing,
the perspiration is pouring off me !

One pound of saccharine ! It will last me till I die, if I live till I
am seventy! It must have cost a fortune ! Thanks very much indeed
for it. I wish salt and tobacco could be done up in the same way !
. . . Common delf teapots are 5*s.* each with them the African
Lakes' Co., 8*d.* at home. Sugar is 8*d.* a pound ; flour, 8*d.* ; tea,
1 *l.* at home, is 4*s.* 6*d.* here ; biscuits, 4*s.* 6*d.* a small tin.
Freight on goods is reckoned by measurement, *e.g.,* I got eighteen

bales of calico the other day, which weighed 1,087 pounds, but the Mission is charged for 43 ft. 6 in., £10 17s. 6d., at £10 a ton from Blantyre.

By the way, this calico is for buying rice here for Likoma and the East Coast stations, as they expect famine. We hear there is famine at the North end of the Lake owing to locusts, and the "*Domira*" has been here for the purpose of buying rice and maize for the starving folk. They have rather spoiled my market, as they have given twice as much as I am giving. I have more than three tons however, and strange to say, some people are so friendly that they preferred selling to us at two fathoms for 40 lbs. to getting four fathoms from the "*Domira*" people ! . . . I have built an excellent kitchen, but it isn't dry yet. The kitchen range consists of three stones, on which rests the pot or pots. The staple meat is fowl (not English, but African). Fowls cost about 3d. each, and really are not bad if killed twelve hours before eating. They are cooked in grease, which comes to us in tins, and is called "cooking-fat." . . . But really we live very well, and now I seldom open anything tinned. I have no great love for tinned things. Dr. Grey of the "*Pioneer*" says Atlay is in a bad way. Butler is dead as I told you. Corbett is at Matope with the "*Charles Janson*" repairing. Johnson and Glossop are on the mainland, travelling from village to village. So, besides the ladies, there is only Matthews to do everything at Likoma. I do hope I shall not be called away. And yet, with such an account from Likoma, perhaps I ought to be ready to go and offer to go. . . .

This place is like a pig-stye, and, tidy as you know me to be, I cannot keep my things at hand. There is fighting down the river, owing I fear to the white man's muddling. Some of the things one hears make one's blood boil, but that is not very frequent.

Remember me to all, . . .

Yours, etc.,

A. F. SIM.

Kota Kota, *February 10th*, 1895.

MY DEAR ——,

This is the first line I have written in my new house. It is the first Sunday I have spent in it, so that I take it as a good omen that it is Septuagesima, and I hope I am adding to these good auspices by writing my first letter to you. Altogether I am

full of thankfulness and very happy in my prospects. I don't
think I have any reason to regret the delay, though it has been a
longer one than I dreamt of. It is exactly five months and one
week since I set foot in this place, and to-day I have been preaching to my first heathen congregation in Swahili—with some difficulty I confess. But I had William, my excellent teacher, to
correct my deficiencies by translating into Chinyanja ; and often,
when I broke into English, he had to interpret. Still I was surprised at my " fluency," and henceforth, please God, I shall go
ahead with my learning of the language. We had a congregation
of about seventy—some Mahommedans, and a very few (about
eight) women. But I had not been able to go round at all to tell
the people to come. By next Sunday I hope to have my arrangements more complete. We had our preaching in the baraza, but
I think that soon we shall move to the shade under the big tree,
where we shall have more room. Our little Chapel is going to be
very nice. I am making the Altar of mud and stones, about 5 ft.
long by 2 ft. wide, and 3 ft. 4 in. high, with re-table and foot-pace
8 in. high. In front of the Altar I hope to be able to pick out a
Cross in the beautiful white quartz stones that lie about here. I
am so thankful for the gift of Vessels which the Parish made me,
and for the altar linen. .   .

It is very lovely here I think and there is plenty of life. Such
beautiful birds—brilliant red aurioles, yellow chaps with black
heads, bright green with long tails. little black and white wagtails,
so tame. which sing very like canaries, only softer. My furniture
is rough but effective ; most of it I made with my own hands. My
bookshelves are packing-cases ; one chair is an inverted box ; the
other was made at Likoma, but I think I prefer the box. My bed
is native made, and cost one rupee. My table, very fine, was made
at Likoma. Other tables, and a cupboard with doors, to keep my
jam and sugar in, are made by myself. This week I shall turn my
hand to other things, and in time I shall be most comfortable.
There is no cause to pity us out here, as far as " roughing it "
goes. I have experienced a little picnicing, but no really hard
times. It seems so strange often when telling the Story of our
Lord ; that for which martyrs laid down their lives among the
heathen one can tell without raising a murmur. I feel as if I ought
to expect stoning. I wonder how the Story strikes them. This
morning, what struck them most was that I said that the God of the

heathen and the Mahommedan and the Christian was one and the same God. They could not make it out, and asked many questions. . . .

It is a matter of doubt among us as to how we are to make Sunday and preaching hours known. A drum, a gun, a dinner bell, are all suggestions. I am thinking of a flagstaff with a particular flag for Sundays. These people, as you can imagine, have but vague ideas of time and days. We have, of course, from the first differentiated between Sundays and other days, and on Saturday those who work for me get a half-holiday, so some know when Sunday comes. Talking of a flagstaff, I am a little bit afraid of lightning here. The other day a pole in the fort was shivered to bits by lightning, not eighty yards from where Mr. Nicholl and I were sitting. Of course one's faith in God serves one in good stead at such times ; and few things give one such a sense of His providence and mercy I think as a thunderstorm. Both our houses, Mr. Nicholl's and mine, are on eminences, and are raised above the surrounding neighbourhood, and one would think that they would attract lightning. At the same time wet straw roofs cannot be good conductors. . . .

February 12*th.*—It is so nice being able to have prayers at regular times. My oratory will be finished by Sunday I hope. I am also making a little room where sick people can come and be treated. Such sores and ulcers—poor things, I wish I could do more for them ; but they are mostly of such long-standing, that even a doctor could not do anything more than dress them and make them keep the place clean. I am also making two rooms at the other end of my baraza, one for the Christian boys to use as a reading and lounging room, and the other a workshop. I don't know what magnificent impressions I may be conveying to you. These rooms are made in a day ; the walls are reeds tied with bark to upright trees and cross bamboos. They require no windows, for plenty of light leaks through the reeds. . . .

I have been opening some boxes, at last, for the first time. One box I opened, expecting to find some delights of my own, contained only shirts for Mr. Johnson. The tin box alone belonged to me ; anyhow it is an accession. This is the most disastrous climate for keeping anything ; everything spoils, even if some creature does not eat it. . . .

February 16*th.*—I have this week built a store-room, a surgery,

a pantry, and a fowl-house, besides a kitchen-range (of mud, of
course). I have also made two roads on the property, and done
countless little jobs. Let me admit that I could not do any of these
things without William, my teacher. He is invaluable to me. . . .
My establishment consists of a cook from Likoma and three
house boys. One of the last is a very smart and hardworking
little chap. It is wonderful how little they smash. The English
kitchen-maid is not in it with them. The cook and three boys do
all the house-work, including washing. We are innocent of an
iron, so it is not so bad as it might be ; and we have soap, but
no blue nor starch. Well, as I never wear a collar, nor a white
shirt, starch is not wanted ; but an iron I require for the Church
linen. . . .

Good-bye.   Pray for us.

Yours, etc.,

A. F. SIM.

Kota Kota, *February* 16*th*, 1895.

MY DEAR ——,

. . . I am in my new house now ; and though I have begun
regular heathen preaching, I have not begun any week-day work
yet, as there is so much necessary work still to be done. I am
pleased with the heathen preaching, which I hold in the baraza,
pleased with my efforts at Swahili, and pleased at the attendance,
seeing that it has not yet cost me any trouble to gather them
together. I trust I shall soon be able to get out on other days and
preach in the village. Yet I fear I shall only be half useful till I
know Chinyanja. I am so thankful to have got started with my
real work. And now the language will improve daily. I have got
beyond books, but I find that does not mean that one is able to
speak a language. . . .

None of the things you mention—needles, pins, saccharine, fish-
hooks—have reached me yet ; but that is not to be wondered at.
Many parcels and boxes which I have heard of have not reached
me—one of them posted from Algiers October 12th. . . .
What has kept me busy is the making of absolutely necessary
furniture, washhand-stand, cupboard, and five tables of a sort ; nothing except tin or iron can stand on the floor here, because of
the white ants.

I rejoice in having a few friends within two feet of my head as I write now—all in a wire frame. . . . I have unpacked my lantern and tried it : it is a huge success. I am really pleased with it. Of course I use oil, but I have never seen oil lanterns give such a good picture as this one does. . . .

We are having heavy rains now almost every day. The roof of my house is not water-tight, so I have to cover everything up when it rains. I imagine we have had a very dry wet season so far, though I believe other places have plenty of rain. We see but little of the locust now, so I hope our fears are groundless.

We are using our little Chapel regularly now, though the Altar, which is made of mud and stones, is not ready yet. I have had one night of fever since I came into this house. I think I am keeping very clear of it for this time of year.

And now, dear boy, I must close. . . . Remember me to everybody. . . .

Yours, etc.,

A. F. SIM.

P.S.—The "*Wissmann*" has brought my box, which I had lost. I am so glad. And now I feel happy once again ! It contains two volumes of *Pusey's Life*, *Browning*, 1st volume of *Edersheim*, and countless treasures ; but what have I done with *Hymns Ancient and Modern with Tunes?* I thought I had it in this box, but I haven't ; also your photo, rather damaged, but as large as life. I thought I had lost it. They have sent me a "Churchman's Almanac" for 1895. The "*Wissmann*" has also brought me some tobacco. We are having a grand thunderstorm at this minute. I expect I shall sit up most of the night. Mr. Williams is here on his way home. I will give him a line to you and to my brother. He is a rough old boy, but full of fun, and knows as much of the Mission as anybody. . . . He says that the four men now at Likoma, Messrs. Johnson, Glossop, Atlay, and Philipps will all have to go home soon on account of health. Mr. Williams has been out here seventeen years in the Mission.

A. F. S.

Kota Kota, *February 25th*, 1895.

MY DEAR M——,

. . . Another want of plan is having no dock at Likoma. It was intended that the "*Charles Janson*" should go down to Matope, where there is a dry dock, to repair. Now she is laid up she won't

be able to go I suppose.   We have engineers, and in Mr. Tulip
a first-class engineer.   The truth is I think that we are learning
by sad experience, that what sufficed for actual pioneers will not
suffice for a settled Mission, where work is of a completely
different nature, taxing people even more than the work of pioneers.
. . .

It is difficult to explain what the wet season means, how everything not hermetically sealed gets damp, and musty, and mouldy.
The atmosphere is full of moisture, and there is no keeping
it out. . . .

Three needles buy a fowl here !   There is a recognised parcel-
post here, and it is at least the speediest way of sending parcels,
though not the safest, perhaps, or least expensive.   It would be
well to insure parcels, if you can. . . .

Mr. Nicholl's house is very fine, with its glass windows and
Zanzibari doors, carved roughly, but effectively, on a site of my
choosing.   It stands in a commanding position and looks very
well.   He has made the same mistake as I have—that of opening
both his doors into the dining-room.   I shall know better another
time.   I wish I could keep up my correspondence as I should like,
but I have so many letters that I can't answer them all.   You
must ask people to be patient with me, and sometimes to be
content with a message through you. . . .

Alas !   the photos I took the other day are all spoiled by cockroaches (or rats).   They have taken a fancy to the gelatine, and
eaten great bits of it off while they were drying.   Isn't this a
nuisance ?   How careful one has to be out here ; rats, cockroaches,
white ants, damp, heat, sun, rain, shade are all dangers ; everything is so extravagant and excessive !   We hear lions at night
now, or did a few nights ago, and of course hyænas and jackals.

Such thunder and lightning as we have !   It is awful ; I think I
told you how one day up at the "Boma," or fort, a pole, seventy or
eighty yards from the house in which Mr. Nicholl and I were
sitting, was splintered. . . .

I rejoice to hear of the condition of the Band of Hope and the
Guilds, especially of the Boys' Guild.   I hope they will continue to
do good service for the Church. . . .

March 16th.—We have begun school.   It began with about fifty
boys and girls, and now is about one hundred strong.   This is
of course only in one part of this big town, and during the wet

season, when most of the people are out in their gardens. The school is pretty informal, and will continue to be so as long as the children know nothing at all. Then it will be a problem how to differentiate them. We have also a flourishing Night School—about twenty-two men, including three petty chiefs. This I have great hopes of. I have written to Likoma for another teacher, who I hope may come by this steamer. I am building a shelter for the preachings, but I have had trouble to get it straight. It is on the site of our Church (I hope), and so I want to get it at its best. I have left room at the East end for a chancel, which will be the beginning of the Church, and may be begun next dry season. I am very pleased with the school ; no doubt of the present number many will be weeded out. They only come from the immediate neighbourhood, and that with very little canvassing, and no coaxing or bribe. We are allowed to bribe the children with the promise of kisibaus ; but I don't intend to mention this unless it becomes necessary. As soon as I can I shall begin to build a separate School. I feel, or begin to feel, my position here perfectly secure. People I think see that I don't tax them, that I have nothing for them but friendship and help, nor anything to do with the Government. I am so thankful that the times of waiting and delay are over ; and now, please God, we shall begin to see progress.

Early this morning I was awakened by the howl, or bark, or whatever it is pleased to be called, of a hyæna ; it seemed just under my window—such a fiendish noise. Yesterday a large cobra was killed by one of the boys, near William's house ; such an evil-looking beast, with a very pretty skin—the first I have seen in Africa. I have at present a great pet in a "dear gazelle." It is thriving splendidly, and now holds the kitten at defiance. Wallace, my cook, killed a puff-adder the other day near the house ; such a brute to look at.

March 17th.—The "*Wissmann*" is in. Mr. Nicholl and I dined on board, and met Baron von Elz, the Governor in German Nyasaland, on his way home ; a nice fellow, rough, but kind I should say. He is taking a little freed slave boy home with him to educate with his brother, who is a minister of some sort. . . .

I am well, and fit, and happy. Do not fidget about me. . . . Good-night. Remembrances and love to all.

Yours, etc.,

A. F. SIM.

Letter to J. B——, dated,—

Kota Kota, *March 1st*, 1894.

MY DEAR ——,

. . . I find Lent rather a hardship here I confess, as we have so little variety. Fortunately it comes in the fruit season. How can one preach to these people about fasting, when they never seem to do anything else? . . . All the headmen promise to send their children to my School. This is *Rammathani* and there are plenty of so-called Mahommedans here, but very few fast strictly. How easy it is to get out of their method of fasting, though it sounds so strict ; and how hard to get out of our Lord's injunctions on fasting ! . . .

You would laugh at my window-frames, as there is not a straight line in them. How this unseasoned wood warps ! Some of them I have made myself. I have made a mistake with the entrance, as both doors, back and front, open into the sitting-room. They ought to be separated . . . Then I have been busy with my road-making, and very successful it is I think. My plan has been to concentrate the roads upon the Church, the site of which I have already chosen. . . .

I am thankful to say we have no burning now, and even trial for witchcraft by poison has ceased. Of course it is forbidden, but there was one case of it since Mr. Nicholl came. The wretched man died, and was dragged round the village by his feet, and then out of it a little way, where he was left for the crows to pick. There was a skull and some bones lying just below my house when I came, which were the remains of a man who had been killed by the poison ordeal and left to rot. Mahommedanism does nothing to stop this or any heathen custom. In fact here the Mahommedans know nothing of their faith, only they are circumcised and taught a few prayers, or rather expressions such as " God is great," and " Mahommed is His Prophet," and that is all.

On the whole I see a good deal of European society, for the steamers all put in here except the " *Charles Janson*," and the officers and what passengers there are come ashore. There are six steamers on the Lake, counting the " *Charles Janson* " and the two gun-boats. . . .

Poor Longhill ! How often I think of those people ! I should like to hear that a little Mission-room was going to be opened up

there, so few of the people ever come to Church. . . . I must
stop, as I have fifteen letters to go by this mail. Keep your heart
up, and pray for us.

Yours, etc.,

A. F. SIM.

Kota Kota, *March* 3*rd*, 1895.
MY DEAR ——,

I cannot tell how touched I am by my letters from home this
last mail. What have I done to deserve such kindness and sympathy? Nothing; it is God's goodness, whose goodness is again
reflected in your hearts. I do hope that by this time you have
grown accustomed to my fevers. I will try and get William to
"shoot" me with my camera, and then you will see that I am not
much pulled down. I wish I had said nothing about them, and in
future I shall be more guarded. . . .

The "*Charles Janson*" and Matope are to blame for our lack of
stores—the "*Charles Janson*" because she is often *hors de combat*,
Matope because it is so far away. Then the mission boat, "*Sherriff*,"
manned by mission boys, brings our stores up, consequently our
stores accumulate at Matope, and Likoma lacks. . . .

My fevers are frequent but slight. Do not please be anxious.
I am in God's hands, and if I were not prepared for this, I ought
not to have come. Besides, what if it be His will to take me?
Am I to grumble, or to shirk His call? Mr. Nicholl does not often
get fever, but he has been laid up ever so much more than I
have. He is laid up now by a fall from his donkey, and he must
have nearly broken a rib, as he was in the greatest pain. . . .

Likoma is seventy miles, or eight hours, from here by steamer,
and I hear from them only once a month, so I might easily be in
my grave before help could come down from Likoma. There are
just two ladies at Likoma, and their hands are as full as they can
hold. No, indeed, I never forget the *Eucharistiá conjuncti* . . .

I have rigged up a cosy little nook for my "study," with a screen
made of calico and a window blind. One is so public here, and
the many doors and windows make one's room almost like the
open air. Here people have to look for me almost. If I have to
build another house for a European, I shall make the entrance
different. . . .

Some people are very shy about coming to the preaching,

especially the women. These people are not at all to be judged by other African races, such as the Zulus, Matabele, etc., as they are very wanting in manly qualities. There is no "*fight*" in them, and I do not find any keenness to hear about religious matters. Yet how soon for me to form a judgment! But I think this is at the bottom of all their faults—a nerveless acceptance of what they are taught. The Nyasa tribes are industrious, not enterprising, nor great drinkers. I imagine our true hope lies in the Yaos, on the East side of the Lake, the most unpleasant people possible. They drink, they slave deal, and do all sorts of abominations, but they are of independent spirit, and the British Administration know this to their cost. They alone of these tribes give any trouble. . . .

I have a lot of my old friends upon my walls now—the choir, and other groups. I count no less than forty-two separate photos on my left hand about the level of my head, just by me as I write. It is so nice looking at one's friends even in photos. . . .

March 17th.—The School numbers a few short of one hundred, and the Night School twenty-two, including three petty chiefs. I am very thankful, and I praise God for this beginning ; but it is only the beginning. When it comes to discipline, the real tax begins. . . .

> Yours, etc.,
>
> A. F. SIM.

Letter to E. L——, dated,—

> Kota Kota, *March 7th*, 1895.

MY DEAR ——,

. . . What a "grind" a new language is! It is so different from our modes of expression. I seem to have got to a certain point in speaking and understanding Swahili, and to stick there. Six months I have been here, and one could learn French by staying six months in France. I think I am too shy to try my hand at chattering with every Tom, Dick, and Harry about the place. It is a difficult language to understand, because the accent is so frequently changed in conversation, and words assume a different aspect altogether, although one knows them in their simple garb. . . .

Alas ! gardening is rather heart-breaking work ; what with a vertical sun during the day, and deluges at night, which wash whole beds away, while the sun bakes like a brick the surface of those which escape the rain. It will come to growing the best native things I expect. I am having shades made for some of my beds. Some flowers however grow — zineas, sunflowers, and stocks. I have other plants (*e.g.*, roses), but I cannot say much about them. Tomatoes do very well, and there are many native things which do well also. English potatoes I find only a middling success. I have a lot of land, and I hope to be able to grow enough for Likoma some day.

It is wonderful how cheap living is in Africa (except tinned things, of which I use as little as I can). I am spending two trusses of calico (equal to £8), and a few beads and some salt a month, and employing fifty men all the time at my building. The only trees a native ever plants are around graves here; though in this particular place the Swahili element has made itself felt by planting many different kinds of fruit trees—mango, cocoanut, custard apple, lime, lemon, etc. I am trying to increase their number, so in twenty years time some one may see my seedlings big trees . . .

I must have exaggerated my difficulties terribly. In pioneer work one has to take one's chance. What if Jumbe had carried out his scheme of cutting our throats ?—you could not have blamed any one. I came prepared for these things, or I should have stayed with my old St. Aidanites. . . .

People of a rather luxurious turn say that glass windows are necessary ; but without going that length I think something fairly air-tight is needful, not so much during the hot season, as now during the wet.

I have a most comical couple of pets—a kitten and a young gazelle. They play together in the most ludicrous fashion. The gazelle can hold its own, but it generally ends up by butting the kitten vigor ously. It is about nine inches high. I have made a bottle to feed it out of—a spare ink-filler used for fountain pens. It sucks grandly, and nearly bursts with milk. We have been troubled with ants in this house. The white ant one has to take as an accepted fact. The walls are already full of them. I can't leave anything softer than tin on the floor. Even our mud and stone Altar in the oratory is full of them, although it has only been finished about ten

days ; and the thatched roof is full of them too. They drop down
in showers at times, upon one's head, down one's back, into one's
cup or plate. They do not bite, and they always work under cover.
They build a mud tunnel as they go along. I have seen it in print
that one queen is responsible for thirteen million ants. Their
nests are under ground, and are divided into cells half the size of a
cricket ball. Each of these cells is filled with a sponge-like formation, which is alive with wee white ants. The only way to destroy
these pests is to get the queen, which is about three inches long ;
but they secrete her down in the earth, so that she is difficult to
find. But there is a more formidable ant, called in Swahili *siáfu*.
It is a brown colour, and millions of them issue forth on the war-
path like a black rope. They killed two of my pigeons, and several
chickens. It is very hard to get rid of them, or to get them to go
another way. They bite like fun, and if you put your foot in their
line of route for a second you find yourself covered with them, and
then it is necessary to change every particle of clothing. Cockroaches and rats too are a great nuisance. I think Africa must be
the natural home of the cockroach. . . .

Pray for me, for it is a big undertaking for such as I am. God
keep me faithful to it !

Yours, etc.,

A. F. SIM.

Kota Kota, *March* 10th, 1895.

MY DEAR ——,

. . . I have hopes of growing some big trees, *e.g.*, blue gums and
Lawsonian pines. Pride of India is successful, and I have planted
about eight of them, also three cocoa-nuts, four mangoes, and
some bananas. The latter is very plentiful in the town, and there
is one mango tree which does not bear, and ten or twenty cocoa-
nut trees, the fruit of which I sometimes taste. I have sown a
peach stone and two sweet almonds for posterity, but some grena-
dilla seeds and Cape gooseberries which I planted three weeks
ago are showing above ground. Several months ago I was given
four seeds which were labelled "English melons," but the only
thing that came of them was a good old vegetable marrow. We
have plenty of maize and rice. I often have "muckacholem," but
I have no butter to make it palatable as I remember it. I have

some English potatoes doing fairly well. I tasted a few the other day, but I shall keep the rest for sowing again next year. . . .

We have a third Englishman here now, a man who was in the Matabele war, and an ex-sergeant in the army. He is digging for gold, and seems quite hopeful. There is however no gold visible yet.

The other day I had the honour of being shown the dead Jumbe's grave. He is buried in the inner room of one of his houses. Hanging in the baraza is the heart and some of the internals of an old enemy of his, who was killed in a fight eighteen months ago about four miles from here. The old house is just as it was, and will be until it falls to pieces. It is the only tomb, and the grave is as it was when it had been filled in. The heart must have been dried in the sun, as it is shrivelled up to about the size of a small apple. There are also bits of cloth hanging in the baraza as offerings to the spirit of the dead. I was very much surprised at being allowed to see it ; but I was with the sheik, so I suppose it is all right. . . .

There are a few sheep here, such funny-looking creatures, brown or black, with no wool and fat tails. They have no fat anywhere else, and don't taste much like mutton. But if you can get them tender they are a change from fowl. I use the fat of the tail for cooking and it lasts a long time. . . . Farewell.

Yours, etc.,
A. F. SIM.

Letter to R. E. P——, dated,—

Kota Kota, *March 25th,* 1895.

MY DEAR ——,

. . . I am full of hope for this station, and yet what purging must take place if it is to become wholly Christian ! The big chief here is said to have a hundred wives, and vice and slavery are upheld by Mahommedanism. One indeed feels helpless when one thinks what conversion means to these people. God only can do it. What wonder that slaves and the poor are, and ever were, the first converts to Christianity ; they have less temptation to the villainous lives of their superiors. We have a good, regular attendance at the preachings of men who for the most part work with us during the week, for we always send the lazy good-for-nothings about their business. We teach a catechism to both young and adults during the week. Of course they learn it much like parrots ; but it means that in coming to us they throw their lot in with us, and understand that we teach them our religion, as well as to read and write.

To-day, or rather to-night, ends *Rammathani*, the fast month of the Mahommedans, during which they are supposed to eat nothing between sunrise and sunset. So they are making a night of it, and guns are going off in all directions (old flint-locks and cap-guns, loaded up to the muzzle, and making a report like a cannon). We have so many coming with gun accidents to be healed with vaseline and iodoform, and we have made some wonderful cures. . . .

We have lost two of our staff since the Archdeacon went home— Butler, a first-rate schoolmaster, and Tulip, a dear old North Country man, who won my heart at once by his North Country dialect and manners, and who was a first-class engineer. However other places and other people suffer, or have suffered, as much as we have. The gunboats have lost three or four men since I came, and they invalid men very readily. Traders suffer too. The Bandawe and Blantyre people do not suffer much, as they take such good care of themselves with brick houses with glass windows, etc. . . .

I have just had a narrow escape from a scorpion : when sorting the wood on my fire I moved a bit of wood he was hiding in, and just missed catching hold of him. I had the pleasure of seeing him scorch himself. There are many of them here, and I kill a great many, but I am thankful I have not been stung yet. . . .

I have a fire lighted every night to clear out the mosquitoes (but they seem to get used to it) and for dryness. Everything gets wet and mildewed in the rainy season. . . .

With love and prayers,

Yours, etc.,

A. F. SIM.

Kota Kota, *March* 31st, 1895.

MY DEAR ——,

I more nearly cried than laughed when I read my last month's mail ; there were eighteen letters and as many papers. . . . I am looking at things rather gloomily to-day with just a little fever and a smaller congregation than usual at the Sunday preaching, but I have no reason for misgivings yet. The hearers meet nightly, and do some "A B C," and then a Scripture lesson. I find some American pictures on the early life of our Lord most useful. These fellows say, "Now our eyes are open." Poor chaps ! I think it will take some time to open them thoroughly. I wish more women would come ; they are shy and timid about facing a lot of men. One old lady who came to us months ago is very faithful, and now we employ her for carrying water.

I have been busy this week sowing English seed as the rains are nearly over and the cold weather is coming in ; but what with goats that will get loose, and fowls that are never tied up, I am in a despairing mood. I have had my little forest cleared, and it reveals what looks like excellent soil. It is so pretty over the Lake now-a-days.

I am rejoiced really by my letters from home to find that nothing is going back, but all going forward. I do not think my coming out has been in vain in that sense. But as for work here, no doubt the prospects are good, but oh ! the patience and the long, long waiting it will require ! Mr. Johnson writes from Mluluka, on the opposite shore, and paints a weird picture of the slave trade and the immorality of these half Mahommedan coastmen. As long as he is here (the coastman) slaving will go on, whether we know it or not. He cannot exist here without it. On Friday a fellow came here with rather a weird history. It was the first day of the new moon after *Kammathani*, and the row—drumming, gunfiring, dancing, and shouting—was all day and night in one's ears. This fellow was bleeding profusely and half blinded, led by three others, injured from what I immediately put down to a gun explosion, which, as they load these old " Brown-besses " up to the muzzle, is not an infrequent occurrence. But it was not so in this case. The man had been deliberately shot with intent to kill ; the gun fired was loaded with sand and gunpowder mixed ! Sand here is as coarse as buck-shot. You remember the murders for which Jumbe was outlawed. This man was the actual executioner, and has now to bear all the evil will of people who think Jumbe's departure a misfortune. And the man who fired the gun at him is a particular pal of mine ; in fact because he married the dead Jumbe's wife he is a big man now, and the chief of the part of the village in which the station is situated. It is an example of the dreadful cruelty of

these folk, and then they took it so calmly and as a matter of fact.
I could have sent them all off to the magistrate, but I should spoil
my influence if I meddled with these matters. Instead I hope to
get this wretched murderer to my class, and teach him a different
spirit.

I am minus a cook these days, but I have a trustworthy heathen
who has been with us a long time, and with the excellent William's
help he does very well. To-night, being Sunday, I am going to
dine with Mr. Nicholl. It is almost a charity to do so, as he has
been, and is still, very seedy, and feels his loneliness much more
than I do. . . .

April 1st.—It is pouring with rain to-day, and after a few days'
drought it is very welcome, especially as I have just put in a lot of
English seed. I am quite the landscape gardener these days,
arranging the estate, planting trees, and looking forward into the
distant future and thinking where different houses shall stand !
. . .

Love to all.

Yours, etc.,

A. F. SIM.

Kota Kota, *April 1st, 1895.*

MY DEAR BOYS AND GIRLS,—

. . . To-day while you are all making "April fools" of
each other I am sitting indoors, and outside it is pouring "cats
and dogs." So there is no work doing and no school, because
of the pouring rain. How the time does fly out here ! Since
writing my last letter to you I have had answers to it. I did not
intend keeping you waiting so long for another letter ; and if I have
time I intend writing another letter to the "*Mail,*" though I quite
forget what I wrote about last time. Well, now all my troubles are
over I think, and I have a big house—not a hut any longer—to live
in, and a solid grass roof over my head, and walls made of mud,
and trees all round me. . . .

The kitchen and boys' bedroom are about twenty yards from the
house on the South side. The class-room I meant to be a dispen-
sary, but now that I have such a big school I have to use it for a
class-room for those boys who are beginning to write. The store-
room of course is necessary to keep my European stores in—
flour, sugar, soap, etc. The pantry ! well, it's nothing to boast of,

but the boys wash the dishes there, that's why I call it a pantry !
As I have so few dishes the same plates are used for each course,
and so the washing up is an important function.   The carpenter's

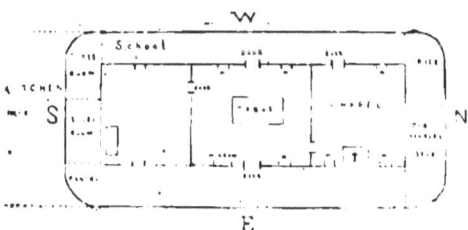

shop is not much to boast of either, but I have made a bench
three feet high and two feet six inches broad, with legs of small
trees and top of packing-cases.   My tools were all given me, when
I left England, by a friend.   They have been useful I can tell you.
Now we are making chairs like this—

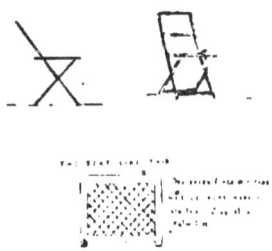

The cross lines are rope—native rope made of the plaited leaves of
a palm tree. So now we need not use empty boxes any more ! You
don't know how comfortable these chairs are !   I am surprised how
fond these children are of coming to school.   It is a good thing,
because we have no " kid-catcher " to get them to come, unless the
football is a " kid-catcher " : but they seem as fond of school as of
football, and some of them have been very quick to learn their
alphabet. A fortnight taught it to six of them, both big letters
and small, and now about fifteen are using slates. A few girls
come, poor little things, but they are not so quick as the boys.

William drills the boys after school, but such stupids they are, they can't number more than five, and none of them know their right hand from their left. Well, all this has to be taught them. Then we teach them Scripture with the help of pictures and a catechism, which they learn very quickly, but like parrots. Anyhow it is the best way to teach them, for one can use the catechism as a text ; it begins, " Who made you ?" "*Nani aliye kuremba ?* " I hope they repeat these things when they go home, it will perhaps rouse people's interest in our teaching. We have had no one wanting to cut our throats lately, and I think we are fairly settled down. Mr. Nicholl is in his house, which is much like mine, only he has glass windows ; but I like my place much better than his—it is so much prettier. His place is three quarters of a mile from mine, so I don't see him very often, and, poor man, he is not very well now. He never has fever, but he has boils and sores, which come from the same source, malarial poisoning, which is the long name they give it. He has much more sickness than I have, although I do get fever sometimes. You will like to hear that I have had no more jiggers in my toes to speak of— one now and then does not do much harm—though the natives who go about with bare feet get them still. We have heard lions roaring now and then these nights, but they have not been nearer than four miles. Hyænas come about us every night, and the other day the boys had a great hunt for a civet cat, which had been making ravages among the fowls in the long grass, which is ten feet high or more, in front of my house. I am cutting this down now, and it will make grand slates for my preaching house : besides it hid a beautiful view of the Lake. We have been planting a good many seeds lately—English seeds—but I am afraid to expect very much of them : radishes, turnips, beans, peas, cauliflower, and cabbage. I have more hope of the native things—sweet potatoes, and so on.

I got such a bit of good news from a friend in London. At one of the big Churches there they have given me £25 to spend just as I like. It is so nice being poor, one can relish this gift so much more ! What shall I do with it I wonder. I think you would probably recommend me to buy an ice machine ! But I think a flying machine would be better, one that will go a hundred miles an hour.

Now the rain has stopped, and the boys have got out the football. It seems so funny to be writing to you and watching these little almost naked black boys playing football with their bare toes.

We have over a hundred children, boys and girls (about ninety boys), in school now. Very soon I shall begin to build a School. The baraza is mud of course, like all our floors, and these scraps sit on the floor and sing out their Ay, Bay, Chey, until they learn it, just like the Infant school at home, and the big men do the same at night. The Scripture lessons fill them with wonder, but I don't think they understand them, although the men say " Now our eyes are open !"

The poor steamer, " *Charles Janson,*" is laid up. She wants something done to her plates and engines. Old as she is, she is still the fastest and best weather boat on the Lake, but she is a little too small ; sometimes the water washes right over her and floods the cabin. The Lake is very stormy. The other day I saw a splendid waterspout from here, towering high up into the clouds, and felt glad I was not too close to it. . . .

Very soon now it will be Easter, and then I shall wish I was with you. These Festivals are rather lonely when there are only three of you to keep them. Just William and his wife and two wee children and I are the Christian congregation here. It will be too late to wish you a happy Easter, but I shall remember you and pray for you. May it be a very happy time to you all ! When I see the state of these people, the promises of Easter—the Resurrection from death, the power of the Holy Ghost—bring me new courage and hope. I can do nothing with them, but God, Who raised Jesus from the dead, can ; and He has said " Lo ! I am with you always."

April 17*th.*—And now Easter is past, and still the steamer has not come, though she was due last week. It is blowing half a gale, and the Lake is very stormy, so that I can see white waves a long way out ; perhaps the wind has delayed her. I am glad she did not come in on Good Friday ; it would have been very awkward. Well, we spent Easter very happily ; there were just three of us, including myself, at our Easter Communion : the Chapel was as bright as we could make it with such flowers as we could get 'but it's such a disappointing place for flowers) ; the mud Altar was covered with a white linen frontal, which the ladies at Likoma had made us, and we had the old Easter promises and old Easter tunes but such strange, unfamiliar words'. It all made me think

very much of the old place, and I think I lived over again some
of the dear old Easter days I remember in the old times, when
we were beginning to think of summer, and I could not help
hoping you were all as happy as you could be.

On Easter Monday and Tuesday we had games—on Monday for
the men, and on Tuesday for the schoolboys and girls—races, long
jump, wide jump, egg-and-spoon races, with limes for eggs, and
three-legged races ; needles, and thread, and blue calico, and fish-
hooks for prizes. So I tried to make it like old days in Mr.
L.——'s field ! And the children were just as noisy and crowded
round one just as you used to do long ago, just as keen, and
the little tots as funny as ever, but the girls very quiet (a little
difference here, I think !). None of them had ever run a race
or jumped either high or wide before, and some of their efforts
were very funny. I think the thing they liked best was the Tug-
of-War. They pulled right well, with no jerking or tumbling. So
you see we tried to think of old times, and do as we used to do
then. It was something like, but so different. We tried however
to make these poor little heathen boys and girls share in our
Easter joy, of which they know so little yet. Then on Easter
Monday we had a feast for the workmen, some of whom have
worked here since I began in November. It is not necessary to
tell them to bring their own pots ! They sit in groups round a
pile of rice and meat, and help themselves with their fingers.
Sometimes the rice was on a big dish or tray, but sometimes on a
mat only. . . .

. . . Now I must say good-bye again. I hope you will have
a bright, warm summer, and lots of picnics and heaps of fun. I
wish I could send you some of our sunshine in exchange for a
little of your rain.

Ever your affectionate friend,

ARTHUR F. SIM.

Letter to Miss F——, dated,—

Kota Kota, *April 6th*, 1895.

MY DEAR ——,

At last the parcel has come—biscuits, sweets, and above
all a piece of Mrs. H——'s wedding cake. I can assure you I ate
to her health and prosperity. I enjoy the lemon drops, and so do
my boys the latter very often on the sly I think. Anything they

fancy particularly goes with wonderful rapidity. I am really puzzled how to grapple with this difficulty. . . .

I fancy mineral discoveries will bring a host of unwelcome visitors here. The Swahili haven't machinery nor capital nor enterprise. They will die out and so will the slave trade, for with the opening of such industries all who haven't the above will have to tuck up their sleeves or go to the wall, and I don't think I see these fellows working. We have had a man here, a wretched fellow, who tried to find gold, but I don't think he succeeded though he professed to be highly satisfied. I suppose one ought to be glad to see the country develop, even if it means a swarm of gold-diggers. I wonder what your white ant was—it certainly isn't the white ant we suffer from if grease would stop its encroachments. I wonder how many tons I should require for this house alone ! No, our ant is a builder and never works, except under galleries of mud. It climbs to the roof, working its way up with extraordinary rapidity inside the mud walls ; but once it faces the open it begins its tunnels of mud. Each ant brings its load and puts it on and plasters it down and makes it even. Under cover of this out-work it eats its way through everything softer than iron, tin, or stone. It not only is in the mud walls of my house, but also in the floor, so that a wooden box placed on the floor falls a prey to it—baskets, mats, etc., have to be moved every day. There is no remedy, one must grin and bear it ! Only one has to take precautions and raise anything that isn't tin off the floor. I have given up the use of mats altogether. Of course tables, chairs, etc., which have legs are safe enough, because there one can see the tunnel being made and can destroy it from time to time, and besides such things are always being moved. How many changes there have been among the Clergy in the North ! These seem to come at intervals, and when they come they come with a rush : five Clergy have moved from West Hartlepool since I left. I shall scarcely know the place, if (or when) I return. The school children are tremendously keen. They come at all hours to the place where the alphabet is hanging in the baraza, and go through their paces : it is a perfect delight to them to get a boy who knows his alphabet to teach those who don't. About twenty know their letters, big and small, and are now advanced to slates and syllables. Isn't this rather quick ? This is the end of the fourth week, and I think nearly all of them can go through their alphabet with only

one or two mistakes.   The preaching is a great problem to me.
One can only lay before them the life of our Lord ; that is I think
what St. Paul did mainly ; let it tell its own story—so strange to
these folk who have no ideal beyond the satisfying of self.   I don't ·
think it ever can have happened among them that one man should
have laid down his life for another.   They have no literature of
course, and their oral tales are only a kind of "Uncle Remus"
jumble.   Well, it's all very interesting, but oh, what patience one
will require ! a long, long waiting time I expect, and even then ?

Yours, etc.,

A. F. SIM.

Kota Kota, *April 8th*, 1895.

MY DEAR ——,

. . . The number of children in the School is rather more
than we can manage, because some are outpacing others and we
ought to divide them up into classes.   William is an excellent
teacher, and I think he really enjoys teaching.   The children make
a huge row chanting their letters and syllables, and take a great delight in it.   Then too our little band of twenty hearers, grown men,
are a source of delight.   All the children are drawn from the poorer
inhabitants of the town, and strangely too most of them are without parents – these have died or been killed.   We could form an
orphanage here for little castaways, whose people do not care two-
pence about them.   Now we have just about finished the *Kibanda*
for preaching, and we are making plans for building a School : so
in time we shall be preparing to receive boarders.   I have a freed
slave boy in my household now.   He ran away from his master,
Selim bin Nassur, who crossed the Lake last week, having been in
the town for nearly a year.   Is it not strange that all his people
have already passed before the magistrate once and declared that
they were not slaves, and that they wanted to go to the coast ?
Now only this last week a hundred and twenty of these very same
men sought their liberty from Mr. Nicholl.   It is a great social
problem.   Hundreds, almost thousands, have passed before Mr.
Nicholl and have, without exception, declared that they were not
slaves : and yet I have no doubt that they were slaves all the time.
Perhaps as they gain confidence more will claim their freedom.

. . .

I am reading "*The Guided Life*" this Holy Week.   It is just what Canon Body is constantly preaching, and I have presumed to preach it too from notes which I have from time to time taken from his lips. It is so true that the gist of Christianity is union with the Person of Jesus by the indwelling Spirit. How patient and loving that guidance is we know, who, like obstinate children, will not submit to it. What is more the guidance is not wanting *altogether* in any of God's children, even in the heathen, though it shines dimly, very dimly in them. . . .

Have I told you of Mr. Tulip's death? It is strange what a number of deaths and invalids we have had at Likoma in a year— Mr. Pearson, Mr. Cowey, Mr. Butler, Mr. Tulip—but I do not think that this is much more than our share if we take the average for eighteen months. But if the number of those invalided home is taken into consideration, I fear it is more than our share. I took a great fancy to Mr. Tulip from the moment I saw him. He was about fifty years of age, with all the bluntness and straightness of a North countryman—the sort of thing one gets to love in them. He was a very clever engineer I believe. They are very shorthanded at Likoma now, and to add to their troubles the "*Charles Janson*" is laid up, and requires extensive repairs. I sometimes rather dread my letters from Likoma, lest I should hear of some new illness or another death. . . .

How things grow in this rainy season! Kaffir corn grows to twelve or fifteen feet high, and grass almost as high. I often think where this and that house is to be built when the work extends, and when perhaps I may have a white companion. I have quite settled on the site for the Girls' School, and all the different houses are already situated in my mind's eye. In the meantime I wish I could get on faster with the languages. It is a very different thing knowing it from books, and talking a language freely and readily as I want to. . . .

It is very nice and of course an enormous help that these people should be so keen on getting on. I confess to get a little tired of an everlasting "A B C" going on close to my head.

Our Scripture teaching is chiefly done by catechism. I hope and pray that their knowledge will be something more than a head knowledge. But the catechism is most useful, and each answer is of course a text to hang a lot of teaching on. It begins :—" Who made you?" and follows much the same line as "*A first Catechism for Children of the Church.*"

Our poor old men complain that all the things they have to do
on the slates are alike, and when they look at them for a long time
they all get mixed up. Isn't this natural? They have no idea of
the difference between a straight line and a curve, as is demon-
strated sadly in my palings and ditches and beds for seeds.

To-day I had given me eight tiny seedlings of the date palm.
How I do hope they will grow and flourish! I see nothing of the
three cocoanuts I planted, nor anything of the mangoes. It is a
case for patience I am afraid. . . .

April 18*th.*—I fear my letters will be very irregular in reaching
you these days; but be sure of this, you will hear of my death by
telegram long before my letters cease to come in, so don't imagine
I am ill or anything like that. . . . The mail always makes me
feel a brute, as I get so much more thought and kindness than I
deserve. . . . Mr. Glossop is here on his way to Unangu, and
Dr. Hine is going to Likoma, as they must have a doctor there
these trying months. . . . I don't forget the dear old place. I
wonder and am amazed that God has been so good to me as to fill
my heart with such affection and love. It is the brightest possession a man can have. . . .

Yours, etc.,

A. F. SIM.

Tuesday in Holy Week. *April* 9*th,* 1895.

MY DEAR ——,

. . . I am thinking a great deal of you this Holy Week.
May your Easter be a very blessed and happy one! We number
three, myself included: but "Where two or three are gathered together"—and here the promise holds as well as at home. What a
contrast—our little Chapel, mud Altar, and congregation of three—
with St. Aidan's, say, on Easter Day. Try and imagine our Good-
Friday Lantern Service! How useful the Lantern is going to be!
I could well have spent the £25 on lantern slides, but I think the
other things I want more, and after all I have two hundred slides
which I have by no means exhausted yet. . . .

I have begun another letter to the "*Mail.*" Do you think they
do any good? I know my first was very uninteresting: but I
think a letter from here might be more interesting describing some
of the social problems, slavery, etc. . . .

I am getting rather a dab at slaying mosquitoes, however it

makes no decrease in their numbers. Rats and mosquitoes, scorpions and the boring beetle are my nightly companions. I think the rats are the worst, for they go on all night, climb my mosquito curtain, rampage round the roof-beams, and make such a row that often I wake with a start thinking that the house is coming down, or that a thief is in (for I have no locks to my doors). . . .

The implements and materials we have tax one's ingenuity I can assure you, and the number of patents we have invented would do credit to Maxim. . . .

How I would like a run on the bicycle with Mr. L—— again to Saltburn and back once more ! How I did enjoy that run ! That sort of thing, so different from anything here, is a bright spot in my memory—the vigour one felt, the green hedges and fields, and the big trees—shall I ever experience it again? Here in the dry season the place is like a barren desert, and in the rainy season the country is impassable. I want to go to see Bua, a place twelve or sixteen miles from here, and as Mr. Nicholl talks of going over in the dhow I shall go with him. It is in my parish, but the road to it is well nigh impassable. . . .

I am very well.

Yours, etc.,

A. F. SIM.

Letter to E. L——, dated,—

Kota Kota, *Easter Day, April 14th*, 1895.

MY DEAR ——,

I must write to you to-day to say how much you have been in my thoughts and prayers. I could not help feeling the contrast a little bit between this Easter Day and last. Three of us in our little Chapel made our Easter Communion together with the countless millions of the whole Catholic Church, and we tried to add our little strain of joy and praise to that mighty harmony that throughout the world ascends to the throne of God. We tried to make the Chapel as bright as the wild flowers and zineas of my own growing would permit. . . .

And we were happy. Who can help it with the glorious Easter promise that puts to shame our doubts and fears ? God grant that you and yours may have spent an Easter of abiding joy and renewed hope and strength !

Lent,--well I could have wished for a little of the spiritual food that one gets so accustomed to and almost to depend upon at home ; but I made the best of it with my books and the Book, although it is trying to be thrown entirely upon oneself. How it reveals one's lack ! Fasting is difficult (where is it not so ?) we have so little variety. Holy Week was, alas ! rather spoilt for me by a smart attack of fever, but I was all right by Good Friday. Perhaps it was the best discipline after all, for it was God's. I read Canon Body's " *Guided Life*," and on Good Friday we read the account of the crucifixion in parallel gospels and sang hymns, and had private prayer in between for the Three Hours. In the evening we had a Lantern Service for the heathen, and told the Story over again, and I am sure they were impressed ; but so cruel themselves, will it appeal to them as it does to us ? And pictures --to those who have never seen a picture in their lives what do they mean ? On the blackboard the men say one line is the same as another, though one curves to the right and the other to the left. But they once said, after seeing some simple pictures of our Lord's birth, " Now our eyes are open." Oh, for the divine gift of patience ! One book I read during Holy Week I think helped me more than any other, and that was the little memoir of Bishop Lightfoot, reprinted from the *Quarterly Review*, which M—— gave me. How inspiring it is to read it and think of it all again !

. . .

Now dear lad, good-bye.

Yours, etc.,

A. F. SIM.

Kota Kota, *April 25th*, 1895.

MY DEAR ——,

The " *Domira* " is running again after repairs, and brought me a huge mail on the 17th--twenty-four letters in all ! . . .

Seeds--the most useful flower seeds are zinea, marigold, sunflower, especially the small kind. I expect the " compositæ " generally would do, as most of the indigenous flowers are " compositæ." Zineas and sunflowers anyhow do splendidly. I have tried many others, but all have failed. What I have in the way of seeds I got from Likoma and the gunboats. If Mr. Nicholl gets any he shares them with me, and *vice versâ*. . . .

I also had heard that Zanzibar had been offered to ——, but

not that he had refused. He was right to refuse. The truth is we ought always to be able to choose a Bishop from our own ranks. The difficulties of the language, the climate, the knowledge of the customs of these heathen necessary to a Bishop — all these ought to be mastered, and it takes years to do so. . . .

You need envy no man his first year out here. The mastering of one or two languages is not only a drudgery in itself, but one feels so hopelessly incapable all the time. Here are the crowds waiting for your message, and you can't deliver it. This oppresses one. . . .

Milk is my chief want now. An African goat gives about a tablespoonful of milk, and most goats and cows have young ones now. . . .

To-day is Sunday, 28th April. It was pouring with rain till 8 a.m., so I thought we should have nobody at the preaching ; but to my delight, it was better than usual.

I reckon the *kibanda* I have built will hold about a thousand people, so I have divided it and made a School at one end and a preaching place at the other. I can't get the women to come into the baraza. Next Sunday I hope to hold the preaching in the *kibanda*, and on Monday to remove the school there. I suppose we must make something like tables if we are to teach these boys to write ! Some forty of them are getting on capitally, and four or five are reading short words ! They require constant change — first alphabet, then drill, then catechism, then sing-song at vowels and consonants, then more drill, and so on. There is nothing to bring them to school except the novelty of the thing at present. We have a fairly steady average of seventy boys. . . .

I shall miss Mr. Nicholl when he goes ; he is very bright and cheery when well. . . .

He is so awfully kind. He is going to spend most of his holiday in America, so probably you won't see him. But if he has any time in England to spare he promises to look you up. His successor, Mr. Swann, is I believe one of the best men as far as administration work goes. I have had no "cases" since Mr. Nicholl went, which is a satisfaction. But he has taken a retinue with him consisting of the men most likely to come to me. . . .

I have a horrid sore toe again ; a jigger got in at the quick, and it has festered.

It has been very cold these last few days—really cold, and cloudy;

and sunless. This weather I am told is going to last till June.
It has rained considerably these last few days, but this won't con-
tinue.
Here's the "*Domira*," and I must close.   Love to everybody.
                                    Yours, etc.,
                                         A. F. SIM.

Letter to W. W——, dated,—

                                Kota Kota, *April 29th*, 1895.
MY DEAR ——,
     Thanks for your antiquarian notes of Hart and Hartlepool.
I only wish I were with you to benefit by your knowledge.   You
know that my house is finished, and that I am in it.   I have had
to have it re-thatched.   Such rain as we have here will find its
way through anything.   The couples I drew a picture of are hold-

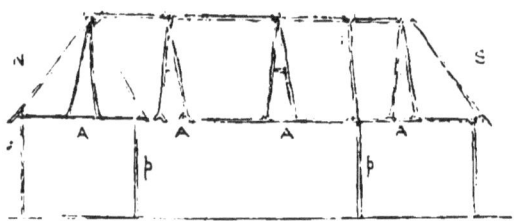

ing well now.   Did I tell you that once during building the whole
roof slid towards the South?   We had to pull it straight with a
rope, and fix it into its place with a rope inside up to one of the
ends from the North partition.   These like A are the couples, or
ties : then from the two partitions (p p) I have a stay, or prop ;
that from the North slants to bear the thrust, for the roof seems
inclined to journey Southwards ; and that on the South partition is
upright.   Four couples and two props carry the roof beam, which
is three trees lashed and pinned together with wooden pins.   The
lashing is hoop-iron off bales of calico.   Most houses out here
have upright trees in the middle, which simplifies all this very
much ; but I don't like that fashion, as it breaks up your floor
space too much : besides at the time I was building I had difficulty in getting big trees.   You will see that the ties or couples

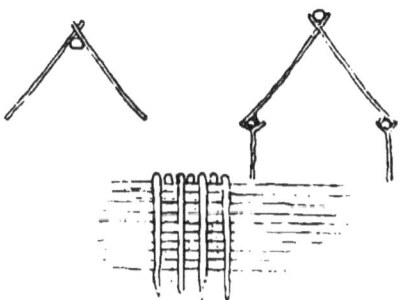

carry the roof-beam, and the roof-beam carries the roof. The roof consists of *chiwalis*, twenty or thirty feet long, and very light and stiff. These are placed as close as they will go, port

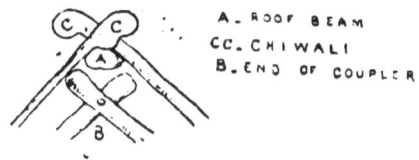

A. ROOF BEAM
CC. CHIWALI
B. END OF COUPLER

and starboard alternately, and they are notched to fit over the roof-beam. Then across these run reeds, called *bangos*, or *matete*. I think they are better than bamboos in the roof, as the boring-beetle does not touch them. We put them three or four together, and tie them with bark rope to the *chiwali*: then on the top of all this lies the grass roof. Lately I have had a pole put in between the two partitions, which are upright trees driven into the ground about two or three feet apart, with *bango* reeds in between. On the top of the trees runs another pole horizontally, fastened at both

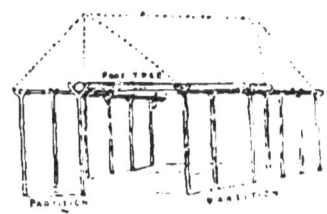

ends to the wall-plate. My new tree jambs these apart, and now there are no more ominous cracks and noises when a strong wind blows, and it has been blowing pretty hard. Of course if we were liable to those Californian tornadoes, a house like this would go to ruin in no time. We have gales but not hurricanes here. Although it feels very cold now, it is not really so as the thermometer goes, perhaps between 55° and 65° in a cold place out of the sun.

Canon Greenwell's discovery is very interesting, although I thought it had always been agreed that that was the old form of the Norman chancel built by Carilef. I wonder if five hundred years hence people of black skin and archæological fancies will be digging up the remains of the Kota Kota monastery, and wondering what was the plan some madman had built or tried to build upon. Never mind. Fountains Abbey was built in wood once.

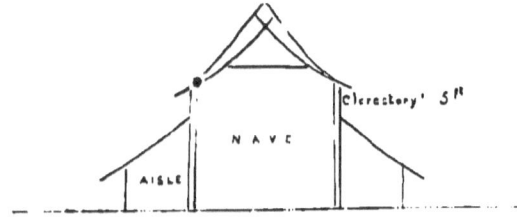

Oh for a run over there again with you! Now mind, that is an engagement this time (or a little later) five years hence, in 1900. Perhaps you will have forgotten altogether about me by then. I hope you will be such a swell when I come home (a builder and contractor) that I shall have to seek a new introduction to you.

I have built a large rough building, sixty by twenty-six feet, on the site where I hope the Church will eventually stand. There I have arranged a temporary School, and one half is for the Sunday preaching. I have begun school there to-day, and I find I have a classroom for women and girls, whom my teacher's wife is going to take. I have built this with three uprights in the middle, twenty feet high. These uprights are very strong, being trunks of the *borassus* palm. They carry the roof-tree, and then the rest goes as before. I have hopes of being able to get more of these for the Church, when I shall make pillars of them, and spring the nave roof from them, leaving five feet of daylight between the spring of the nave roof and the start of the aisle roof for a clerestory, which would give sufficient light probably for the whole building. But these palm-trees are scarce here. What am I to do with the ends of the building? Draw me plans, please Mr. Architect, economizing these palms, and remembering we have no lime and cannot build *high* walls. These palms are about twelve or eighteen inches in diameter, and they are excellent for our purpose, if we could only get plenty of them. Like all palms they grow from the inside of the stem, so the outside is the hard part, and the inside soft, therefore it does not do to cut them up. They are a mass of fibres, and have no grain like other wood. My head teacher (for I boast a second teacher now) is away in the country with about fifty men superintending the cutting of trees, as I have

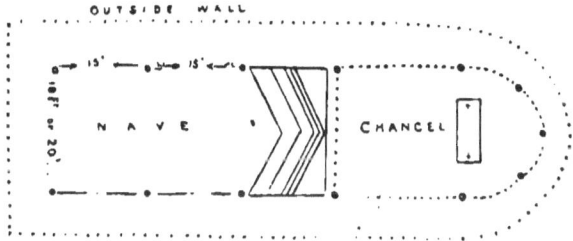

to build a married couple's house. These small houses we build very quickly and easily—first the uprights in the wall, then the wall-plate, then a cross-tree from front to back wall-plate, and up from this a prop which carries the roof-tree. With mud walls you have to build wide eaves, so as to keep the rain off the mud. And with most native houses, even the little round beehives, these wide eaves form the day-room, where they sit in the heat of the day and do nothing, or weave baskets, or make nets, or sew. The weak point of our houses is in this cold weather the impossibility of keeping out the cold wind both at night and in the daytime. In the daytime one wants light, and that can only be had by opening windows. Of course glass is the remedy, but in our Mission we rather set our faces against luxuries of that kind. In fact at

Likoma they build walls merely of *bango* reeds, which are the reverse of air-tight, and for window space they carry the *bangos* only to within three feet of the wall-plate. So willy-nilly you must have air, which is trying on a cold night, and also when you are having your "tub." My house is far and away better than these, but still I feel the disadvantage.

A word about my tools. I wrote for a bench-screw. I have two vices with a grip of about three inches, and I am using these for all my woodwork. I hope to be able to cut planks one of these days, as I am told there are trees to be had with some difficulty, so I have asked for a pit-saw. The screw-tap if it comes, and if it will make a screw with a good, deep thread, will be very useful. We have blacksmiths here, but they have no tools. They use charcoal, and their bellows are made out of a goat skin, and to keep up the continuous draught they use two bellows, working them alternately. I have got them to make me hinges of this sort ;

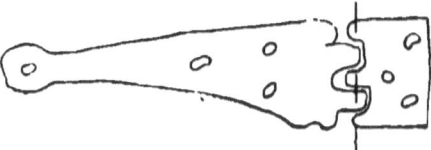

they are pretty rough, but they answer their purpose for windows. Also I had a trowel made from a broken hoe, but I used it for a garden spud, as the ladies who do the mud plastering prefer their fingers to any trowels. I also tried to get sickles made, but they were a failure. For a saw-set we use a steel punch and hammer to set our saws ; but the wood here wears saws out in a terrific way, and it is generally so sappy that it is very hard to get the saw through at all. I had £5 worth of tools given me before I came away, and I think I made a very happy selection, except for bringing carving tools with me, which will be of very little use I fear. These big trees I spoke of are like mahogany, a red wood without quite such a "pernicketty" grain as mahogany has, but very hard.

I see you are making arrangements to come and build my Church for me, so I will stop making plans. Yes, "Early African" is an excellent style for the country. "Crockety pinnacles!" I think you must mean crotchety builders. The place where the cloister ought to be is the place where the boys at present play football. I shall have to see about this, or no trees will grow there ; but I think I can find them a good place when the grass goes down ; it is about twelve feet high just now, but it (the grass) makes good slates. I should like to know something about thatching, also something about brick-making. What a boon it would be to have lime here ! It would be an effectual cure for white ants. . . .

Barrows and shovels ! The only implements they know of besides their hoes are those with which nature supplies them in the way of hands. They fill baskets with clay or mud, and carry them on their heads. No doubt they would do the same with a barrow. Grass-cutting is a slow job, as they use a hatchet about three inches or less at the edge, and cut against a bit of wood. They manage to cut about half a dozen stalks at a time. I am sorry you don't appreciate my patent for getting up in the morning. Try it, and you will never miss that early train on Choir Trip days. Talking of hens, I have great difficulty in getting any to eat now, as I have run out of calico, and the people won't take anything else for them. . . .

I think you had better pack up and come straight out here. I want a companion badly, and if we can't do anything else we can teach these folk "*Kelway.*" I have left my *Hymns A. & M.* behind, but I have my old chant-book with all the variations in manuscript, and few things please me more than to sit and ponder over it, and go over them all again.

April 30*th.* You are wrong about Likoma. It is the hottest place on the Lake, because it is all stones and rocks, and the heat is radiated from them. The boys just come from Likoma say this is much colder ; also this is more exposed to the South-East wind, which is our cold wind. It is a strange thing how one's habit changes out here. If I were to take a dip in the Lake I believe I would certainly have fever. I have to have a warm bath every day ; I could not stand a cold one, although in England I never missed my cold "tub" every morning.

St. Hilda's Church is very interesting. How strange that they should have to buttress the tower in that fashion ! I suppose it is true they had no foundation. In Hart Church how the organ spoils the chancel ! Where organs ought to be placed is a real

difficulty. On a screen, as at York, to my mind spoils the look
of the Church, breaking it up too much. Durham is the best
solution, but who can afford electric and pneumatic couplings,
etc.? St. Aidan's is not satisfactory. The organ is a bit drowned,
and the organist altogether "obsquatulated." . . .

Good luck to you, old boy, and best wishes.

Yours, etc.,

A. F. SIM.

Letter to A. E. M——, dated,—

Kota Kota, April 30th, 1895.

MY DEAR DOCTOR ——,

I will begin about the fever and the tabloids. The fever
generally fetches me in the afternoon ; I feel disinclined to eat, drink
a little tea or lemon water, and then my temperature begins to
rise. When I get the pains and aches in my back, loins, and head
I go to bed, having taken 20 to 30 grains of quinine. Eventually
I go to sleep and perspire through everything. In the morning
generally I am normal, sometimes not quite. The highest temperature I have reached has been 106°, and that twice ; then a rather
high temperature lasted two days. The attack I had last Sunday
(the common sort) began about five o'clock, when I took 20 grains
of quinine. The pains came, so I lay down, but got up for Evensong and went to bed afterwards without my dinner. I tried my
temperature out of curiosity, not thinking it would be much, but it
was 104°. However on Monday I awoke normal, ate well, but
with that horrid mouth, and tongue nothing extra. I took 10
grains of quinine and a tonic tabloid or two—quinine 1 grain,
ferri hypo 2 grains, arsenic $\frac{1}{30}$ grain, strychnine $\frac{1}{30}$ grain (Bur-
roughs and Wellcome I think). To-day (Tuesday) I am quite fit,
but I shall take quinine again after lunch, which is about the time
it came on originally. I perspire with great ease which is my saving ; but you see I am still in my first year and must expect a lot of
fever I fancy. I think it is most like an influenza kind of fever,
only influenza leaves more weakness and of course lasts longer. I
feel little weakness after these attacks, though sometimes I feel
a hankering for a good beefsteak and a glass of port-wine or
beer ! Neither of these are obtainable here, so I suppose that is
why I hanker for them.

The tabloids—I am glad to have the quinine, opium, paregoric, Dover's powders, and in fact all of them, but there are plenty to last a long time. M—— talks of sending more ; he must think my capacity for swallowing medicine is enormous. I don't understand what *trinitrine* is for—a doctor here told me it was dangerous, being a compound of mercury ; it is said to be for peritonitis. I hope I am not going to have peritonitis. Tell me too what salicylate of soda is good for. If I am in time to stop those other tabloids you might order me some more paregoric, tonic tabloids, chlorodyne, and carbolised vaseline.

I wish you could see Dr. Robinson, who is in England now, and have a talk with him about all our little troubles. He is a capital fellow, and I should think a clever surgeon.

We have fearful ulcers among the women here. There is one case of cancer—old Jumbe's brother. And there has been a case of small-pox, which ended in the patient disappearing in a moment when his watcher slept. He has not been found since, which is a good thing, for if he had died they would have buried him in his house probably, and the disease would have spread like wildfire. There has been much small-pox at Forts Johnston and Maguire ; I don't think any Europeans died, though one or two got it. I was vaccinated, but it did not take. It is very hard to get vaccine out here, as it quickly congeals. . . .

I am so glad to hear of the great success of your Boys' Brigade, for now that your old boys are capable of becoming officers, you have attained your highest point of merit. Of course they won't do without superintendence, but still it is a great step. But best of all, and without which anything else is unavailing, is what you say about the moral and spiritual tone of the bigger lads, and specially the communicants. It is grand ; and what an effect for good it must have in the town ! Even if these fellows only cease to do actual evil, it is so much cut off Satan's power in the yards and shops. . . .

Our success here is said to be great. I wish I could think so. Anyhow they show a willingness to come, which is something.

Yours, etc.,

A. F. SIM.

Kota Kota, *May 1st*, 1895.

My dear ——,

My heart is at home at St. Aidan's, but I don't think this is wrong, nor do I think it militates against effective work. Still it is my main difficulty—permanent difficulty I mean. The language is a temporary one, which, please God, will soon be forgotten now, but it is a very real one while it lasts. To have a message and not to be able to deliver it is hard and depressing. . . .

I am picking up Chinyanja pretty well, but I have a multitude of counsellors in the shape of four books, each representing a different dialect, and none of them exactly that of this place. It is not half the language Swahili is, but easier I suppose. . . .

When the "*Domira*" was here I had a lady visitor with her husband, a Free Church missionary. It made me look round my bachelor establishment ; I fear she must have thought it rather untidy. It was such a change to have a lady to speak to, even for a moment. It is only about seven months since I saw ladies, but it seems years, though I had not thought of it before. She was a great wonder to the natives, being the first English or white lady I suppose that many of them had ever seen. I have moved the school out of the baraza into the *kibanda*. The latter will I reckon hold one thousand people, so I have divided it, and now one end forms the School— three rooms divided by reed partitions. The numbers still keep up, and when the hot weather returns I fully expect they will increase. Now with much sickness in the shape of coughs, and many away fishing and hoeing, they number eighty regular attenders, beside a class of women, which Monica, William's wife, and Kathleen, the cook's wife, take between them. Our School furniture is very inadequate—one blackboard, one card of the alphabet, and twelve slates. The women have a blackboard, home made, about the size of a sheet of letter paper. I have written for more things to Likoma. About forty boys are doing syllables now. The phonetic spelling is a great boon and makes it easy for them. Some of the scholars too are beginning to learn the multiplication table. They are so fond of drill and singing 'tonic sol-fa', but we have no modulator. I am turning the drill to some use, as the elder boys are marched out with baskets and do a good half-hour's work collecting and laying mud for the floors of the new houses. They seem to enjoy it almost as much as football, but of course they won't stick to it long.
. . .

May 10*th.*—I have had a disturbed time since I last wrote, not through natives, but Europeans. The gunboat "*Adventure*" has been here for Mr. Nicholl, who was away, so it waited till he returned yesterday. It brought Mr. Swann to replace him. These good officers have kept me going. Well, there is one result anyway ; one of them is a keen photographer, and so he took the house, several groups, and myself. Mr. Nicholl went up to Likoma in a dhow. The magistrate of Kota Kota has Likoma under him, and so Mr. Nicholl has had to go once or twice to settle matters

A. F. SIMS HOUSE AT KOTA KOTA.
With shadow of the big " Preaching Tree" at 4.30 p.m. Rev A F. Sim, Mr. Swann and Captain Rhodes in the foreground.

among the natives. This time he has brought away two prisoners, implicated I believe in some of that superstitious poison-drinking to detect witchcraft, which is against the law in British Central Africa. Mr. Nicholl had a great reception ; large parties of men and women came up from the village and danced ; many pounds too of gunpowder were blown off. I shall miss him very much when he goes. He is kind and thoughtful. . . .

Please remember me most affectionately to all my old friends. Give my love to the children.

Yours, etc.,

A. F. SIM.

Letter to S. F. S——, dated,—

Kota Kota, *May 2nd*, 1895.
MY DEAR ——,

. . . I have not yet had need of water, and having much
else to do I have not begun my well. I had occasion however to
dig a hole eight feet deep on high ground, and even at this depth
water percolated through a foot or two deep, but this was in the
rainy season. I can get a good many feet lower down to get a start
with the well, where in the wet season the water stands. Of course
I should build a wall (mud) and a shed over it to keep out dirty
water. I expect I shall find it necessary to timber the top while
the men are digging, as if left to themselves they are so inclined
to undercut. We have no bricks, but if I knew how I could of
course make them ; however as yet I don't want to spend time and
money on that. . . .

The movable railway was tried in the " *Wissmann* " (German)
Expedition, and for many reasons had to be given up, though I
don't know the whole story. .   .

May 18th.—The German steamer brought in Mr. Corbett from
Likoma on his way home after three years out here, and I had to
show him all the buildings, etc. He is the third Likoma person I
have seen since I came to Kota Kota, so you can understand we
generally have something to talk about. He has had most of the
building work to do at Likoma, consequently he is regarded as an
authority. He was good enough to compliment us on our buildings, but I shall take a hint he dropped about expenses and stop
building when I have finished two native houses. . . .

The children here are awful beggars, and I have nothing I can
spare. They like soap, salt, and sugar ; but these are precious
things to me, more than they are to them. . . .

Remember me most kindly to all my old friends.

Yours, etc.,
A. F. SIM.

Kota Kota, *May 3rd*, 1895.
MY DEAR ——,

. . . Here is a gunboat with Mr. Swann to replace Mr.
Nicholl, who is away, as I have told you in my last, but he is returning. I expect him back overland to-morrow or Sunday, when
he will pack up and go as straight as circumstances will permit for

England. I shall miss him sorely I am sure, although I shall get on with Mr. Swann well enough. . . .

May 5th, Sunday.—The gunboat is still here and I have been busy entertaining the sailors. One man, the senior officer, an old " P. and O." and R. N. R. man, is very nice indeed. The other, who will captain the "*Pioneer*" when she is ready, is quite nice, quiet, and keen on stones ! No. 1 is keen on photography and is named Cullen, so I made him take a "shot" at my beard ! To-morrow I will develop it and see what it is like. No. 2's name is Rhodes. Mr. Swann seems very anxious to please, but he is quite different from Mr. Nicholl. Captain Cullen came up at 7.30 to our Celebration, which I Anglicised a good deal as he does not understand either Swahili or Chinyanja ; but it was nice, and he is the first outsider who has ever done so here. He stayed to breakfast and I have had peace ever since. I used the *kibanda* for preaching in this morning for the first time. It was windy and cold as I have no walls to it, but this week I think I will be able to mend that. William, who was away last week cutting poles, has managed to get about 250 poles, 300 *chiwalis*, and bark for tying purposes, so this week is going to be a busy one. I shall start a married couple's house, measure for a more permanent School, and make arrangements for another house for Hamisi, my foreman of outside work, who as a youth was with Livingstone. That will keep us going for a bit ; other things, such as railways, etc., have to be done. Mr. Nicholl is still away, and will be awfully grieved to leave this place I know. I got a letter from him dated from Chingomanji's opposite here April 23rd, on Friday, May 3rd. . . .

Two men, engineers, have come for Likoma I hear—Mr. Crouch, who was out before, and another, name unknown. I heard there was a box for me waiting at Fort Johnston, and I am in a perspiration to see it. There is another man I heard of as coming to Likoma—a carpenter named Sims. If he arrives I trust our letters won't get mixed ! Mr. Crouch and the other man can hardly have left on March 2nd, can they ? They went up from Fort Johnston in the sailing boat. The Commissioner is expected every day. I wonder if he will pay us a visit here ; I am very curious to see him. . . .

The East Indians here do not get on with the natives, and will never settle nor put any money into the country. . . .

I think I must send you a specimen of the fibre these people make their fishing net twine with. They have quite a different knot from our netting—it is a reef knot. They use no mesh, and make an excellent net which only needs tanning (and in some places they do tan it) to keep it. . . .

Yours, etc.,

A. F. SIM.

Kota Kota, *Ascension Day*, *May 23rd*, 1895.

MY DEAR M——,

. . . The "baccy" came in splendid order. I have written to thank Mr. Crouch for fetching it . . . The seeds— I fear the apples and pears will come to nothing here, but I will send some of them to Unangu. Don't they want grafting? I hope the raspberries, and possibly the gooseberries, may come to something. Thanks also for the book, "*Mr. Will's Widow*," and the foreign note-paper. I still have a good deal left, but at my rate of writing a big store soon goes. This I got when in England, and yours came in time to replenish my original failing supply. . . .

Mr. Nicholl left this morning in the "*Ilala*." . . . He has been kindness itself to me. . . . He could tell you the latest of me and of the Mission generally, in which, though not a Churchman, he takes a personal interest.

My dear boy, what a dreadful time you are having in the matter of Church Defence; how it must bore you ! Don't commit yourself. Come it must and will I believe. The question is, how and when ? I think the historical argument may be pushed for more than it really is worth. I believe in it, but it doesn't go for much with voters I imagine. It requires a technical knowledge to appreciate it. It is horrid having to take up a political question, but I believe it is your duty. . . . Is there any talk of co-operation among the Schools of the diocese after the fashion of Box No. 13 at Alnwick in the Newcastle diocese?

Tools again. Probably if you could have sent me a grindstone and handle we could have mounted it. . . . I have only glanced at the fruit-growing book ; it looks about as useful for elephant rearing as far as this place is concerned. However I may get tips about pruning (of which I know nothing) and perhaps manure. . . . I am awfully amused about W. D—— and the sugar. Thank him for it, and tell him that it has come, and that now I have plenty. I am always touched by the children's letters. I wish I could write to them all, but it is impossible ; indeed writing as much as I do will have to cease in some measure soon. I have a huge number of letters to answer. I had such a jolly one from M—— last mail, with many interesting enclosures from Mr. L. J—— and boating men of Sunderland A.R.C. . . .

I am going to send you a pair of lion's claws (the lion was killed near here after eating one or two men), and also a leopard skin, if it can be properly cured, of which I am afraid, as it has been badly shot by natives in this neighbourhood, where it was killed. Leopards are an awful nuisance in some places, though we are free from them here.

I am very glad to hear that Archdeacon Maples has accepted the Bishopric. In my view of the situation here, Likoma is most inadequate as the headquarters of our Mission. I can see nothing to recommend it, except that it has a good harbour, and is free from war scares. The impression is growing that it is unhealthy, owing to its great heat. This is due to the stoniness of the place and the radiation of heat. There is a very noticeable drop in the temperature about 2 a.m. every night—at least so I am told. The people are not of a specially lofty character, and as a central school it is said to be neither far enough from nor near enough to the boys' own homes. No boy I believe going to Likoma from the East shore stations takes to it, and they soon get homesick. . . .

May 31st.—We have had the excitement of having a gunboat in. She brought the new Sikhs, and has to-day taken the old lot. It seems a farce to send a force of seven Sikhs to a place like this. They are useful as being well disciplined, and they can be trusted to keep guard at night and so on, which the natives cannot.

We have had another excitement ; a lion was killed on Monday, and brought in to the Boma. I photographed it, and the doctor on the gunboat carried off the skin. By the way, if you could send a pound or two of arsenical soap, I could probably preserve some of these skins for you. The native way of stretching them in the sun and drying them spoils them for setting up in England. You might also send some corrosive sublimate in tabloids. Alum is good, but more bulky I should imagine than arsenical soap. A few brushes like paint-brushes would be useful. . . .

Yours, etc.,

A. F. SIM.

Letter to E. F. E ——, dated,—

Kota Kota, *May 24th*, 1895.

MY DEAR ——,

. . . We have lions about four miles from here, and two men were taken a few days ago. I often wish I had the right weapons ; but of course at this season of the year, with grass 10 or 12 ft. high, it would be a case of a large party and beaters ; to go otherwise would be madness. My Martini-Henry sticks, as nearly all seem to do—the ejector won't act. . . .

The arrival of a steamer causes all the people to shout what is supposed to be "Hip ! hip ! hurrah !" but they make it, "Hupplah !" I think the people here have learnt it from the Atonga, who have come under the Bandawe missionaries' influence. The Atonga supply the labour market of British Central Africa, and they are so far enlightened as to know the advantages of leaving home and going to other places to obtain work and the calico with which they are paid. They are, on the other hand, the most lustful and bullying people of this part, unless you reckon the coastmen, who do not belong to this part. . . .

May 31st.—The gunboat has departed to-day with the old lot of Sikhs, whom she has replaced with new. . . .

One can buy here two fowls for a yard of calico (sixpence), and eight or ten eggs for a dessert-spoonful of beads or salt—it is not table salt, but a darkish, coarse kind. . . . This is said to be the unhealthy season ; but I find it agrees with me, as it is nearly two months since I had any fever. . . .

June 3rd. Yesterday we killed an enormous lizard, fully 14 ft. long, which inhabits water, and sometimes comes about where fowls are. It was a most exciting chase, as it got into the drain which runs round my house. I am having it skinned, as it has such a beautiful skin, and the fat is said to be good for sprains. Probably there is a little superstition attached to this. . .

And now farewell,

Yours, etc.,

A. F. SIM.

Letter to Mrs. F——, dated,—

Kota Kota, *May 28th,* 1895.

MY DEAR ——,

. . . A box sent from Zanzibar in December has not
arrived yet ! You can imagine how it is that sometimes (really
wonderfully seldom) we run short of European eatables. I shall
be always content if I can get salt and flour. Tea too is useful, as
the water is not very safe to drink unless it is first boiled ; but
what with wars and lions and scares and thefts, it has been very
difficult to get carriers, and I believe there is a glut of goods at
Katunga, where the lower river journey ends. Talking of lions, I
went up to the Boma to see a lion this afternoon, which had been
killed to-day four miles from here. It had eaten a man and part
of a child, so they got the other part of the child and baited a trap
with it, and to-day the lion was found dead with two bullet
holes through his body—one bullet went right through him from
end to end. What do you think of the bait ? Of course the
magistrate knew nothing of it till they told him after it was done.
Such a great brute—very old, and with very little mane, and very
gaunt. I believe it is generally old lions that take to hunting men.
They find it easier work than stalking four-legged game. How
helpless one would be with such a beast it is not hard to imagine !
I am going up to-morrow about daybreak to photograph him, and
then he will be skinned, though his skin isn't worth very much.
As to the bait, I don't suppose they would have caught him with
any other. I feel pretty confident now that all my troubles, as far
as the political situation goes, are over. There is a chance of
course that the Commissioner will not leave a magistrate here ;
but even then I should not contemplate any trouble myself, though
I might have to witness many barbarities and injustices which
might get me into trouble, if I felt it my duty to interfere in any
way. But from the point of view of stopping the slave-trade, I do
think it is important to occupy this place. I daresay from a
missionary point of view, if there was no Boma here, my position would be better. In looking up some absent scholars the
other day I found that they were fully persuaded that they would
be sent to prison for having missed school. However after assurances to the contrary, most of them have come back. We are
better supplied now with school materials, and can make school a

little more varied and interesting to them. I feel as if I were beginning to get the mastery over my fevers ; and though I have to
put in a saving clause about boasting, I think that in time I shall
be almost as well here as at home—not so full of activity, but
feeling pretty fit and well. I am trying now taking quinine regularly, about four or five times a week, ten grains each time ; and
though it is said to be the fever season, I have had no fever since
April 28th. I have never been so long without it, and then it was
very slight.

May 29*th.*—Fancy, it is more than a year since I left England.
I don't know that it seems a short time ; but you see I have had
no winter, no Christmas trees, no particular holidays to mark the
flight of time. It is more strange than you can imagine, and it
seems to rob life of its reality somehow. To-day has been cold
enough for November in England, pouring rain, very little sunshine, and a gale of wind. How these poor people feel the cold
in their almost naked skins ! They look pictures of misery, and
hug themselves with their arms crossed from shoulder to shoulder.
The school too suffers considerably in such weather. I went up
before 7 a.m. this morning to photograph the lion, but it was eleven
before I got a chance, owing to the rain and no light. I can't say
the royal beast looked very dignified with his head propped on a
tin biscuit-box ! Here is a gunboat in sight, on the roughest day I
remember seeing here ! She is getting a tossing. The gunboats
are much too small for this Lake ; you can't imagine how rough
it is at times. They have been handed over from the Naval
Authority to the Foreign Office, *i.e.* the Administration ; and
now they are manned, not with R.N. men, but with a couple of
R.N. Reserve officers, one of whom at least is very clever and
experienced, so perhaps he has come out this rough weather to try
the gunboat's paces. The sea is breaking a long way out, and
the whole hull of the boat disappears from sight. . . .

June 10*th.*—I am keeping awfully well this cold weather. At
that *moment* I believe we had a slight earthquake shock. It seemed
like a slight tremor, and there was an unaccountable noise in the
roof, as if a sudden blast of wind had struck it ; but it is quite still
outside. I wonder if it was : I believe they are frequent here.
The Bandawe people often feel them seventy miles North of this.
I hear that one of the ladies with whom I travelled up the river,
belonging to the Scotch Free Church Mission at Bandawe, has

become engaged to a doctor[1] in the same Mission. The poor
Blantyre people (Scotch Established Church) have been having a
bad time of it lately ; one of the principal missionaries died, and
the wife of the head of the Mission went out of her mind and died
on her way home at Zanzibar ; her husband was with her, very ill
himself. They have had war in the neighbourhood of their stations,
and the excitement and exposure is said to have caused the trouble.
. . .

How thankful I am that in our Mission, statistics have their
right place—*i.e.* nowhere. They will be made up some day, but
that is not yet ! I wonder if people at home realize what conversion is. Out here at a new station for instance, we seldom
baptize any who have not been two years under instruction. At
least we try and make sure that they are genuine cases. What
experiences you have had with the frost ! I at least shall never
get my main frozen ! I wish I could ; but I have always to send
for my water. . . .

And now with all good wishes and thanks,

Yours, etc.,

A. F. SIM.

Kota Kota, *May 29th*, 1895.

MY DEAR ——,

. . . I have one rose tree flourishing (it evidently enjoys
this cold weather), six guavas about a foot high, two fig-trees
and one hybiscus ; but my cocoa-nuts are a failure.

May 31st.—I have sown a lot of peas to-day ; those I sowed
about a month ago are coming on splendidly, just coming into
flower. . . .

I think you would be amused at the musical instruments the
natives use. The most common is a three-stringed affair, which
they play with their fingers. The sounding-board is made of
an enormous gourd, and the stem has three keys which they
finger to alter the notes. The music is most monotonous. Then
there is another instrument, the notes of which are composed of

---

[1] News of the death of Dr. Steele, referred to above, reached A. F.
Sim on the 30th of June. "He was going home for a holiday, when he
died of jaundice, a common cause of death among white men here, and an
awful death, I believe."—A. F. S.

bits of hard wood of various sizes, which rest on the stalk or stem of a small banana-tree. Perhaps a whole octave is obtained in this way. Two men play at it, sitting opposite to each other. The tune is a kind of "chopstick" affair; but they play very

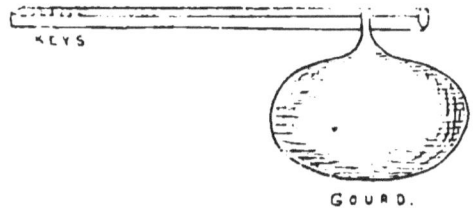

KEYS

GOURD.

quickly, striking the notes with sticks of hard wood. Some of the notes are a foot long. Then there is the interminable drum, which *never* ceases. It is of various sizes, and each kind has a different name. Some belonging to the chief are "spirit drums," and are only used on very special occasions (I think perhaps when they are conciliating the evil spirits). . . .

June 3rd.—I have just had a jigger taken out of my toe. I fear when the dry season comes they will be very bad here. The only pet I have now is a cat; it is indispensable for keeping down the rats, which swarm especially in the roof. She is very fond of me; but the black boys, although she is a native herself, frighten her dreadfully—I expect from her old experience of their cruelty. The cats are treated very badly in native houses. . . .

I wish you could see my accounts. I never was any good when I had to keep them in £ s. d.; but when it comes to calico, beads, salt, hoes, and sometimes soap, I get into a hopeless mess. I have been trying to unravel these awful things for hours, and I cannot make them square. I think we ought to have a business man here to keep us straight. . . .

I wish I knew something of Kindergarten work; I am sure it would do splendidly with these children. . . .

I do believe that many of these people will in time come to love Christ; but there is no sense of sin yet—nothing to appeal to. All one can do is to preach a personal Lord, Who loves and calls for love, and that every breach of His commands is an injury to Him. Alas! they know so little of love. Family love, one is almost brought to think, is wanting among them. These people are nothing like the Uganda people, as they are also far removed from the Matabele and Zulus—a happy-go-lucky lot, fairly industrious, most peace-loving, and I think ease-loving and unambitious. I am prepared to believe that the Yaos, who live on the East side of the Lake (*e.g.*, Unangu), are different. They are cheeky, warlike, troublesome, with lots of push ; and I think we are quite right to spend a lot of time and patience upon them. . . .

We have had a death among the children, and there is some chickenpox about. This cold weather thins the school and the preaching and the hearers' class. I don't wonder ; how can they stand it when they are almost naked ? They are very fond of football, and are quite as full of spirits as English children. . . .

The feeling of influenza is very like malarial fever ; but in its effects, as far as I am concerned, influenza is much worse. Probably if I had to stay in bed ten days on end with fever I should never get up. . . .

And now farewell.

Yours, etc.,

A. F. SIM.

Letter to C. H. B——, dated, —

Kota Kota, *June 4th*, 1895.

MY DEAR ——,

. . . I believe I am getting fond of my life here. If only I had some one to laugh with, or cry with (!) how different it would be ! But it would be hard to get the right man, and one might be worse off with the wrong one. You must not be too hard on us out here for sending men alone. Dr. Hine is not alone, nor is Mr. W. P. Johnson, nor of course are the people at Likoma ; mine is an exceptional case. We were in a hurry to occupy this place, and there has been a dearth of men at Likoma. Besides it was thought that the magistrate's presence would count as companionship, and of course all the time I was staying with Mr. Nicholl it did (except when he was away). Now I do want another white man, because, having finished my necessary buildings, I shall wait for the Bishop's return before starting anything more, and in the meantime I want to get out into my Parish of 2,000 square miles. . . .

If I had a free hand and plenty of help I should start Schools in many places, and visit them frequently. They form a nucleus, and the School is useful for gathering people together. They begin by

working at it, and grumbling, and striking, and swindling until
they get to know one.

What nonsense it is for people in England to ask for a list and
statistics ! It is ghastly to think of having this sort of thing to
deal with. Conversion among these people is a gradual dawning
which may take years. They have no idea of sin ; they have very
little family love. What can one appeal to ? My idea is simply to
go on hammering out the Old, Old Story, and God in His own
time will reveal to them what love is. They are a cruel people ;
poor things, they have been brought to it by lives of persecution.
But the native proper is a peace-loving, indolent creature, living
from hand to mouth, cultivating with something like industry
during the proper season just as much as will suffice, and no more,
Sometimes the locust comes, and then he starves with a good grace,
and dies by hundreds. Thank God we have plenty of food here,
in spite of the swarms of locusts that passed over us. Now the
bairns are different. I think I see lots to hope for in them ; they
are so like our youngsters at home, full of fun and spirits, and they
come up here and gather together to play football and handball
with all the noise English boys are capable of. But I do think in
their homes they are quiet and subdued. They have good spirits,
but no enterprise. *Whip-tops* and kite flying so far I have found
indigenous, and handball, two games of which I have seen, one
with sides, which is a fearful romp (the only romp I have found yet
among them). Fancy coming upon the homely whip-top ! Generally
two boys whip the same top. Among the elders there is a game
something between draughts and halma, which they play on a big
board with holes in it, or in the ground with stones. But they
take to football like ducks to water, and quickly learn the rules of
Association and all the tips and points. A big shout goes up when
a goal is kicked. They have recognised leaders among them (who
rather bully their following), so I suppose there is a rudimentary
hero-worship. I don't know enough of the language to find out if
they have any historical heroes. They have no worship (except
the Mahommedans), only a fear of the spirits of the departed. I
think they have a dim idea of the Unity of God. They have lots
of stories of the " *Uncle Remus* " kind—I shall try and collect
them some day. The funny part of their relation of stories is the
gesticulation and noises they make, and the click with their fingers.
I have seen images made of mud and baked in the fire ; I wonder

what they use them for—charms I expect. They have a great belief in charms. A man brought me a ball of lion's hair wrapped
up most carefully, which he wanted to sell for *dawa*, or a charm
against lions. . . .

When the children first came to school not one of them could
count more than up to *five* correctly. We are teaching them the
Swahili numbers and now they can count up to a hundred. Fancy
in Chinyanja consecutive numbers go only up to *five*, and then begin
again; six is five plus one (*sano ndi mozi*), ninety-nine is *makumi
sano ndi naie ndi sano ndi naie*—imagine what nine hundred and
ninety-nine must be ! It is a barbarous tongue. . . .

The steamer has come so I must close hurriedly . . .

Yours, etc.,

A. F. Sim.

Kota Kota, *June 18th*, 1895.

My dear M——,

. . . Dear old J. R. H——. He will be a fearful loss to us
and to Cambridge, but a gain to the Church at large. It is a painful
process losing our brothers or parting with them ; but how like it
is to a family growing up, and getting separated as each goes out
into a wider world. I am awfully sorry for Cheltenham that Dr.
James is leaving. In many ways I sympathise with the outcry
against clerical monopoly in Headmasterships. Plenty of most
able men as Headmasters must be lost in this way. Who will go
to Cheltenham ? . . .

Very soon you will be making arrangements for leaving the
Parish in C——'s hands for three days, and spending them at
Auckland ; I wish I could wire greetings. My letter to the Bishop
will arrive too late. Anyhow, though I have the same difficulty in
remembering how long it takes letters to reach you at home as
you say you have, you will easily imagine that I shall be with you
in spirit on that day. Being on Saturday this year I wonder when
you will keep it.

I am awfully pleased to see my name on the front page of the
St. Aidan's Magazine again. It quite fulfills one of my theoretical
ambitions. Thanks for granting my request. Well now, if it is
possible, could you get the parishioners to do more to support this
work here ? You know my impression was that all should go to
the Common General Fund, but it seems that anything beyond
the most absolute necessities have to be begged for. Could they

make me all the kisibaus I want ? Kisibaus always sounded like "*Miss Toosey's Mission*" sort of things, but you little know how large a part they play in making a boy's character ! For instructions—*vide* cover of "*Central Africa*" ; for materials—use strong unbleached calico. This is one suggestion. Another is, Altar Frontals—serviceable rather than ornate, the same size as St. Aidan's, made by some volunteer.   . . .

Welch off to Canada—that is Welch Disestablishment and no mistake ! . . .

I am glad to hear my letters arrive regularly ; I write by all opportunities. Don't believe I am dead till I tell you.   I will have it wired to you, and you wire to D——, and he can make it known in the family ; though the alternative is to have it wired to the Office ; and I gave them both your and D——'s address.

The German steamer is very late now ; she has been undergoing repairs.   I am looking forward to her arrival as she may bring me a companion. Things would be so different then, for one can never absolutely trust or possess the sympathy of even the best native. . . .

My cook distinguished himself by picking a dishful of my precious peas under the impression they were beans, and cutting them up and cooking them like beans.   They are not half-ripe yet, and I have been watching these very pods, my first, with angelic patience.   . . .

We killed a water lizard four feet long the other day, whose skin has gone to make a drum.   He looked like a young crocodile with a huge long tail ; he was after my fowls.   The attendance at school has been nearly halved by the cold.   This morning I was shivering, and had to take a sharp walk to warm myself, with a shooting jacket on over my white cassock.   All the boys have colds : how they can stand it in their naked pelts I don't know.   This is one reason why I want kisibaus.   I want to get hold of a few boarders, but I intend to go about it cautiously.   I shall probably be asked a price for them by their parents, after the fashion of a slave dealer ! I have bought the dead Jumbe's widow's bracelets, or armlets, for ten fathoms, equal to ten shillings —solid ivory, nine of them.   They were the price of a slave in old days.   I shall send them to you ; perhaps they will go towards the Museum.   If you care for it I will buy curios for this purpose.   . . .

It seems to be necessary for the members of the Staff in our

Mission, if they want anything but the bare necessities of life, to
have to beg for it in the " *Central Africa* " Magazine. If I were to
do so (I have had no need at present) I know some in the Parish
who would not like it, and some who would volunteer to supply my
want, whatever it might be. Well if I want anything I shall write
to you. . . .

Directly I get a Church built, which won't be till after I have
seen the Bishop, I shall want an Altar Frontal, say eight feet by
three feet three inches, and a credence bracket ; but wait—it would
be heavy and awkward to send, and I might be able, with my new
tools, to make a very decent one. Altar Frontal—red (Sarum red)
serge, with simple stoles or orphreys ; cloth—not velvet or silk.
Then when other needs are supplied we can talk about changes of
colours. I may some day ask for a harmonium, so will you consult
those who know about the kind to stand damp ?

Last Monday when I ought to have taken my men's hearers'
class, I could not attend myself as my lord the Malarial Fever had
me by the leg ; but William tells me there were seven new men,
which makes me glad. It was a very slight touch of fever, and
I am hungrier than ever. . . .

June 23rd.—The gunboat " *Pioneer* " brought me some tobacco
from Mr. Nicholl. He is a most generous-hearted fellow. He
imagines I have a claim upon him for kindness, etc., rendered, and
there is nothing he can do for me which is too much or too extravagant. He says he is sending me hams and a case of liquor ! I
have one letter from England—a long type-written letter from the
Bishop Designate—a copy of one written to Dr. Laws, the head of
the Bandawe (Scotch Free Church) Mission. From it I gather I
must go quietly, as the whole question of our occupation of Kota
Kota may be re-opened—not that I for a moment expect it will be
given up.

Mr. Nicholl tells me he is to take up his headquarters at Kota
Kota eventually, and Mr. Swann is to go to Bandawe ; I am glad
and sorry. Mr. Swann is very nice, and getting on well with the
people here. Mr. Nicholl will be able to do more for the place. . . .

The " *Ilala* " is in here to-day from the North. There is no news
as she has not been to Likoma. I expect to see Captain D—— of
the same this evening. Your little parcel, with Clergy Mutual
Almanac and cuttings, has come ; thanks also for news of the Boat
Race ; they made a good fight considering. I don't know what

the state of affairs is at Cambridge now, but this time last year they had a huge row—observe no Third Trinity men in the boat; I imagine they have refused to row; it practically means no Eton men. Last year they were nearly all Third Trinity men. There was a strike against Third Trinity after the race of '94, and W. B. C—— was made President—an ancient President of the 70's. . . .

I got a bite yesterday morning from a big spider; it was in my towel when I began to dry myself. I got him against my shoulder; it was sore all yesterday and is itching a good deal now. We have chicken-pox or measles among our boys. School is reduced by this and cold to about fifty. . . .

When the steamers come in, especially the gun-boats, I get the right time. I was just an hour too fast this time! I guessed as much beforehand, for when I got up at sunrise I found my clock at 7.30 always, or nearly. We have about eleven hours of sun, but longer twilights than at any other part of the year. . . .

Remember me to everybody. Thank Mr. R—— for the obituary card and S—— for the photo.

Yours, etc.,

A. F. SIM.

Kota Kota, *June 20th*, 1895.

MY DEAR ——,

. . . I am so rejoiced to see my name restored to the Parish Magazine cover; it brings me a lot nearer home, as now I feel I have a home and a claim upon somebody, and not so much the outcast I might have felt if many of my old friends left, or died, or what not. . . .

I hear rumours of one of our lake shore villages, where most of the people are Christians, being raided by a Yao chief, and many Christians carried off. What will be done I don't know. There is no strong hand of law in Portuguese territory. . . .

June 30th. Third Sunday after Trinity. I took the "lost sheep" and "lost coin" for my subject to-day with the heathen, and they seemed very much interested in it. . . . The right way to preach in these Oriental tongues I am sure is to use illustrations very largely, like our Lord's parables. I am not good at this, but I must try and acquire it. . . .

What with five steamers (including two gunboats) on the Lake I see many passengers; but the people I seldom if ever see are the Likoma people. The Mission steamer never calls here, and consequently I feel isolated because so few fellow-Churchmen ever come near me. . . .

For the last few days there has been a strange game or dance going on, called *Vinyau*. It consists in making a few counterfeit presentments of wild beasts. These are made a little distance from the village by young men. Then the excitement consists in bringing these wild beasts, ghosts, etc. (generally made out of straw), into the town at night. There seems to me to be a trace of what is found universally in Africa, namely, initiatory rites.

July 2nd.—The raid to which I have referred above was by a big Yao chief, the very man to whom I was within an ace of being sent when I first came out (not at Unangu, but at Chisanga). This, as Mr. Johnson feels, is probably the beginning of a new era in the slave-trade on the East shore. This side has been practically closed to them, and now they are beginning to find a supply for their demand of slaves in the peace-loving and timid villagers along the East coast of the Lake. If Mr. Johnson could get the people to build Bomas, or strong stockades, and arm them, he would be perfectly justified in doing so. There isn't a single Portuguese in the country. Let us hope it may end in our acquiring that strip of land. Nothing else will put an end to slave-trade in these parts. . . .

Continue to pray for us.

Yours, etc.,

A. F. SIM.

Letter to T. C. G——, dated,—

Kota Kota, *June 21st*, 1895.

MY DEAR ——,

. . . I am quite sure that whatever are the faults of our methods of sending out Missions, the results here justify the existence even of the most European-civilization-running Missions. To the Missions of East Africa we are largely indebted for the exclusion *entirely* of liquor from those parts affected by the Brussels Act. Natives here drink, but none of them know the taste of rum or gin, or any other European drink ; and what drinking there is, is but trifling in amount. The evils of civilization are not very apparent, I am thankful to say, among the natives of these parts. No, the problems that faced St. Paul and the Apostles of the

Gentiles were very different from those which face the missionary
in Central Africa. Yet if the forces of good government that are
coming in under British or European auspices were not present
(and remember they are Christian, modelled upon, and influenced
by the teachings and principles of Christ), no doubt these people,
as they became Christians, would learn to govern themselves by a
righteous law ; but it would take a long time of course. They
have no idea of justice ; they submit the most serious causes to
poison test. In places there are chiefs who exercise a despotic
power, and where they are strong enough they hear all cases.

But the introduction of European (i.e., Christian) force is essential in this part of the world, for the weak is more oppressed here
than in any country or in any time known to history. I don't
think the missionary can afford to refuse the help of its presence.
It saves him any amount of trouble and worry, and puts an end to
the question as to whether weapons in his hands are justifiable.
Of course there are many cases where a young, inexperienced, incapable, or even wilfully unjust administrator of the law does a lot
of harm and makes blunders ; and perhaps it is even true to say
that at present few only of our magistrates and collectors know
much of the native or native ways of thinking ; yet that is due to
the youthfulness of the enterprise. Of nearly all Central Africa I
think it is true that no European country, which has grabbed a
protectorate, will get her money's worth out of it, or at least for a
long time. I think and hope that it is an act of justice to the
downtrodden that Europe has stepped into African politics. As a
missionary, like any other property-holder, I am benefiting ; for
I have bought the site of our Church, School, houses, etc. (and
paid a good price for it—300 rupees), and the Administration steps
in and grants me a deed on behalf of the Mission, and I feel safe,
so that I need not bother my head any more about it. So with us
the problem of government (though not an easy one for the
Commissioner) as far as the welfare of the people is concerned,
is to my mind settled. When you hear of the Government fighting with native chiefs, you must remember that these chiefs are
really the curse of the people whom they tyrannise over. They
are responsible for much of the slaving and raiding and destruction
of their neighbours' crops. . . .

Have you taken an interest in the correspondence in the " *Church
Times* " on the question, " Why the Working-man does not come to

Church"? I notice the editor rather condemned the idea of starting an organization after the Religious Order style. It seems to
me to be all a part of our all-present difficulty—the sudden growth
of population in towns out-growing the Church's organization ; and
added to that, the inheritance of a century of coldness and indifference and deadness. Nothing but work, work, work will get
the working-man, or any other man, to come to Church, and to
become a true Christian with the help of God. Nothing but this
will drive the spirit of scepticism out of him. . . .

I use the Sermon on the Mount a good deal in my heathen
teaching. With the "hearers" I am taking at present the Being
and Nature of God—His Unity, Omnipotence, etc. They don't
ask questions or discuss ; they only grunt sometimes, which I
think is a kind of acquiescing surprise. They listen well I must
say. . . .

Farewell. *Dominus tecum.* Thanks for your prayers

Yours, etc.,

A. F. SIM.

Letter to Miss G——, dated,—

Kota Kota, *June 21st*, 1895.

MY DEAR ——,

Let me begin business at once. Kisibaus did you say?
Are you making yours for any one in particular, and if not, why
not for me ? I want them even now, and cannot get them from
Likoma. I should like them all of one kind, not coloured ;
strong, unbleached calico ; machine sewn ; sizes mostly small ;
measurement from back of neck to bottom hem, 15 in. and 19 in.,
with sleeves 10 in. ; and 20 in. and 26 in., with sleeves 15 in. A
few coloured ones would not be amiss. You little know how
practical and useful an article they are, and how large a part they
form in making an African boy. He has some idea of himself
and a glimmering of self-respect when he has a kisibau on.[1]
Scarcely a boy in school has escaped having a cough, and about
twenty are too ill to come to school. Poor little bairns ! they
come up hugging themselves with one hand on each shoulder,

---

[1] "They (kisibaus) are most useful articles in the development of the
African boy, and by no means the useless thing one is inclined to imagine,
and so are blankets. We have not got so far as top hats and boots yet,
and we do *not allow* our people to wear trousers" !—A. F. S.

looking the picture of misery from the cold. This is a very exposed place, and now the wind from the South-East is very cold.
. . .

In a country like this if well-disposed people (philanthropists)
are sent out—even hunters, if their standards are high—it does
the people good. I daresay the people welcome them more than
they do us, for they spend more in the country. I think the
Society system is not theoretically perfect, but like many other
modern anomalies it has two sides, and for the present seems the
only way possible to us. . . .

May I tell you one way in which I think you could confer a
boon on me personally? Will you write out a few cooking recipes,
remembering how few articles we have—milk puddings, eggs, and
what ways to cook them, stews, rissoles, cakes, rice cakes, drop
cakes, scones with soda? We have sugar, currants, flour, eggs,
milk, rice ; we use tinned fat and we have tinned butter, which I
never use for table. Rice is practically my only " vegetable," and
I can get it very cheap ($\frac{3}{4}d.$ a pound). Lemons and limes I can
also get, and generally onions. A really useful cookery book for
Africa would be a rare boon. I never quite recalled how much
one is bound to the flesh until I had to do without salt and sugar,
and very occasionally flour. . . .

Please remember me to any inquiring friends. . . .

Yours, etc.,

A. F. SIM.

Letter to W. W——, dated,—

Kota Kota, *July 2nd*, 1895.

MY DEAR ——,

. . . I shall not take boarders on a large scale till I
build a proper School. I have first my own house—which, let me
tell you, is a big success—it houses not me only, but fifteen million
ants of different sizes, some millions of mosquitoes, some hundreds
of scorpions and cockroaches, which I have not counted, and a
cat. The jiggers are irregular in their attendance, so I don't call
their register. Besides my house then, which we may call the
" Noah's Ark," I have William's house, another teacher's house,
and two more like it for my principal workmen. Also I have a
big thing, mostly roof, with walls of reeds, 60 ft. by 20 ft. inside,
which is School and Preaching-house combined. I am now adding a spare room at the corner of my verandah for my white

companion when he comes, though I shall probably go into it myself. I cannot run to another house. . . . Mud is our only mortar at present, as so far we have not discovered any lime. There is some at Deep Bay at 2*s*. 6*d*. a cwt., unburnt, carriage by steamer £6 or £8 a ton. The Universities' Mission carries most or all of our goods from Matope, about 250 miles above the Rapids, and saves a small fortune every year.

There are seventy-one boys in school this afternoon, divided into four classes. We are going to buy some old canoes and make tables of them, as they are flat-bottomed and more or less wall-sided and of very hard wood. We shall be very well off then—as well as Likoma School, though a little rougher. They had proper deal flooring-boards from England to make their tables, etc., out of. We have made everything ourselves—chairs for teachers, small tables, blackboards, stands for ditto, etc., etc. You can imagine their being rather *rough*. Our planes are worn into awful shapes, as the men never sharpen them properly ; and when they are so blunt you know what happens. An adze (of which we have two) is one of the most useful tools ; it is an improvement on what the natives use themselves, so they get on pretty well with it. One fellow, whom I have kept at carpenter's work, is quite decent with a saw—jolly hard work it is too, with wood like mahogany, and green, unseasoned stuff. . . .

I wish I knew how to make windows out of my spoilt photographic plates ! Will you, next day you have " off," run over and show me ? . . .

Goodbye. . . .

Yours, etc.,

A. F. SIM.

Kota Kota, *July* 11*th*, 1895.

MY DEAR ——,

. . . The gunboats came in late, after dark, on Tuesday night ; and when I was fast asleep in bed a note came to me from Mr. Swann, which gave me a fright, as I thought he was ill, saying that the Commissioner and Major Edwards had arrived in the " harbour." Well, I managed to go to sleep again under the burden of such a piece of news, but was wakened up by the " Town Crier " (meaning a horn, and a drum, and a loud-voiced man), shouting that the *Bwana mkubwa* had come, and all owners of guns were to go down in the morning to salute him ! Such is the paternal nature of our government out here. Well, when I had just finished breakfast, and was preparing to go up to the Boma and see him, they brought a man with his hand blown to pieces by an exploded gun ; it almost invariably happens when these gunfirings go on that some one is hurt by a bursting gun. It was a nasty sight, but I did not feel a bit sick, as I rather thought such sights would make me feel. I applied a tourniquet to stop the bleeding, dressed it with iodoform and vaseline, and this morning he has gone in the gunboat to Bandawe to see Dr. Prentice. The thumb, or perhaps the hand, will have to come off. I was afraid he would get tetanus. . . .

After finishing off this poor fellow I went up to pay my respects to the Commissioner, and had a long talk with him about the affairs of State, about the Chisanga raid, the future of the Eastern shore, the Yaos, etc. I found he entirely agreed with me about the position of Likoma as our head Station, and went so far as to say if Mponda's were chosen he would guarantee the money to build the Church. This of course was nothing to bind him to ; but he would lend his name to begging for it in home papers. He was quite nice about this site here, and said it would be made over to the Mission under the Government seal, etc. He came over with me to see the place, and expressed himself delighted with it. . . .

Major Edwards is commander of the armed forces out here. There are several bullying chiefs that have to be wiped out, so you will see his name in the papers probably. After lunch I saw a big camera coming along, and somewhere in the rear was the Commissioner. He is a small man and inclined to be stout, with a little moustache and beard, very artistic, a really good painter and drawer. He wrote, among other things, " *The History of a Slave*," and illustrated it himself. He has also written the " *Life of Dr. Livingstone*," in the " *Great Explorers* " series. He is an able little man. . . .

July 17th.—The " *Ilala* " came in from the South on Sunday, the 14th, with a party of sportsmen, who had chartered her for a fortnight—very decent fellows—they dined here. They had a letter of introduction to me from Mr. Nicholl. That wretched man with the hand blown off did not go to Bandawe. I got the doctor who came with the sportsmen to look at him. He fears tetanus, so do I, as the silly fellow will not come up to have it dressed every day.

If I had had all the knowledge I want, I should have cut off his thumb at any rate. Even then it might have turned to tetanus ; but we must do our best for him. . . .

W. W—— sends me full plans for building my Church ! But I don't know if I can get the wood, etc., to carry them out. I think it will have to be rather rougher than he contemplated. I don't know yet what I shall do. I think a Church will be necessary before next year ; and yet I don't want to go in for great expense until the Bishop returns, because he has promised Dr. Laws to reconsider our position here. I do not for a moment think we shall give it up, but letters I have received from the Archdeacon bid me not to launch out too far, and not to push beyond the bounds of Kota Kota. . . .

My dear chap, if any one is in a generous mood and wants to send me something nice, tell him to send me a roll of bacon ! I had a taste of a piece sent from Likoma, and life assumed a different hue ! I am sure it would reach me in splendid condition packed in salt, as they send hams, and I could use the salt. Mr. Nicholl, knowing how one yearns for these things sometimes, has sent me a couple of hams. I haven't begun them yet. They are sewn up in canvas and packed in salt. . . .

Patience must be my motto for some time to come. Kindest remembrances to all my old friends. . . .

Yours, etc.,
A. F. Sim.

Letter to F. C. M——, dated,—

Kota Kota, *July* 20*th*, 1895.

My dear ——,

. . . To-day I have been making a flagstaff. The people naturally don't know the difference between one day and another, so for their benefit I am going to hoist a flag on Sunday, and another when they are to come to class. My big bell is cracked so badly that I cannot use it. I think the flagstaff is a great success, forty feet long, with a topmast cross-tree, truck and all. In a strong wind it bends like a fishing-rod. The flags are home made out of calico. . . .

Mr. Swann and I are starting a slave village on my land. We start with about ten families. This being till lately an emporium for slaves, they still come in small numbers, and are still set free to look after themselves. Natives must have some one to look up

to, or their freed state is worse than bondage, as they go near to
starving and then pawn or sell themselves again. I want to let
them build round my place, and they and those who follow them
can look to me as their "Baba" (Father). This would not involve
trouble I think, seeing that we live under the shadow of the brave
old flag of England. All future freed slaves are to be added to this
settlement, so it will in time become a growing concern. . . .

It is all very well for you to talk about beards. Just set yourself
to grow one on the top of your head, and then I will tell you
whether it goes inside or outside the sheets—sheets, no, I have
forgotten what they are. . . .

"Skipper" has gone ere now to Liverpool. It will be hard work
for him, poor old boy, but such a nice lot of men. I am so glad I
know them. I helped him (a little) in the Liverpool Mission
eighteen months ago. I am very glad, yet I can't help feeling
anxious for him ; I do hope Liverpool will agree with him. Whatever it does for him, he will do Liverpool good. It is a grand
sphere, and no mistake. . . .

In reference to a Parochial Missionary Organization, I think it
is best to stick to one Mission, but to bring in another now and
then to talk about and perhaps give a little help to. People can't
become thoroughly interested in more than one, though they can
be made to understand there is more than one. . . .

If I were a philanthropist I could amuse myself with much profit
by making a big village refuge for the freed slaves ; but I should
have to be prepared for political troubles, and fight my people's
battles, etc., etc.   However one white man is not really capable
of doing this, and I doubt if it would really succeed. We did it I
suppose with some success at Mbweni, in Zanzibar, and now those
people are spreading across to the mainland, where there is a little
colony of them near Kichelwe, with a native Deacon. . . .

Give my love to old pals, especially the boating men. . . .

Yours, etc.,

A. F. SIM.

Kota Kota, *July 20th*, 1895.

MY DEAR ——,

. . . I have just returned from my daily instruction of a
convicted murderer the man who killed a Makua soldier some
time ago, and who was sentenced to death when the Commissioner
called here. I have been up each day to see the poor fellow,

and have taken William with me to ensure his understanding the message. He listens, says he believes, and he knows the short Creed, Duty to God and his neighbour, and the Lord's Prayer, so I cannot take him so far without giving him the full privileges of the Church on earth. . . .

July 25th.—Yesterday the gunboat brought the Commissioner on his return, and to-day I have celebrated my first Baptism in Africa. At daybreak this morning, in the presence of three Christian boys, I baptized him, giving him the name "Jacobo," this being St. James's Day. He died painlessly at 7 a.m., and now I have buried him in the first Christian grave in our little God's Acre. Is it not a strange firstfruit of one's stay here—a penitent, I believe so far as his knowledge went, really penitent murderer? I need not say how awful and solemn the days of teaching and preparing him have been. I think he was brave at the last, and seemed much comforted that he had friends about him, and, as we assured him, a Friend above. . . .

The Commissioner was very kind to me, and when I showed him the plans I had drawn for the brick Church he was quite enthusiastic. He believes, as I have come to believe, that wattle and daub is as expensive (*more* in the long run I think) as bricks. . . .

Well, my determination, if God spares me, is to build a Church worthy of His honour. I want it also to be an object lesson. I shall use nothing (unless glass after a little time) but what comes out of this soil and country ; and I am confident I shall be able to build very cheaply, strongly, effectively, and more worthily of our great cause. . . . I want to do no more in the way of temporary building, and when I begin again, I want my first building to be the choir and chancel of a brick Church ; and so contributions, however large or small, will be thankfully received by my "Commissary," the Rev. A. A. McMaster, towards the permanent Church of Kota Kota. I don't want to draw upon Mission funds, so I am going to beg from my friends. £50 will build the sanctuary ; £80, or £100, will build the sanctuary, choir, and aisle ends. This is the appearance I want the Church to have from the East--apsidal—no ornamentation is required in that grand old Norman work. Small windows suit this country, as they suit Norman architecture. I think with this we can get dignity and effect. Chancel will be 15 ft. high to wall plate, aisle roof springs 15 ft., and the outside walls of the body of the Church 10 ft., or

9 ft. 6 in. Width of chancel 20 ft., nave 20 ft., aisles 10 ft. each, length such as is necessary. The roof is of course my principal difficulty, and I fear I shall have to content myself with a grass roof, although, if I can make bricks here, I do not see why one

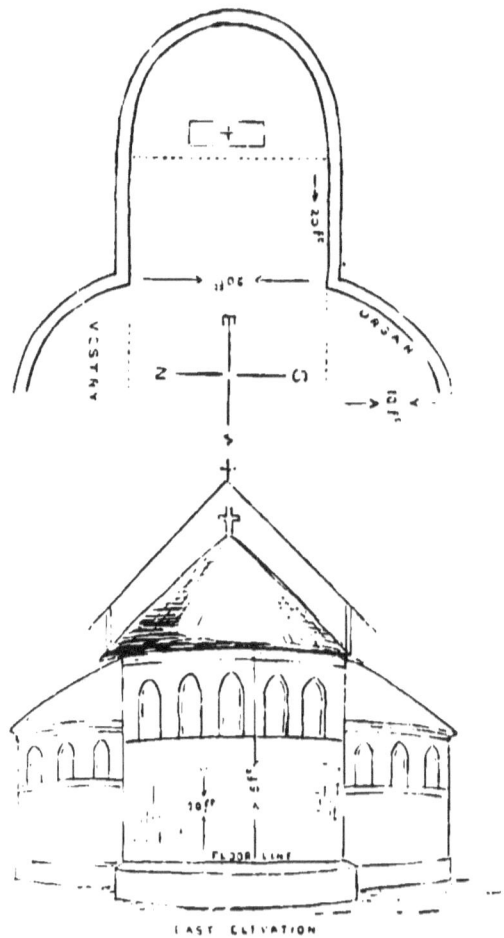

should not make tiles. An iron roof naturally occurs to one, but the freight would be enormous ; even a ton would cost £20 or £30, and how many tons should I require? I shall not begin till next dry season ; in fact not till I see the Bishop on his return. Mr.

Swann is quite keen about it, and takes great interest in my soaring ambition. The Commissioner said I could appeal to him for "advocacy," but I hope to be able to do without that ; in fact among my personal friends I hope to be able to get enough to build the chancel ; then I shall be content for a long time, though probably when I get so far I shall be fired with further enthusiasm. Whenever we have our Offices and Celebration in the little oratory, I cannot help dreaming of a day when, please God, we shall have a large congregation of communicants and a seemly Church as far as the fabric goes. . . .

If I could get lime to make mortar—and it is only a question of cost—of course the building would be ever so much more permanent, and the walls would defy white ants. . . .

Mr. Swann came over this afternoon for a game of football, at which he is very keen. Oh, how we do sweat, to put it in plain English ! Some of the boys, two from Likoma, are too much for us ; they never tire. It is doing wonders for them, as they are naturally cowards ; but the football is making them more plucky, and already they don't like to show that they feel a kick. One of the gold prospectors came over too, a huge man, sixteen stone or more. We could not persuade him to keep goal, but he stayed to dinner. . . .

July 31*st.*—To-day there is a story of war to tell. A Yao chief, on the other side of the Lake, butchered in cold blood some people who lived under a neighbouring chief, for the sole reason that they had paid customs due on ivory, which they had brought through Kota Kota. So Kota Kota is going to be avenged on him. The "*Pioneer*," which happened to come in the same day as the news, steamed out again to fetch Sikhs and a gun (seven pounder), under Captain Hamilton, who is coming back here for the Kota Kota contingent of seven Sikhs and two hundred irregu- lars (very irregular). They are going to surprise the good man and burn his village. The people's glee at the prospect of an assured victory and plunder is horrid to look upon. . . .

August 2*nd.*—The expedition found the man whom they had gone to help in such a state of terror of his friends that he refused to go with them. In fact he and his people fled and would not come near them, so they had to spend the night cutting firewood : for on a lea shore with no firewood, they ran a good chance of becoming a wreck if any wind had sprung up. They have had

all their trouble for nothing, and now the man aimed at will say that the white man came and went away because he was afraid.
. . .

I have been out here nearly a year (ten months), and have seen only four of the Likoma people since I left Likoma last September ; three of these passed this place on their way home, and three of the staff there I have never seen. In days to come communication will be much improved, as railways and telegraphs will mend matters a little. . . .

The last time the "*Domira*" passed here she had on board a white man as a prisoner—six months' hard labour, if you please, for cruelly beating a black servant. He had given him seventy-five lashes with a hippo-hide stick, and then he rubbed salt in the raw wales. The boy's wrong-doing was what we should call right-doing, as he had reported his master's beastly lust and vice to the Administration magistrate at Deep Bay. The white man was a servant of the African Lakes Co., and I think he richly deserved his punishment, don't you? I am glad to see that justice is sufficiently impartial out here to take that line with a white man.
. . .

I am about to build a room in my baraza for my white companion, and Mr. Swann has given me 1,000 bricks to try my hand with them ; but I have no trowels and no mortar, and none of my men have ever seen a brick wall ! . . .

Yours, etc.,

A. F. SIM.

Letter to Mrs. F——, dated,—

Kota Kota, *July* 25*th*, 1895.

MY DEAR ——,

We have had a visit from Commissioner H. H. Johnston. He is one of those who takes an interest in our Mission, and who is strongly impressed, as I think I told you I am, with the inadequacy of Likoma to the needs of our Mission as its head-quarters if our work is to grow and be a large organization. This too is a dream I fear I shall scarcely see realized, namely, the removal of our head station from Likoma to Mponda's village, opposite Fort Johnston, which is on the main artery of the trade of this country. Being in the midst of a large, thickly populated country, it would give all those newly joined missionaries, who of course at first congregate at the head station, a sphere in which to work off their zeal. The first year of a missionary's life is his most trying time, and the zeal which burns brightly when he first arrives has a chance of being extinguished when he is set down to learn a language, and has nothing else to do except looking after stores and counting the spoons and forks once a week ! Have I told you that I am expecting a white companion—a Mr. Faulkner, who was working at Zanzibar when I passed through ? I met him there, and liked what I saw of him very much. He leaves England after his holiday in August, so I may expect him in October or November. He is a practical man and will be exceedingly useful, enabling me to get about much more than I can do at present ; besides, if my dream of building the Church comes true, he will be exceedingly helpful I expect. I shall build another room in this house under the baraza, which is 12 ft. wide ; this will do for one of us, and so we shall both be under one roof, and there will be little or no expense. The Commissioner on both occasions paid me a special visit, and was most gracious. He compared this station most favourably with Likoma. I have built a bigger and a stronger house than any there. The initial cost may have been greater, but I expect my house to outlast two of their kind, and when it begins to tumble down, it will I think be time to build a brick house.

To-day is Saturday, *July 27th,* a day of more or less peace and quietness, when I prepare for Sunday, and the school has a holiday ; but on this day the morning is made hideous by the boys cleaning and sweeping my house out. Mud floors require much sweeping, and there is a horrid dust while they are being done. That is the only part—the floor—which I wish was brick.

An interesting question is arising here ; at this place especially many slaves are released ; the question is what to do with them. African customs and habits lend themselves to slavery in a peculiar way. All ordinary natives live under the protection of a recognised chief, or headman. He is the Father ; he protects them, clothes them, and they in return cultivate his land for him, etc. He also sells his people sometimes. The result is that no African can live independently ; he must have some one in whom he can recognise his Father. When slaves are released far from their homes, they often voluntarily go into slavery again, simply because they have no one to look after them. The question is brought forward here by the release of 120 men who declared themselves slaves. These men have again been beguiled into practical slavery. But the man who has done this is now in durance vile, and has been sent to Fort Johnston in irons. Now what is to be done for them? They want a home and ground to cultivate. I am much tempted to put my finger in the pie and start a freed slave village, and become in some measure their Father! But I think I might get into trouble, for no doubt it would cost some money—more than I have to spend upon such an experiment. The magistrate here is greatly interested in the matter, and the end will be that together we shall do what we can to provide for them. But it is an interesting development—the point at which the spheres of the Administration and of Missionary work touch. You will like to hear that our magistrates are fairly impartial out here to black and white.

August 2nd.—Since writing we have had exciting preparations for war. News came from the East shore that one of the Yao chiefs, living a few miles from the Lake shore, had killed three men for the sole reason that they had paid Custom dues for their ivory passing out of this country. So immediate preparations were made, and the gun-boat "*Pioneer*" went down to Fort Maguire and took sixty fighting men, including Sikhs, under Captain Hamilton and Major Edwards, and made their way to this place; but they found the very people, whose cause had been espoused, in such a state of terror that nothing but empty houses were left. So they came away. It is so like a native—he is completely at the mercy of quick movements. Such consternation was spread by the gun-boats that the rumours reached other villages and everybody fled —even the crew of a Government dhow which happened to be over there. Well, nothing was done, and the guilty chief was not punished, and it remains to be seen what he will do next! It was just the same here when young Jumbe was arrested; the "*Adventure*" came in to take him away, and everybody fled, innocent or guilty. One old headman has become a fast friend since then. And now he will even dare to go on board a gun-boat! Of course, this expedition was to have gone into Portuguese territory, but there is not a single Portuguese there.

The Yao Chiefs, finding this side of the Lake closed to their slave traffic, have begun to raid the Nyanja villages along the Lake shore on the East side. Thus they are brought into immediate contact with our Mission.

Will you remember me most kindly and affectionately to all my
Sunderland friends, and especially to your own family ? Thanks
again and again for the papers to which I look forward eagerly by
each mail. How I miss the trudges, and bicycle rides, and out-
ings, etc. ! Here the country is a blaze of grass fires—grass 8
or 10 ft. high. It is getting on towards the very hot season. I
am extraordinarily well ; jiggers alone trouble me, and they are
numerous, but even to them I am getting accustomed.

Now farewell, with all kindest wishes.

Yours, etc.

A. F. SIM.

August 5th, 1895.

MY DEAR M——,

. . . The "*Domira*" passed here on Saturday, August 3rd,
with a large expedition—ten white men with two Maxim guns—
exploring for gold and taking up a concession in British Central
Africa of a territory of 600 square miles. Another similar party
is here under a cousin of F. L——'s, of Pembroke College. He
gets £1,000 a year and all expenses until the land is broken up ;
and then he is to get 10 per cent. of the profits and a fixed stipend
of £300 a year—I suppose as long as he likes to stick to it.
Another concession further South, just behind this, perhaps three
days' journey, has been floated for a million ! The shares were
sold in twenty-four hours. . . .

It is jolly to hear of the old hands coming back into the choir.
Tell W—— I will send him plans by next mail of my new brick
Church ! Tell him it is the kingpost couples I shall have to use,
as I understand the foot-beam can be divided in that style. If
any money comes in, will you pay it into the bank, and I can
draw by cheque out here ? . . .

The "*Domira*" brought news of the death of the manager of the
African Lakes' Company. He has been out here eighteen years,
and was on his way home to get married. He was one of those
you would have considered quite inured to Africa, and he looked
as healthy as a farmer. He was universally respected and liked.
He started life as a blacksmith. . . .

My dear boy, if you want to get rid of the influenza, come out
here and listen to the boys doing the tonic sol-fa—it is ex-
cruciating in its present stage. Though if we can teach them to

sing head notes instead of bawling, there is some hope for them.
. . .

So farewell.   With all kind wishes to yourself and old friends.

Yours, etc.,

A. F. SIM.

Kota Kota, *August* 14*th*, 1895.

MY DEAR ——,

The heat is growing greater every day.   I do not like it so
much as the cold weather ; and the country, and especially my
garden, is becoming a wilderness.   . . .

I have made an experiment in bricks and mud, and am building
the spare room for my future helper.   I am following a curve round
the outside end of the baraza to give an idea of what an apse will
turn out, and I am very pleased with it.   It is a "mudlark" if
nothing else.   We have no lime here, and so we have to be content with mud for mortar.   The mud from the old ant hills is very
sticky, and hardens in the sun ; but it is a very dirty job, and you
may be able to imagine me a mass of mud from head to foot.   I
find bricklaying, of which I have to do most myself, very heavy
work, as our bricks are ten by five inches.   I wish I knew something about bricklaying, and carpentering, and thatching, and
gardening.   Common sense is the only experience I have of any of
these things, but I confess I am often puzzled.   . . .

August 20*th.*—On Sunday I had two little freed slaves sent to
me by Mr. Swann ; they are cheeky and as happy as the day is
long, though at first they were awfully frightened.   One little fellow
delights to cheek the big boys and then run to the kitchen, which
is his present home, for refuge.   The other is rather sickly—I
expect it is whooping-cough, so I keep him separate from the
rest.   . . .

What with building, carpentering, tinkering, writing, teaching,
and preaching, I have little time for reading, and but little to read,
except when the mail comes in.   I have read every biography I
can lay my hands on, the last that of that extraordinary man,
Laurence Oliphant.   I have also been reading *Dickens' Life*, and
two or three of his books over again in the light his Life sheds
upon them.   It is as well to be busy, as otherwise one might have
time to think of fever.   . . .

I have had a dozen pine apples from my garden, and ten more
or so are coming on.   They are the most satisfactory fruit to grow

here, as they do so well in dry soil. I daresay I have a hundred plants now. I am trying some pomegranate cuttings, but they don't look up to much. I shall devote myself to getting cocoanuts this next season, and planting as many as ever I can in every direction. The two little mango trees are coming on well. I wish I had orange seeds, but I can't get them, so please send me some out of the next oranges you eat. Send only good seed ; try them by floating them in water first. Mr. Swann has been very generous to me. He made me a present of a cow and a calf last week, and also two goats. It is strange to think that a goat costs less to kill and eat than a tin of tongue or corned beef. The reason I kill so few is that I can't get through them. I have one or two sheep, and they are capital eating ; of course they are not much like mutton, yet ever so much better than goat's flesh. . . .

September 2nd.—It is a year to-day since I reached Kota Kota. All best wishes.

Yours, etc.,

A. F. SIM.

Kota Kota, *S. Bartholomew's Day, August 24th,* 1895.
MY DEAR ——,

. . . To-day is a Festival in our Mission, commemorating the first Baptisms I believe, or something of that sort—*vide* Almanack, which I don't possess. So we begin a week's holiday from school to-day. I am thinking of trying to see if I can hit an elephant next week ; but it is difficult to get away when one is alone. Last week we held an examination of the children (seventy-five in all), and the Report is fairly good, seeing that what progress they have made they have made from nothing. I gave three Scripture prizes, and all the school received a bit of calico to wear. They are huge swells to-day in their white calico. You can call this what you please—bribery, if you like. Anyhow those that have come hitherto had no promise of anything, and did not expect it. Of course they look upon it as wages for coming to school, just as if they had been doing some work for me ! I can't help that ; we must gradually get to a better state of things ; anyhow it is a great thing to see the boys decently clothed. How long it will last I do not like to predict. To-day we have a feast. Two goats, a gift from Mr. Swann, are in the pot boiling, and also rice ; so we are bent on having a good time. I expect when we begin school again the whole juvenile population will try and attend ! It is and has been blowing a gale for the last few days. It is a rough time for the boats I know.

The freed slave village is growing and will grow,—sixteen or eighteen houses now, and more in process of building. Last Sunday two little fellows were sent over by Mr. Swann, freed from a caravan passing over. Nearly every caravan that passes brings a few slaves. Mr. Swann is a capital hand at finding them out. He takes them unawares by some apparently innocent question, and it generally comes out that they have slaves. These are freed and sent over to me, and their captors are put in chains for twelve months or so. I am keeping these little fellows in the house.

I am busy making preparations for Mr. Faulkner. My building operations are delayed for lack of more bricks, so I am engaged upon furniture for him—a writing table and a washhand-stand ! I am looking forward keenly to having him. We shall be able to double the work by extending our visits to parts of the village further away.

The bell is just going for the feast. The food does not look savoury, but filling. The children sit in rings with a round mat in the middle, on which is piled the rice and a bowl of goat, and into which they all dip their fingers. This is an idea for your Sunday School feasts. When they have eaten their fill they think of drinking, and each washes his fingers—there is an Oriental simplicity about it.

We are digging a well, which is rather an interesting bit of work. I thought I saw gold once, but it was only yellow mica. There is a peculiar blue clay, the formation in which, Mr. Swann says, diamonds are found. So if I make a fortune out here, don't say I didn't tell you about it. . . .

August 25th.—This is Sunday, just after the heathen preaching. There was a large congregation, how many I can't say ; but I was surprised as it is blowing a gale and very cold. I have been blowing these lazy, do-nothing people up, calling them all sorts of names, anything to stir them up to a divine discontent with their surroundings. The freed slaves turned up well. . . .

It is so nice to see these youngsters decently clothed, wearing a good large bit of white calico instead of a filthy little bit about two inches wide. Now that I have given them calico I suppose I shall have to give them soap to wash it with. Jiggers are an awful nuisance this dry weather. It is a matter of daily occurrence both with Mr. Swann and myself to have one or two or even five taken out of our feet. Sometimes they get into one's fingers. However, I know the feeling so well now that I can generally spot them when they first enter the skin, but even so they often choose tender spots about the quick of the nail, and it is painful work to get them out.

Yesterday afternoon we had a great game of football. Mr. Swann delights in it and gets quite excited. We have two Likoma boys who can knock the sparks out of both of us, even with our boots on. We have great fun, and it is satisfactory to find the boys getting a little more manly, and some of the little fellows will stand up to one and charge the biggest boys. When you send me the balls—small balls—we shall have to begin a course of cricket. I want to rig up a gymnasium of a mild kind—a swing, horizontal bar, and so on—anything to make the boys take an interest in school life and to attach them to the school.

Mr. Swann has been particularly generous to me of late. He gave me a cow and calf the other day, and two goats for the feast. This he says is in return for some furniture I have made him— chairs and a table, both of a most primitive sort. Thus I have milk of my very own now. I have always had plenty, as Mr. Nicholl used to send me some every day, morning and night, and Mr. Swann has kept it up. The people just here are by no means pastoral. They know nothing about cattle, and I get very riled to see them driving the cows at a canter. One of the little freed slave boys —"Feruzi" is his name—is playing football like a "good un." He at any rate feels himself at home. He has a mother somewhere, but his father was killed in war—some slave raid I suppose. He belongs to a tribe at the back of the hills behind Kota Kota, upon which the Angoni make constant raids. It is from the Angoni that the Yaos and coast people buy most of their slaves on this side of the Lake. It is very striking how seldom these youngsters squabble among themselves. Some of the smallest among them were the best attenders at school, and got a fathom of calico for a prize. They cut the most comical figures with this stuff wrapped round them—nothing but their little black heads and arms and legs appearing. They have such a comical way when they are mutually pleased, or tickled with something, of shaking hands—"Tip us a flipper, old chap" sort of

thing. Old and young do it, and to see a couple of wee scraps
doing it is the best part of the joke I think. . . .

I should appreciate a big School or Church bell which could be
heard all over the village from the Mission. The flag-staff is a
huge success. In these heavy winds it bends almost like a fishing-
rod, but it is so light and strong that I have no fear of its breaking. I am rather afraid to leave it up when the stormy season
comes round. I wish you would make enquiries as to copper or
other metal for a lightning conductor. At Likoma the station is
in a hollow between hills and so they don't get the lightning as we
do. There is real danger of fire I believe ; houses more than
once have been set on fire at Bandawe, besides other accidents,
and there are few long residents in this part who don't number
such incidents among their experiences. At Bandawe they have
lightning conductors now. I wonder what would be the cost of
100 feet—at least less than that of a new house. But I think the
Mission should supply me with this. Don't go further than making
enquiries as to price. Mr. Swann has offered to make me 60,000
bricks at 10s. per 1,000, and I have promised to take them ; so I
hope somehow or other I shall be able to pay for them ! I expect
my wisest course is to be patient about building my permanent
Church. I had better I think get my hand in over the School,
and teach one or two men the art of laying the bricks straight.
In this case I think I should have to be content to build a small
temporary chancel, outside of which I could build the permanent
brick chancel ; and yet I don't think this would be the cheapest
way. Only you see I have not a bricklayer at hand, and my
skill, as you can imagine, is limited, though I am not frightened
of trying. . . .

For the present Farewell, or " Kwa keri," as they say here.
Ask —— for the rest of my news.

Yours, etc.,
A. F. SIM.

Letter to E. L. ——, dated,—

Kota Kota, *August 28th*, 1895.

MY DEAR ——,

. . . We have been digging a well, and it is a great success.
At twelve feet we came to solid bed rock, and the water stands

at present about two feet deep. This is very fortunate, and it is
good water, so that I can now see the bottom of my basin when
it is full of the well water—a thing I have not succeeded in
accomplishing for a long time. I think of bricking the walls up
to keep the mud from tumbling in. Those four men, who worked
down the pit, succeeded so well that they broke both crowbar and
pickaxe over the business and so we have had to stop. To have
this water near will be a great saving of trouble, as hitherto we
had to send a great distance for it, and it was only poor stuff
when we got it. Now that the freed slaves' village (eighteen or
twenty houses are now in process of building) is growing, and my
hearers' Classes number about eighty men and a hundred women,
when I have a helper I hope to be able to do much more work.
I have a plan simmering in my mind of starting a Girls' School,
separate from the boys, under my teacher's wife, who is a capital
scholar and motherly body. She was a freed slave, and was
brought to Zanzibar very young. It is a pity her training should
be laid aside. She has two children—both girls. I do not care
about the girls learning very much, but they might get a little
humanised. A few come to the Boys' School, but I don't think
it will do them much good, and it can't go on for ever. . . .

August 24th was the festival of St. Bartholomew, and we have
a holiday for a week in commemoration of the first Baptisms at
Zanzibar. Previous to this I held an examination (in which
seventy-five boys took part) in Reading, Writing, and Scripture.
Arithmetic only extends to counting so far with most of the
scholars. On the whole I am well satisfied with their progress,
especially as they began from nothing. So I gave three prizes
for Scripture, and to each scholar a prize for attendance ; the
prizes consisted of calico. You may call it a jolly good bribe if
you like, or something done in the way of a corporal act of
mercy—clothing the naked ; anyway the boys are great swells
these days. I want to encourage as much self-respect as will
make them keep themselves clean, for they are a dirty lot of little
urchins at best. I think there are even now a few of the best
boys and a few men and women whom I could present for ad-
mission to the Catechumenate. You can imagine this a step of
some importance in such a new state of things. Their ways of
thinking, etc., are so different from ours, and ours so unintelligible
to them. . . . We also had a feast for the scholars on St.

Bartholomew's Day—a boiled goat and rice, followed by a game of football as a digestive. The feast was a great success.

August 29th.—On Sunday I had a capital congregation, rather to my surprise as there was a cold wind blowing. I should think there were a hundred men and women, and a hundred children. . . .

Mr. Swann like myself is in hopes of getting an assistant, so we shall double our number of white men here this year. What with old houses and those now building in the freed slave village there must be nearly forty just outside my paling on the Mission property. An old lady, who had escaped from a caravan of slaves passing through, made her way up here with her child this afternoon ; and so it will go on growing, house by house, until there is quite a town here. It will be very interesting work to watch, as they look upon me as their " *Baba.*" It would of course be impossible to do anything like this but for the magistrate here. There is no such thing as a freed slave settlement except where there is a European power to protect it ; and if any large number of people attached themselves to a missionary, say in Portuguese country, he would have to have an armed force to protect them and look after them. The magistrate has the armed force, and I look upon him as one would look to the Bench and police in England to protect us and maintain order. Although the country on the East shore, on which most of our stations are planted, is painted Portuguese in the maps, it is as lawless and slave raiding and slave dealing as any in Africa. It is a perfect farce calling it protected by a European, or civilized power, in any sense. Poor Dr. Hine has a hard time there at Unangu, bullied by the chief, Kalanji, and with the insolent Yaos as his neighbours and parishioners.

I am very anxious to see the Bishop, and to have a talk with him as to my future policy. I wish all my boys might be boarders, so as to take them out of heathen surroundings ; but how this fits in with our policy I don't know. I don't suppose we want to break up family life, and our first duty to our neighbour is to honour parents. We cannot teach them to despise their homes and their elders. This seems a difficult and ticklish subject. The Roman Missions out here started their work in an almost un-inhabited country. They bought little slave boys—in fact they got Tippoo Tib to provide so many boys of a certain age at so much a head, and with this nucleus they started a school, leaving

adults practically alone. They also armed such adults as came
under them as workers or what not, and in fact started a new
nation or tribe, providing them with arms to defend themselves,
and such implements of civilization as they thought necessary or
useful, teaching them trades, etc. Thus they founded a centre,
and threw off from it ever increasing circles of villages and settle-
ments as their boys and girls grew up. Mr. Swann says that in
this way the whole of the West of Tanganyika will be Roman
Catholic. They are called *Watu wa Msalaba* (people of the Cross)
and own the Roman Mission as their chief—a somewhat temporal
though very powerful sway, but one which we have always shrunk
from and which is scarcely primitive in its style. . . .

There, dear lad, I have filled up six pennyworth. I am very
well in every way, and happy, and deeply interested. . . .

Yours, etc.,

A. F. SIM.

Kota Kota, *August* 30*th*, 1895.

MY DEAR ——,

The "*Domira*" came in from the South with no mails, the
story being that a new sorter (a native) had been appointed at
Blantyre. He succeeded excellently till the bags were closed,
when he put the wrong labels on them, sending back the English
mail on its way home again, and the African letters were returned
to Fort Johnston! Isn't this barbarous? It was a great disappointment to me. I have not heard from home since the end of
May. Perhaps also my letters to you will be delayed in consequence. . . . It is interesting to think that Bishop Steere's
great idea of having a chain of stations in the direction of the
Rovuma is completed by the new station at Mtarikas—it is seven
days from Unangu, and twenty from Masasi. So though the
chain is more or less complete the links are rather long ones. . . .

I fear the Bishop may look aghast at our freed slave village.
It has however cost me nothing. I shall give them all the
employment I can, and Mr. Swann too has promised to employ
them. When he and I first talked about starting this village, I
must say I thought it was rather a dream, and that it would be
difficult to accomplish; but it has been no difficulty whatever, and
no expense. . . . Three more freed slaves have come in to-
day, and I have apportioned them "building sites" (bits of ground

about as big as your sitting-room). The settlement numbers about seventy souls, including children.   . . .

September 1st.—It is a year to-day, the first Sunday in September, since I put foot in Kota Kota—last year it was September 2nd. What a different man I am in myself and all my surroundings since then ! How thankful to God for all His mercies I ought to be, and am ! Africa is a different place to me from what it was. I begin to see a little of the habits of thought of the people, as I begin to know more of their language. You see I had been ill-prepared for the life out here by all the kindnesses and super-fluities of home ; but I am more than content with God's dealing with me now that I begin to see my way a little. These boys are very lovable, and as I get to know them better, and they me, I think I shall have a very happy lot. None can accuse them of not being keen, and when well treated I think they will do anything for one. I have been slow to encourage them too much—think-ing it best to get to know them a little at first, for of course they differ the one from the other as English children do, and some will take advantage of one.   . . .

I have written to Mr. Nicholl to-day ; the news of Kota Kota interests him very much. It has a charm of its own, although it bears a very bad name. Mr. Swann and I are greatly pitied for having to live here, but we laugh in our sleeves ! I think the truth is this place is not "Anglicised," nor is it purely native. It has the glamour of Orientalism about it. The people wear Arab dress (the best classes at least) and the profuse manners of the East still remain in minute degree here. To-morrow work begins again with us, and I shall not be sorry ; living for a week like a hermit, without a hermit's habits and graces, is not much to my liking.

Mr. Swann sent me the first cabbage to-day from his garden, and a bunch of radishes, which my cook at once began to boil. Try a boiled radish, do ! Mr. Nicholl began a garden down in the town in a kind of marsh, and this hot weather it has been a great success. Fancy even wheat surviving and flourishing there, and potatoes, hot-house melons, onions, etc. ; but none of these are ripe yet, and there is many a slip betwixt cup and lip, or between the "*shamba*" (garden) and the table. The moon here, though it is very bright, does not scorch one. I believe it is very bad to sleep in its rays, as it occasions blindness. I do not know the meaning of the

passage in Psalm cxxi. 6. The Revised Version has "The sun shall not smite thee by day, nor the moon by night." May it not be a purely poetic way of expressing God's guardianship?
. . .

Will you tell my old friends I never forget them, though I treat them so badly in the matter of letters? I am sending ten letters home by this mail, most of them longer than this, so I have little time to spare, and there is a rather large correspondence to be carried on locally. At least I do not forget them, and I pray for all my old friends at home every day. . . .

With all best wishes . . .

> Yours, etc.,
>
> A. F. SIM.

September 2nd.—They have sent me Mr. Philipps, a young lay-man who has not been long out here, as my companion. It is rather strange that he should come here exactly a year to the very day after I arrived. It is so hard to realize the first state of things in those old days when we were living in little round native huts. . . . There is a rumour of the murder of Mr. Atlay while away from Likoma on a holiday, but do not mention this unless it is corroborated.

> Kota Kota, *September 5th*, 1895.

MY DEAR ——,

Poor Atlay! We have not had final confirmation of his fate, but I fear there is no ground for hope. He went from Likoma to the mainland for a little shooting during his holidays, and camped a day's journey from the shore, when it is said a party of Angoni (Magwangwara) came upon him and his men. Atlay was asleep in his tent about noon. The drift of the rumours point to his being clubbed and stunned. Since then his boots, kettle, a tin of flour, and a towel have turned up. Two of the boys who were with him have not been seen since; the rest returned, one wounded. I am afraid our worst fears will be confirmed. Mr. Crouch and others went up at once, and though they found the things mentioned above, they could see no trace of Atlay. Conse-quently Mr. W. P. Johnson has gone up to follow the track of the Angoni, and of course it is a great danger to him. The men will be desperate, but we have begun to think that he has a charmed

S

life, and yet we cannot help feeling very anxious for him. We here shall have no more news till the return of the German steamer, a month hence. The Commissioner has been written to, but what can he do, as the affair happened in Portuguese territory? . . .

They have sent me Mr. Philipps, a young layman who hopes to be ordained, from Likoma. I am absolutely unprepared for him, as I did not expect any one for some two months, so I have had to set up my tent in the baraza and sleep there. I have given him my room as both bedroom and sitting-room. Fortunately I had table and chairs ready, and now I am making other furniture for him. On the whole I think he is pretty comfortable. I do not look on him as a permanent fixture, for, as you know, the Bishop has other plans for this place, and if he brings Mr. Williams as far as Nyasa, he will send him here. . . .

The book Mr. L—— sent me on " *Building Construction*" is after all most valuable to me, even to the burning of bricks. I am sadly coming to the conclusion that great doings in the way of brick-building are beyond my powers ; in fact, I could not leave the work a moment. I still hope to be able to build a brick School, but the Church will be a different thing. I must wait I fear till I can get a practical man who can put in his whole time at that. . . .

September 8th.—The grindstone which you sent me I have set up, with a biscuit tin for trough, and soldered it with Mr. R——'s soldering irons, etc. Will you tell him how grateful I am? I feel ready to undertake furnishing and upholstering for the community at large ! I have done so in a small degree. I made six chairs for Mr. Swann, and six for a planter at Zomba, and an armchair of my own patent. The credit side for these shows one cow, a calf, two goats, a cheque for £3 3s., and a lot of seeds. Now I can turn out better work, for with this vice I can cut a decent mortise, and with these soldering tools I can set up a tin-smith's shop. A blacksmith lodges outside in the freed slave contingent, so here we are with all the conveniences of civilization. I want a glazier, a bricklayer, a brick-maker, and perhaps soon a telegraphist. The telegraph is complete to England now I believe from Blantyre. I paid a shilling as my contribution for the first telegram to be sent by the Commissioner to the Queen.

My dear boy, if you knew the almost constant state of anxiety we live in here you would wonder that my hair is not grey. After what I have told you about Atlay, a report comes by native sources, which are very correct on the whole, that a boat belonging to Likoma has been upset at Kajuro, three days South of this, in a squall of wind, and that two white men were drowned. Yesterday a large empty box covered with zinc and locked was brought to the Boma ; some fishermen had found it a day and a half North of Kajuro. Mr. Philipps says that we have many of these at Likoma, and some new ones were expected. The natives on board the boat were taken to Fort Maguire to be examined, as Kajuro is in that district. We are living in fearful suspense. Who were the two white men ? I fear that this will prove true, as native rumours fly very rapidly, and are, for the most part, well-founded. We are expecting no one just now. The Bishop and Mr. Williams are coming overland. Mr. Faulkner is coming with the ladies and is not due here till the end of October. Why was the boat at Kajuro, a long way out of her course to Likoma ? The wind then was southerly. I don't think the boat can possibly have been going South. It has been a week of very heavy winds from the South, so much so that the " *Wissmann* " had to put out two anchors, and was delayed here two days. It was the hardest blow I remember having experienced.

Later.—We have seen this box that I spoke of above, and Mr. Philipps recognises it as just like those at Likoma. It is an anxious time waiting for news. I fear the worst almost, as report says it was a Likoma boat. There are no others like those belonging to Likoma on the Lake, but I have heard that one of the small traders was starting just such a boat. But who the two white men are is a mystery until the German steamer brings news on her return journey. Mr. Swann has sent men, under one of his policemen, to do all they can to get news, and to gather up such things as may wash ashore, and to find out all they can about the bodies. At any rate, if news arrives at home about two men being drowned in a Likoma boat, you will know it is not I. In fact don't believe any reports about my death, for I have given instructions that a telegram should be sent to Mr. Travers, and you will hear as soon as anybody, at any rate before letters could bring you the news. . . .

We are all well here. The school is I think very flourishing. The calico prize has had a good effect, as it serves as a uniform. Now all our boys are quite recognisable in the town by their white cloth. On Saturdays they go down to the Lake with one of the teachers, armed with a bit of soap, and get their cloth washed. A few new boys have come, and some old ones have returned. Mr. Philipps is going to take an English class every day. It is a difficult problem how best to teach English. They pick up such a doggerel in the ordinary way, *e.g.*, " box " is called " *bokosi*," and even spelt so ; "slate" is called "*silati* " ; "steamer," "*siteamer.*" These they take as their own names, so you can imagine our roll call is rather a funny one. . . .

I do wish I had a good practical all-round man like W—— with me, for of course I cannot do everything myself. The amount of carpentering we want is huge, and no one I have, except perhaps William, is capable of measuring anything. Well, anyway they have learnt to saw, and the adze is their natural tool, and one man has learnt to plane in a rough way. On the whole, so far we have been rather successful with our doors and window-frames, tables, chairs, bookcases, etc. So love to all. Don't believe I am dead till I let you know. . . .

Yours, etc.,

A. F. SIM.

Kota Kota, *September 15th,* 1895.

MY DEAR ——,

Perhaps you will know from other sources, before you receive this, how only too true the news is, which I hinted· at in my last letter to you. Bishop Maples and Mr. Williams are dead—drowned in Leopard Bay on their way to Kota Kota. On September 4th we heard the first news, but did not believe it was one of our boats. On September 7th another token, or message, came in the shape of a big wooden box, such as we use at Likoma for stores. Still we thought it possible that some one else might have such a box. At last on September 13th at about noon, after Sext, the message came from the Boma that the crew had come in, having walked from Kazembe (the chief's name) or Kajuro (his village). You can imagine how hard it was to believe it until then. We expected Bishop Maples by the mainland, and I did not look for him till October or November, and no one dreamt of his sailing up to Kota Kota ; but he was in a great hurry to get on as fast as he could. . . .

The natives are steady, trustworthy fellows, but they know nothing about sailing a boat with European sails. They had lowered the mainsail, but kept on in a gale on the quarter under foresail and mizzen—an impossible rig. When the actual capsize took place they were keeping the boat out to avoid the rocky point that runs out at Kazembe's. She must have "broached to." They passed Monkey Bay at 11.30 p.m. ; it was consequently pitch dark, and none of the men knew that coast. I cannot tell you how much we feel this blow. . . . These (including Atlay) are three of our most experienced men, all taken from us in eight days. We have Wimbush and Glossop at Likoma, and Dr. Hine at Unangu is going home this year I believe, as he is not in a fit state of health to remain any longer. But Mr. Faulkner is expected in November, so we are not so short-handed as we might be. . . .

I have scarcely had a fever since I got into this house, and Mr. Philipps is as well as possible, which he was not at Likoma. . . .

All the natives belonging to the crew were saved, but they had to swim four to six miles, and were two hours in the water. . . . All sailors on the Lake speak of Leopard Bay as a dangerous place. Captain Cullen says the depth is from thirty to fifty fathoms—quite impossible to get down to, even if we had divers. . . .

September 27th.—I am thankful to say William was successful in his search, and returned on September 21st with the Bishop's body, which was only identified by the few rags of clothing remaining on it. He arrived at 4.30, and we buried the Bishop's remains at 5.30. I wish we could have by any means sealed up the body hermetically, and sent it to Likoma ; but it was almost unapproachable, and we had no wood to make a coffin. We have buried him under the spot where we intend the Altar of our Church to stand. I intend almost at once to build a temporary chancel, on measurements within those I sent home, so that we can start the permanent building when we are ready. . . .

Have you read Canon Scott Holland's speech at our Anniversary Meeting? It is strange to read it now in face of another Bishop's death, and he was present to hear it. We are crippled without our Bishop ; I was waiting for him to endorse what I have done, and to give me leave to go ahead. With Bishop Maples buried here, I feel it to be a forecast of final success. We have not been allowed hitherto to consider our occupation of Kota Kota as finally settled, owing to the Free Church Mission claiming a first footing on the West side of the Lake, though they had not touched Kota Kota ; albeit they have gone to Lake Tanganyika almost, and South to Livingstonia. Now our seal is set on this place. I aspire to having

the whole Marimba country conceded to us, of which Kota Kota
may be called the capital.   .   .   .

You will not omit to pray for us in our sore need.   .   .   .

Yours, etc.,

A. F. SIM.

Kota Kota, *September 19th*, 1895.

MY DEAR ——,

It is with a poor heart I bring myself to write my letters by
this mail. Before you get this you will hear of the terrible catas-
trophe that has fallen upon us. First there was the awful death of
Mr. Atlay. It is impossible to blame him for carelessness, for no
one would think such an occurrence possible nowadays ; and I
expect if we knew the natives' side of the story we should find it to
be some extraordinary accident on their part, although it does seem
so deliberate.   Mr. Atlay happened to have built his temporary
shelter where the road passes, and to have closed the path of the
Magwangwara.   This to the raiders was itself a challenge ; he was
equipped for a shooting expedition, and perhaps they thought he
was man-hunting.   A raiding party of young irresponsibles is not
accountable for their actions, although they rarely kill a white man
in these days.   Mr. Johnson and his party brought Mr. Atlay's
body to Likoma, and it has been added to the muster now growing in that little graveyard.

The other accident following in eight days makes one ask how
much we who are left, through our sins, contributed to it.   It is
an awfully solemn thing to be entrusted with God's Gospel to the
heathen.   Perhaps we deal with our opportunities too lightly.   God
gives us many a hard, solemn lesson of how near our work is to
His heart, for He casts us upon Himself again and again ; difficulties and losses are the stones of which the spiritual temple is built.
It is not any easier out here than it is at home to live a recollected
life.   Nay it is harder, for sometimes fever and the climate dispirit
one.   I have two hundred souls, young and old, upon my hands to
train in the knowledge of God.   Is it not a great task ?   You will
not forget to pray for us and ask others for their prayers, and have
many an Eucharist with missionary intention.   .   .   .

Sunday, September 22nd.—We have found the Bishop's body.
.   .   .   I cannot tell you what a relief this is to us.   It was almost
with joy that I heard that the body had been recovered.   William
had wrapped the body up most carefully to carry it, and covered it

with a flag with a red cross upon it, which he had taken with him.
. . . Is it not strange that the only bit of personal property belonging to the Bishop which has come to hand should be his holy
Vessels? One of the boys in the crew happened upon them in the
water when the boat sank, and brought them ashore. Tired and
worn as the boys were they would not leave the case containing the
Vessels, but brought it here when they came in. . . . The day
on which the crew arrived at Kota Kota was the 13th of the month.
It struck me at the time how appropriate to the occasion were the
first few verses of the evening Psalm, " Save me, O God ! for the
waters are come in, even unto my soul." William made it known
to all the villages he passed that a big reward would be paid to any
one who brought in or found Mr. Williams' body. And he also
made a complete search to the South of where the boat sank. . . .
It is inexpressibly sad to think of the Bishop's plans for the future
of the work out here. To-morrow (Monday) we are going to offer
a Requiem for all the three who have died by violent deaths. I am
afraid it will be a great shock to all our friends in England. . .
I had hoped Bishop Maples would have admitted a few to the
Catechumenate here. . . . The blow of these three deaths has
had a crushing effect at Likoma. It is heartrending to read all
their letters. . . . Poor Mr. Brooke, I hear, is another victim to
paralysis in the legs—a disease almost peculiar to Likoma. Even
Mr. Philipps had symptoms of it while there. We are very well
here. All things are going well. I feel every day more and more
that God has called me to this work. I feel too that I can be a help
to these poor people, and in time perhaps a help in the counsels
of the Mission. You will I know pray for us at this time. It is
a sad time of trouble and anxiety. I trust none of us will lose
our heads, or lose heart, or courage. And now, farewell. . . .

Yours, etc.,
A. F. SIM.

Letter to A. J. K——, dated,—

Kota Kota, *October 1st,* 1895.

MY DEAR ——,

. . . We have lost three of our oldest men in a week.
G. Atlay was not an old man in years, but he was so heart and
soul in the Mission that one associated him with the work almost
as much as the other two—the Bishop and Williams, who had been
out here nineteen years. When at Blantyre, and talking about the

death of some old Africans—Mr. Fotheringham, of the African
Lakes' Company, in particular—the Bishop was heard to say:
" Well, Williams, we have been in Africa nearly twenty years ; we
cannot expect to live very much longer out here !" Poor Williams
went down in the boat without a word ; he was asleep at the time
in the cabin aft—a temporary erection in the stern sheets. . . .

Nothing has been seen of Williams' body. The accident occurred
sixty or seventy miles South of this ; and, with the prevailing wind,
some things have been found eighty miles from the spot, i.e., sixteen
miles North of this, but the Bishop's body was found among the
rocks almost at the spot where the boat went down. I have done
all that could be done by sending out search parties and offering
rewards. And now we must keep our heads cool and work on and
wait. . . .

Well, old chap, we have many faults and sins, and God teaches
us by many a hard lesson how solemn our work is. How near we
should live to Him ; but it is not easier out here than at home to
be recollected—you will not be astonished to hear that it is harder
indeed. We have long times to wait for visible fruit—two years
at least before any are made Christians. The classes are interesting, and so is the school ; but, unlike the Uganda people, these
people do not evince the keenness for the Gospel or for "reading,"
such as one hears is the case in Uganda. They are "sair hadden
doon," and all keenness about anything seems driven out of them.
To eat, drink, sleep, and dance contents them. To eat they must
cultivate, but it is not much trouble ; they never dream of manuring,
or dressing their gardens. They are scared out of their lives at
the very thought of war. It is not deeply interesting to have to do
with such sluggish people ; but they are God's creatures, and they
have waited long for the Gospel, and it is our work to preach to
them. . . .

My ideal head station is a community with an experienced
representative of every essential trade, e.g., carpenter, mason,
builder, and agriculturist. We have still the terrible consideration
of health with us daily ; but with brick, or stone, or even good
mud houses fever might almost be forgotten. Cultivation means
drainage, and good buildings mean an even temperature. . . .

My feeling about Kota Kota is that it will be considered an out-
station of little importance, because it is not among the Yaos.
The possibilities here are I think very great. If I felt that a

proper and adequate staff would one day be spared to come here, I could work with a better will, for myself alone the work promises to be overwhelming. At present we have our hands full with a hundred hearers and over a hundred school children. I am quite conversant now with Swahili, and getting on with Chinyanja ; the two mix themselves up in my head rather, though Swahili comes most readily to my tongue. . . .

To-day Mr. Swann has started upon a tour of inspection through his district called the Marimba country, the whole of which I should like to be able to reckon as my Parish—a very interesting one, the fountain head of the slave trade at one time. But what could I do with all these people " by my lone " —as the Vicar of St. Aidan's would say ? They call us the people of the Bishop, as opposed to the Presbyterians. . . .

It is hardly credible what a change the coming of the white man here has wrought in a year. The down-trodden are holding their heads up, and beginning to feel that they are as good as their betters. The old influence is being scattered ; most of them have gone to the coast. One of the most important Arabs who was here when I came, with three or four hundred people—presumably most of them slaves—is dead. About eighty of his people, who ran away from him, now form the nucleus of a slave village under my fatherly wing, with Mr. Swann in the background to support me, and really take all the dirty work off my hands. It is an interesting experiment, and indeed a necessary one, for if you free slaves and do not provide them with homes, they are in a worse case than formerly. It is very hot these days, and night and day one is in a continual state of melting away. If this ceases you get fever. Poor Mr. Philipps is not a very healthy subject ; but it is still his first year, and one wants a year to get settled down to the perpetual melting. I expect at the end of this month we shall have some rain, thunderstorms, etc. I look forward to the rains to work a miracle among my trees, fruit, and other plants. They are doing awfully well as it is. I hope in a year or two to have some of all the best fruit that can be grown. Only I have no oranges -will you send me some seeds ? They want grafting ; but I think I could get grafts from Blantyre, or even Zanzibar. In course of time I shall have avenues of limes, lemons, guavas, and custard apples. Flowers are a disappointment. Some beautiful lilies exist for a short time, but not for long ; and zineas and sunflowers do well, and that is about all ! I have already had a dozen pineapples, and another dozen are coming on. I have also cows (two), and calves, and goats. I think of buying more cows and sheep. All this I enjoy very much, and to see to them is my principal recreation ; but I also think they are necessary to existence here. Our people are no good with cattle unfortunately.

I wonder if I have told you anything interesting. I can't give you missionary stories yet. The influence is only general as yet. Hearts are still unquickened ; but by God's grace one will see light entering if you will continue to pray for us. . . .

When these souls begin to have ideals it will be a hard task for their Priest. I trust I have not made you think my life arduous or difficult. I am very happy, and have excellent helpers in my two teachers, and some nice and clever boys coming on. I am indeed happy to have such capital health. As work increases the interest will deepen.

Now let me close by wishing you and your wife a truly happy Christmas. I can't send Christmas cards ! Give us a thought at your Altar on Christmas Day, for you may be sure old friends will be very present to us, if God spares us.

Yours, etc.,

A. F. SIM.

Letter to Mrs. F——, dated,—

Kota Kota, *October* 5*th*, 1895.

MY DEAR ——,

You have doubtless heard of our terribly sad losses. Bishop Maples, George Atlay, and Mr. Williams—the last a layman— all met their deaths in a violent manner within eight days. George Atlay, on August 26th, was killed while out in the midsummer holidays shooting, by a raiding party of Magwangwara (Angoni or Zulu). On September 2nd, about midnight, Bishop Maples and Mr. Williams were drowned coming from Fort Johnston to Kota Kota in one of our sailing boats.

It is a hard lesson God is teaching us. May we by His grace open our hearts to it ! Ours is a solemn work : we are very close, the strongest of us, to the borderland between the work of this life and that of the next. Our time for work is short. May He give us grace to redeem our opportunities ! It is so easy to say that each case was due to their own rashness. It does not minimise our loss, and in each case I don't know that exceedingly great rashness can be proved. In Mr. Atlay's case, it is true he had warnings, but they were vague ; and I doubt whether any one would have felt ready to give up an expedition of that kind for vague rumours of war, which are very rife and generally baseless.

In the Bishop's case, no doubt any sailor would have sought shelter. In either case the immediate loss is ours, and it is very sad to think of the Bishop's death, with all his new plans of work. He was never so full of good spirits and hope as when he came up the river. He was in a fever of impatience to reach Likoma, and had intended coming overland ; but something had prevented this, and I think he was all the more anxious to get to Likoma at once. Mr. Williams was a man about forty-five, a layman, who had been in the Mission for eighteen or nineteen years, and was to have come to me here to help me. The Bishop was not aware I think that I had already got a white companion ; but I think he would have consented to leave both of them here, for if I had a really large staff I could immensely increase this work.

Mr. Atlay was a young man—a Priest—with I always thought great promise of making an invaluable missionary. How long shall we have to wait for a new Bishop ? These are the kind of difficulties which I suppose a missionary's lot is always cast among. It is of no use pretending that they are not trying.

. . .

You would be surprised to know how cold it is and has been these last few days. It is getting on for the very hot season, and it has been raining—a most extraordinary occurrence at this time of the year. We are clothed in our warmest clothing. This is the time one wishes we had glass windows ; for open windows mean cold, and when they are shut there is no light ! The school keeps up to about a hundred still ; I think these children are on the whole wonderfully keen about learning. I don't know what else there is to bring them to school. The hearers too number over a hundred when they are all present. I have four classes in the week for them. Some are very regular ; but there is a fringe of those who have to work in the gardens, etc., and are prevented from coming regularly. How I would like lots of money to develop this work. Once the outlay is made it can be carried on for very little I am sure, labour is so very cheap. I long to build a proper Boarding School, and have all or most of these boys to live here constantly under one's eyes. I wish I could found a

monastic establishment here—lay brothers who would each have
his proper work to do, and a sisterhood for the girls and women.
By such means England, nay Europe, was Christianized, and the
plan is not effete or obsolete for such countries as this. It came
to an end in England because its day was over ; but in these
lands to be won from heathendom I fully believe the old monastic
system still has a work to do.

N.B.—I believe Bishop Westcott is of the same opinion in a
modified sense. Besides the Gospel to preach and teach and the
education of the natives in letters, there are arts to develop—
agriculture, building, farming. All these must be brought into
the natives' own lives to raise them out of their indolence and
animal-like sloth. I do not think the country is capable of
developing very much, and that must be very slowly ; but we are
doing very little in this direction. However simple our aim, yet it
will require properly trained and devoted teachers, for not in our
generation will any return be made. Alas, that we should want
for money ! But who does not? . . .

Yours, etc.,

A. F. SIM.

Kota Kota, *October* 10*th*, 1895.

MY DEAR M——,

I am postmaster in Mr. Swann's absence. His patent, like
Mr. Nicholl's, for keeping the place quiet while he is away on a
tour of inspection, treaty making, etc., is to take all the troublesome ones with him. . . .

It is a bad job you don't improve faster. I can go up to 105'
and back to normal all in about twelve hours, and be well in
thirty-six hours.

Well now, my news is that I may go to Unangu for the wet
season so as to allow Dr. Hine to go home. It is wrong to
allow him to remain out here, and there is no one else to send
(now) so well qualified as myself by reason of my cast iron constitution and knowledge of Swahili. Dr. Hine would come here
in the meantime and be ready to take the steamer on the first
symptoms of fever. I have myself offered to do this. I am not
glad at the prospect. I don't pretend to be, but I hope I am
ready to do anything required of me. I believe that almost any
place is "livable" in, if you make it so. I shall only go for a
short time, and I shall still remain in charge of Kota Kota. I

shall hope to return, if God wills, next year, after about six
months. I shall probably cross the Lake in a dhow, which is
safe, if slow, in the hands of its own crew. There is another
good serviceable boat here, the property of a trader. Anyhow I
will do the best I can by myself. Strange discovery at this period
—Likoma is a bad starting place for Unangu. A letter of mine
reached Unangu in five days from here on one occasion. The
only thing I have to regret about it is the leaving this place ;
for not being properly in charge I can undertake nothing new
at Unangu, but simply go on Dr. Hine's lines. Alas, that our
new "health resort" should be unable to preserve even a doctor's
health ! . . .

I am very comfortable now. I have built Mr. Philipps a new
brick room and whitewashed it, and it has a brick floor. The
whitewash is made of a disintegrated stone almost like pure white
clay here, not lime—would it were ! I have 20,000 first-rate bricks
in hand, and I am going to brick the dining-room and common-
room floors. I shall move the writing table, books, etc., into my
bedroom, making that my bedroom and study—it is quite big
enough. I shall whitewash it to-morrow and Saturday. I have
been sleeping in my tent at the end of the baraza, and but for the
tent it would be exactly like a Likoma house—the tent makes all
the difference. We shall have a spare room when the chancel is
built.

I trust the new Government at home will do some sober, decent
work for working people, the unemployed, and agricultural
labourers, *e.g.*, the reform of land tenure, drink, etc. Can we not
expect more liberty for Convocation ? You see I am old fashioned.
I have got " *Merrie England,*" but I have not had time to read
it. . . .

It is quite idyllic to be penniless, but a little awkward at times,
especially as the Mission is so poor. . . .

As time goes on we shall be able to get more stores out here.
Two men, one financed by Wiese, a big man who has started a
Company for £1,000,000 to take up a concession, and the other an
old-fashioned trader, have gone shares, so far as this place is concerned, and we, I think, will be the gainers. We can get most of
the things, for which we are now dependent on Likoma, from
them. I think it will work if their prices are anything decently
within the limits of a millionaire, which the African Lakes'

Company's are not.   Fancy, the latter charges £15 passenger fare from Fort Johnston to Kota Kota—two days' journey and no night travelling—cargo, £7 a ton the same distance.   The charges on the German steamer are £8 per passenger and £5 per ton cargo.

What wonder that we try and escape these by using our own boats ! But the days of monopolies are drawing to a close ; more traders and big companies are coming in.   Some day a telegraph wire will be here, and Kota Kota will have a post office. . . .

We have come to the end of our wholesome water, so I employ a man to bring two buckets twice a day from the hot-water springs —excellent water, running as powerfully now as immediately after the rains, and almost tasteless. . . .

I am going to try and get paint out here and a pit-saw before I begin serious building.   I see no difficulty in the way of plenty of bricks at 8s. or 10s. per thousand.   I believe £50 or £60 would build us an excellent School. . . .

Mrs. R—— sent me "*Beside the Bonnie Briar Bush.*" It is charming.   I cried over it. . . .

The school numbers over one hundred now, and so do the hearers.   The children are very keen, and the attendance is good. The slave village is growing every day.   It is very hot just now. . . .

It is rather like a battlefield out here.   However safe one feels oneself, there are those one cares for and looks up to falling all round us. . . .

October 13*th.*—The "*Domira*" came in at 9.0 to-night, so that is all this mail.

Yours, etc.,

A. F. SIM.

APPENDIX A

THE LAST SERMON PREACHED IN ST. AIDAN'S CHURCH BY
ARTHUR FRASER SIM. ST. AIDAN'S, *Third Sunday after
Easter*, 1894.

"*Christ is all*" (Col. iii. 11).

In this text we find both the Christian's aim and his source of
strength. When he fails it is when he loses sight of Christ.
When he succeeds it can only be in the power of Christ.

THE CHRISTIAN'S AIM.

To succeed in this—who can do so here? None perfectly; yet
all can in measure.

It may be that I speak to you from this pulpit for the last time.
And with this in my mind, and fully realizing the relative importance of last words, let me reiterate my earnest conviction that a
Christian's success is not measured by his wealth or his position,
or the name he has won for himself, but by his struggles after the
likeness of Christ. Christ is all, all to him, all that will last, all
that he cares to have. To lose Christ is to lose all. To win Him—
by patient struggle with known sins, by the conquest of self, by
love for others—to win Christ is his only aim. What matters
pain, what matters disease and sorrow, if Christ alone is your
aim? What matters death itself, if by death we may win Christ?
Nay, will not these things be welcomed, courted, triumphantly
borne, if they will but bring us nearer to our goal?

"Nearer, my God, to Thee,
E'en though it be a cross that raiseth me."

True, good fortune may come to the Christian as to a man of
the world. Success in worldly enterprise comes not by chance.

GOD alone can place it in our hands, and GOD alone can permit it to be withdrawn.

True also that Christians are found in lowly walks in life, in poverty, in sickness ; sorrow attends them as well as joy.

Be it the one or the other, yet not in these directly, but in the slow, gradual, grinding discipline of life is Christ to be found. Not by great deeds of heroism, not by great sacrifices, but by the daily, hourly, constantly-repeated, unseen acts of self-denial and self-conquest is Christ won. Not every one has the opportunity to do great things, but every one can do little things. Nay, 'tis easier to do something great, and so win the applause of men, than to faithfully strive with the daily temptations as they arise, and do the hourly duty and continual drudgery unseen and un-applauded. Let us ever remember this—it is greater heroism in GOD's sight to conquer selfishness by an hourly struggle than in a moment of impulse to go to the stake. It is nobler to face the offence of the Cross of Christ in the daily life, in the home, in the shop, in the yard, than by fits and starts to awake up to some gigantic effort and then relapse again into torpor.

I say this, brethren, because I want you to realize that we can all be heroes though no man applauds us or all our acquaint-ance revile us. It is better to give the angels cause for joy than to win a name in a nation's history. Let us rather fear success ; let us flee from men's applause. These are dangers ; they take our eyes off from our failings. To the Christian Christ is all. If he is not gaining a better knowledge of himself, and a firmer grasp of Christ's comfort and peace and joy, success is not his though men speak well of him. GOD grant us failure and disappointment if only we may win Christ. The Christian's aim is Christ : no-thing short of this—to know Him, to grow in likeness to Him. And though this aim may not be realized fully here, yet we may all grow more like Him than we are, and know Him better than we do.

And this is your aim and mine, and this is the purpose for which GOD has put us into the world. This is the meaning of all our surroundings - this disappointment, that illness, this loss, that sorrow, this friendship, that loss of a friend.

I think if our life is placed in pleasant places, it is perhaps be-cause we are weak and GOD is gentle with us. Yet even in smooth paths we must seek GOD's will, and not impatiently try to tread a new and difficult way. GOD will show us His will for us in His own time. His voice will be unmistakable, His guiding clear, His command peremptory, and not to be set aside without terrible danger to the soul.

The Christian's aim is Christ, and oh, how Christians fail, not only in attaining that aim, but even in apprehending it ! And the test question we must put to ourselves is this—To me is Christ, or self, the first object of my life? And here, let me repeat it, the choice comes not in great events, but in the daily, hourly discipline of life. It is St. Paul who gives the Colossians and us this text for our life, and yet how does he advise it should be carried out? Listen. Not "go to the stake," not "go and make a profession of your Christianity," but " Put on therefore, as the elect of GOD, holy and beloved, bowels of mercies (or, as in R.V., a heart of compassion), kindness, humility, meekness, long-suffering ; forbearing one another and forgiving one another, if any man have a complaint against any : and above all put on love, which is the bond of perfectness." And then he goes on into the outward home life : "Wives, be in subjection to your husbands. Husbands, love your wives, and be not bitter against them. Children, obey your parents. Fathers, provoke not your children, that they be not discouraged. Servants, obey your masters. Masters, give unto your servants that which is just and equal."

Brethren, the world won't applaud many of these conditions of winning Christ. Even a half-Christian world will call you a fool for your humility, meekness, long-suffering, your forgiving spirit. Yet this, the practical Christianity of your daily life, is the way to win Christ. Without it, though you give your body to be burned, or all your goods to feed the poor, you cannot win the Christian's goal.

If Christ alone then is the Christian's *aim*, if the method is self-discipline in daily habits, unknown and unnoticed, of self-conquest—what, then, are *the means*? For we may be sure that it is not enough to say, " Do this little thing or that ; develop this habit or that "; but, because these so-called "little things" are the real battle of life, it is just here we need most the grace of GOD to enable us not only to win the battle, but to undertake it at all. What are the means? And here again, brethren, if it were GOD's will that I should never preach to you again, after some years of experience now let me put *first*—what to me, and I am sure to every Christian who is making any fight against his sin must be first—the Communion of the Body and Blood of Christ. If by GOD's grace I have made any progress in my spiritual life during these last few years, I am confident that the strength for the conflict with self has been drawn from this GOD-given food. If any one is conscious of a besetting sin to be conquered, here he will find strength to meet it. If any has difficulty in keeping up the high standard of Christian endeavour, here failings may be confessed, broken vows renewed, waning strength reinforced. If it is a sorrow or a disappointment or anxiety that robs life of its brightness, here, on the Lord's bosom, all may be poured out, and His " Be of good cheer " will lighten the heavy heart, and bring again the sunshine of a new fresh courage into the drudgery of life. If it is a dear one's absence that fills the heart with disquiet and a yearning for his safety or his return, here we may come to Him in Whom absent and present are one—nay, in Whom even the dead are not lost. To Him we may confide the anxiety, to His care leave all that is dearest to us on earth.

But, brethren, let us be careful how we approach GOD's Altar, and let us be careful when we are there. Remember Who is there to meet us, and give Him the reverence due to the world's Creator and mankind's Redeemer. Let us welcome Him into a heart prepared to receive Him; humbly, as all unworthy of so great a boon; with a clean heart, a heart cleansed by confession of sin, and earnest prayer for the presence of Christ—" none of self, all of Christ." The quiet hours spent at the Altar of this Church have been to me the happiest of all these happy years, and I were ungrateful not to confess it. But they have sometimes been clouded with this sadness—that more who, I know, are able to come, who, I know, are desirous of conquering sin, do not seek here the Divine strength for their trouble. And this sadness is intensified when I remember that from this Holy Table goes forth the Leaven that is to work a change in the world immediately around us. If every worker in this Parish were a regular *weekly* communicant (and this is the Church's standard—a standard, I think, within the reach of nearly all of us), if every worker were a regular communicant, then I am confident we should make a greater change in the lives of those around us, and the work of the Parish would be better done, and when it was done it would be lasting. For let us never forget that GOD has set us here as " a city set on an hill," as a light in a dark place, and from *us* men gather their knowledge of Christ. By us, whether we will it or no, they judge of our Lord's character. We are in a measure sacraments of Christ—outward and visible tokens of the Lord who dwells invisibly within us.

But the communicant's life must be a life of prayer and of meditation. In these let us examine ourselves ; let us strive to bring them up to the high standard of Christ.

Let our prayers be real ; let us take trouble with them. Let each have his or her daily subject for prayer, taking pen and paper, and using the same real thought as a tradesman uses for his business. And meditation—this I know is hard ; but in a word, it is the devotional study of Holy Scripture, reading our portion on our knees, asking GOD to enlighten our minds to behold the beauty of His love, His truth, and His holiness.

Brethren, these are the means. We know them already ; we have used them ; but we are very apt to accept a low standard. Yet if we do not make the most of the means, how shall we ever attain the end ? And if the level of our attainment in the use of means be low, how shall we ever attain to Christ ? However much we assent to the fact that Christ is all to the Christian, yet if we neglect prayer and the Holy Scriptures and Holy Communion it is folly—nay, is it not sin ?

I have tried to realize that this probably is the last time—perhaps for years, perhaps for ever—that I shall speak to you from this pulpit, and I have tried to be practical and matter-of-fact. I would, by GOD'S help, that my last words might help some one here to attain more nearly to the Christian's ideal, which is Christ.

For myself I am convinced that the step I am taking is GOD'S will for me. I have shrunk from it ; I have tried to count the cost. But of all the difficulties or the possible dangers which in that field I may have to face, there is none I fear so much as increased temptation. If it is true that bodily strength is sapped in a hot malarial climate, how much will that add to the power of temptation—temptation to despondency, for the work is a slow one, temptation to lower the standard of Christian attainment, even the temptation to sloth. These I fear, and if by personal friendship or by ministerial contact I have any claim upon your prayers, I ask that you should remember me and all missionaries in our temptations. For if the battle is hard here, I think it will be much harder there.   I do not I think fear sickness, and I think death may be faced as well by the Christian Priest as by the tradesman or the sportsman ; but I do fear lest I be going into a battle with sin too keen for my weak powers of resistance.

I know that work for Christ is the same, whether it is undertaken at home or abroad ; and I beseech you not to imagine that this work is nobler than work at home.   It is not taking the step which is the difficult task ; but it is there, as here, the slow daily discipline under perhaps greater difficulties.   It is the growing in grace, the slow advance which wins Christ, which here as much as there will try one's strength.   Let me have your constant prayers in this.

And let my last words from this pulpit be this reminder : To the Christian, whether abroad or at home, CHRIST IS ALL AND IN ALL.

GRAVE OF A. F. SIM, KOTA KOTA.

APPENDIX B

c. S. XIV aft Trinity 1845.

... give us peace and joy . here on earth
and afterwards life with Him in Heaven
to know love. serve. without death. weariness
sin or temps . The man who pleases
God does not fear death
death comes but the beginning of life .
after death he will come closer to God . see
Him . hear his voice .

We have had sorrows - we have lost
3 ... we have ... for our
loss . but they have joy ...

What is this life of ... . Here on
Earth is a trial . if we pass through it
well we obtain our reward . and death
is not the end - but we live with death
nearer to God.

What shall we give in exchange for soul
...
... honours. pleasure . ...

The above is a fac-simile of one page of the Sermon-notes found in A. F. Sim's Bible at Kota Kota.

APPENDIX C

APPENDIX C

EXTRACT FROM PARLIAMENTARY REPORT (1896) OF COM-
MISSIONER SIR H. H. JOHNSTON, K.C.B.

THE Universities' Mission has had a chequered career in Nyasaland. . . . Its ill-luck culminated last year in the deaths of
Bishop Maples and Lay-Assistant Williams from drowning, of
the Rev. George Atlay, who was murdered by the Magwangwara,
on the mainland, and the loss of the Rev. A. F. Sim, who died
of fever at Kota Kota after a year's most successful work in the
Marimba district, on the south-west of Lake Nyasa. It appeared
as though Mr. Sim were going to build up in a short space of
time something like a native church, so great was his influence
among the natives and the personal affection towards himself
with which he inspired them. Kota Kota is an exceedingly
Muhammadan place, with several mosques and mollahs, but
even amongst the Muhammadans the death of Mr. Sim was
deplored with real feeling. . . .

No person who desires to make a truthful statement can deny
the great good effected by missionary enterprise in Central Africa.
There are some Missions and some Missionaries out here of
whose work nothing but praise can be uttered, though much just
criticism might be written on their mode of life, which in some
instances, is singularly and needlessly ascetic and uncomfort-
able. . . .

About Mission work in other parts of the world I have no direct
knowledge, but I can say of all mission work in British Central
Africa that it has only to tell the plain truth and nothing but the
truth to secure sympathy and support.

PERIODICALS, LEAFLETS, PHOTOGRAPHS,

AND OTHER PUBLICATIONS.

TO BE OBTAINED AT THE OFFICE OF THE UNIVERSITIES' MISSION,

9 DARTMOUTH STREET, WESTMINSTER, S.W.

Books, Pamphlets, etc.

The following are kept on sale at the Office. The prices given are net prices, and include postage.

The History of the Universities' Mission, 1859-96. 467 pp., with numerous illustrations. 3*s.* 9*d.* Superior edition, 5*s.* 3*d.*

Memoir of Bishop Steere. By Rev. R. M. HEANLEY. 2*s.* 9*d.*

Livingstone : an interesting short biography by T. HUGHES. 2*s.* 9*d.*

Diary of a Working Man : an interesting account of the beginning of work on Lake Nyasa. By the late W. BELLINGHAM. 1*s.* 9*d.*

Autobiography of a Slave Boy. Edited by Archdeacon JONES BATE-MAN. Fourth Thousand. 2½*d.*

Mission Heroes.—Bishop Mackenzie. 1½*d.*

,, ,, **Bishop Steere.** 1½*d.*

,, ,, **Bishop Smythies.** 1½*d.*

An Heroic Effort. By H. RIDER HAGGARD. 2*d.*

The Capture of the Slaver. By Rev. D. GATH WHITLEY. 2*d.*

CENTRAL AFRICA.

The Illustrated Monthly Magazine contains letters from the Missionaries in Africa, articles on subjects bearing on the work of the Mission, and all news of the Mission in Africa and at home. In it are also acknowledged all contributions to the Mission Funds, and all parcels received at the various Mission Stations. Full directions are given for the address and despatch of letters and parcels to the Missionaries, a list of whose names, with the stations at which each is working, is included.

Price 1*d.*, *by post* 1½*d.* ; *special terms for quantities.*

Bound volumes from 1883 *may still be obtained, price* 1*s.* 9*d. each.*

Covers for binding the yearly volumes, 7*d.*

AFRICAN TIDINGS.

A CHEAP AND POPULAR ILLUSTRATED HALFPENNY MONTHLY.

Twelve copies post free for 7½*d.* ; *special terms for quantities. Bound volumes,* 1*s.* 6*d. Covers for binding, or reading cases,* 7*d.*

Leaflets.

The Series of Illustrated Leaflets provides a cheap and interesting means of circulating information about the work of the Mission. They are recommended for distribution in Church before a sermon or meeting, and for circulation in parishes and schools.

PRICES : 1*s. per* 100 ; *except* 16 *and* 17, 2*s. per* 100.

Swahili Books.

A collection of Books of Devotion and School-books in Swahili, Bondei, Chinyanja, and other African Languages may be seen and obtained at the Office of the Mission. The following are a few of the principal Swahili publications of general use and interest :—

Msimulizi. The bi-monthly magazine. Edited and printed by the Kiungani boys. 4½*d.*
Swahili Handbook. 4*s.* 9*d.*
Swahili Exercises. 2*s.*
English-Swahili Dictionary. 7*s.* 9*d.*
Swahili Grammar. 1*s.* 9*d.*
The Holy Bible. Old Testament. 2 vols. 2*s.* each. New Testament. 1*s.* 9*d.*
Book of Common Prayer. 3*s.* 3*d.*
Treasury of Devotion. 1*s.* 9*d.*

Lantern Slides.

The following sets of slides may be borrowed for use at meetings on behalf of the Mission if carriage to and fro is paid :—

(*a*) Zanzibar and Slave Trade.
(*b*) Zanzibar and Magila District.
(*c*) Zanzibar and Rovuma District.
(*d*) General Set.
(*e*) Lake Nyasa.

At least three weeks' notice should be given to prevent disappointment.

A pamphlet containing description of the slides, to assist in the preparation of lectures, price 6*d.*

The Report

is issued annually on May 1st, and contains an interesting record of the year's work, with a complete account of the Mission Funds for the past year.

Price 3*d., by post* 4*d. Copies of the Report from* 1860 *may still be obtained.*

Butler & Tanner, The Selwood Printing Works, Frome, and London.